The first solo
the *New York Tim*
of the Dragonland
and Sovere

MISTRESS OF DRAGONS

"Intriguing characters . . . clashing cultures . . . fascinating personalities."   —*VOYA*

"Best known for her successful partnership with Tracy Hickman (*Dragons of the Vanished Moon*, etc.), Weis launches a new series on her own that's sure to please high fantasy fans . . . In the world of Dragonvarld, an ancient race of dragons with its own parliament has kept apart from the race of men and refrained from meddling in their affairs. Since a renegade dragon, Maristara, seized the human realm of Seth three centuries earlier, an Amazonian order of priestesses with magical powers and the Mistress of Dragons have kept the peace. But evidence that Maristara and a partner-in-crime have indulged in their taste for human flesh means renewed trouble . . . *Mistress of Dragons*, will keep readers turning the pages and will leave them eager for the next installment."
                                                        —*Publishers Weekly*

MISTRESS OF
DRAGONS

MARGARET
WEIS

TOR®
fantasy

A TOM DOHERTY ASSOCIATES BOOK
NEW YORK

This is a work of fiction. All the characters and events portrayed in this novel are either fictitious or are used fictitiously.

MISTRESS OF DRAGONS

A Tor Book
Published by Tom Doherty Associates, LLC
175 Fifth Avenue
New York, NY 10010

www.tor.com

Tor® is a registered trademark of Tom Doherty Associates, LLC.

ISBN 0-765-34390-8
EAN 978-0765-34390-1
Library of Congress Catalog Card Number: 200304618

First edition: May 2003
First mass market edition: May 2004

Printed in the United States of America

0 9 8 7 6 5 4 3 2 1

Dedicated to Brian Thomson,
with affection!

1

EVERY MORNING, BEFORE THE SUN ROSE TO GILD the white marble columns of the monastery with flecks of gold, the High Priestess went to the Chamber of the Watchful Eye to perform the Rite of Seeing. She alone could conduct the ancient ritual—that was her duty, her privilege.

As the other priestesses murmured morning prayers in their cells, Melisande, the High Priestess, walked the chill, dark pathways that led from the monastery proper to the small temple where she would perform the rite. Built out on a promontory overlooking the valley and the city below, the Chamber of the Watchful Eye was circular in shape, constructed of black marble, its domed roof supported by black marble columns. The temple had no walls. Standing within its columns, Melisande could look out to the fir and cedar and hemlock trees that formed a natural wall around the monastery.

Another wall—this one of stone, man-made—surrounded the monastery, its extensive grounds, and outbuildings. The Chamber of the Watchful Eye lay outside this wall. Melisande let herself out through a wicket gate every morning to perform the ceremony. Female warriors atop the wall kept close watch on their priestess, prepared to hasten to her defense, should that be needful.

The temple housed one sacred object—an enormous, white marble bowl. Inside the bowl, lapis lazuli had been inlaid into the marble to form the iris of an Eye. The Eye's pupil, in the very center of the bowl, was jet. Every day at noon, the youngest acolytes, virgins in both mind and body, came to wash and polish the marble Eye. Every dawn, before the sunrise, the High Priestess came to see what the Eye saw.

Though the sun's dawn colors smeared the eastern sky with pink, those colors had not yet driven away night's shadows that clustered thick and heavy, tangled in the boughs of the fir trees. Melisande brought no lamp with her, however, but walked the path in darkness. She had no need for lamplight. She had walked this path every morning for the past ten years, ever since she was eighteen. She knew every crack in the flagstone, every dip and rise of the hillside, every twist and turning of the ridge along which the path led. When she stepped out of the shadow and into the fading starlight, she was close to the temple. Four more steps along the path, round a small coppice of pine, and she could see it silhouetted against the gradually lightening sky.

Melisande wore her ceremonial gown, put on in the morning to perform the ritual and removed on her return, to be smoothed and neatly folded and laid at the bottom of the bed in her small cell, in readiness for the morrow. Handwoven of angora yarn, the gown was dyed black, then dipped in purple. Melisande was one with the night when she wore the gown, another reason she preferred not to carry a light. When she removed the sumptuous gown every day, exchanging it for her daily garb, she shed the sacred mysteries of the night and took on the mundane chores of the day.

Arriving at the temple, Melisande slipped her feet out of the leather sandals before entering. The marble was cold, but she had grown used to treading on it barefoot, even enjoying the thrill that went through her body as her flesh touched the chill stone. Whispering prayers, she ascended the three steps that led to the dais on which stood the Eye. Melisande knelt before the bowl, said the ritual prayer, then lifted up the flagon of holy water that rested on the floor beside the Eye.

She poured the water into the bowl. The blue iris shimmered in the expanding light of the dawn. The Eye shimmered with unshed tears.

Melisande waited until the ripples ceased, the water was still and smooth, to say the ritual words, taught to her by the Mistress of Dragons on the day Melisande had been named High Priestess.

"Open wide, you that guard our realm, and let my eye see what you see."

Every morning for ten years, Melisande had looked into the lapis lazuli iris and every morning she had seen what the Eye saw: the valley in which nestled their realm; the mountains that surrounded and guarded and sheltered it; the city of Seth at the northern end of the valley; the farmlands that surrounded and supported it; the castle of the king built in the foothills of the mountain; and ruling over all, the monastery of the Sacred Order of the Eye, perched atop the mountain known as the Sentinel.

This morning, Melisande saw all that and more.

She saw the dragon.

Melisande gasped, stared in disbelief. Though the daily ritual was designed to keep watch for dragons, she herself had never see one. Twenty years had passed since the previous High Priestess had looked into the bowl and seen eight dragons descending on the valley. Melisande recalled that event clearly. She had been eight years old at the time and she could still recall the thrilling terror and excitement as the warriors carried all the little girls to the catacombs beneath the monastery, to keep them safe and out of the way.

The other girls had been in tears. Melisande had not

cried. She had crouched in that whimpering, stifling darkness, feeling the ground shake from the powerful forces being unleashed above, and in her mind she was in the Sanctuary of the Eye, alongside the sisters, using her magic to drive away the ferocious beasts bent on destruction. She had not been formally taught the magic; her instruction in that would not begin until she was twelve. But she knew the words from listening to the sisters' daily chants and she had repeated them then, whispering them to herself. The colors of the magic spread in vibrant sheets across her mind—luminous reds and flaring orange, meant to dazzle and confuse the dragons, lure them into range of spear and arrow, or send them crashing into the mountainside.

The battle of the Sacred Order against the invading dragons had been hard fought. Eventually, the powerful magicks of the Mistress and her priestesses and the arrows and spears of the warriors had driven the dragons away from Seth. Emerging from the catacombs that night, Melisande saw splotches of gore being cleansed from the flagstones. Reaching down, she dipped her fingers in it— dragon's blood.

Melisande placed her hands on the rim of the stone bowl, stared into the center. The Eye vanished. The blue iris was blue sky, clear and cloudless. The dragon's green scales glittered in the newly risen sun; the eyes, set on either side of the massive head, seemed to look straight at her, though Melisande knew that this was a trick of the Eye. The dragon was still far distant. He could see the mountains of Seth, perhaps, but nothing more. Not yet.

Melisande sat back on her heels and drew in a deep breath to stop herself from trembling. She was not afraid, for there was nothing to fear. The trembling came from the shock of seeing what she had not expected to see. Rising swiftly, she left the temple, running back up the narrow, flagstone path that led to the monastery. As she ran, she went over in her mind what she must do. There were many actions to be performed and she could not do all of them at once. She had to prioritize, determine the order of importance of each, and this she did as she hastened up the path.

Reaching the gray stone wall that surrounded the monastery, Melisande drew forth the iron key that hung from a silken cord around her waist and used it to open the lock in the wicket gate. She was pleased to see that she had so far disciplined herself that she had stopped trembling. She opened the gate with a steady hand, shut it behind her, and ran through the garden. She could hear a stir on the battlements.

The warriors had been standing guard all night. Their shift was almost over and they yawned as they walked their beat, looking forward to a meal and then their beds. The astonishing sight of their normally dignified High Priestess running barefoot through the wicket gate (she had forgotten her shoes), startled them into wakefulness. An officer called down to her, demanding to know what was wrong, but Melisande did not take time to answer.

She did not enter the monastery. She continued at a run through the garden that completely encircled the four white marble buildings and passed through another iron gate that led to the barracks—a large block house made of the same gray stone as the protective wall that surrounded the monastery. The flagstone path between the monastery and the barracks had been worn smooth by centuries of booted feet. Reaching the barracks, Melisande pushed open the huge wooden doors, and entered into darkness that smelled of leather and steel and the almond oil the women rubbed onto their bodies. Bellona, as commander, was the only warrior to have a private chamber, located in the front of the barracks, so that she could be wakened quickly at need.

The room was small, square, furnished with a wooden bed on which was laid a goose-down mattress. The mattress was a present from Melisande; warriors usually made do with straw. Bellona's polished steel cuirass and helm had been hung neatly on a wooden stand near the bed, her sword and shield placed alongside. A table and two chairs beneath a slit window were so placed as to catch the first rays of the sun.

Bellona was still asleep. She would not waken until the bells rang the end of night, the beginning of the day. She lay on her back, her head turned sideways, her dark hair mussed and tousled. A restless sleeper, she had kicked off the light woolen blanket that had also been a present from Melisande. As usual, the blanket had slithered to the floor. Bellona slept naked, for at any moment the alarm might sound and she must be up and armed and armored.

"Bellona," Melisande called softly from the doorway. She entered the room, shut the door carefully behind her. She had not wanted to startle Bellona, but the timber of her voice must have given her away.

Bellona jolted awake, sat bolt upright, her hand already reaching for her sword. "Melisande? What is it? What is the matter?"

Drawn to strength, drawn to warmth, Melisande sank down on the bed beside the warrior, who regarded her with concern that was starting to deepen into alarm.

"By the rod, you are shivering!" Bellona put her arm around Melisande, held her close. "And your feet! They're bleeding. Where are your shoes?"

"Never mind my shoes. Bellona,"—Melisande drew back to look into the woman's dark eyes—"a dragon is coming. I saw it."

"Melis!" Bellona gasped, gripping her arm tensely. "Are you certain?"

"I am," said Melisande firmly.

"Have you told the Mistress?"

"No, I came to tell you first. I knew you would need time to ready your defense."

Bellona smiled, her dark eyes warmed. "I thank you for thinking of us. Not many of your sisters would have."

"None of my sisters have been instructed by the commander," Melisande answered. She slid reluctantly from the warrior's warm, strong, and reassuring embrace. "I must rouse the Sisterhood, then go to the Mistress."

"Tell her we will be ready," said Bellona, reaching for her armor.

"You must make certain that the little girls are safely removed to the catacombs," said Melisande, still feeling close to those memories.

Bellona nodded absently, her thoughts on all she needed to do. "You can count upon me, Melis."

"I do," said Melisande, squeezing her hand. "Always."

The two exchanged a parting kiss.

"Should I send a messenger to the king?" Melisande asked, turning back as she reached the door. "I hate to disturb him. His youngest child is ill, they say, and not doing well. Both he and the queen are frantic with worry."

"His Majesty should be informed, nevertheless. I will send a runner," said Bellona, lacing up her boots.

"Reassure His Majesty that he need not be concerned," Melisande said. "We are well prepared to deal with the dragon."

"Of course," said Bellona, matter-of-factly.

"I will not ring the great gong, though," Melisande continued, thinking aloud. "Not unless something goes wrong. The people in the valley will still have time to flee if we fail."

"Nothing will go wrong," said Bellona, standing up. "You will not fail."

Her brown-skinned body was all muscle, lithe and powerful, with small, tight breasts. Her body differed from Melisande's, whose was soft and delicate, with the pale skin of one who spends her days inside walls among her books, working her mind, not her muscles.

"You and the Mistress hold us in your care, Melis," Bellona added. "Our trust is in you."

Hastening off to summon the Sisterhood and wake the Mistress, Melisande wished she had as much confidence in herself as her lover had in her.

* * *

The kingdom of Seth, in the valley of Seth, was nominally a monarchy, ruled by either a king or queen, as determined by the sex of the eldest child born to the ruling family. The monarch was nothing more than a figurehead, however, someone for the crowds to cheer on festival days. The Mistress of Dragons was the true ruler of Seth and had been for three hundred years. Everyone knew and acknowledged this fact, including the monarch.

Three hundred years ago, the kingdom of Seth had been held in thrall by a dragon, who had taken up residence in the Sentinel Mountain. The dragon had repeatedly attacked the kingdom, stealing livestock, setting crops ablaze, slaying or carrying off to her lair any person unfortunate enough to be caught out in the open. Hundreds fell victim to the marauder. Hundreds more fled the kingdom, traveling to distant lands. Seth came perilously close to being wiped out of existence. Then came a savior.

One of the festivals still celebrated in Seth commemorates that blessed event. The townsfolk construct a dragon in effigy and carry the huge wooden monstrosity through the streets, accompanied by players dressed in black wearing skull masks, to represent the dead. At the end of the festival, a player clad in white, with the golden mask of the sun, fights the dragon in a mock battle. The figure in white is the Mistress. She destroys the dragon, using a golden sword. The effigy is then burned in a huge bonfire in the middle of the fairgrounds to great rejoicing.

This was symbolic of the event. In reality, the Mistress fought the dragon in a less dramatic but more effective manner, using magic to drive away her foe. The dragon was vanquished, never seen again. The grateful citizens offered the Mistress the wealth of the kingdom. They offered her the kingdom itself, but she refused.

She would not become their king. She would become their goddess. She built a temple on the mountainside and placed inside it the stone bowl known as the Watchful Eye. She asked for nine maidens, virgins all, to volunteer to serve in the temple and learn the art of dragon magic, so that when the Mistress died, she would leave another to keep the kingdom safe.

Down through the centuries, many women assumed the mantle of Mistress, ascended to godhood. The monastery grew in size and in power, so that now twenty-five women, sixteen of whom were virgins, served in the temple. The most senior of the Sisters of the Eye, as they were known, was the High Priestess, the woman responsible for keeping watch for the ancient foe. When the Mistress died, the High Priestess would assume that position.

Her services were still needed. Several times, over the years, the kingdom of Seth was attacked by dragons. The worst assault had been twenty years ago, when eighteen enormous dragons had laid siege to the monastery itself. The battle against them had been fierce. Many of the Sisterhood had died, as had many of the valiant warriors. Dragon blood fell from the skies on that day and so it was known in the annals of history as the Day of Black Rain.

In the end, the dragons were repelled. Never again had the dragons attacked in such numbers, but, every so often, one or two would appear.

"They come to see if we maintain our vigilance," said the Mistress.

The vigilance of the sisters never faltered. The people of Seth lived in peace and prosperity in their isolated valley, looking to the Sisterhood to guard them.

Ten years ago, the Mistress of Dragons had chosen Melisande to be High Priestess. At eighteen, Melisande was the youngest to be selected for the honor, but few disputed the fact that she deserved it, for she was reputed to be the most powerful in dragon magic of any woman yet born in the monastery. The current Mistress was very old, nearly seventy, and in poor health. Melisande was aware that the mantle of godhood could fall upon her at any moment and she strove always to be worthy of the honor.

This day would see if the Mistress's faith in her protégé was justified.

The monastery proper, consisting of four buildings, was built in a square around a central courtyard. In the middle of the courtyard stood two gongs—one enormous gong made of iron and another, smaller gong made of silver. If the iron gong were sounded, the deep booming call would be heard in the city far below and in the farms and forests beyond that, warning the people of Seth that they were under attack, giving them time to flee for their lives into the caverns in the mountains. The other gong was smaller and made of silver. This gong alerted the Sisterhood to the coming of their foe.

Melisande lifted the silver hammer, prepared to strike. She could hear, in the distance, Bellona bellowing commands. Feet pounded as the warrior women raced to their posts. A few of the Sisterhood, hearing the unusual commotion, peered out their windows, wondering what was going on. Melisande did not leave them long in doubt. She struck the silver gong, sending a shivering peal of alarm through the monastery.

More heads looked out the windows of the monastery's east wing that was the dortoir, where the sisters lived.

"Make haste!" Melisande called to them. "I am going to the Mistress."

The heads disappeared, as the women hurried to don their sacred garments. Melisande returned the silver hammer to its stand. The gong continued to vibrate, the notes dying away slowly.

Warriors ran past her, heading for the south side of the monastery, where lived the nine mothers. The mothers—or "cows" as they were known disparagingly among the warrior women—were those sisters chosen by the Mistress to bear children, sacrificing their virginity in order to perpetuate the Sisterhood. Babies were taken away from the mothers shortly after birth. The male babies were given to families in the kingdom who had been denied a male child and needed an heir. Girls were kept in the monastery to be raised by the Sisterhood as sisters or mothers or warriors, depending on the bent taken by the magic in their blood. This wing also held the "mating" rooms (used once monthly) and the birthing rooms.

The warriors emerged from the south wing, escorting the children and mothers to the catacombs beneath the monastery.

Melisande hurried past the west wing that would be empty now. Here were classrooms, where the sisters were taught the sacred magic that kept their kingdom safe. This wing also housed the kitchen and dining hall, the school-rooms and playrooms for the little girls.

The fourth wing, the north wing, belonged to the Mistress. Here were her chambers. Beneath this wing was the Sanctuary of the Eye.

The Mistress of Dragons lived apart from the Sisterhood, as was right and proper for a goddess. She came among them only rarely. Her life was devoted to the magic and she spent a large part of every day in the Sanctuary, working her powerful magicks that kept the kingdom safe. Two bronze doors barred entry to everyone in the monastery except the High Priestess and chosen members of the Sisterhood, and even they could enter only by invitation. The eilte of the warrior women stood guard.

The warrior women saluted as Melisande approached. They had heard the silver gong and, although they had not received direct orders from the Mistress, this was an emergency and they had standing orders to allow the High Priestess to pass. Melisande was not strong enough to shove open the huge bronze doors; the warrior women performed that office for her.

"Good hunting, High Priestess," said one, as Melisande entered the Mistress's residence.

Daylight entered with her, shining down a long narrow corridor of wood and painted murals. The eyes of the dragons portrayed in murals gleamed with borrowed life in the sunlight. The light vanished as the bronze doors closed with a dull boom, stealing away the life briefly granted them. Windowless, the corridor was lit only by small cresset lights placed at intervals along the wall. Part of the task of the warrior women was to lower the lights, fill them with the oil that kept them burning. The darkness was redolent with the scent of incense, and had a thick, warm, comforting feel.

Running was not permitted in the chambers of the Mistress. Nor was shouting or talking. One was expected to enter with bowed head and sacred thoughts, move with seemly decorum. Melisande had to force herself to slow her steps. She wished that she had not forgotten her shoes. The Mistress would think she lacked discipline. Calming herself with prayer and the thought that the dragon was yet far distant, she decorously walked the shadowy corridors to the Mistress's bedchamber.

She was surprised to find the Mistress's door closed.

The opening of the bronze doors tripped a wire that rang a bell in the chambers of the Mistress, alerting her to the presence of a visitor. Ordinarily, she would open the door in preparation of receiving a guest. Finding the door still closed, Melisande assumed that the elderly Mistress was still sleeping and had not heard the bell's clang. Melisande raised her hand to the bronze knocker, which was in the shape of a dragon, but at that moment, the door swung open.

The Mistress stood within. The golden threads embroidered into her ceremonial robes shone in the light of an oil lamp that stood upon a richly carved wooden table. Her seventy years had sapped the strength of her body. Her hair was snowy white, her face wizened and deeply lined, her thin body bent and stooped. Her voice was strong, however; eagerness flickered in her dark eyes.

"You have seen a dragon," she said.

"I have, Mistress," said Melisande, ashamed to be unable to control a tremor in her voice.

In this sacred place, the enormity of the situation, the danger and the peril for her people, and her own responsibility fell suddenly upon her and she faltered beneath the crushing weight. For a brief moment, she wished fervently that she was once again that eight-year-old girl, being carried to safety in the strong arms of a warrior.

"How many?"

"Just one, Mistress."

"The dragon is coming here? Are you certain?"

"The beast was still very small within the Eye, Mistress. But he grew larger as I watched. He is coming closer. And his gaze looked straight at me."

The Mistress smiled. Her smiles were rare and always inward, so that Melisande was never certain if the Mistress was pleased with something she had done or if her joy rose from some secret held within.

"I knew you would be among the blessed," said the Mistress. She moved toward the door, grasped hold of Melisande's wrist. "I knew when you were small. I could see the magic dancing in your mind. You must describe the dragon to me."

"A young male by his bright coloring, golden green on his back and shoulders and mane, tending to blue scales on his belly and his legs and tail. Should I summon the sisters—"

"Yes, summon them." The Mistress's hand was skin and sinew and bone. She clasped Melisande's wrist tightly. "Send them to the Sanctuary. Alert the warriors—"

"I have already done that, Mistress."

"Ah, yes, you would." The Mistress smiled again. "Then it seems you have done what is needful, Melisande. I will go to the Sanctuary to prepare. You return to the Eye to keep watch. When the dragon's head fills the bowl and it seems that you cannot hide from his sight, the beast will be nearly upon us. Come to the Sanctuary, for we will have need of you."

The Mistress did not let loose her grip. She kept fast hold of her with her hand and her dark, bright eyes.

"This will be your test, Melisande. I have faith in you. Have faith in yourself."

"I will try, Mistress. I have much yet to learn."

The Mistress's hand relaxed, her touch grew gentle, caressing. "Your time will be soon, Melisande."

"No, Mistress, do not say so," Melisande said, truly grieved. "You will be with us many years—"

The Mistress's smile grew sad, poignant. She shook her head. "We are always given to know our time, Melisande. So it will be with you, when your hour comes."

The Mistress gave Melisande's hand a brisk pat. "Still, that hour will not come today. Now we must prepare to meet our foe. Go do your duty, Daughter. I will take up mine. And remember, as you can see the dragon, so he can use his magic to see you. Do not let him intimidate you."

The Mistress gave a gesture of dismissal. Melisande bowed her way out and the Mistress shut the door behind her.

Melisande paused a moment in the fragrant darkness. As she closed her eyes and prayed silently to the Mistress for courage, the thought came to her that soon she would have no one to pray to. She would be the Mistress and all prayers would come to her. The thought was startling, daunting. She wondered why it had never occurred to her until that moment.

"Probably because I assumed the Mistress must live forever."

Her prayer ended suddenly, half-spoken. If her time to be a goddess was coming soon, she had best get used to acting on her own.

She pulled the bell rope to alert the guards to throw open the bronze doors. Blinking in the bright sunlight, she drew in a deep breath of fresh air. The warriors had manned the battlements that ran along the tops of all four walls. Other warriors were carrying the last of the children to safety. Melisande saw the little girls clinging to the warriors, their arms clasped around them tightly, their sleep-drenched eyes wide with the novelty of it all, and she smiled at them reassuringly. The "cows" followed closely, soothing those children who were fearful, telling them to pray to the Mistress.

The members of the Sisterhood were waiting outside to be admitted to the Sanctuary. At Melisande's nod, they filed past her, out of the sun, into the darkness. They wore their white robes, their cowls cast over their heads, their eyes lowered, their hands clasped in prayer.

Absorbed in their prayers, they did not speak to Melisande, nor did she speak to them. She continued on her way, hastening back to the Chamber of the Eye. As she passed out the wicket gate, she saw Bellona, walking the battlements, inspecting every warrior, making certain that all were ready. Glancing down, Bellona caught sight of Melisande and the two shared a smile and a loving glance, then each went back to her duties.

Walking the path in the sunlight, Melisande looked back at that little girl, who had summoned the magic in the darkness. She looked back at the little girl and her self-doubt vanished. She sent her blessing to that far distant child, and went with confidence to face the dragon.

2

MELISANDE KNELT DOWN AGAIN BESIDE THE BOWL
that was the Watchful Eye. She paused a moment before
she looked into the water to try to calm herself and focus
her thoughts—a difficult task. Her thoughts refused to
stay in this quiet, sacred place, but ran away back up the
mountain, to Bellona, to the Mistress, to the sisters, wondering how they were faring, wondering if there was anything she should have done that she had left undone,
wondering if the little girls were safe . . .

"Stop it!" Melisande commanded herself sternly. "The
Mistress is with us. She has matters well in hand. My
duty is to watch the dragon."

She put her hands on the rim of the enormous stone
bowl and bent over it, looking into the still water.

Two eyes looked back. Living eyes.

The dragon's head filled the bowl; his red eyes with
their pupils, narrow slits like murder holes, staring unblinking into hers. The sight was unnerving and Melisande jerked away, unwilling to let those terrible eyes see
into hers.

And remember, as you can see the dragon, so he can

use his magic to see you. Do not let him intimidate you.

The Mistress's final command came back to Melisande. She must defy the dragon, show him she was not afraid . . . yet she hesitated. She could see again the intelligence and the guile in the dragon's eyes, as they had looked up at her from the calm water. If he penetrated her mental barriers, he would be able to see clearly the doubts and fears that crouched there in the darkness.

"Let him," she thought. "I am not afraid. I am High Priestess and he is but a monster." She looked back into the water, looked directly into the dragon's eyes.

"I am the High Priestess of the Temple of the Watchful Eye," she said to him, her courage growing. "I give you fair warning, Dragon. Do not trouble us and we will not trouble you."

"We?" the dragon asked. "Who is this 'we' who threatens me? I see only one and a puny one at that. Summon your Mistress. I will speak with no one but her."

The dragon did not speak aloud, or at least his mouth did not move. His words were brightly colored visions in Melisande's mind, so that she saw his meaning more than heard it. The sight was unnerving, for the colors were too bright, jarring, and vivid, with sharp points that jabbed at her painfully. She flinched and longed to turn away, but she held steadfast to her duty, held the dragon's gaze.

"My Mistress does not deign to speak to the likes of you. We are the Sisters of the Dragon and we await your coming with powerful magicks. Be warned and turn back."

The dragon's eyes glinted. "Do what you must. I *will* speak to your Mistress. I come for that purpose and that purpose alone."

The dragon's eyes shifted away from her; the colors smeared and ran and washed away, leaving her gray and exhausted. The dragon had no more use for her. She was a human, a lower form of life. Melisande searched behind the lone dragon for others of his kind, but saw none and she began to understand. This was no well-thought-out, planned assault by a troop of dragons. This was an attack by a single dragon—a young male—out to test himself.

Melisande was angered. This dragon was here for self-aggrandizement, attacking them to make himself look good in the eyes of his superiors or perhaps gain the approval of some female of his species. His demand to speak to the Mistress was a ruse, a trap.

Melisande sat back on her heels, stared into the Eye, concentrating on the dragon, for the Mistress would want to know as much as Melisande could tell.

Part of the training of the Sisterhood was devoted to studying dragons. "Know your enemy," was the dictum of the Mistress and she had taught them all she knew, including what she had leaned from the Mistress before her, and so on back to the very first Mistress of Dragons.

Like humans, dragons vary in shape and size, in height and weight, in coloration of their scales and their manes and eyes, in temperament and personality. Bellona had dusky skin, black hair, and brown eyes, whereas Melisande was blonde and pale with eyes the color of the lapis lazuli in the bowl. The current Mistress was dark-skinned, like Bellona, but the one before her had been as fair as Melisande. The same was true of dragons.

Within the classrooms were stone jars filled with the scales of the dragons who had sought to invade the kingdom. That same little girl who had whispered the magic had been fascinated by the scales. While the other girls were playing, Melisande had often gone to the classrooms to watch the dragon scales glitter and sparkle in the sunlight.

The scales in one jar were blue-black, like the juice of blueberries. Another jar held scales that shimmered green-yellow as new leaves in springtime, and yet another jar held scales that were red as blood or flame, and still another amethyst. She had found it hard then to equate creatures of such beauty and magnificence with evil, but she had only to look at the paintings on the walls of the Mistress's chamber to see represented in vivid detail the destruction that dragons wrought on humans.

"The scales of young dragons," said the Mistress, "are brighter in hue than the scales of elder dragons, for a dragon's color deepens over time. This is one way to tell a dragon's age. The scales of very elder dragons may have darkened to the point where they appear almost black, no matter what color they were born with."

The scales of this dragon were a bright, iridescent green. His eyes were red, as are the eyes of all dragons, but the eyes of this dragon had an orange glint to them that bespoke youth, rash courage, reckless bravado. The spiky mane was a deeper shade of green, darkening to turquoise. Melisande could not see the wings now, for the beast's head filled the bowl, but she remembered them as being a light green, leathery, like a bat's. The beast had four legs—the front two smaller, used in a manner similar to a human's arms; the back two large and muscular, used to propel the dragon's massive body into the air. The tail was long, as long as the body, stabilizing the dragon on land and acting as a rudder during flight. The spiky mane ran the length of the tail.

The dragon's head was sleek and graceful and reptilian. The shining scales formed a V-pattern with the darker colors of the mane slanting down between the eyes, giving way gradually to brighter green scales that covered the snout and the powerful jaws. Four of the dragon's fangs protruded from the mouth—two upper and two lower; the rest of the sharp teeth were hidden.

Melisande rose to her feet. She no longer saw the dragon's beauty. She saw only the beast's careless cruelty, which could sport with human life. She had no doubt that the dragon was coming to attack Seth, the only kingdom in Dragonvarld that dared stand up to the dragons who terrorized and dominated the rest of the world. Hidden in their valley, the people of Seth cut themselves off from the rest of the world, barring admittance to their realm.

"For if the rest of the people of Dragonvarld knew

about the peace and the prosperity of Seth, they would flock here by the thousands and we would lose all that we have fought so long to gain," the Mistress warned.

Her anger burning away her fear, Melisande left the Eye. She knew all she needed to know. The dragon was coming to do battle. She was calm enough to remember to retrieve her shoes and she ran back to the monastery, eager as a young warrior for her first battle.

The women on the wall cried out to her as she came within sight, demanding to know if the dragon was coming. Furious at such a breach of discipline, Bellona shouted them to silence. Melisande entered the wicket gate, ran across the courtyard. Two soldiers stood beside the great iron gong.

"Sound the alarm," said Melisande, and as the first booming notes rang out over the valley, the warrior women cheered and clashed their spears on their shields.

Melisande flashed a quick glance at Bellona, pacing up and down the wall, exhorting her warriors to fight bravely, die gloriously, and add more scales to the stone jars.

As Bellona's words "die gloriously" rang out, Melisande faltered. She felt a pang of fear—not for herself, but for Bellona. Melisande had never before imagined losing her beloved and she now knew that possibility was very real, for if the magic failed and the dragon succeeded in his attack, Bellona would be in the front of the fray, the first to attack, the first to fall.

"Blessed Mistress, do not let it come to that," Melisande prayed.

Her resolve hardening, she hastened to the Sanctuary.

The bronze doors to the north wing stood open and unguarded. The Mistress had ordered the warriors to the walls to aid in the defense of the monastery. The sisters would be inside the Sanctuary now, preparing their powerful magicks to fight the dragon.

Never mind decorum. Melisande ran through the dark corridor. The door that led to the Sanctuary of the Eye stood near the Mistress's chambers, so that she might have easy access at any time. Usually the door was closed and locked. The Mistress was the only person in possession of the key. This day, the door was open. Firelight streamed out into the corridor, shining bright on the evil faces of the dragons in the murals.

Entering the door, Melisande descended a long flight of stone stairs and ran the length of another corridor that delved deep into the mountain. Carved out of the mountain's bones, the corridor's walls were rough and irregular, the air chill. The smell of the earth mingled with the fragrance of incense and perfume wafting down the corridor from the Sanctuary that lay ahead.

A cavernous chamber, crudely built, the Sanctuary looked as if it had been dug out of the rock by a single swiping scoop performed by a gigantic hand. The chamber was oval in shape, its walls and domed ceiling formed of jagged, broken, and crumbling rock. The stone floor was smooth, worn by the feet of the countless numbers of sisters.

At the north end of the chamber stood an altar made of white marble. So large was the altar that a man could have rested his body full-length upon the altar and still found room to stretch. The altar was known as the First Miracle, for it was so wide that it could not have fit through the door and so heavy that a hundred men could not have lifted it. Yet, here it stood. According to the teachings, the earth itself had given the altar to the First Mistress as a gift.

The marble altar was wonderfully carved in relief, portraying images of dragons. The altar was obviously old, for the white marble was starting to yellow with age. Dust had crept into cracks and crevices so that each carved scale of every dragon was clearly outlined in black.

The top of the altar was smooth. An iron brazier, formed in the shape of two nurturing hands, stood beside the altar. One of the most important duties of the Sisterhood was to keep the sacred flame burning, for, the first Mistress had prophesied, if the sacred flame was ever doused, the dragons would win and Seth would fall. The fire's fuel was peat, dug from the bogs down in the valley, formed into bricks and hauled up the mountain by peat men, the only males ever permitted to come close to the monastery (with the exception of the men chosen monthly for breeding). The men brought the peat to within five miles of the Sanctuary. The warrior women hauled it from that point the rest of the way.

The sisters themselves carried the peat down the stairs to a small cavern off the main Sanctuary, where the bricks were blessed and sanctified by the Mistress. Incense and perfume were added to the peat to further purify the fire. A shaft in the ceiling carried the sacred smoke out the top of the mountain. On a cloudless day, the people in the city of Seth could look up into the mountains and see the thin curl of smoke rising from the brazier and take comfort in the knowledge that the Mistress was watching over them.

Each sister knelt on a small wool rug decorated with the symbols of the Watchful Eye, the Nurturing Hand, and the Hand Defending. In one hand was the spear, in another the thunderbolt, symbolizing the two means of combating the dragons—the spear of the warrior and the thunderbolt of the Sisterhood's magic.

Melisande entered to find the sisters at their stations, kneeling, forming a circle around a large Eye that had been carved into the granite floor. The Eye was the Second Miracle, for it was said to have appeared the day the Mistress knelt before the altar and proclaimed that here she would fight the dragons. The sisters arranged their rugs so that each faced inward, toward the Eye. Their heads were bowed in prayer, their voices murmuring. All were here. All except the Mistress. Melisande wondered uneasily if the strain had proved too much for the elderly woman, if perhaps she had fallen ill. She was about to go search, when several of the sisters caught sight of her and bowed low to their High Priestess.

Melisande could not leave now. Her sudden departure

would cause consternation among the sisters, disrupt their concentration. The Mistress was a proud woman. She would not thank Melisande for coming to fetch her, as if she had forgotten or neglected her duty. If the Mistress was detained, she must have her reasons.

Melisande bowed to the sisters. Gliding across the floor, she took her place at the head of the circle, in front of the marble altar. The sisters wore their sacred garments— gowns of pure white lamb's wool, embroidered with symbols of the Hands and the Eyes along the hem of the gown and sleeves. Melisande's gown was similar, except that her gown was black and trimmed in golden thread, to mark her standing as High Priestess.

She inspected each of the sisters, to make certain that each had come properly prepared. Finding all in order, Melisande sank down thankfully onto her rug. The warmth of the fire from the brazier felt good. She realized only then that she was chilled to the bone and shivering. She had not noticed before now.

She began to speak the ritual words of prayer, "O, Mistress of the Dragon, come to us in our time of need . . ."

The words held new meaning for her now and she prayed them with a fervor she had never before felt. And, as if in answer, the Mistress of Dragons entered the chamber.

She wore the trappings of her high office: a full-length gown of wool that had been decorated with thousands of tiny beads, designed to resemble the scales of a dragon. Twenty women had worked for five years to construct the gown. Every color scale in the stone jars was represented in the colors of the beadwork and the gown shimmered and gleamed in the firelight. The Mistress wore a golden crown formed of clasped hands, holding the Watchful Eye, a beautiful sapphire.

The sisters bowed low, their heads touching the stone floor. Melisande bowed, then, rising to her feet, she took the Mistress by the hand and led her ceremoniously to the altar. The Mistress took her place beside the flaming brazier. Melisande bowed again and left to return to the head of the circle.

One of the sisters spoke. Her voice was low, but so silent was the chamber that it could be clearly heard.

"Melisande has blood on her sacred garment, Mistress."

Some of the sisters sucked in their breath, so that a soft sibilant gasp went through the chamber. Melisande had no need to search for the speaker, for she knew quite well who had spoken. Lucretta was five years Melisande's senior and she had been certain she would be chosen High Priestess. The Mistress had chosen Melisande, however, and Lucretta had been furious. She had taken out her wrath on Melisande, who suffered her slights and insults in silence, knowing, as Lucretta should have known, that petty jealousies must not ever be allowed to break the divine unity of the Sisterhood.

Melisande looked down at the hem and saw the gold thread stained with red, probably from the cuts on her feet. Lucretta must have looked very hard to have seen that. Her body suffused with an unpleasant warmth, Melisande glanced back to where the Mistress stood behind the altar.

"Mistress, I—" Melisande began.

The Mistress made a swift negating motion with her hand, and Melisande fell silent.

"The blood upon the sacred garment of our High Priestess proves her devotion to the cause," said the Mistress, her tone and expression stern. "Melisande, take your place and lead us in prayer."

As Melisande knelt upon her rug, she cast one swift glance at Lucretta. The woman's face was hidden, but the back of her neck was flushed an ugly red. This incident would only further enrage her. Melisande put Lucretta and her petty jealousies firmly out of her mind. They had to battle the dragon.

She faced into the center of the stone Eye carved into the floor and began to recite the ritual Battle Prayer, asking the Mistress to grant them the magic to fight their foe. As she spoke, she extended her hands, one to the sister on her left (thank the Mistress it wasn't Lucretta!) and one to the sister on her right. Behind her, she could hear the creaking voice of the Mistress reciting the words to the magical spells that were known only to the Mistress of the Dragons and taught to her successor on her deathbed.

One by one, the sisters clasped hands until they had formed a ring around the stone Eye. As Melisande prayed, her elation grew, her voice gained in strength and in power. The sisters joined in the chant and their voices were strong and fervent, so that the chamber rang with their chanting. The sisters began to rock back and forth, holding hands, swaying with the words. The Mistress raised her own voice, her words counterpoint to the chanting of the sisters.

Melisande felt the sisters' hands she was holding burn with unnatural warmth. The magic, called the "blood bane," acted on her and the others like a fever, making the skin hot to the touch, sometimes bringing on delirium if the sisters were weak. The colors burned in her mind, shimmering and whirling and sparking.

Louder and louder the chanting grew. The Mistress's magic fed the fire in the brazier. The flames leapt high. Those in the valley below, waiting fearfully for the battle, would see the smoke belching from the mountain and they would cheer. The dragon would see the smoke, too, but he would not know its portent.

The Eye carved into the stone blinked and then began to widen and Melisande wondered fearfully if she was delirious and then she realized, with a thrill that banished pain and fever, that this was the miracle of the magic. Melisande had never seen the miracle and she was awestruck.

The stone floor vanished. Blue sky appeared with the snowcapped peaks of the mountains. The chamber filled with sunlight.

From behind the mountain flew the dragon.

The Mistress gave a great cry that seemed torn from

her frail body, a cry of fury and hatred and triumph. The dragon heard it or seemed to, for he turned his head suddenly and stared with narrowed eyes directly at them.

The colors of her mind, colors imprinted on the backs of Melisande's eyes, took shape and form—spiking yellows and sharp iron grays, stabbing and piercing. The colors blended with the colors of the other sisters, working on the dragon's mind, confusing him while protecting them from the spells he might cast.

The Mistress unleashed the power of her magic, a burst of energy that rose, swirling, with the smoke.

The dragon tried to veer away, but it was too late. The magic caught the dragon in its vortex. Trapped in the maelstrom, the dragon flapped his wings violently in an effort to escape, but the magic spun him as if he were a foam bubble churned up by the spell's whirling torrent. The energy whipped his head back and forth and beat against him, buffeting and pummeling his body, and he roared in pain and anger. Round and round the magic tossed the hapless dragon, dragging him downward, to dash his body on the jagged rocks.

He was young and strong and he fought to avoid his terrible fate, but Melisande could see that he was weakening. He was within range of the warriors now. Spears and arrows soared upward in deadly arcs, one tearing through a wing, another bouncing off his scaled hide. He was being sucked down, inexorably, and there was no escape.

Suddenly, the Mistress's words faltered, became garbled. Melisande glanced over her shoulder, saw the Mistress clutching at her throat.

"Mistress!" Melisande cried, frightened.

"Maintain . . . the spell!" the Mistress gasped. Clasping hold of the altar, she struggled to remain standing, but she was too weak. She slid to the floor. The sisters faltered. The chanting petered out. Panic-stricken, they stared at the Mistress, lying on the floor behind the altar. One began to scream hysterically, another burst into tears.

Melisande tried to keep the chanting going, though she knew it was hopeless. Without their Mistress, the sisters were no match for the dragon. The fire in the brazier sank down, so that the smoke was a thin trickle, barely visible.

The dragon realized he was free.

A flap of his leathery wings carried him safely out of range of the spears and the arrows. As he flew off, Melisande noted that one foreleg sagged limp beneath his body, the skin of one wing was torn, and countless arrows stuck out of his flanks. Blood marred the bright green of his scales.

That was the last she saw of him, for the Eye shut out the view, closed on the sunlight and blue sky. The light of the brazier failing, the chamber was dark, filled with the smell of smoke.

The fever of the blood bane left them all weak and drained, yet many of the sisters managed to stagger to their feet, crying out for the Mistress. Melisande heard hysteria in their voices and she feared that this would lead to panic.

"Stop it!" Melisande ordered sharply, blocking the way to the altar. "Regain control of yourselves. Your mad raving will do our Mistress more harm than good."

Glancing behind the altar, she saw the Mistress lying on the floor, mouth open, feebly gasping for air. "Fetch me cool water and blankets. Make haste."

The sisters stared at her, helpless to obey. Those who had strength enough to stand were being forced to lean on each other for support. Like them, Melisande was weak and light-headed as a patient rising from a fever bed. None of them had the strength to fetch anything.

"Then pray for her," said Melisande.

Most of the sisters looked ashamed of themselves and, sinking to their knees, began to pray fervently. Lucretta alone did nothing. She glared at Melisande, her hatred and envy plain in her eyes.

Melisande had no time to worry about Lucretta. Weak and shaking, her body covered with sweat, Melisande made her way to the altar and to the Mistress. She sank down beside her.

The Mistress could not speak, but she formed the words with her lips. "The dragon!"

"He was grievously wounded and he fled," said Melisande. Taking hold of the Mistress's hand, she pressed it to her lips. "Dear Mistress, you saved us from the beast. The people are safe."

The Mistress struggled to speak. "*Not* dead?"

"You drove him away and he will not be back soon," said Melisande. "You must think now of yourself, of resting and getting well."

The Mistress shook her head in frustration. She fell back, limp and exhausted. She motioned to Melisande with a crook of a shaking finger.

"Come closer."

Melisande caught back the coil of her hair, bent her head to hear.

"I have failed you," the Mistress said in a gasping breath.

"No, Mistress, please—" Melisande could not go on for her tears.

"Come to me . . . tomorrow. We start . . . the final training."

The Mistress fell back. Her eyes closed. Her body went limp.

"She is dead!" cried Lucretta, and a wail rose from the sisters.

"No, she sleeps," Melisande returned, her voice firm to quell the panic. "She cannot remain here. She must be carried to her chamber."

But how she was going to manage that, she did not know. She would be lucky to walk ten steps, much less try to carry the Mistress.

The sisters gazed at her in dismay. Their training had not prepared them for this. They had never supposed the Mistress would fail them, that she would need their aid.

"I will go for help," said Melisande. "The rest of you

wait with her, do what you can for the Mistress while I am gone."

Placing her hands on the altar, she used it to support her weight and pulled herself up. She paused a moment to gather her strength, then, bracing herself, she walked toward the door. Dazed and ill, the others watched her. They could not help her. They could barely help themselves. Melisande concentrated on her destination. Slowly, slowly, the doorway drew near. She couldn't even think about the long walk through the corridor, back to the bronze doors. She managed to reach the entrance, before her strength gave way. She leaned against the wall, clutched at it to support herself. Her one thought, that she could not let herself fall.

"I'll rest . . . a moment . . ."

Strong arms caught her, lowered her gently to the floor. Bellona's voice, giving orders, echoed through the Sanctuary. Warriors surged past her into the chamber. They carried litters with them, blankets, water, and brandy wine.

Melisande looked into Bellona's dark, anxious eyes.

"I am all right," she said. "Don't worry. It is just the weakness of the blood bane. You must tend to the Mistress."

"She is being cared for," said Bellona. "I will take her to her chamber, then send for the healers. Rest now, Melis, and leave all to me."

"The Sanctuary is sacred. You should not be here," Melisande said, trying to sit up.

"You can clean the chamber of our defilement later," returned Bellona, pressing her back down.

Melisande gave up the struggle. "How did you know there was trouble?"

"When the magic failed, I knew something had gone wrong."

The warriors placed the Mistress on a litter and bore her to her chamber. Other warriors helped the sisters, aiding their faltering steps, carrying those who were too weak to walk.

"You see?" Bellona told her. "All is in hand. The dragon fled. It was a glorious battle, even if we did not kill the beast. You should rest now, Melis. You are exhausted. I will take you to your chamber."

"No, my love," said Melisande, as sleep, strong and warm as Bellona's arms, enfolded her. "Take me to yours."

3

MANY YEARS HAD PASSED SINCE HE HAD RECEIVED
a summons. Their silence had not surprised him, for the
world was lurching along fairly well—as well as could be
expected with humans running it—and his services had
not been needed. He'd spent the years roaming the world,
moving from place to place, watching, observing, reporting back if circumstances warranted.

His reports were reassuring. The humans were doing as
they had always done down through the centuries—
making a mess of their own lives, yet somehow managing
not only to survive as a species but even to progress. Thus
he wondered about the summons. Nothing was amiss, so
far as he knew. And they never summoned him unless
something was amiss.

His was, by necessity, a stoic nature, and he felt nothing
more than mild curiosity as he walked the dark, subter-
ranean corridors that led to the Hall of Parliament. He
carried no lamp or torch. He did not need light. He had
the ability to magnify ambient light and so the darkness
was light to him, albeit a gray-silver, hazy sort of light,
as on a night when the light of a full moon can be seen
through low-lying ground fog.

He was strong, well-muscled, bronze-skinned from his years of sojourning. He had gray-streaked black hair that he wore clubbed and tied at the back of his neck with a leather thong. He wore leather breeches and a leather vest and leather boots. He bore no sword. He carried a knife, which he used for hunting and eating, and a walking staff, which served to settle any difficulties he might encounter. He had brown eyes hooded by low, dark brows. In some light his eyes glinted red, but he tended to keep out of that sort of light. He had a mouth that was tight-lipped, rarely smiling, never laughing. He spoke little and then always to purpose. He made no friends, took no lovers, for that would mean becoming involved with humans.

He was the only one of his kind in the world.

He walked the winding corridors carved out of rock that led deeper and deeper underground and he was comfortable and at home. At times, the cavern tunnels were so cramped and narrow that he was forced to crawl through them, at the cost of cuts and scratches and scrapes on his fragile human flesh. More than once rock slides blocked his path, forcing him to stop to clear them. He jumped chasms, waded a dark river. All around him was silence, except for the occasional drip of water or the fall of a pebble somewhere in the distance. He liked silence, preferred silence.

He could not hear them, and he might have thought himself alone, but he could feel their movement in the ground that shuddered sometimes beneath his feet. They were here and they were waiting for him—the Parliament of Dragons.

He squeezed through a narrow tunnel that opened up into a vast cavern. Although he had been here many times, he tended to forget, over the years, the magnificence, the grandeur. Standing upright, he paused, as he prepared to enter the Hall of Parliament, to catch his breath and to marvel.

The cavern was immense. He had been in human cities, teeming with thousands of people, that could have been picked up whole and dropped into this cavern. The ceiling was far, far above him, so far that it seemed like heaven's dome, without the stars. The dragons had constructed an entrance at the very top of the mountain, hidden from sight by clouds and magic, and dim light filtered down from above. A dragon was just arriving. He watched the massive body soar through the entryway far above him, watched the great beast slowly spiral round and round in the dim, gray light; head peering downward to find a place to land. He lowered his gaze, looked around him. He could see them now and hear them. Eleven dragons of the twelve houses of dragons, the elders of each house: the Parliament.

The twelfth dragon landed on the cavern floor and settled himself, bowing his head to the others, shifting his bulk to make himself comfortable, pulling his wings into his sides, adjusting his tail so that it wrapped around his legs. He made his apologies for being late. The others murmured their acceptance.

Dust, disturbed by his fanning wings, clouded the air. Had the dragons been in the sun, the light would have sparkled and danced on their bright scales. A brilliant sight, one to dazzle the eye and the mind, for when a dragon moved, the gleaming scales rippled, clashing golden as the sunlight on ocean waves. He saw the wondrous image in his mind, not here in the cavern, for in the dim light the scales of all the dragons were gray, the same gray as the stone walls surrounding them. Only the slit eyes gleamed red.

He stood at the entrance to the Hall, waiting patiently. The twelve arranged themselves in a circle, with the Minister at the compass point, north. The dragons were recumbent, resting on all fours, their tails wrapped around their hind legs, the tips touching the front talons planted firmly on the ground in front of them. They held their heads upright. The eyes gazed at him, unblinking. He heard their breathing, the rasping of their wings, the scrape of claws. These were the only sounds that broke the silence, the only sounds that would break it. Dragons communicate with thought alone, not with spoken words.

As such, the language of dragons is a language of images, textures, shapes, color, and emotion, playing upon all the senses. A dragon hearing of a storm from another dragon would be able to feel the cold rain, hear the clash of the thunder, and see the wind-driven waves crashing upon the shore. The brush that paints the images conveys the feelings of the dragon and the dragon receiving the image knows if he is being warned of an approaching storm or merely hearing the tale of a storm long past. Thus the dragons, living solitary lives, can communicate with their brethren if need arises.

A human mind is not made to communicate in this manner. When he had first undertaken this task, the images and colors and emotions had seemed to explode in his brain, splintering into many colored, sharp fragments, like a stained-glass window struck by lightning. He had very nearly gone mad until he had learned to distill the thoughts into simple words and pictures and shapes.

The dragons, for their part, took care to keep their thoughts gray-tinged, with rounded edges, so as not to overwhelm him.

He had not communicated with any dragon for a long time, and it took some moments for him to transition himself from human speech and thought patterns to those of dragons. He saw himself in the Minister's mind, saw himself walking to the center of the Hall, saw his image surrounded by bright sunlight.

"Approach, Draconas," said the Minster, adding, politely, "It is good to see you again. Thank you for coming."

Draconas walked forward to stand across from the Minister at the southern compass point. He made his bow. The members of Parliament bowed their heads.

"I am honored to be called," Draconas answered in the same silent language. Distilled through his human mind, his thoughts would appear to them like the scrawlings of a child. "I look forward to serving this august body in any way that I can."

The fact that he could not have ignored the summons if he'd tried made this pointless, but dragons are invariably polite and aware of the importance of formality and ceremony, particularly within their own society. Dragons are not given to interaction with other living beings, including their own kind. A mated pair may love each other dearly and yet not live within several hundred miles of each other. They may communicate on a daily basis, but see each other only once every few centuries. Hatchlings are sent into the world as soon as they are able to hunt on their own and they are generally as glad to leave the nest as the parent is glad to have them depart. If forced to come together, dragons grate on each other's nerves. Tempers flare and things are said that were never intended. The icy waters of polite speech and observance of the formalities keeps the fire in the belly under control.

Such formality also means that dragons come straight to the point. They do not blather on about nonentities as do humans, for which Draconas was grateful.

The Parliament of Dragons was an ancient institution, dating back to the fourth and final horrific Dragon War, at the end of which the exhausted dragons realized that unless they developed some means for keeping peace among the noble families, dragons as a race would vanish from the world that they had ruled for centuries, a world that bore their name.

Few humans know of the Dragon Wars, for they were fought when humans were still primitive beings, wandering the primordial forests with clubs in their hands, living in caves, and dancing around their campfires. In those caves, however, can be seen primitive paintings, depicting enormous monsters battling in the skies, with blood raining down upon the land and fire lighting the heavens.

The Dragon Wars had ended by the time the humans moved out of their caves and into villages. The Dragon Parliament established laws by which the dragons governed themselves and, later, laws that were used to govern the fledgling race of wingless creatures known as humans, who had developed an intelligence which, while not approaching that of the dragons, made them a species worthy of some notice.

The Parliament elected one of themselves to serve as Prime Minister. The dragon elected held the office for life. Anora was the current Prime Minister. An elder dragon, she was matriarch of a powerful family—Draconas's family, she being his great-aunt. Anora had been Minister for many centuries. She was old by the reckoning of dragons, which meant that she was ancient by the reckoning of humans.

It is difficult to tell a dragon's age by appearance, for there is no hair to go gray, as on humans, no skin to wrinkle or brittle bones to snap. Draconas could see that Anora had aged in the years since he had last seen her and he was saddened. She had always held her head proudly upon its graceful, curving neck. Now her head sagged forward, as though it had grown too heavy for her to bear. The skin around her eyes was puffy, the eyes had sunken. When she spoke, he noted that the upper and lower fangs and teeth were worn, smooth and rounded. On her body were patches of bare flesh, where scales had fallen off and not grown back, as they would with a younger dragon.

Anora turned her gaze again on Draconas and her eyes shone with the same bright intelligence he had come to know and respect. Her jaw was just as firm, her thoughts strong and resonating.

"We have summoned you, Draconas," said the Minister, "because something must be done about Maristara."

Draconas flexed his hands, his mouth twisted into a grimace. So that's what this was about. How long had it been? Three hundred years? An eye blink to a dragon, though generations of humans had been born and died in that time. Something must have stirred the pot to cause this foul thing to come floating to the surface.

"Yes, Minister," said Draconas, there being not much else he could say, aside from, *What the devil has taken you so long?*, which would not have been well received.

The Minister's red eyes flickered. Her tail twitched. Anora knew quite well what Draconas longed to say. She made an oblique gesture, lifted a talon, cautioning him to maintain his composure. She had no need. Draconas knew. He understood. He waited.

Another dragon shifted his head to look at the Minister. He was a young dragon, with shining green scales, muscular, strong, and dangerous.

"I ask for the wand," said this dragon.

"If there are no objections, I hand the speaker's wand to Braun," said the Minister.

There being no objections, she handed the jeweled wand that she held delicately in a taloned forefoot to the young male dragon. Draconas did not know him. Braun was new to the Parliament and quite young to be head of a noble house. Draconas knew, though, which house Braun represented. He felt a tingle at the base of his spine.

"I am Braun," said the dragon in tones that were smoldering red and sharp-edged. "As you undoubtedly know, Maristara is my grandmother."

Draconas inclined his head in acknowledgement. Again, there wasn't much to say, except *I'm sorry*.

"I am going to begin by reciting the history of events that have taken place over the last three hundred years. In this, I beg the Parliament's indulgence, for all of you know the history. You have lived it. I have new information, however, that I daresay none of you know."

The dragons settled themselves. Some exchanged glances, but all curbed their thoughts. If Braun wanted to publicly review his family's shameful past, that was his prerogative. Draconas, being a servant, had no say in the matter. He didn't mind hearing the story again, just to refresh his memory, especially as it seemed he was now going to be a part of it.

"First," said Braun, "I would remind you of the laws

of Dragonkind, the laws that were written at the very first meeting of Parliament, thousands of years ago.

"The first law: Dragons may not take human life.

"The second law: Dragons may not interfere in human affairs. Dragons may not coerce, intimidate, force, threaten, resort to trickery or extortion in their dealings with humans.

"The third law: Dragons, with one exception, should have no dealings with humans."

Here Braun paused to nod politely at Draconas, to acknowledge him the exception.

Braun then continued. "Three centuries ago, the dragon Maristara broke all the laws of Dragonkind by seizing a human realm known as Seth. She established herself as ruler of that realm and the humans who inhabit it. At that time, the Parliament acted, sending a strongly worded document informing Maristara that she had broken the law and ordering her to give up her conquest and depart. No word came from Maristara. That was her answer.

"A delegation was sent to speak to her. She raised magical barriers to keep them out and the dragons, having no authority to try to break through these barriers, were forced to withdraw. Time passed. The subject of Maristara was brought up at every Parliament, but no one knew what to do. Nothing like this had ever occurred in our past. None knew how to handle it. The matter was debated for well over a century, with some saying that if we let her alone, she would tire of her toy and depart, and others advocating most strongly that she be attacked and driven out.

"Eventually, the Parliament took action that was really no action. My father was given authorization to fly to the realm to try to reason with his mother. He attempted to penetrate the magic, but could not succeed. Once more, the Parliament dithered and debated. At length, after another century or so had passed, the Parliament decided that they had no choice, they must remove Maristara by force."

"We all remember what happened then, Braun," said Anora. "I do not believe you need go into it."

The other dragons looked round. Red eyes glinted. Horrific images of blood and pain filled Draconas's mind. He firmly shut them out.

"It is because we refuse to face unpleasant facts that we are in this situation," Braun stated. "I relate this for the sake of Draconas, who perhaps has not heard it before."

Anora looked at Draconas, who lifted one eyebrow. She sighed and said, "Very well, Braun. Continue."

"Twenty years ago Parliament sent a troop of dragons to the kingdom to try to free the humans and bring Maristara to justice. They combined their magicks and managed to penetrate the barrier or thought they did. It was a trap. They were attacked. Not by a dragon. By humans. The result," Braun stated, his mental colors green, poisonous, "was disastrous. The law forbade them to fight back. Several of our brethren were slain and many more injured. We were soundly defeated. It was the worst massacre of dragons by humans in our history. But it did accomplish one thing. It proved that Maristara had done something even more heinous than seizing control of a kingdom. It proved that she had taught humans dragon magic."

"That was never established," said an elder member, one Malfiesto, sternly.

"Of course it was established," returned Braun, thoughts flickering with impatience. "How else do you account for the fact that we were so utterly repulsed? That many of our kind were slain? Show me the humans who could do that without magic. Isn't that true, Draconas?"

He had his own ideas, but he was not going to be dragged into taking sides. Fortunately, the elder dragon spoke again, and Draconas was forgotten.

"Even if she has done this, I can't see what you expect us to do, Braun."

Anora brought this to a halt. "Do you request the wand, Malfiesto?"

"No, Minister," Malfiesto replied. "I have said all I wanted to say. All that is needful, I believe. Except this is a fool's errand, for us and Draconas. What's he going to do that we haven't tried already?"

Anora frowned and Malfiesto subsided, his thoughts taking on a green-gray shade that among humans would have denoted grumbling.

"Please continue, Braun," she said.

"Thank you, Minister," said the young dragon. He cast a defiant glance at the other members. "I will tell you why I have brought you here and why I requested the presence of Draconas. As all of you know, I am here today, a member of this august body, because of the unexpected death of my father."

Braun cut short the soft, muted colors of sympathy by adding, "My father was murdered."

The dragons exchanged uneasy glances. They did not know what to say. Rumor had it that the family's terrible shame had driven Braun's father—Maristara's son—mad. No one knew precisely what had happened. The dragon's broken and twisted body had been found at the base of a cliff. It was assumed that he had gone crazy and ended his life by flying headlong into the mountain.

Braun knew what they were thinking. He could see into every mind and he said defiantly, "He was not murdered by his mother, Maristara. She never leaves her realm. Yet he was murdered by a dragon. Someone who is in league with Maristara, protecting her and shielding her."

"This is a most serious accusation, Braun," said Anora. The images in her mind flickered orange. "Not since the Dragon Wars has one of our kind shed the blood of another. I find it very hard to believe. What possible motive—?"

"A taste for human flesh," Braun answered.

The dragons shifted, restless, uncomfortable. They didn't want to hear this, the dirty secret of Dragonkind.

All dragons have a taste for human flesh. Once in the long ago, humans had been hunted nearly to extinction. One reason for the Parliament, one reason for laws, one reason for Draconas.

"What proof do you have, Braun?" said Anora, clearly skeptical.

"My father had long been trying to find some means to bring about Maristara's downfall. He said that it was plain to him that Parliament was incapable of dealing with her—"

Rumblings at this, but no one spoke outright.

"—and so, as her family, the responsibility fell to us. He began to investigate, to find out everything he could about her, about this unfortunate kingdom, about the ill-fated attack. He studied the attack, spoke to survivors, and he reached two conclusions: The first, that the humans had used our own magic against us. The second, that Maristara had been warned of our coming. The only being who could have warned her was one of us, another dragon."

He halted, glanced around, but no one contradicted him.

"My father theorized that whoever was spying on us for Maristara was being well paid for the information. He asked himself, what does she have that any of us could possibly want? Gold, jewels. Bah!"

He paused as images of sweet flesh formed in their minds. "She has humans."

The silence was profound. Everyone kept his or her thoughts submerged.

"My father began to ask questions, to pry and meddle. 'He's gone mad'—that's what you said. 'Let them think me mad,' he told me. 'They'll soon see true madness.' He received information that pointed to a certain dragon."

"What is the name?" demanded Anora, sharp-edged.

"I don't know," said Braun, and a sigh of relief passed softly among the dragons. "He wouldn't tell me, wouldn't blacken the name of a noble family until he was certain. The night he left to question this dragon was the night he died, a death that came very conveniently for someone."

"He should have come to the Parliament," said Anora.

"Would you have listened?" Braun countered.

"We are listening—"

"Now that he is dead."

Anora looked around. No one met her eye. Tails twitched and wings stirred. Talons scratched the floor, tails thumped, and scales rippled.

"We need proof," said Anora.

"And that is why I am here, Minister. Members," said Braun, lifting his head proudly, "I did not come seeking your pity. I came because I have a plan."

His bright eyes fixed on Draconas, who stood calmly, resting easily on the balls of his feet, waiting patiently for his part.

"Well, what is this plan?" Anora asked, when Braun did not immediately speak.

"I would ask to tell it only to you, Minister," said the young dragon. "You and Draconas."

Colors of anger and outrage from the assembled dragons burst upon Draconas. He instinctively raised his hand to shut them out, as he might raise his hand to block out the searing rays of the sun.

"Are you accusing one of us of being a spy?" Malfiesto demanded. "The elders of the twelve houses!"

Braun stood steadfast against the fury. "I do not accuse anyone here. But someone did warn her before and the plan was discussed only among the members of Parliament."

"I'm afraid that is not precisely true," Anora interposed. "Some of us might have told our mates or spoken of it to others."

"Yet, I think I am right in this," said Braun stubbornly. "But I leave it to you to decide, Minister. I will abide by your decision."

"I do not want to put us at odds with each other," said Anora, "as must surely happen if I do as you request. We

are the Parliament. Each member's loyalty is unques-
tioned. Tell us this plan."

Braun was not pleased. "So be it," he said. "I traveled
to the kingdom of Seth—"

"That was foolish, young one," stated Malfiesto with a
snort.

"I know that, but I was half-mad with grief over my
father's death. I wanted to talk to Maristara, to ask her—"
Braun broke off. "In any event, I nearly paid for my folly
with my life. Yet, while I was there, I did manage to
accomplish something. I managed to penetrate the magic
long enough to view one of the humans, a female, sent to
repel me. I saw into her mind, only a glimpse, but what
I saw there intrigued me. Her mind was filled with an
image of a woman she knows as the 'Mistress of Dragons,' who is, I believe, the kingdom's ruler.

"My idea is this: If Draconas could capture this Mistress of Dragons, he could bring her back here for study
and questioning. We would know for certain that Maristara has broken the law by teaching humans dragon magic.
The Mistress might know who among us is working with
Maristara. We might be able to find out where Maristara
has her lair and we could bring her to justice."

The Minister liked the proposal, as did the others. They
were all relieved, glad to be able to hand their problem
to someone else. There was just one small detail.

"Your plan is good, Braun," said Draconas. "But you
have overlooked one important factor—a factor that is
easily overlooked, I admit, due to my appearance. Maristara's magic is just as effective at keeping me out of the
kingdom of Seth as any of the rest of you."

The dragon was baffled, confused. "I am afraid I do
not understand, Draconas. You are human—"

"He looks human," Anora corrected. "He is, in reality,
a dragon. Surely you knew this, Braun? He is the chosen."

"I am not a hatchling," Braun returned, blue-white and
chill. "I thought that perhaps because he has was given
human form, the dragon magic wouldn't affect him."

Anora shook her head. "The clay is the same, whether it is molded into the shape of a human or a dragon. Draconas's body is different, that is all. Thus he retains his powers of magic, his strength, his ability to communicate with us, and so forth."

Braun's head slumped. His talons dug into the stone, his tail slashed. Dejected, frustrated, he glared at Draconas, irrationally blaming him for not being what the dragon wanted him to be. The other dragons unleashed their thoughts now, offering suggestions, arguing, dithering, and debating. Anora, her images vibrant and imposing, endeavored to restore order, but without much success. The dragons were outwardly affronted and inwardly disturbed by the accusations and the thought that one among them could be a killer of his own kind.

The bombardment made Draconas's head ache. This might go on for days or weeks and he was frustrated. He'd long thought the Parliament had been lax in its dealings with Maristara. He'd long advocated that they do something, take some sort of action. Of course, they said, that was the human part of him talking.

He stood in the midst of the maelstrom of thought, his gaze fixed on the dejected Braun, mulling over in his mind what to do. There was a way, but it would mean doing something he had carefully avoided doing for six hundred years. It would mean bending the law, if not outright breaking it.

It would mean meddling in the lives of humans.

"But then, after all," Draconas told himself with a wry grimace, "I *am* the exception."

He stepped forward. "Minister," he said, holding out his hand, his human hand, "I request the wand . . ."

4

THE ROAD LEADING TO THE GREAT WALLED CITY of Ramsgate-upon-the-Aston was generally well-traveled, for the city was the capital for the realm of Idlyswylde, one of the most prosperous nations on the continent. Merchant caravans, their mule-drawn wagons loaded with goods of every kind and variety, rolled ponderously down the road, the fat merchants smiling broadly on all they encountered, for every person they met was a potential customer. Knights with hawks upon their wrists traveled in company, laughing and jesting as they rode in search of glory. Tinkers, mendicants, gypsies, noble ladies peeping out from behind the curtains of their sedan chairs, thieves, assassins and cutpurses, minstrels, bards, and traveling actors all walked the old highway or rather, all had walked it in the past.

This day, though the midsummer's morning was fine, with the hot sun beaming through lazily drifting clouds, the lone traveler had the road all to himself. Not a fat merchant in sight, nor yet a single mendicant, shaking his begging bowl. Draconas might have thought himself alone in the universe, but that he came upon three small, ragged boys sitting on a bridge that spanned the Aston river. Draconas had a good view of the boys for quite a distance, as he walked toward the bridge. Every so often, one or more would leave off swinging his bare feet and throwing rocks in the water to lift his head, shade his eyes with his hand, and peer up into the sky. Then, with a shake of his head, the boy would go back to his heel-swinging and rock-tossing.

Knowing that there is no more knowledgeable person in the universe than a seven-year-old boy, Draconas stopped to speak to them.

"Do those towers I see ahead mark the city of Ramsgate-upon-the-Aston?"

One of the boys looked up. Children have an innate sense about people. The boy cast Draconas a shrewd glance, that took in everything from his knife, thrust into his belt, to his leather jerkin and leather boots and his green breeches made of the fine strong cotton known as moleskin, to his nondescript walking staff from which hung a leather pouch. The clothes bespoke a huntsman, maybe even a poacher. The man's dark, hooded eyes bespoke something else. The boy jumped respectfully to his feet.

"Yes, master, that is the city," said the urchin. "I can guide you there for a copper."

"I am hardly in need of a guide, since I can see the towers for myself," said Draconas mildly. Seeing the child's face fall, he added, "I would gladly pay a copper for information, however."

"Yes, master," said the boy.

There was a minor scuffle, as the boy's two friends, hearing the word "pay," leaped up to join him and an argument ensued. When the dust settled, the first boy emerged as the winner. As the others rubbed their jaws and noses, he turned triumphantly back to Draconas. "What do you want to know, master?"

"I have heard that this Ramsgate is a large city, wealthy and prosperous, and that its markets are famous throughout the realm."

"That's true, master," said the boy proudly.

"Yet, I find the highway empty. No one travels to Ramsgate, it seems, except myself. Can you tell me why that is?"

"Why, the dragon, master," said the boy, looking as astonished as if Draconas had expressed a wish to know what that strange yellow orb was, blazing in the heavens. "You mean to say you ain't heard what's been going on? S'all anyone's been talkin' about."

"No, I am sorry to say, I haven't," said Draconas. "A dragon, you say?" He glanced skyward.

"Yes, master." The boy jerked a thumb at his companions. "That's why we're here. We're hoping for a sight of the monster."

"He's come every day for a fortnight," added another boy, younger than the other two, probably a little brother, tagging along. "Joe, the miller's boy, seen him. Green, he was, and huge, with fire a'blazing from his mouth and the blood of those he slaughtered a'smearing of his claws."

"He didn't slaughter Joe, I hope," said Draconas.

"No, sir. Joe run for the bushes when he saw the monster and hid there 'til it flew past. But the dragon's killed thousands of people and set fire to all the villages up and down the river." The boy looked positively thrilled.

"No wonder no one is on the road," said Draconas. "Killed thousands, you say? This dragon does sound a fearsome beast. Still, you lads do not appear to be afraid of it."

"We're not," said the first boy, though he kept looking warily at the sky.

"Is anyone going to fight this dragon?" Draconas asked.

"The king and his knights set out in search of him. We seen 'em ride out of the city gates and then we seen 'em ride back in, all hot and angry and a'swearing that they didn't get a sniff of the monster the livelong day."

"And they wasn't even out of the saddle a'fore a farmer

comes running in a'crying that the dragon has made off with his herd," chimed in the little brother. "And then they swore some more. The king swore, too. I heared him."

"The markets and shops is all closed," spoke up the third boy. "People are a'feared to stick their noses outen their windows. Joe said that the miller said that the monster will be the ruin of us, even if he don't kill us all in our beds."

"A wise man, the miller. Here is a copper for each of you," said Draconas, removing the pouch and doling out the coins. "And one for the intrepid Joe."

He started off across the bridge.

"Wait, master!" cried the boy. "You're a'headin' into the city."

"Well, what of it?" said Draconas.

The boys ran alongside. "Even after we told you about the dragon? Ain't you a'feared?"

"I am," said Draconas. "But I need the work."

"There ain't much work to be had," said the boy. "Not since the dragon come. What work do you do?"

"I'm a dragon hunter," said Draconas.

He continued on down the highway, the towers of the city of Ramsgate-upon-the-Aston before him and the empty road behind. The boys, after a moment's conferring, left the bridge and scampered along the banks of the river, to take Joe his copper and tell him the exciting news.

Draconas arrived at the city gates, which should have been standing wide open to welcome all and sundry. This day, the gates were closed and barred. Draconas shook his head, amused.

"They must think the dragon is going to fly in through the front door," he muttered. The irony of his statement struck him and he gave a shrug. "Well, well. Perhaps they are not so foolish, after all."

The city walls were heavily manned. Sunlight gleamed off the helmed heads that peered at him over the ramparts.

Only a few looked down at him. Most were tilted upward, searching the skies.

Eschewing the enormous main gate, Draconas made for a wicket, set off to one side. The door opened as he drew near. A large man, armored in plate and chain from head to toe, a dazzling sight in the noonday sun, waved the traveler to step inside.

"You're a bold one, mister, to be out in broad daylight," said the guard, fixing Draconas with a keen look.

"Not so bold as in need of work," Draconas answered. "I heard that my talents might be of use in Ramsgate and so I made haste to travel here."

"Ramsgate-upon-the-Aston," the guard corrected dourly. "We're particular about the name, there being a town called Ramsgate about twenty miles south of here. A low sort of town, if you take my meaning. We don't like being confused."

"I beg your pardon," said Draconas. "And I beg the pardon of Ramsgate-upon-the-Aston."

"In fact," continued the guard, frowning, "you might be best advised to take yourself to Ramsgate. They welcome beggars, I hear. We do not."

"I am not a beggar," said Draconas mildly, maintaining his pleasant demeanor.

"You said you had no work."

"I said I was looking for work and I'm fairly certain of finding it here. My name is Draconas. I am a dragon hunter."

The guard's eyes widened in astonishment, then narrowed in suspicion. "Here, now, if you're a dragon hunter, where's your great sharp sword and your armor and your shield? And where's your horse?"

Catching sight of Draconas's staff, the guard leapt to a conclusion. He backed up a pace, made the sign against evil. "You're one of them devil-serving warlocks, aren't you?"

"I have come to Ramsgate-upon-the-Aston to offer my services to your king," Draconas stated. "As for how I deal with the dragon, that is my concern. Though I would point out that sharp swords and shields and horses have not done you much good thus far."

The guard's forehead furrowed in a frown. Rattling his sword, he said in threatening tones, "Be gone, foul wizard! Our king has no need for the services of those who worship the devil."

"On the contrary, your king is the one who sent for me," Draconas said coolly. "Let me speak to your commander."

The guard hesitated, then shoved his blade back in its sheathe. "Wait here," he ordered and clanked off.

He returned with his commander. "You say His Majesty sent for you, sir. I suppose you have proof?"

Draconas removed the leather pouch from the end of the walking staff, opened it, took out a letter, opened that partway, and pointed at the signet at the bottom.

The guard peered at it closely. "That's His Majesty's," he said, straightening.

Draconas folded up the letter, placed it back into the pouch.

"Now, sir," he said, "I have told your cohort who and what I am and I assume he has told you. I have told him my business—I am here to deal with the dragon. And I have showed you a letter with His Majesty's seal. I am expected at the palace and I intend to keep my appointment with His Majesty. You may send an escort with me, if you do not trust me."

The commander looked past the dragon hunter to the empty road, down which no travelers had come this day nor would any come another day, so long as there was a marauding dragon about. The commander's thoughts went to the market, whose stalls were empty as the road, to his friends and neighbors who were starting to grow restless. His gaze shifted to the gleaming towers of the palace, where—it was said—the king was at his wit's end.

"Take him along," the commander ordered the gate guard. "His Majesty will decide whether to see him or not. If His Majesty turns him out, bring him straight back here." He turned to Draconas. "Will that do, sir?"

"More than fair, Commander," replied Draconas.

"You had best make haste," said the commander, opening the wicket. "One never knows when or where the foul monster will suddenly appear."

"One never does," Draconas agreed politely.

Draconas had visited many human realms in his six hundred years, but Ramsgate-upon-the-Aston had not been one of them. He could see that he had missed something. He was impressed with the cleanliness of the city, its obvious wealth and prosperity—both of which were being threatened by the presence of the dragon. Braun had really been outdoing himself. The boy's tale of the dragon slaughtering thousands wasn't true, of course. Braun and Draconas were to bend the laws of Dragonkind, not shatter them.

Nor did they need to. The sight of the dragon sweeping down from the skies, slaying cattle, burning barns and hay ricks, was all that was needed to terrorize the populace.

"In a week's time," Draconas predicted, well aware of human foibles, "a hundred dead cows will become a hundred dead people. A single barn burned will be a city ravaged."

He was glad to see his faith in humanity had been upheld.

The guard was sullen and uncomfortable in Draconas's presence and refused to be drawn into discussion. He walked the streets in grim and clanking silence, always at Draconas's elbow, though the guard took great care not to touch him. The only time the guard deigned to speak was to point out the local abbey, where he laid great emphasis on the fact that the priests would be more than happy to save Draconas from demonic influence. The guard also took Draconas past the town square where, so he said pointedly, they burned witches.

Draconas paid scant attention. He was taking in every

detail, making note of every street, every building, making his evaluation. Above all, he was interested in the ruler of this fair land of Idlyswylde.

His castle was typical of those Draconas had visited in other realms. Built on the high ground, it had started out as a motte and bailey structure established on a hill above the river. The now proud city of Ramsgate-upon-the-Aston had probably begun life as a ramshackle collection of thatched-roofed huts, huddled close to the wooden bailey for protection.

Over the years, the wooden fortress had been transformed into an imposing castle of white stone with turrets and towers and ramparts and crenellations, courtyards and outbuildings, stables and barracks. Scaffolding raised on the south side of the castle walls meant that improvements to the palace were ongoing. The city had crawled out of its thatched-roofed huts and moved into grand stone and timber structures, with plastered walls and garishly painted signs, paved streets and flowers in pots.

Draconas was not one to be impressed by architecture— dragons live in caverns, where the temperature remains unchanged year-round, perfect for cold-blooded reptiles, and he found that even after six hundred years, he still felt most at home in caves. He was more interested in this proof that the castle and the city had grown and prospered and thrived. Prosperity indicated a realm at peace with its neighbors.

A realm at peace, until now. Now that the dragon had come.

Arriving at the palace, Draconas and his escort walked through the main gate and into a vast courtyard crowded with young men, half-in and half-out of their armor, shouting and gesticulating and proclaiming loudly that the dragon had seen them coming and been too scared to fight. These must be the knights who had ridden out in search of the dragon. Draconas inclined his head as he walked past them. The knights paid him no attention, but kept on talking.

The surly guard led Draconas to the main entrance of the castle. Keeping Draconas under close surveillance, the guard hallooed at the top of his lungs for someone to come.

After several moments, a man appeared, emerging from a side door, ducking underneath the scaffolding.

"Ah, Gunderson," the guard grunted. "Just the man."

The two conferred. Draconas heard the word "devil" used several times. Gunderson was an older man, missing most of his front teeth and an eye. His remaining eye, fixed intently on Draconas, held intelligence enough for six. He had the air of a military man.

"You bear the king's letter, sir?" Gunderson asked, leaving the guard and walking over to Draconas.

"I do," said Draconas, reaching for the pouch.

Gunderson waved his hand. "This way, sir."

The guard cast Draconas a glance of loathing, "You're walking with the devil, Gunderson," the guard warned.

"I'll soak myself in holy water, Nate, if it'll make you feel better," Gunderson replied.

" 'Tis no joking matter," the guard said and, muttering underneath his breath, he made another sign against evil and stalked stiffly away. "I'll be speaking to Brother Bascold about this."

"I'm sorry to be the cause of any trouble," said Draconas, falling into step beside Gunderson. "I guess I shouldn't have been so open about my calling. Where I'm from, the people are not so backward—the people are not so close-minded," he amended tactfully.

"You were right the first time, sir," said Gunderson with a grin. "Backward is the word for it. Nate is a country boy and he still believes witches eat babies and dance naked in the forest in the moonlight."

"I assure you," said Draconas, "that I have never danced naked anywhere, in the woods or out of them."

Gunderson laughed. He had a fine laugh, broad and rolling.

"Wait here. I'll inform His Majesty."

Gunderson brought Draconas into a large hall, then left him to go in search of the king. Draconas looked curiously around. The stone walls kept the air in the cavernous hall as cool as the air in the Hall of Parliament, and the room was nearly as dark. Slit windows let in only a small portion of sunlight and, since the room faced east, even that had been cut off by the sun's sojourn to the other side of heaven. Several pieces of fine furniture decorated the hall and these, including leather, high-backed wooden chairs and a small table, were arranged before an enormous fireplace placed along the center wall. A huge rectangular table, intended for serving meals to a large company, stood at one end of the hall, with benches at the low end—below the salt—and chairs at the other. This was the public hall. The family's private rooms would be elsewhere.

As Draconas looked idly about, taking note of this or that, a child of about seven years of age came to have a look at the dragon hunter. The child was a male, with fair hair and large eyes. His chaussures and tunic were well-made of fine fabric, but not frilly or ostentatious. By his somewhat rumpled, disordered appearance, he'd thrown off his everyday clothes to change hurriedly into more formal clothing on hearing of a guest in the house. He'd apparently done Draconas the honor of washing his face, though he'd missed a spot around his right ear.

"My father will be with you shortly, sir," said the boy. "He asks that I offer you refreshment."

"No, thank you," said Draconas, guessing that he was in the presence of the heir to the throne. Two other blond heads peeped around the corner of a door at the end of the hall. "I take it you are Prince Wilhelm?"

"I am, sir," said the prince with becoming dignity.

"And I am Draconas."

The prince nodded and bit his lip, apparently trying to remember what to do next in order to make his guest comfortable. The answer came to him.

"Please be seated, sir," said the prince with a gesture toward the high-backed chairs.

Draconas bowed, but remained standing.

The prince realized that he must seat himself first, before his guest could sit down. Wilhelm perched on the edge of a chair, then jumped back up eagerly, his princely manners forgotten. "I heard Gunderson tell my father that you are the dragon hunter. Is that true? Do you really hunt dragons? How many have you killed?"

Before Draconas could answer his questions, a woman came bustling into the room, and Draconas was on his feet again. The woman was dark as the young prince was fair. She was short and well-rounded, where he was tall and slim. There was enough resemblance between the two, especially the slightly pug nose and the large, wide-open eyes, to mark them as mother and son.

"Queen Ermintrude," said Draconas. "I am honored."

She was attractive in a soft and motherly way, with her broad hips and ample bosom. The expression of her face was sweet and wholesome. Her dark hair, thick and luxuriant, was her one beauty, and she wore her hair uncovered, bound up in an elaborate braid, not hidden beneath a wimple as was the current fashion.

"His Majesty asks your pardon for the delay. He will be with you shortly. In the meantime, would you like to wash after your journey?" She looked sternly at her son. "Or did Wilhelm ask you that already? He knows he's supposed to."

The prince flushed. "I am sorry, Mother. I forgot I was supposed to offer that first. I did ask him if he wanted refreshment—"

"I would like to wash up," Draconas intervened. "Not a bath," he added hastily, remembering that it was the custom in some realms for the lady of the castle of offer her guests a bath, sometimes even assisting them to bathe with her own fair hands. "Just splash some water on my face and hands. Perhaps Prince Wilhelm could show me—"

The prince's glum face brightened. "I will be glad to, sir."

"You will be our guest this night, of course," said the queen. She paused a moment, her brow furrowed in thought. "We've a great many guests at present, but I believe there is a room available in the east wing, at the far end of the corridor."

"Please do not trouble yourself, Queen Ermintrude. A blanket in the stables will suffice."

The queen smiled, her face dimpled. "You have the air of well-traveled gentleman, sir. You have probably been to far grander royal courts than ours." She spoke very fast, not giving him time or space to answer. "Neither my husband nor I are much for ceremony. You aren't either, apparently. You didn't bow, you know, when I entered and you don't call me 'Your Majesty' or 'Madame.' I came from the royal court of Weinmauer, where my father is king. Have you been there?" she asked, but sped on before he could reply.

"He is very formal. I found it all quite stifling. So did my dear Ned, when he came to marry me. Our marriage was arranged, of course, but we found that we suited one another excellently. My first act as queen was to ship home the twenty ladies-in-waiting my father insisted on sending with me."

The queen laughed again.

Draconas opened his mouth, but she was off again. "Take Master Draconas to his room, Wilhelm. When you have washed and relaxed, sir, come back here and we'll have some spiced wine. I make it myself. Shocking, isn't it?"

Wilhelm made a dash for the door at the end of the corridor. As Draconas prepared to follow, the queen halted him with a look. Casting an oblique glance at her son, Ermintrude walked hurriedly to Draconas, rested her hand on his arm. Her dimples vanished and so did her flighty air.

"Gunderson tells me you are a dragon hunter, sir," she

said softly. "I hope that you can help us. Ned has not slept in a fortnight. He eats next to nothing. He is so worried about the people and he feels so helpless. The merchants are in an uproar . . ."

Ermintrude paused, regarded Draconas intently. He was being judged. She had something confidential to impart and she was trying to decide if she could trust him. After a moment's searching gaze, she made up her mind.

"I'm telling you this, sir, because Ned won't. My husband is being pressured by his ministers to ask my father, the king of Weinmauer, to send in soldiers, proclaim us a protectorate. My father has long had his eyes on our rich kingdom. He means to have it for his own. That was his view when he married me to Ned. My father was sadly disappointed when I refused to go along with his plotting and scheming. I know he's heard about the dragon. His spies tell him everything. If he sends in troops, there will be war, for Ned will never permit our kingdom to come under the sway of Weinmauer. We suspect that at least two of the ministers are in my father's pay—"

A sudden shocking thought came to her. She drew back, regarded Draconas warily. "Perhaps you, too—"

"I know nothing of politics, Queen Ermintrude," said Draconas. "Of that I assure you. I am here only to do a job."

A tear rolled down her cheek and more glimmered in her eyes.

Draconas stepped back hastily, half-turned, and thrust his hands behind his back.

"Why, blessed angels save us," exclaimed Ermintrude. "Are you one of those men who fall apart at the sight of a woman's tears?"

Draconas's mouth twisted. "You have found me out, madame," he said with a bow.

"You needn't worry," said Ermintrude, wiping her eyes. "I won't cry anymore. It's just . . . you're the first person who has ever claimed he could help and sounded as if he truly meant it. But what was that you said about my husband trusting you? Why wouldn't he?"

"My methods are somewhat unorthodox—"

"I understand that they do *not* involve dancing naked in the moonlight," said Ermintrude, a hint of the dimple returning.

"No, madame," said Draconas with a half-smile. The dimple was infectious. "They do not."

"Ah, too bad." Ermintrude sighed. "I might have enjoyed that. He's coming, Wilhelm," she called to the prince, who was shuffling this feet impatiently. "Please don't say anything to my son about what I told you, sir. We don't want to worry him or the other children."

Manners required that Draconas kiss the queen's hand, but she—in her distraction—did not offer her hand to be kissed and he made no move to do so. Her tears were still wet upon her fingers. Bowing, he took his leave of her, pleased with what he'd found out.

"This is better than I had expected," he remarked to himself. "A threat of war, all because of a few burnt villages and some dead cows."

Going off to wash his face and hands and satisfy the young prince's curiosity with some amazing lies about hunting dragons, he added inwardly, "Humans work so hard to complicate their lives. It sounds as if this wretched king is every bit as desperate as I hoped."

5

EDWARD IV OF THE HOUSE OF RAMSGATE-UPON-
the-Aston was young to be king, only just turned thirty.
His father had died in his mid-fifties from drinking tainted
water while on a hunting expedition. Edward had almost
gone with his father on the trip, but had stayed home at
the last moment when the young prince Wilhelm had
come down with a fever. Had Edward gone, he would
have undoubtedly drunk the same water and succumbed
to the same illness, leaving his son, then five years old,
as king.

Wilhelm related the family history to Draconas as he
washed his face and his hands in the large bowl the servants brought to his bedchamber. Wilhelm rather prided
himself on having saved his father's life.

As he washed and Wilhelm chattered, Draconas could
hear other people, guests of the king and queen, coming
and going about the castle, which was crowded with
knights and their ladies, visiting nobility, entertainers and
servants, and hangers-on.

The knights were loud and boisterous. They had decided to make up for their disappointment in regard to the

dragon by organizing a grand boar hunt, which was to take place on the morrow, and they were making ready. Their dogs trotted at their heels, occasionally barking and snapping at each other, adding to the commotion in the corridors. Wilhelm would have taken Draconas to the stables, to show off his very own horse, but Gunderson tracked them down.

"Master Draconas," said the old soldier, "His Majesty is at liberty to see you now."

"I'll see this remarkable horse another time," Draconas promised.

The prince was disappointed at first, but then he thought how he could lord it over his younger siblings by telling them how he had spent the afternoon with a real dragon hunter, and he ran off in search of them.

Gunderson led the way to the family's quarters. They passed through the main hall, now filled with young men and their dogs and retainers, all discussing the upcoming hunt. Conversation halted as they entered. They stared openly at the man everyone in the castle now knew was a dragon hunter. Some of the looks were curious, some intrigued, some openly hostile or suspicious. Draconas paid no attention to any of them.

Gunderson preceded him up a spiral staircase cut into the stone of the west tower. The stairs opened into a comfortable chamber, small and snug and private. Several finely woven rugs covered the floor. A large fireplace stood at one end, not in use on this fine summer's day. Oil lamps provided light and scented the room with a pleasing aroma. The king sat at a table strewn with papers, dictating to a man clad in the somber garb of a clerk.

Draconas looked around. This was the king's own private room, his favorite room, where he came to transact his business, came to think, came to be alone. A man's possessions tell a great deal about him, at least so Draconas had come to believe, and he was intrigued by the fact that the king's study was littered with instruments of a scientific nature. A very fine astrolabe had a prominent place on a table. Beside it was a sextant. A telescope was positioned on the balcony. Draconas wondered briefly and with some amusement if the king had shifted the telescope's use from observing the stars to observing the dragon.

Edward glanced up at them as they entered and gave them a brief nod, to show that he knew they were here. He continued his dictation. Gunderson took Draconas to a window, where they were out of earshot, and Draconas knew now why the king had made this his chosen room. Doors paneled with glass opened onto a balcony. Below was the castle courtyard. Beyond the courtyard was the castle's walls. Beyond the walls the city of Ramsgate-upon-the-Aston, and beyond Ramsgate, the world. Green fields gave way to the darker, mottled green of the forest that gave way to the misty purplish blue of the distant mountains. Draconas looked to those mountains, with their white snowcaps, and his pulse quickened. He could not have arranged for a better setting if he'd had the workings of it.

The secretary departed at last, the sheaf of papers now in his keeping. Edward rose to his feet and stretched. Hearing the scraping of the chair being pushed back, Gunderson and Draconas understood it was proper to turn around.

"His Majesty, King Edward IV," said Gunderson.

Draconas inclined his head.

Gunderson's face flushed. "You are in the presence of the king, sir. You will bow to His Majesty."

"I beg your pardon," said Draconas, "but he is not my king and therefore I do not bow."

He spoke to the king, who was regarding him not in anger, so much, as with amusement. "You sent for me, King Edward, because you have a problem and you believe that I may be the one to solve it. You are looking to me for help, not the other way around. If you want to hire me, that's fine. If not, that's fine, too. But it is important to me and to my job to know that we meet on an equal footing."

Draconas watched the king closely, waited for his reaction. If Edward threw a tantrum, stormed and raged, then Draconas would know he'd been wrong in his assessment of this man and he'd have to find someone else.

Edward's mouth quirked. "He has a point, Gunderson, or rather, several points. We're not his king. We did send for him. We are planning to turn to him for help. It's hard to force a man to bow under those circumstances."

Draconas was satisfied and he took the opportunity to study the man upon whom, all unknowing, the hopes of the dragons rested. Edward was poised, confident, self-assured, and handsome, according to the standards of the day. He wore his chestnut-colored hair shoulder length, as was the fashion in this part of the world; it fell in soft waves from a center part. His features were regular and well-made, with high and prominent cheekbones; a strong, straight nose; and large hazel eyes that met other eyes with disarming frankness. He was tall, his body well-formed and muscular, for although his kingdom had been long at peace, he was always mindful that he might have to fight in her defense.

"I hear there's to be no naked dancing," added Edward. His smile was warm and generous, immediately making the stranger a friend, yet, at the same time, maintaining a cool reserve, reminding one always that he was in the presence of a king.

"Since this seems to be a source of major disappointment, I could arrange it," said Draconas.

Edward grinned. He had a grin like his young son's, a mischievous smile that lit the hazel eyes, charged them with flecks of greenish-gold.

"I fear the naked dancing would have no effect on the dragon," said Edward.

It might, Draconas thought, but not the effect he's looking for. The image of the plump, dimpled, and well-endowed Ermintrude dancing naked with wild abandon in the moonlight was not without its attractions.

Draconas was honest, however. "I fear not."

"Ah, well," said the king with a feigned sigh of regret. "Another time, perhaps."

The smile in his eyes did not last long. The hazel darkened to brown. The handsome face was drawn, careworn, plainly revealing his anxiety and worry. Another man might have tried to hide such feelings. Edward's feelings and thoughts would always be plain upon his face, out in the open for all the world to see and judge.

"I believe that my wife explained the situation to you," said Edward. He gestured toward where the clerk had been sitting. "Those letters you saw me dictating. One was a dispatch from a baron who has holdings on the border of our land and that of Weinmauer. He warns me that Weinmauer's castles along the border are being reinforced. My father-in-law is preparing to ride to my rescue and, in doing so, will swallow me whole. I would almost rather," he added with a glint in the hazel, "be swallowed by the dragon."

"I understand," Draconas replied.

"And you have a solution for this?" Edward asked, regarding Draconas intently. "You can dispose of this threat? Kill this monster or drive it away?"

"Before I answer that, I must teach you something of the nature of dragons," said Draconas. " 'Know your enemy,' is a common dictum among military men, or so I am led to believe."

He cast a glance at Gunderson at this, careful to include the soldier in their conversation, guessing—rightly—that in the absence of his father, Edward would look to the older man for advice and counsel.

"I am eager to learn," said Edward. "Let us sit by the fire. I'll send for wine."

"Tell me exactly what depredations this dragon has committed," said Draconas, once the servants had been dismissed. "That may seem irrelevant, but it tells me something of the nature of the beast."

Edward took a moment to organize his thoughts. "The dragon began by attacking the village of Apfield in the western part of the kingdom."

"Excuse me," said Draconas. "But I believe that we can label the dragon a male. Female dragons rarely commit these sorts of wanton acts of destruction. Female dragons tend to be more subtle and cunning."

"Women are the same the world over, I guess," said Edward, the smile returning briefly to his eyes.

Draconas did not comment. "I like to be precise in the details. Please go on."

Gunderson took over. "After the attack at Apfield, we began receiving reports from almost every part of the kingdom: cattle slaughtered, sheep stolen, people terrorized, homes destroyed. Despite rumors to the contrary, no one has been killed yet," he stated, "but it's only a matter of time."

"I see. And what measures have you taken against the dragon?"

"We summoned His Majesty's knights and waited for the monster to appear. When it did, we set out in pursuit. Our horses are no match for a beast who can fly with the speed of the winter wind."

"Wherever we were, the dragon wasn't," Edward said with fine irony. "The beast seemed to take delight in striking places either just before we arrived or just after we left, making us look like fools."

"The dragon can keep track of your movements from the air," Draconas said, agreeing. "A large mounted force is easy for him to spot and, as you say, he can move much more swiftly than you can. You will never catch him that way."

"Then how?" Edward demanded, slamming his hands on the arms of the chair. "What *can* be done? This dragon must be stopped!" He jumped to his feet, began pacing the room restlessly.

Draconas affected to give the matter serious thought. "I would say that you have a very serious problem. A male dragon—undoubtedly a young one—has taken up residence in your kingdom. Probably in a cave somewhere along the river."

"Residence!" Edward's jaw dropped. "You mean, he plans to *live* here?"

"I am afraid so. Dragons are not that much different from humans in how they think and act. Young men are young men, the world over. You yourself undoubtedly engaged in rash or reckless actions from time to time in your youth."

Edward exchanged rueful smiles with Gunderson, both harkening back to some fond memory. "I may have done so."

Returning to his chair, he flopped down, thrust out his long legs, and stared moodily at his boots.

"I take your point, Master Draconas. This dragon is young and reckless and foolish."

"Precisely. He has no idea of the hardship he is causing, nor would he care if he did. He cares only for his own pleasure and to draw the attention of young females."

"How long will this go on?" Edward demanded.

"Dragons live a very long time, Your Majesty. A dragon's youth may span hundreds of years—"

"God's breath! Something must be done, sir! We must find his cave. Strike him while he sleeps. You shake your head, but—"

"Impossible. First, you might search the rest of your lifetime and never find his lair. Dragons are quite cunning in the manner in which they hide their dwellings. Second, an immense force would be required to battle him. A thousand knights would not be too many."

"A thousand." Edward groaned. "I had trouble enough scraping up twenty."

"Even if you had a thousand, the dragon would hear you and see you from miles away and have time to either prepare his defense or make good his escape. However," Draconas added, seeing the king sinking into despair, "there is a way to rid yourself of this menace."

"Yes?" said Edward, hope propelling him forward in his chair.

"It will require courage on your part, courage and commitment and sacrifice."

"I am prepared to do anything to save my kingdom," said Edward resolutely.

"And you must put your faith and trust in me," said Draconas.

Edward glanced sidelong at Gunderson at this, then looked back to Draconas.

"I do not know you, sir," said the king. "What I have seen of you I like, but as to trust . . ." He shook his head. "I am not prepared to give that now. Perhaps when I have heard your plan—"

"Fair enough," said Draconas. Rising to his feet, he gestured to the window. "If you would be so good as to accompany me, Your Majesty, there is something I would show you."

Mystified, the king did as Draconas asked, with Gunderson ranging closely alongside.

"Do you see those mountains? Those far away, with the snowcapped peaks?"

"Yes. That is the Ardvale mountain range."

"Have you ever traveled there, Your Majesty?"

"Merciful heavens, no," returned Edward, amazed at the question. "The Ardvale mountains are outside the boundaries of the realm. Our border ends at their foothills."

"So you do not know what lies beyond?"

The king shrugged, uninterested. "The mountains are said to be impassable. Nothing but snow and rock. I fail to see—"

"There is something beyond those mountains—a kingdom. The kingdom of Seth."

Edward struggled to be polite. "I had no idea. A kingdom there, you say." With a rolling-eyed glance at Gunderson, the king turned away. "Now, Master Draconas, we were discussing this dragon . . ."

"The kingdom of Seth was once attacked by a force of dragons," Draconas continued imperturbably. "More than twenty dragons laid siege to the city."

Edward halted, turned to stare, appalled.

"The dragons were repulsed. Three were slain. I tell you this, Your Majesty, because the kingdom of Seth is the one place in the world feared by dragons. It is the one place in the world that dragons avoid."

Draconas pointed back at the mist-shrouded mountains. "There, in that realm, you will find the person you need. The person who can drive away the dragon and keep him and his kind away from your kingdom forever."

"How?" Edward demanded. "Who is this person?"

"A woman who is gifted with powerful magicks. You must travel to that kingdom and persuade this woman to come back to Idlyswylde with you. Only her magic can drive away the dragon."

"Magic . . ." Edward exchanged amused glances with Gunderson, who smiled tolerantly. "Are we back to naked dancing, then, sir?"

Draconas cast a significant look at the astrolabe. "Has science helped you so far?"

Edward appeared nettled. "We haven't tried. I was thinking of importing several cannons. We could place them on the battlements—"

"What do you expect the dragon to do, Sire? Wallow in the fields while you pummel it with cannonballs? Or perhaps you propose to knock it out of the skies?"

Edward flushed in anger. He wasn't accustomed to being ridiculed. "I think it would work as well as shaking a chicken's foot at the dragon and chanting *abracadabra*."

"You do not believe in magic," said Draconas.

"No," said Edward, but then he added with a sudden flicker of gold in the hazel, "but then, I didn't believe in dragons, either." He walked over to the balcony, gazed out at the mountains, and took a squint at them through the telescope.

"I am willing to try anything at this point," he added,

turning. "I will dispatch a delegation to fetch this woman. Gunderson, you will go as my personal representative. We will send gifts. Jewels. Fine silks. Women like that." He halted, regarding Draconas with some impatience. "What is wrong now, sir? Again you shake your head. Are jewels the wrong sort of present?"

"There is a reason that you have never heard of the kingdom of Seth," Draconas said in reply. "I am one of the few people in the world who has heard of it and that only after years of searching for clues to its existence. The kingdom is held in thrall, its borders enchanted by this very woman. Thus she keeps out the dragons and all others who might do her people harm. Your delegation could spend years searching those mountains and they would never be able to penetrate the magic that hides the entrance to its borders. And even if, by some miracle, they did happen to stumble across it, they would not live long enough to profit by their discovery. Warriors guard the borders, with orders to slay all who attempt to enter."

Edward stared, amazed. "I seem to have fallen into some sort of fairy tale! Enchanted kingdom. People held in thrall. Borders hidden by magic."

"The man is mad," said Gunderson, frowning. "This nursery tale has gone on long enough, Your Majesty. I am sorry I wasted your time with such nonsense. Let me toss the fellow out on his ear."

Edward waved him to silence. "I find this hard to believe, Draconas."

"Then let me ask you a question, Sire. Has science been able to prove the existence of God?"

"Of course not," said Edward shortly.

"Yet you believe in God?"

"I am a man of faith. And, yes, I understand what you're saying." The hazel eyes were quite dark, with glinting flecks of green. "You hand water to a man dying of thirst and then dash the cup from his lips. You tell me in one breath that in that far-off kingdom lies my only hope and in another that my hope must rest on the supernatural. And what does it matter anyhow," he added, with an impatient gesture, "for it can't ever be attained?"

"I did not say that," said Draconas. "A delegation would not be able to enter that kingdom. They would all be killed. But one person might, provided he is armed with the proper magic. One person to plead his cause."

Edward gazed long at Draconas. "Armed with magic. Merciful mother of God. If I sent Gunderson—"

Draconas was again shaking his head. "The Mistress of Dragons is exalted by her people. High and puissant, she is worshipped as a god. Only you, a king in your own right, would have any chance of obtaining an audience with her."

"You're not seriously considering this, Sire," said Gunderson, eyeing his king.

He drew Edward aside. They spoke in low tones, but Draconas had quite good hearing. Turning his back, he gazed out the window, pretended to be absorbed by the view.

"I don't like this, Your Majesty," Gunderson told him. "What do we know of this fellow? Nothing! And he proposes that you go with him on some wild-goose chase of a journey. Magic!" He snorted. "It is likely a trick of Weinmauer to lure you away."

"Whatever it is, I don't believe it is that," said Edward dryly. "My father-in-law could never have made up such a tale—a priestess with magical powers hidden away in some enchanted kingdom." He sighed softly. "If it is true, what an adventure, Gunderson! Think of it!"

"*If* it is true." Gunderson laid heavy emphasis on the "if." "First there is this business of the magic. Your Majesty knows, as do all educated people, that it is not possible for humans to possesses supernatural powers. That what these charlatans who call themselves warlocks and witches pass off as 'magic' is really nothing more than trickery—sleight of hand, illusion, gimmicks."

"True," Edward admitted.

"Second, I do not like his arrogance. He does not show you the proper respect."

"You know, Gunderson, that's the one reason I tend to trust him. He has made it clear that I must take him as is. If he were up to some nefarious scheme, wouldn't he be slavering and fawning all over me, like those toadies sent by my father-in-law?"

"Unless he thinks that is what you would think—"

"Oh, come now, Gunderson, this is getting a bit thick!" Edward smiled. "I'm rather considering going with him."

"Your Majesty can't be serious!"

"You were the one who recommended I meet with him—"

"Meet with him, yes. Hear what he had to say. Not go off alone with him."

"I have an idea," said Edward. "You spoke of the magic. Let us make a little test." He raised his voice. "Master Draconas, you say I must be 'armed with magic.' What sort of magic? Who is to arm me?"

"I will, Your Majesty."

"I trust you do not think it untoward of me to ask for a demonstration?" Edward cast a sidelong glance at Gunderson, as much as to say, "We have him now."

Draconas shrugged. He drew the leather pouch from the end of his staff, thrust in his hand, and brought out a yellow topaz. As large as a hen's egg, the topaz had been cut so that it was smooth upon the top, beveled about the edges, and flat on the bottom. Draconas walked over to the table the king had been using for his work and laid the jewel flat upon a sheet of vellum.

"A lovely gem," remarked Edward, coming to inspect it. "Are we going to see it levitate? Go floating out the window?"

Draconas made no answer. He held his hand over the jewel, spoke a soft word. The topaz began to gleam with an eerie yellow light. The king and Gunderson stood staring with some amusement at the glowing jewel, neither approaching it.

"Remarkable," Edward said. "What is it supposed to be doing?"

"You mentioned the window," said Draconas. "This jewel is a window. A magical casement that I alone have the power to open. Come forward and look through it."

Edward glanced at Gunderson, whose expression was very dark. "It's some sort of trick."

"If so, it is a very good one," Edward remarked. He looked up at Draconas. "Come, sir. How do you cause it to glow like that? Ah, I know. Is this one of those prisms that has the power to store up sunlight?"

"It does more than glow," said Draconas. "Look into it."

With a laugh and a shrug, Edward bent down, gazed into the jewel.

His eyes widened. He gave a soft gasp, moved closer, staring intently. The eerie yellow light cast a radiant glow upon his face.

"There's . . . there's someone in there!" He lifted his head, awed and incredulous. "Who is she?"

"I do not know her name," said Draconas. "All I know is that she is a priestess who serves the Mistress of Dragons. She is beautiful, isn't she?"

"I have truly never seen the like," murmured Edward, drawn to the jewel. "Her lips move. She's starting to say something . . ."

Draconas swiftly clasped his hand over the topaz, and broke the spell. The light vanished and with it the image of the priestess who had looked into the magical stone bowl and seen the dragon Braun, and had spoken to him. Draconas had no intention of permitting the king to hear that conversation. Although the kingdoms of Seth and Idlyswylde had been separated for hundreds of years—so many years that each had forgotten about the other—once there had been traffic between the two. They shared a common language.

"I want to hear what she says!" Edward stated.

"Now is not the time."

"It was a trick, Your Majesty," Gunderson said gruffly. "Here. Let me see that thing."

Draconas handed the topaz to the steward. Gunderson shook it, peered at it. Fetching a jeweler's glass, he inspected the gem from every angle. "It is an ordinary topaz," he said at last. "Not even very valuable. The gem is flawed."

He offered it to Edward, who shook his head. Gunderson handed the gem back to Draconas, who dropped it into the leather pouch.

"How did you do that, sir?" Gunderson asked again.

"As I said, magic." Draconas shrugged. "My magic. The magic that will carry you inside the enchanted kingdom."

Edward sucked in a breath, let it out slowly. "What is your plan?"

"All in good time. There is first the matter of my payment. One hundred gold pieces. Fifty now and fifty on completion of the dragon's removal."

Edward blinked, amazed. "That is an immense sum, sir."

"One might almost say, 'A king's ransom,'" said Draconas. "Or in this case, a kingdom's ransom. The dragon is costing you much more than that in lost revenues every day."

"Very well," said Edward, wincing. "And now that we are agreed, I ask you to tell me how this magic of yours works."

"Magic is not a waterwheel, Your Majesty. I cannot draw you a diagram or show you the mechanism. It is what it is. If you could send someone for the gold . . ."

"Gunderson, go and fetch it from the strongbox."

"Your Majesty, I beg you to consider what you are about. Your kingdom is threatened from without *and* from within. The barons on the border are preparing for war. The merchants cry that their businesses are failing. They have no money to pay the taxes, which means we have no money to pay our soldiers, much less money to pay this man. As for his so-called magic, I don't know how the trick was done, but there must be some rational explanation!"

Gunderson talked on, and Draconas sat down in a chair and let him.

Watching the king closely, Draconas saw the hazel eyes darken until they became unreadable. The expressive face, previously open to all, slammed shut its doors, quenched the inner lights. The king listened politely to the older man, but his gaze strayed to the leather pouch hanging on the staff.

"A young man," Draconas mused, "beset early in life by the burdens of kingship—burdens that grow heavier every day. He was married young to a woman he barely knew with the object of reducing him to a nonentity. Now he must be husband and father, not only to his family, but to his people. He stands knee-deep in their muck, bent double beneath the load. Here am I, offering him an adventure spun of moondust and topaz and a mysterious beauty. Like the chivalrous knights of old, he goes forth with a noble cause, to save his kingdom. I offer him the chance to cast off the burdens, forget for a brief time that he is king, husband, father. He would be more than human if he refused."

"My mind is made up," said Edward, cutting Gunderson off in midsentence. The voice he used was the king's voice, cold and impersonal. "I will go with Master Draconas. I know I run a great risk, dear friend," he added, relenting, "but it seems to me that if there is the slightest chance that this might work, that I can rid our kingdom forever of the dragon's scourge, then the risk is one that I must take."

"Let me accompany you, Your Majesty," Gunderson pleaded earnestly. "Do not go off alone with this stranger."

"I need you here, my friend," said Edward, "to look after the kingdom. Ermintrude is more than capable of dealing with her father, but she will need you at her side if the worst should happen and he invades the realm."

"Yes, Your Majesty," said Gunderson in heavy tones. He turned to Draconas. "See that you take excellent care of King Edward, sir. Or I promise you, there will be the devil to pay." Gunderson tapped himself on the chest. "Me."

That night, the marauding dragon struck again.

Though the hour was late, the knights were still sitting at table when the alarm was raised. Everyone present grabbed shield and sword and raced outside, clambering up the stone steps to the ramparts to see for themselves.

Off in the distance, the dragon's enormous green-scaled body gleamed in the light of the flames of burning wheat fields. The knights cursed and struck their swords against their shields, shouting challenges to the dragon to come and fight. Braun, of course, disdained their challenge and flew away with a flip of his tail, that looked for all the world as if he were deliberately insulting them.

His face dark with fury, Edward pressed his lips together in a firm, straight line, turned on his heel, and left the wall. A short time later, the king announced in quiet, level tones that he was planning a pilgrimage. He was going to seek divine help to find a solution to their problem.

Edward had wanted to keep his journey secret, but, as Gunderson had quite reasonably pointed out, "If you suddenly turned up missing, Sire, with no explanation, the people would panic. They might think that you fled in terror. Your absence would most certainly open the door to the king of Weinmauer."

"But if," Edward had argued, "I announce that I am traveling to another kingdom on a diplomatic mission to seek help about the dragon, I will be expected to take along armed guards, servants, my ministers and advisers, my scribes, my hawks, and my knights."

"Go on a pilgrimage," Draconas had suggested. "Even a king may go upon a sacred quest alone. In fact, it is almost expected."

Edward was struck by the notion, one that touched his romantic and adventurous nature. The age of chivalry had passed from this part of the world. Ramsgate-upon-the-Aston was starting to think more about commerce and trade than "worshipfully winning worship" which had been everything to the chivalrous knight. Those days were in the recent past and were now much celebrated. Minstrels sang of them, poets wrote of them, women sighed over them, and men spoke with regret that the chance to do gallant deeds and undertake heroic actions was gone forever.

Not even Ermintrude could say a word against it when Edward announced his intention of leaving upon a holy pilgrimage to a distant realm, though she obviously had her doubts and fears. Edward's knights begged to accompany him, some of them going so far as to prostrate themselves before him and plead with him. Edward was steadfast in his refusal. He had to undertake this alone. He asked only for their prayers and their blessing. The knights gave him this and a rousing cheer.

Having no fear now that the king would change his mind—or have it changed for him—Draconas went to bed. Edward and his wife left the hall early that night, as well. He was probably with Ermintrude right now, doing his best to reassure her that he would return to her safe and sound.

"I wonder," said Draconas to himself, with some amusement, as he stretched out on the straw-stuffed mattress, "if Edward will tell his wife about the beautiful face in the topaz? I'll wager he keeps that to himself."

6

THE KING MANAGED TO ESCAPE THE PALACE AND
the city with a minimum of fanfare, much less than Draconas had expected.

Dawn had yet to break when Edward mounted his horse for the journey. A priest was present to bless and anoint the king. His family was there, Ermintrude with a brave, supportive smile and anxious, troubled eyes; Prince Wilhelm bitterly disappointed that he couldn't go. The knights gathered, and so did many townsfolk, for the rumor of the king's departure had spread like dragon fire, as one wag said. No one cheered, for this was a sacred pilgrimage. Many murmured blessings as their king rode past. Draconas was not present. He had arranged to meet the king on the road outside the walls. The less notice he brought to himself, the better.

Gunderson rode with His Majesty as far as the city walls, where he turned his king over to Draconas with a baleful look, a final clasp of hands. Edward had with him three horses—a pack horse, a horse that was to be a gift for the Mistress of Dragons, and a horse for Draconas.

"Gunderson told me that you arrived in the kingdom

on foot," said Edward, handing over the reins to a less-than-enthusiastic Draconas. "Accept this with my gratitude for all you have done."

"I haven't done anything yet," Draconas pointed out, eyeing the horse, who eyed him back.

Draconas did not like to ride. With his dragon-gifted strength and endurance (far beyond that of normal humans), he had no need. He could run long stretches at a time, covering as many miles in a day as a horse, without stopping to rest. That was one reason.

There was yet another.

Animals and Draconas did not get along. Some beasts took fright and fled. Others attacked him on sight. Most animals appeared perplexed. They didn't know what he was, but they knew what he wasn't. He wasn't human. Village dogs would follow him for miles, sniffing at his heels and whining. There had once been a cat, a small tortoiseshell, who sat in front of him for hours, her head cocked to one side, her golden eyes staring and staring.

He had to be especially careful with horses, who would flatten back their ears, snort, stamp, and roll their eyes at his approach. Once he was near, however, he could usually soothe them with his voice and firm touch, so that they would permit him to mount, as he did with the king's horse. The filly was restless and edgy, however, constantly swiveling her head to regard him with deep suspicion.

"I've never seen Falderal act like this," Edward said. "Perhaps there's a burr under her saddle."

Draconas could have told the king that it was not the burr under the saddle that was bothering the horse, just the dragon atop it. Since he could not very well say that, he dismounted and was starting to remove the saddle to check, when he heard hoofbeats.

The day was incredibly quiet. Animals had gone to ground for fear of the dragon; the birds hid fearfully in the trees, their songs silenced. Even thieves and brigands had fled the kingdom, or so Edward said. Draconas's acute hearing picked up rhythmic pounding behind them, pounding that continued on for a bit, then suddenly ceased.

Draconas looked south, back down the way they had come. The country through which they were riding was open grasslands, extending beyond both sides of a road that rose and dipped among small hills. The road ran straight, and it was well-maintained, for it led from Ramsgate-upon-the-Aston to the town of Bramfell located in the northern part of the kingdom, famous—so Edward said—for its wool.

A glint of light in the distance attracted his attention. Draconas's eyesight was as keen as his hearing. A dragon in flight can spot a mouse in the fields hundreds of feet below. His vision was not quite that good—his human eyes limited him—but it was better than that of the average human. Atop a hill some distance behind them were five riders. The glint he saw came from the sun shining on the lens of a spyglass one of them was holding.

In the next eye blink, the riders were gone. He did not hear the hoofbeats.

"What is it?" Edward asked, noting Draconas's preoccupation. "The dragon?"

"I thought so, but I was mistaken," said Draconas. He replaced the saddle, bent down to cinch it, all the while listening for the hoofbeats.

Nothing.

"I don't want to be caught out here in the open by that foul beast," said Edward, looking grim.

"No," said Draconas, glancing around. "Not out here in the open."

He remounted and they started off. Draconas listened intently and very soon he heard a muffled echo, distant hoofbeats, coming along behind. He and the king traveled a good five miles and all the while the hoofbeats remained behind them, not drawing nearer, keeping their distance.

Draconas developed a theory. A small roadside shrine, nestled in a stand of trees, provided him a chance to test it. The king halted to make an offering, for, he said, he needed all the help he could get. Draconas led the horses to a nearby stream for water and listened and watched back down the road to the south. He heard the hoofbeats for several moments before they came to a halt. He thought he caught the glint of light, but he couldn't be sure due to the dust they'd raised and the haze of a warm afternoon.

Edward proposed they remain here for lunch and to rest the horses. Draconas agreed.

They both drank from the stream, laved water over their faces and necks, then Edward brought forth a luncheon "fit for a king," as he said laughingly. He laid out bread and two whole roasted capons, wrapped in cheesecloth, and placed a skin of ale into the stream to cool. Edward handed over one of the capons, tore the leg off the other, and began eating.

"By my faith, this is good," he said, gnawing on a chicken leg with as much gusto as a small boy. The king gazed contently out over the green meadowland. "No one wants me. No one needs me. No one is hounding me to fix this, answer that, sign this, don't sign that, listen to the same grievance for the hundredth time . . ."

He paused, gave a great sigh of contentment that came from somewhere deep inside him. "No one can find me."

Draconas gave the king a moment to enjoy this peaceful interlude before he shattered it.

"Do you have any enemies?" he asked.

"A king always has enemies," said Edward cheerfully.

"I mean, enemies who would want to do you serious harm."

Edward looked intently at Draconas, then said, more somberly, "If you mean enemies who want to see me come under the thumb of Weinmauer, then the answer is yes. If you mean enemies who want to see me dead, then the answer is . . . well . . ."

He pondered, thoughtful. "I suppose no man wants to think there is another out there bent on taking his life, but

I guess there could be, though none come to mind at the moment."

"Would your father-in-law want to see you dead?" Draconas pursued.

"He wouldn't be prostrate with grief if I died of natural causes. Weinmauer is not a dummy. He knows he would be the first suspect if I were to die by foul means. He would earn the undying hatred of his daughter, for one thing, and he would find himself with a war on his hands. He doesn't need that. Why should he? He is certain of gaining what he wants by peaceful means."

Edward tossed the chicken leg into the brush. "Unless your plan works and I can bring back this Mistress of Dragons, my father-in-law will march in to 'protect us' and the people will line his route, cheering. Why do you ask?"

"Because we are being followed," said Draconas.

Edward stared, astonished. "The devil we are! Followed? Are you sure?"

"I'm sure."

Edward frowned. "I told those young hotheads that I must do this alone—"

"I don't believe it is any of your knights. They would have raced after us and caught us up by now."

"Some fellow traveler then—"

Draconas shook his head. "You yourself said even the bandits had fled for fear of the dragon. Whoever is following us is hanging back, keeping track of our movements, stopping when we stop, riding when we ride."

Edward peered down the road. "I've heard nothing, seen nothing."

"I have," said Draconas.

"But why?" Edward demanded. "Why would they follow us? Robbers would just attack. They wouldn't risk discovery trailing after us." He frowned, recalling Draconas's questions. "You don't think they're ordinary footpads, do you?"

Draconas regarded the king intently. Edward was either

an exceptionally good dissembler or he honestly did not know why someone might want to send assassins after him.

"No, Your Majesty, I don't." Draconas washed off the grease from the capon in the stream. "What is the lay of the land like ahead of us?"

"Open, like this, for several more miles, then we enter a thick woods along the riverbank. After that, we cross the river and more open meadowland. This is sheep country—"

"The woods, that's what they're waiting for," said Draconas.

Edward finished off his capon. He removed the ale skin from the water, uncorked it, swallowed deeply, and handed it to Draconas.

"You think they'll attack us once we're in the woods."

"They haven't attacked us yet. They're waiting for something. Cover for their deed is the most obvious explanation."

"Why would they need cover? There's no one around for miles and miles. No one except the dragon," Edward added with a wry smile.

Draconas had to admit that the king had a point. Why not attack them here and now? Why wait? They were two alone, only one of them carrying a sword, and there were five of them, all undoubtedly heavily armed.

"And you're certain they mean to kill us?" Edward asked.

"I'm not certain of anything," Draconas admitted.

Edward shrugged. "I find it very puzzling."

He took another pull at the ale skin, squinted up at the heavens. "It's noon or thereabouts. I believe I will take a nap. I didn't get much sleep last night. Ermintrude wasn't thrilled at the idea of my making this journey. I'm afraid if I keep going, I'll fall asleep in the saddle."

Draconas nodded. "I'll keep watch."

Edward removed his sword, laid it beside him, and flung himself down on the ground beneath a tree. He pulled his hat over his eyes to block out the sun, relaxed, and gave a deep, contented sigh. "Wake me if we're attacked," he said, grinning.

Draconas regarded the king with a frown. *Assassins hot on his trail and he takes a nap, leaving me—a perfect stranger—to keep watch. Is he a dolt? I'm beginning to wonder if I picked the right man for the job.*

Leaving the slumbering king, Draconas walked out to the road. He saw nothing. He heard nothing, yet he felt their pursuers out there.

Draconas returned and sat down beside the stream. Judging by his relaxed posture and even breathing, the king slept soundly. The horses flicked at flies with their tails and nibbled on the long grass. Draconas amused himself by using a chicken bone to catch crayfish. He found his mind going back to the matter of their pursuers again and again, which meant that he wasn't as sure of his assumptions as he tried to convince himself. He ended up throwing the bones and the crayfish into the stream in frustration and, in an irritable mood, he woke up the king, shaking him roughly.

"Time to ride," he said.

Edward removed his hat, blinked up at Draconas, then squinted at the sun. "Already?" He yawned, sat up, stretched. "I didn't wake up dead," he added lightly. "Therefore I take it nothing happened while I was asleep."

"I wouldn't say that," said Draconas, swinging himself up in the saddle. "I think I learned something."

"I know I did," said Edward, mounting his horse.

Draconas shifted restlessly in the saddle, ready to get started. "What was that?"

"How to catch crayfish," said Edward and, with a wink and a grin, he galloped off.

He was testing me, Draconas realized. *Six hundred years among humans, and they can still surprise me.*

They were deep in sheep country now and they should have seen the green hills dotted with the white flocks. The shepherds were keeping their sheep closer to home, now, for fear of the dragon, and the hillsides were bare, empty.

Another hour's riding, and the long grass and heather gave way to oaks and maples, linden trees and stands of white poplar, their leaves golden in the rich light of the sweltering sun.

"I can hear them now," Edward reported.

"Yes," said Draconas, who had been listening to the pounding of hooves for the past hour, as regular as a heartbeat. "They're coming closer. And they don't care if we know they're back there."

Edward glanced up at the overhanging branches of the trees. "Gunderson says that if you know you're going to fight, you should be the one to choose the ground. He was talking about armies, but I assume the same applies here."

"You have ridden this road often, so I leave that to you," said Draconas, having now a much better opinion of the man he'd chosen. "Since they are five and we are two, we need to keep them in front of us. Otherwise they will try to circle around and attack us from all directions."

"Yes, that's what I was thinking." Edward frowned thoughtfully. "Up ahead, there's a place where a large oak was struck by lightning. Half of it fell across the highway, completely blocking the road. The people of Bramfell spent days clearing it. They hauled the trunk of the tree to the side of the road. If we were to put our backs to that tree trunk, anyone trying to come up behind would have to climb over it to reach us."

"A good plan." Draconas nodded.

"Why are you so certain they're out to kill me?" Edward asked.

"If they wanted to stop for a chat," Draconas answered dryly, "I think they would have done so by now."

Behind them, the horses' hooves broke into a gallop.

"How far is that tree?" Draconas cried.

"Up ahead," said Edward, and kicked his horse in the flanks.

The hooves pounded closer. There was no doubt that they meant trouble.

Reaching the lightning-blasted tree, Edward remained mounted, his sword in his right hand, a dagger in his left. He wore his traveling clothes—a belted, embroidered tunic, tall leather boots, short pantaloons, and woolen chaussures. He had not thought to wear armor.

Draconas jumped from his horse. A staff was no weapon for a horseman and he was accustomed to fighting on foot. Neither he nor the king were in any real danger, for Draconas had his dragon magic and while he could not kill these humans, he could confuse them with illusions or frighten them with fire. He preferred not to use his magic unless as a last resort, however. Edward knew Draconas had magical powers, but no human on earth possessed such powers as did Draconas and he was loathe to reveal himself.

He was confident that the two of them could handle these cutthroats without the need for magic. Gunderson had trained his protégé well. Edward sat his horse with confidence, handled his weapons and himself with skill.

Five horsemen appeared in the distance. Seeing their quarry waiting for them, they spurred their horses forward. The road did not narrow, as it passed through the forest on its way to Bramfell, for large wool carts traveled this route. The five could have ridden abreast, but they did not do so. One rode ahead. Four followed at a short distance, as if they'd been ordered to keep back.

This struck Draconas as an odd strategy for a band of hired thugs. He concentrated his attention on the lead rider and he was startled and confounded by what he saw. So was Edward, apparently, for he lowered his sword.

"By Our Lady," he said in astonishment, "it's a holy father."

The lead rider was tall and lank, with the thin, wasted body of one who spends much of his time fasting. He wore long black robes, belted around his waist with a rope. His over-large eyes shone with a wild light in his gaunt face.

He was not used to riding, apparently, for he jounced up and down on the galloping horse, seeming likely to tumble out of the saddle at any moment. Clinging to his horse with his knees and the grace of God, the monk raised one hand to heaven and pointed with his other hand at Draconas.

"God smite the demon!" the monk cried.

A blow as from a gigantic mailed fist struck Draconas, flung him back against the tree trunk with such force that it knocked the breath from his body and very nearly dashed the wits from his head.

He lay on the ground on his back, stunned as much by the impossibility of the blow as by the blow itself. The monk had used dragon magic, magic no human was supposed to know. The sounds of shouting and cursing and the clash of steel impelled him to his feet.

The other four men bore down on Edward, ignoring Draconas.

The king had been taken aback to see a monk attacking them, but he'd recovered and was meeting his opponents' attack with enthusiasm, his sword cutting and slicing and parrying, all the time keeping his back and that of his horse to the log. For the moment, Edward was in no danger. Draconas looked about for the more deadly foe.

Unable to control his horse, the monk had gone careening off down the road. Horse and rider were now about half a furlong away, the monk struggling frantically to bring his horse under control so that he could return to the fray. Draconas had time to assist the king and reduce the number of their enemies before he had to deal with the monk.

Running up behind the thugs, Draconas swung his thick, oaken staff like a club, giving one man a clip on the helm that set it chiming like a church bell. The man fell from his horse. Edward thrust his sword through the throat of another, who slid from the saddle, choking on his own blood.

The monk regained a modicum of control and managed to turn the horse around. He came galloping back for another pass and Draconas had to leave the remaining assassins to Edward.

Taking up a position in the middle of the road, Draconas watched in bemusement to see the monk come charging straight at him, attacking mindlessly, arms akimbo, feet flying out of the stirrups. His eyes, wide and lit with madness, stared at Draconas. Howling again about demons, the monk pointed his finger.

Draconas was prepared for the magic. He spun his staff in an arc. A shield of silvery blue energy formed in front of him, shielding him. He crouched behind the shield, ready to spring.

The monk's magic struck the shield. Light sizzled. There was a crack like thunder.

The monk's horse panicked, reared back on its hind legs, front hooves pawing at the air. The monk went flying, head over heels, and landed with a thud on the hardbaked dirt.

The horse galloped off. The monk tried to struggle to his feet. One arm dangled useless. He couldn't put his weight on his leg. He half-dragged himself to a huddled crouch, then thrust his good hand into the folds of his ragged robes.

Expecting a knife, he halted, watching and wary. Madmen are frightening opponents because there is no telling what they're going to do. This one obviously felt no pain, for he continued to glare with ferocious hatred at Draconas, gibbering and cursing him as "demon spawn."

Keeping his staff raised, Draconas edged forward.

"I don't want to have to kill you," he told the monk. "I just want to talk to you."

"The devil take your foul kind!" the monk snarled.

His hand darted out from his breast. In it he held a small glass vial.

Draconas dropped his staff and lunged, but he was too late. The monk yanked the stopper from the vial and dumped the contents down his throat.

The monk gagged. His tongue burst out of his mouth, swollen and purple. His eyes bulged and he grabbed for his throat. Choking, the monk pitched forward, dead.

"Damnation," swore Draconas.

Hearing booted footsteps running up behind, he whipped about, raising his staff.

"It's me," said Edward, scratched and bloody, dirty and sweaty, but otherwise unhurt.

Draconas relaxed and turned back to the dead monk.

"What did you do to him?" Edward demanded, coming up to stand beside Draconas.

"Nothing," said Draconas. Bending down, he lifted the man's hand, exhibited the vial still clasped in the clutching fingers. "He drank poison."

"But"—Edward gasped—"that's a mortal sin. And he was a holy father—"

"Bah!" Draconas snorted. "He's no more a holy father than I am. He's just dressed up to look like one." He lifted the head, indicated the bald pate encircled by the tonsure. "Sunburned. A true monk's skin on top of his head would be tanned from the sun. That tonsure was newly cut."

"You're right," said Edward, puzzled. "But why should an assassin disguise himself as a monk? I could understand if he'd been trying to sneak up on me, but he came riding straight at—" He halted, and eyed Draconas thoughtfully.

"Maybe he's carrying something beneath his robes." Draconas tore the black fabric from the man's back, then halted, appalled at what he saw.

Red, roped, ugly wheals crisscrossed over the monk's spine and shoulders, the type of scars made by a whip or lash. Some were old. Some were fresh.

Not much in this world fazed Draconas. He'd seen every sort of cruelty man could inflict upon man, some of them highly creative, and he had not blenched. This sickened him. He replaced the robes with a gentle hand, and rose to his feet.

"Good God," said Edward, shocked. "I wonder who did that to him?" He glanced back at the other men, lying in the dust.

Draconas shrugged. "No way of knowing."

"I wonder something else," said Edward coolly. "He attacked you, not me."

Observant bastard. Draconas had been hoping the king hadn't noticed that fact.

"He was a madman. Who knows why he did anything?"

Edward stood staring down at the body, shaking his head. "I don't believe it. Those other four were mercenaries, hardened soldiers, well-trained and, from the looks of this"—he held up a bloody money pouch—"well-paid. I found this on one of them. Silver coins, twenty of them. These men were professionals and such veteran sell-swords don't work with lunatics. Yet, he was obviously one of them."

"Truly a mystery," said Draconas. He bent down to pick up his staff, and gazed speculatively down the road. "I know you planned to stay the night in Bramfell, but I don't think that would be wise. I say we leave the road, detour around the city, and strike off directly through those fields to the northwest."

"The way will be much more difficult to travel," stated Edward. "And slow our journey considerably."

"Better we arrive behind time, than not all," Draconas said. "Whoever hired these men is probably sitting in a tavern somewhere in Bramfell, waiting to hear how they fared. When the assassins don't show up, he'll come looking for them." Draconas glanced around at the dead and the wounded. "And he'll find them. Nothing we can do about that. But at least he won't be able to find us."

"You think whoever did this will try again?"

"Don't you?"

"Do you know what I think, Draconas?" said Edward,

his hazel eyes golden as the sun in the leaves. "I think kings aren't the only ones with enemies."

He walked back to his horse, wiping the blood off his sword as he went.

"That's true enough," Draconas said to himself. He stood staring down at the body of the lunatic, who *had* been a madman, if he hadn't been a monk. What had driven him mad? The dragon magic burning in his blood, the ill-usage, the terrible sights he'd seen. His last words echoed in Draconas's mind.

The devil take your foul kind.

The monk had known the truth about Draconas. He had known where to find him. He'd been taught how to use the dragon magic against Draconas, though not taught very well.

Only twelve dragons had known the plan to find the Mistress of Dragons, the twelve who sat on Parliament. One of those was either in league with Maristara or was passing on information to the one who was.

"Which means that I owe you an apology for doubting you, Braun," said Draconas grimly. "We all do."

Now, at any rate, he had his answer to the nagging question that had been bothering him ever since the king had mentioned it: With no travelers on the road to interfere or see them, why did the assassins wait to attack them until they reached the shelter of the trees?

The answer was simple.

The assassins weren't hiding their deed from the eyes of man.

They were hiding it from the eyes of the dragon.

7

BEFORE THEY COULD CONTINUE ON THEIR JOUR-
ney, Draconas had to chase after his horse. When he had
caught the beast, he had to dissuade Edward from giving
the bodies a decent burial. As Draconas pointed out, they
were paid killers and, if they had been caught by the law,
they would have been hanged, their bodies left to rot on
the scaffold to serve as a warning to others. Leaving them
here was no different.

"Plus," said Edward, struck by a new thought, "leaving
them will give the sheriff of Bramfell the chance to investigate the matter. When next we stop, I'll send a message to the duke, telling him what happened and urging
him to find out who paid these men to kill us."

"An excellent idea, Your Majesty," said Draconas, who
had no intention of allowing anyone to investigate anything.

He searched the body of the monk, but did not find
anything useful; not that he had expected to do so.

"What happened to the bastard I hit on the head?" he
thought to ask.

Edward glanced about. "I didn't see. Probably came to
his wits and ran off."

"All the more reason to be leaving, before he reports back to whoever hired him that he failed. The sun sets late, we have another couple of hours at least."

They left the road, moving slowly at first, for they were forced to guide their horses through the tangle of bramble and bracken that lined the roadside. Once free of that, they struck open meadows and they were able to ride more swiftly. Draconas had the very great satisfaction of seeing the road and the forest surrounding it dwindle in the distance.

Topping a rise, they halted to let the horses rest. The king glanced back over his shoulder and stiffened in the saddle.

"Smoke," he said, pointing. "Back there."

The sun was near to setting. Shadows filled the valley. Red-orange light gilded the high hills and the treetops. Black smoke curled in a straight line into the still air.

"A campfire," said Draconas.

"That is no campfire," said Edward grimly. "The dragon has set fire to the forests around the road." He squinted to see into the sun. "Must be close to where we were when we were attacked."

"All the more reason to make haste, Your Majesty," said Draconas.

The king watched the smoke another moment, his lips compressed in a straight, tight line.

"I'm glad you're on my side, Draconas," he said abruptly. "You *are* on my side, aren't you?"

"I'm never on anyone's side," Draconas responded. "But I like to be paid."

Edward eyed him a moment, then he burst out laughing, a hearty laugh, that rang among the hills. "I like you, Draconas. Damned if know why, but I do." He galloped off, his gaze fixed on the twilight-touched mountains.

Draconas cast a final glance back at the smoke. Braun, doing his job. Destroying the bodies.

* * *

They rode hard for five days. Draconas insisted that they rise early and sleep late, pushing themselves and the horses to their limit in order to cover as much ground as possible. Braun and Draconas kept watch for anyone following them—Draconas from his vantage point on the ground and the dragon from the air—but no more mad monks appeared.

Draconas guessed the reason why. They had tried to kill once and failed. They could try again—chasing him all over the countryside—or they could harbor their resources, wait for him to come to them.

Maristara knew where he was bound and why. She would have her trap set for him at the point where she figured he would have to cross—the pass that led through the Ardvale mountains.

Maristara had sealed off the pass three hundred years ago, using her magic to create a rock slide that effectively blocked the old road. The ordinary traveler would not think of trying to cross, but a persevering adventurer might be able to climb over and clamor around the boulders that filled the cut. Since her magic prevented him from entering, Draconas had planned on trying to send Edward, cloaked in magic, through the pass at that point. He had to rethink this plan, however. Maristara would be on the lookout. She'd have guards posted, probably more deranged magicians.

As for Edward, if he was worried about assassins or breaking through enchanted barriers, he didn't show it. The king might have been on a holiday outing. He was in a good humor, talking and laughing and looking eagerly about him. They crossed the border of his kingdom, entered a strange land—a land strange to Edward. Draconas had traveled here once before only a short time ago. He'd made the attempt to cross the border, braved the enchantment. He still had the fresh scars to show for it.

"My life was once quite pedestrian," said Edward on the evening of the fifth day, as they sat around the fire. "I plodded along the road, one foot in front of the other.

Then came the dragon, and suddenly I am doing cart-wheels and handsprings."

Draconas was doing cartwheels and handsprings—mental gymnastics. The king talked. Draconas only half-listened, said "yes" or "no" or "Is that so?" every so often. He was thinking about Maristara, what to do now that she knew they were coming. Abandoning his goal was not an option. Before the attack by the monk, Draconas had been skeptical, as were the other dragons, of Braun's claims and accusations that Maristara had a partner and that these dragons were using humans for some nefarious scheme. The monk possessed of the dragon magic (or by the dragon magic, as the case may be) had changed Draconas's mind.

Braun is wrong about one thing, Draconas reflected. It is not human flesh the dragons are after. It is human talent. We suspected that Maristara gave women the dragon magic. Now it seems as if she is doing the same for men, only not quite as well. Perhaps human males do not adapt to the dragon magic . . .

No, that's it! Draconas realized, struck by sudden insight. She's teaching the males to use the magic to kill. Human females are taught defensive magic, to protect the monastery and the dragon. Human males are being taught to use the magic to destroy. No wonder it's driving them insane.

"How do you feel about it, Draconas?" Edward asked, jolting him out of his reverie.

"I'm sorry, Sire. I was wool-gathering. What were you saying?"

"That I used to long for adventure," Edward repeated. "I used to hope for a war to break out. Not a big war, mind you. Just a small one. Anything to dispel the monotony. Then, when the dragon came, I felt guilty. I said to myself, 'God is punishing me for those evil thoughts.' Do you think God would do that?"

"I think we should get some sleep," Draconas said. "Dawn comes early. Will you take first watch or will I?"

"I will," said Edward. "It's good just to be able to sit quietly and think, without being constantly interrupted."

"Yes, it is," said Draconas pointedly, but he had the feeling Edward hadn't heard him.

Wrapping himself in his blanket, Draconas laid down on the grass near the dwindling fire and shut his eyes, hoping the king would heed his own counsel and remain silent. Edward sat staring into the dying fire, silent and pensive, his thoughts turned inward, for which Draconas was grateful. He was thinking he should have another mental talk with Braun. They now had proof that Maristara had given humans the forbidden gift—dragon magic. And that these humans were no longer being kept cloistered in Seth. They were being sent out to hunt him.

What is Maristara up to? What is she after, she and her partner? Draconas was trying to settle these questions in his mind, when Edward again broke in on his thoughts.

"I love Ermintrude, I truly do," Edward said suddenly. "We're lucky in our relationship, I suppose, considering that neither of us had any say in the matter of our marriage. We met each other, were wedded, and bedded all on the very same day. Our love isn't the love you hear about in the minstrel's song, love that aches and burns and drives a man to either do glorious deeds or drown himself in the river."

He hummed a few bars of a minstrel's lay, then sang part of it in a rich tenor.

Great anguish locked in the weary heart
fierce bitterness borne secretly,
mournful expression without joy,
dread which silences all hope,
are in me and never leave me:
and so I can neither be healed nor die.

"Still," he added lightly, when he was finished, "that type of love can't be very comfortable and I am quite comfortable with Ermintrude and the children."

His tone grew more serious, his voice softened. "I would give my life for the children. They are my future. They are my immortality. That's why I must do everything in my power to drive away this dragon. If our children are our future, I have to make certain that their future is secure. Isn't that right, Draconas?"

Draconas said yes and went on following his own bleak trail of thought. Humans with dragon magic. Humans were more than capable of destroying themselves without dragon magic. He could not imagine what they would do to each other if they possessed this powerful weapon.

"Or what they might do to us," Draconas said to himself.

For that was, of course, why the dragons were nervous. A human with dragon magic might not be a dragon's equal when it came to battle, but he would certainly be far more formidable than he was now. And an army of humans possessed of dragon magic . . .

They will be waiting for me at the pass. These strange monks, armed with dragon magic . . . the enchanted barrier, keeping me from entering . . .

And keeping anyone inside that kingdom from leaving.

Draconas was so struck by this realization that he sat up and threw off his blanket.

"What is it?" Edward asked, mildly alarmed.

"Anthill," Draconas answered, covering. Standing up, he shook imaginary ants out of his blanket and changed places. Lying back down again, he added, "That was a charming song you were singing. Perhaps you'd go on with it."

"It is not a charming song. It is a very doleful one, but anything to shut me up, right?" Edward said easily. "Very well. I'll sing and you think. I trust that eventually you'll tell me what it is you're thinking about. Eventually," he added with a grin, "you'll have to."

The king began to sing, his tenor rolling out into the darkness.

And as her lute doth live or die,
Led by her passion, so must I;
For when of pleasure she doth sing,
My thoughts enjoy a sudden spring . . .

**There is going to come a time when Edward is going
to dig in his heels and refuse to budge until all his questions have been answered. Knowing humans, that time
will be a most unpropitious one,** Draconas said to himself.
He made a mental note to be ready for it and then went
back to examine his earlier premise.

*No one is able to cross the enchanted barrier to enter
Maristara's kingdom, but people are able to get out. Hu-
mans possessed of dragon magic are in the world and
Seth is the obvious source.*

A taste for human flesh, so Braun had claimed. Perhaps
that was how it had started. *A dragon spies for Maristara.
She pays him with humans intended for his dinner table.
But then this dragon discovers that the humans can be of
more use to him than to his stomach. If he has been on
the receiving end of human slaves for three hundred
years, he might well have an army of men possessed of
dragon magic. He and Maristara could be plotting to take
over cities, countries, nations.*

What intrigued Draconas was the fact that these humans
were being smuggled out of the kingdom. There had to
be some way to remove them so that they were not
missed. At some point in or around Seth the barrier must
have a "gate" left open. And Draconas had an idea where
that might be.

Dragons are cave dwellers. They are born in caves, the
hatchlings breaking through the leathery shells of eggs
that have been deposited in the darkest recesses of the
deepest caverns. Here the younglings remain for a hundred years, living off food brought to them by their par-
ents, sleeping and eating and growing until they are strong
enough to leave the caves and catch their first painful
glimpse of sunlight. The sight of light is terrifying for

most young dragons. Draconas remembered it clearly, remembered hiding his head, longing to creep back into the comfortable, safe darkness. He remembered the way being barred by his mother. He had no choice but to suffer the light.

Over time, he grew used to the sun and came to enjoy it. But when he dreamed, he dreamed of cool, dark caverns.

Maristara is no different. She is comfortable in underground rooms and tunnels and what better place to hide that which she does not want others to see, for most humans loathe and fear dark, confined spaces. Upon first arriving in Seth, Maristara would have done what any dragon would do—she would take up residence in a mountain cavern, tunnel it, build it, shape it to suit herself. Which meant that there would be an entrance . . . and an exit.

"Braun," called Draconas, his thoughts tinged with sweet, warm colors of satisfaction, "the dragon must have a back door to her lair. I'm guessing her lair is in the Sentinel peak in the Ardvale mountains. The back door must be easily accessible to humans. See if you can find it."

The sixth day dawned hot and sultry. No breeze stirred the limp leaves. The air was humid. Sweat poured off their bodies. The horses' heads drooped as they plodded along. Edward fanned himself with his hat and said he smelled thunder.

They were in the desolate foothills of Ardvales, picking their way among scrub pine, fallen timber, and bits of the mountain that had broken off and tumbled down the steep slope. The river Aston flowed in the valley beneath them, to their east. The river circled eastward round the mountains from its source far to the north. A part of the river stole into Seth, rising to the surface to form a large lake in the western part of the valley, then diving underground again. They had crossed the Aston several times on this journey, for it was a winding, meandering river, with innumerable branches and tributaries.

"Once commerce between our two kingdoms must have traveled up and down this river," Edward remarked. "Strange that all has been so long forgotten. Perhaps I can change that."

Draconas answered, "Yes." He ceaselessly scanned the mountains, searching for the "back door," though he didn't really expect to find it. It would be concealed, at least from those whose eyes were at ground level. Braun would have a better chance at spotting it from the air.

The day wore on. The sun blared, brazen and oppressive. Draconas, who generally cared very little for his physical comfort, felt as if he were being slow-roasted. Waves of shimmering heat rose off the rocks. The mountains wavered in his view.

Edward abruptly reined in his horse, jerking on the reins so that the animal whinnied and shook its head in irritation.

"The dragon," he said in a tight voice. "It's up there."

Draconas squinted into the cobalt sky to see Braun, massive wings outspread, soaring upon the thermals, gliding across the face of the mountain, his neck curved, his head bent. He was close to the borders of Seth. Maristara and her priestess—the beautiful face in the topaz—must be on alert.

He hoped they were. Keep the pressure on. Humans under pressure often acted carelessly or foolishly and, in this regard, dragons were no different.

"You're mistaken," said Draconas coolly. "That is a heron."

"A heron!" Edward scoffed. "Don't you think I know a dragon when I—" He stared, blinked his eyes, stared again. "You're right, by Our Lady. It *is* a heron. But I could have sworn . . ."

"It's the heat," said Draconas. "It plays tricks on a man's eyes. I have seen what I thought was a blue lake in the middle of a desert, only to find nothing but sand.

Look," he added, changing the subject, "to the west. There is your thunder."

Blue-gray clouds, shimmering with white lightning, bubbled and boiled and roiled rapidly over the tail end of the mountain's spine. The storm moved so fast that with a crack of lightning and a crashing boom it was on them, soaking them with rain in an instant.

Edward laughed for the sheer pleasure of the cool water on his hot skin and from the exhilaration that comes from witnessing one of nature's spectacular furies. Taking off his hat, he tilted his face to the sky, enjoying the feel of the water rolling down his sweat-soaked body. Draconas cast half a glance skyward, saw Braun riding the storm winds.

The dragon spoke to him, glee-tinged images appearing in Draconas's mind.

"I think I have found what we seek. I'll show you where to look. Watch for my sign."

Draconas wondered how he was supposed to see anything in the lead-gray murk. He lost sight of Braun in the trailing clouds, but kept an eye on the area where he'd last seen the dragon. The rain pelted down harder. Draconas cursed beneath his breath.

A sudden blaze of light flared on the mountainside, drawing his eye. Draconas stared hard, marked the spot where the pine tree had caught fire, presumably struck by lightning. Draconas gauged the distance, searched for other landmarks, although a burnt and smoldering pine should not be that difficult to locate.

Braun veered off, steering clear of the mountain so that the strange eddies of the storm winds did not catch him and slam him into the rock face. The dragon took to the air, climbing through the rain, seeking calmer skies.

"Be wary," Braun warned, as he flew away. "I knew to look in this location because last night I spotted torch lights wending their way up the mountain. Maristara is entertaining visitors."

"I was right," said Draconas.

"So it would seem," Braun replied.

The leading edge of the storm passed quickly, taking with it the black clouds, the blinding lightning, the booming thunder and torrential rains. Gray clouds and gentle, steady rain settled in. Draconas watched the darker gray smoke rise from the burning tree, mentally calculating the distance and the time it would take to travel to that place.

When he found a route he liked, he turned his horse's head and started off to the northeast. Edward put his sodden hat back on his head, thought better of it and removed it, draped it over the pommel of his saddle to dry.

"I thought you said the pass was over there." He pointed to the west, the direction they had been traveling.

"It is," said Draconas. "I've changed my mind."

"Just as you changed a dragon into a heron?" said Edward.

"You know that such a feat is impossible, Your Majesty."

"I know that you call me 'Sire' or 'Your Majesty' only when you want to lull me into good behavior. I have seen you do the impossible—in a flawed jewel you showed me a flawless woman. I am not a child, Draconas. Nor am I a fool."

You are neither child nor fool, Edward. You are a pawn. A small and insignificant piece in a very large game. You see only the square on which you stand. You are not capable of seeing the entire board and thus you must move as I direct. And if I must sacrifice you to the greater cause, I will not hesitate to do so. Humans wielding dragon magic have the power to destroy us all.

Lifting his head, Draconas looked into the gray mass of clouds, beyond which Braun had flown. The dragon flew in blue skies and calm winds, leaving Draconas on the ground, in the rain.

"On thinking the matter over, I have decided to see if I can find another route into the kingdom," he said, continuing to ride, not looking back. "An underground passage—one that might be free of enchantment."

"And free of crazed holy men?" suggested Edward.

Draconas smiled, but he kept his smile to himself, his back to Edward.

"I could stop here and refuse to budge until you tell me what is going on," Edward continued, "but I won't. Why, do you ask? Do I trust you? No, not particularly. You are a man of secrets. You make it impossible to trust you and that's fine with you because you don't want to be trusted. Perhaps you think I ride with you out of curiosity. That is true. And you think I am desperate. I am, I freely admit it. This blasted dragon has my kingdom by the short hairs. But there is another reason."

Edward paused, then said quietly, "If I made my stand and you refused to answer me, I would have no choice but to turn my horse's head and ride back home. And I am not ready to go back. Not yet. I have enjoyed these days. For the first time in my life, I am free. I am not king. I am not husband. I am not father. I am not the bearer of sins. I am not the answer to questions. I am not the solution to problems."

Edward paused again. The rain had let up, but the clouds remained bunched above them. The smoke from the burning pine rose to clasp the storm's chill trailing fingers.

"I must go back to that," Edward said. "I want to go back. But not yet. Not," he added, with his sudden, mischievous smile, "while I have such an excellent excuse not to. So, lead on, Draconas. I follow."

Six hundred years ago, when he'd first taken on this form, Draconas had made a mistake. He had come to like and admire a human. Because of him, the human had died and Draconas had nearly lost his sanity. He had sworn to himself, never again.

He repeated the words. Never again.

8

AN IMPORTANT CEREMONY WAS BEING CONDUCTED in the monastery in the mountains of the kingdom of Seth.

Tonight was Coupling Night, as it was known. On every night of the full moon, twelve men selected by the Mistress of Dragons from a list presented to her monthly by Seth's king were brought into the monastery under heavy guard. Twelve priestesses, chosen by the Mistress, awaited them. Men and women would pair off and spend the night together. The next morning, the men would be escorted out. Nine months later, if all went well, twelve babies would be born.

The selection of the men was strictly adjudicated by the Mistress. No nobleman was able to whisper into His Majesty's ear that a worthless son should be chosen, nor could a wealthy merchant offer bribes to so honor his family. The men had to be of high moral character and must have performed a deed of heroism, compassion, or self-sacrifice that could be attested to by witnesses. Although the men chosen would never know their children, the honor of being selected would follow them throughout their years.

Each man was dressed in his finest, arrayed as a bridegroom for his wedding. No raucous laughter or crude jokes accompanied this bridegroom's party, however. The people of Seth honored the sisters who protected them from the dragons. The ceremony, which would insure the continuation of the Sisterhood, was a sacred one. The bridegroom and escorts proceeded up the mountain in hushed reverence.

They came at twilight, after a day of heat and torrential rain. The sky had cleared at last and the evening star glittered on the rose-red and saffron horizon. Bellona's warriors, clad in metal armor that had been polished to high sheen, met the men at the gate that led through the high wall into the monastery.

Bathed and shaven, their hair combed and adorned with garlands, the men were dressed in simple white robes and walked barefoot, to show their humility. One by one they entered, to be searched for weapons by the guards. Their names were checked against the list and, if all was well, they were admitted. Friends and family bid them goodbye and called blessings upon them, though wives sometimes gulped back their tears, for this honor was a bittersweet one to the woman who would spend the night alone.

The men were escorted by the warriors into the monastery's garden, where the sisters awaited them. All the members of the Sisterhood were present; those with whom the men would mate lined up on one side of the quadrangle, the remaining sisters standing opposite them. This night, Melisande would be the one to greet them and welcome them in the name of the Sisterhood. Customarily, the Mistress of Dragons would have performed this duty, but she was so ill that she could not rise from her bed.

As the Mistress's body grew weaker, her spirit burned stronger, or so it seemed to Melisande. The Mistress's voice was a thin, quavering whisper, but her orders were clear and coherent. Her hand trembled with a palsy, but the grasp of that hand on Melisande's was firm.

"This night is so important to our future," said the Mistress, lying back among the pillows. "I should have given the instructions before now. But there is so much to do . . . so much . . ."

"Rest yourself, Mistress," said Melisande. Seated on the edge of the bed, she smoothed the gray hair back from the woman's forehead with a gentle hand. "You will be with us for many more Couplings. You are ill from the strain of driving away the dragon we saw today. You should not have risen from your bed so soon. Soon you will be well again."

"The shadows draw close around me," said the Mistress. "Tomorrow morning you will come to me, Melisande, and we will begin the death watch."

"Mistress, no!" Melisande choked back her tears. The Mistress would be displeased with her for crying. "Not yet. We cannot manage without you. I cannot! I am not ready."

"You proved your readiness during the battle with the dragon."

"I have so much yet to learn . . ."

"You will manage, Melisande. We all do, when the time comes. And know that I will be with you," said the Mistress, patting her hand. "I will always be with you. Now," she added briskly, "dry your eyes and attend my words.

"When you make the ritual greeting, welcome the men and praise them for the deeds they undertook to win this honor. Keep the greeting short, so as not to try their patience. When you have concluded, dismiss the women, send them to their chambers to make ready. After a decent interval, have the guards escort the men. When each man has entered a room, the doors are locked and sealed."

The Mistress seemed to want to say more, but she had to use her breath for breathing, not for talking. Her eyes closed. She gasped, coughed.

Melisande rose from the bed. "Do not tire yourself, Mistress. I know how to perform this ceremony. I have been witness to it often enough. I will leave you to rest."

The Mistress grimaced. "I will rest soon enough, Melisande. I have all eternity. . . . What was I saying? Remind me, Daughter."

"The men escorted in and the doors locked."

"The food and drink—"

"—all prepared, Mistress, and I have ordered that it be taken to the rooms."

"With the special herbs. You did not forget—"

"No, Mistress. The food and the wine are both laced with aphrodisiacs."

"And the fertility potions," the Mistress said. "The women must drink the potion this night." She tried to rise. "I should go . . ."

"I have seen to it, Mistress," Melisande assured her. "The women know what to do. I will check each personally in the morning to make certain they have obeyed. They know the importance of the Coupling. We all do."

Frustrated at her lack of strength, the Mistress sank back down among the pillows. "You and the others will spend the night in prayer, Melisande. Pray for fine, healthy children to be born of his union."

"Yes, Mistress. The omens are good. Five healthy babes were born this day and last night."

The Mistress's eyes brightened. "Five?"

"Three girls and two boys. And four babes were weaned this day, taken from their mothers into the nursery."

"I recall the day they were born. All boys."

"All four, Mistress."

"Ah, well." The Mistress sighed. "At least we have three healthy girls born to us this day."

"The boys are ready to go to families, but you have yet to tell me the proper procedure. I understand that they are taken away during the night and that no one knows how or when—"

"For the sake of the mothers," said the Mistress gently. "This is a difficult time for them. Removing the children in the night, without their knowledge, makes the separation easier."

"But how is that accomplished? If I am to be responsible—"

"Tomorrow," said the Mistress, closing her eyes. "I am very tired, Melisande. Please leave me."

Melisande gave an inward sigh. She had so much to learn and it was always tomorrow.

"Can I bring you anything, Mistress? A glass of wine? Some food? You have eaten hardly anything for days."

"I have no hunger anymore. No hunger for anything. Not even life. Place a glass of wine by the bedside. That is all I want."

"I will do that and I will send someone to sit with you—"

"No!" The Mistress was fretful. "The others fidget and whimper and worry me to distraction. You are the only one I can tolerate."

"Then I will come back to see if there is anything—"

"You will not." The Mistress's voice was sharp and the tone startled Melisande. "I am sorry, Daughter. I did not mean to snap at you, who have been so devoted to me. You have not slept in nights, however. Did you think I didn't see you slip in here every hour, hour after hour? This night, I will sleep and so shall you."

"Yes, Mistress. If that is what you want."

The Mistress's voice softened. "I am so very tired. No one is to disturb me. Come to me in the morning."

Melisande bent down, whispered a heartfelt prayer, and kissed the Mistress's wrinkled hand. Blinking back her tears, she washed her face with cold water, then left the chamber.

Dusk layered the garden in blues and purples. The moon would rise shortly. It was time for the ceremony.

Melisande made her speech of greeting, repeating words she'd heard spoken every month of every year for all the years of her life, words that held deep meaning for those who heard them—or so she hoped. The words held no meaning for her this night. She might have been speaking a foreign tongue. She had so much to do, so much to think about, so many responsibilities falling on her, and no time to think clearly about any of them.

When she stepped into the quadrangle, taking the Mistress's customary place upon the raised dais at the north end of the quadrangle, a wave of dismay rippled through the Sisterhood. Where was the Mistress? The sisters clutched hands. Some gave audible gasps and one actually burst into tears. The priestesses who were soon to be coupling with the men started to wilt like cut blossoms. The men had no idea what was going on, but they could feel the tension. They cast swift glances at each other, shifted uneasily in their places.

Melisande had to seize control of the situation, keep it from spiraling into disaster. She was thankful for the discipline of Bellona and her warriors, who stood calm and steadfast. Walking over to take her place beside the dais, Bellona gave Melisande a reassuring smile that warmed her like spiced wine.

"The Mistress sends her regrets," said Melisande in ringing tones. "She is sorry she cannot take her accustomed place before you this night, but the battle with the dragon has left her fatigued. Men of Seth, I bid you greeting in her name."

She continued on with the traditional speech and though she could not have repeated afterward a single thing she said, the words had the desired effect. Her explanation, delivered in a cool, strong tone, spread soothing balm upon the fears of the sisters. Her praise for their deeds of heroism heartened and strengthened the men, while her expressed admiration for the women who were soon to be mothers caused them to preen themselves with pride.

Her speech concluded, Melisande relinquished control of the evening to Bellona. The sisters went to the nave to recite their prayers. The women went demurely to the coupling rooms, there to wait in a flutter of nervousness for their chosen companions. Some had already borne children and knew well what to expect. They looked forward to the act of love eagerly or with dread, depending on past experiences. Some were virgins. This would be their first experience and they waited in trepidation.

Bellona's troops escorted the men, saw to it that each was locked in a room with a mate and given food and wine, heavily laced with potions and spices known for their ability to loosen the inhibitions and strengthen a man's potency. Guards were placed at either end of the hall and nature was left to take her course. Soon the night air would dance with the sounds of giggles and deep laugher, which would give way to grunts and sighs and cries of pain or pleasure.

Melisande should have been in the nave praying with the sisters, but she needed a moment to talk with Bellona. Over the years, only a few untoward incidents had threatened to mar a Coupling Night and these had been dealt with swiftly and quietly. But there would be no rest for Bellona or her troops this night, so long as there were men present in the monastery.

Melisande slid into the fragrant shadows of an alcove created by shrubbery and a twining honeysuckle vine and waited for Bellona. The commander was still inside the coupling chambers, making certain that all was well. Within a few moments, the door opened and Bellona stood outlined against the backdrop of lamp light, giving final orders. This done, she shut the door. She headed across the compound at a brisk walk. Melisande did not speak. She did not have to. So close were they that she knew Bellona would find her.

Bellona had gone only a few paces past where Melisande stood when she stopped, turned, and sent a piercing gaze into the shadows.

"Melisande? Is everything all right?"

Melisande shook her head, and Bellona was by her side in a moment.

"You're chilled, shivering." Bellona drew Melisande into her arms. "What is it? Tell me."

"Oh, Bellona," said Melisande, holding fast to her lover. "We are to begin the death watch tomorrow!"

Bellona whispered a swift prayer, tightened her grip. "I will take charge of everything in the monastery. You do what you must do and give no care or thought to anything else."

Bellona hesitated. "Thirty years have passed since the last death watch. Few here are old enough to remember what needs to be done. Has she told you?"

"Yes," said Melisande. "I was going to tell you, but I thought I would wait until after the Coupling Night. I didn't know it would happen this soon."

"I have time to talk now."

"But I must be at prayer—"

"Hang the prayers, Melisande," said Bellona roughly. "Your voice will not be missed. Lucretta will take great pleasure in leading them in your absence."

"And make snide remarks about me later," said Melisande with a faint smile.

"She would not dare," said Bellona in low tones. "Not about the new Mistress."

Melisande shivered. She pressed closer against Bellona.

The fragrance of the honeysuckle was sweet in the warm night. They could hear borne on the still air the murmur of prayer on one side of the compound and the sounds of high-pitched laughter on the other. The two sides of life, thought Melisande, the spiritual and the physical. And over both is raised the hand of death.

"When did you last eat? Or sleep?" Bellona demanded.

"I can't remember. Don't scold me," Melisande said wearily. "You don't know what it's like. I hold onto her hand, trying to hold onto her, but she slips a little farther away from me every moment. She is our mother, Bellona. The only mother most of us have ever known . . ."

"I know, dear one. I know. But it is her time. We all must come to it."

"Spoken like a warrior," Melisande said bitterly.

"That is true, dearest one. We warriors give ourselves to death and perhaps that makes it easier for us to accept. A warrior's death is quick and clean, or so we pray. This lingering, wasting death must be terrible to see. I wish you were not alone with her, Melisande. You've been closeted with her for days now. You do not eat. You do not sleep. You are half-sick from fatigue. Can't you persuade her to allow some of the other sisters to share this sorrowful task?"

Melisande shook her head. "Only the High Priestess may oversee the death of the Mistress. Thus it will be when it is my time."

She leaned her head against Bellona's strong shoulder, let her eyes close for just a moment. "Though I can't understand why it should be this way, Bellona. It would be different if she taught me things—how to perform the ritual, for instance, or gave me instruction on dragon lore, passed on to me her wisdom. She does not, however. I don't understand . . ."

Her voice died away. She sank into the darkness, into the honeysuckle sweetness of the night and Bellona's embrace.

A voice calling for Bellona roused Melisande. "What?" she gasped, starting suddenly awake, sleep-drowned, and fuddled. "What is it? What is wrong?"

Bellona cursed. Standing up, she walking out of the shadows of the trees so that she could be seen. "I am here, Nzangia. What do you want?"

Halting, the warrior saluted, her fist to her chest. Melisande recognized Bellona's second-in-command, a young woman of twenty years, tall, raw-boned, awkward in everything except fighting.

"I am sorry to disturb you, Commander, but you asked to be kept informed—"

"Well, then, what is it?" Bellona snapped.

"The strangers at the pass are still there."

Bellona frowned, displeased. "Your last report said that they departed."

"We thought so, Commander, for we saw no sign of them for a fortnight, but we were wrong, apparently. One of the scouts spotted one this morning. I rode back to tell you."

"How do you know it was the same?"

"They are easy to distinguish, Commander, with their black robes and bald pates."

"What are you talking about?" Melisande asked, now wide awake and tense. "Strangers near the pass? For a fortnight? And I am only hearing about it now?"

"The Mistress asked me to say nothing to you," said Bellona. "We reported this to her at once, of course. She said they were probably wayward travelers lost in the mountains. But no lost traveler hangs about for over a week."

"And these are strange travelers," said Nzangia. "There is something sinister about them, fey. I don't like it."

"I don't either. I want to think about this, Nzangia. You are dismissed. I will have orders in the morning."

The warrior saluted and departed. Bellona sat back down on the bench, hunched over, her arms on her knees, her chin in her hands, staring unseeing into the night.

Melisande waited patiently for an explanation, but none came.

"Are you going to tell me what is going on?" she asked at last.

Bellona stirred, shook her head. "I'm not sure I should. The Mistress said I was not to worry you."

"It is too late for that," said Melisande dryly. "You will worry me far more if you say nothing."

"It is not important, really. Except"—Bellona frowned—"it is very odd—"

"Bellona!" Melisande exclaimed, exasperated. "Tell me!"

"A week ago, the border patrols reported seeing a party of men riding near the pass. There were eight in all. Five were cloaked and hooded, so that it was difficult to tell anything about them, but three were very strange looking. They wore black robes and their hair had been tonsured."

"Like the old paintings of the monks who once lived in this monastery," said Melisande. "What did they do?"

"They stared at the pass and stared at it and stared at it some more, all the while pointing and talking. They investigated the area around it and then left, or so we thought."

"They did not try to cross there or anywhere else?"

"No, and that in itself is odd. It was almost as if they knew that trying to break through the enchantment would be futile."

"And now they are back."

"Yes, and they shouldn't be. The enchantment works by filling the mind with lethargy. A person eager to enter the pass through the mountains suddenly realizes that it is not worth the effort. He has no care for what lies beyond. He forgets why he was ever interested in the first place. And so he departs and never gives the matter another thought."

"But these did give the matter more thought."

"Yes," said Bellona. "And not only that . . ."

She rose abruptly to her feet, walked a pace or two, stood with her back to Melisande, staring up at the stars, as if seeking guidance.

"What is it?" asked Melisande, a catch of fear in her voice.

"These strange people aren't the only ones to take an unusual interest in the border. I wasn't going to tell you now. I was going to wait . . ." She paused, irresolute, then turned to face Melisande. "A dragon made the attempt. Not the green dragon we saw and drove away. Another."

"Impossible," said Melisande crisply. "I would have seen it in the Eye. The Mistress would have seen it . . ."

"You have been occupied with other matters," said Bellona, looking gently on her lover. "And so has the Mistress."

Melisande reached out, grabbed hold of Bellona's hand. "I would have seen it, I tell you!"

"But you didn't, Melisande," said Bellona softly. She brushed back the tendrils of fair hair that straggled down the careworn and sorrow-softened face. "I don't know why or what went wrong. A dragon did try to cross. The enchantment kept the beast out. A border patrol saw the lights and heard the blast of the angry magic. They hastened to the site and found scorch marks on the rocks and a rock slide and smears of blood."

"Some person . . ." said Melisande stubbornly.

"The enchantment doesn't react violently to people. Only to dragons. Dear Melisande." Bellona put her arms around her, drew her close. "You didn't fail! Never think that."

"But I did! I should have seen . . . Without our prayers, the dragon might have won its way through . . ."

Tears welled up in her eyes and burned in her throat. She never cried. Not in front of Bellona. Not in front of anyone. Angrily Melisande blinked the tears from her eyes, pressed her lips together until she had mastered the painful swelling in her throat. She drew back from Bellona's embrace, put aside her lover's caressing hands.

"You must ride to the pass," said Melisande. "I want you to personally investigate this."

"But the death watch—"

"The Mistress's quarters are cordoned off. No one may enter or even come near until she . . . she has passed."

"Except you."

"Except me. Nzangia is like your right arm, Bellona. You've told me that often enough. You can leave everything in her charge. There is nothing to do here except give the guards their orders. It's not like anyone would dare disobey."

Bellona remained irresolute. "The men are still here—"

"They will be gone by morning. You can escort them out and then depart. You must see to our defenses, Bellona. The Mistress has assured us that we could repel invaders if we needed to, but it has never been tested. I would feel better if you went there yourself, made certain that all is well. There is nothing you can do here. We can only wait."

"I will go on one condition," said Bellona. Taking hold of Melisande's hands, she brought them to her lips, kissed them. "That you spend this night in our bed."

"Bellona, I must say prayers for the success of the coupling," said Melisande.

"Bah!" Bellona snorted. "Either the battering rams will thrust through the gates or they will go limp and fail and if that happens I doubt if the prayers of the likes of Lucretta are going to stiffen their resolve."

"Bellona!" Melisande exclaimed, shocked, but before she could continue the reproof, the ludicrous side of praying over fornication struck her and she started to laugh. Horrified, she clapped her hands over mouth.

"There, see what you made me do."

"Forget the prayers. Come with me," pressed Bellona, kissing her lover's cheek and her neck.

"No, I mustn't," said Melisande, sighing and relaxing beneath the warm caresses.

The two held fast to each other, Bellona rubbing her cheek in the soft, fair, and fragrant hair, Melisande giving in to strong arms and the gentle touch.

"Melisande," said Bellona softly.

"What?" Melisande murmured, half in a dream.

"You were asleep. Standing up. While I was holding you."

"No! Was I?" Melisande blinked and shook herself.

Bellona regarded her sternly. "You have to get some sleep, Melisande. You go on ahead. I'll take a last look around. And I'll tell Lucretta that you are not well."

"Don't be long," said Melisande, yielding.

"I won't," said Bellona with a kiss.

*   *   *

Bellona made her rounds, saw that all was well. The soldiers were in good spirits. Coupling Night was a sacred tradition for soldiers and sisters. Every woman there owed her birth to one such night in the past. Still, the soldiers did not look upon it with quite the same reverence as the sisters. Each month they made bets on the "bulls," staking a share of their food rations on which would plow his furrow more than once and which would be lucky to plow at all.

They told the same crude jokes and stories that had been told for three hundred years on these nights and added some new ones, sharing them all gleefully with Bellona when she made the rounds. She laughed, but did not linger, as she might have done, to join them in their fun.

Hopeful that another Coupling Night would pass without incident, Bellona went to the nave, gave her message to Lucretta, who screwed up her mouth in disapproval and sniffed. Bellona had one more stop to make before she went to her quarters.

"All well within?" she asked the guards at the door of the Mistress's chamber.

"Yes, Commander," replied one. "All is quiet."

Bellona looked at the windows that were always dark, their heavy curtains always drawn. The Mistress might die in there alone and no one would know it. Yet, perhaps she was not so near death as they all feared. Melisande had a great deal to learn before she was ready to take over as Mistress of Dragons. The current Mistress had not yet begun to teach her.

Bellona was still uncertain about whether or not to travel to the pass. Looking at the dark windows, she made up her mind. The journey was about thirty miles. A day's ride with a change of horses en route. A day there, to inspect the defenses and find out more details about who it was who had tried to enter. A day's ride back. If the Mistress died, there would be little for Bellona to do, except to keep the sad news from spreading out into the

kingdom until the sisters were ready to announce it. And
the last death watch had lasted weeks, or so Bellona recalled hearing.

Her mind made up, Bellona returned to her quarters.
The hall was dark. The barracks quiet. Accustomed to
coming and going at all hours, Bellona found her way
easily in the moonlit dimness, entered the room quietly.

Melisande lay on the bed. She had not undressed. She
had not removed her robes or her sandals, nor unbound
her long flaxen hair. A band of silver moonlight slant
through the slit window and fell across her face, which
looked worn and sorrowful, even in sleep—the haven for
the troubled. Sweat glistened on her face and neck. The
room was stifling.

Bellona took off her sandals and removed the white
robes. Pouring cool water into a bowl, she dipped a
sponge into the water, wrung it out, and laved Melisande's
arms and breasts, her face and hands. Bellona used long,
slow strokes, moving the sponge gently, so as not to wake
her. Melisande shivered, but she did not waken. Bellona
carefully loosened the heavy coil of braided hair and
brushed out the waves that were gold in the daylight,
white by the moon's reckoning.

This done, Bellona drew the blanket over Melisande's
damp body, so that she would not take a chill. Leaning
over, she kissed Melisande on the forehead, on the eyelids, and the mouth. Melisande never stirred, but the lines
of weariness had smoothed, the tension in her body relaxed. She slept deeply and peacefully. Somewhere in the
night, a woman gave a drowsy, satiated laugh. A man's
deep chuckle joined her. Somewhere in the distance, thunder rumbled. It would rain before morning.

Bellona crawled into bed, flung one arm protectively
over Melisande, and shut out the moonlight.

9

"WE'LL LEAVE THE HORSES HERE," SAID DRA-
conas, tying the reins around a tree limb, "and go in on
foot."

He could not see Edward's face, for he was turned
away from him, but he could tell by the quick, deft movements that the king was eager for action. Edward did as
instructed, and swiftly joined Draconas.

The fire-blasted pine tree, still smoldering, was a furlong away, growing on a ledge that jutted out from the
rock face. The moon had lit their way up the side of the
mountain. An easy climb, for the slope was gradual, not
steep; the trees flung about with a sparing hand. Distant
thunder presaged more rain. As they neared their destination, the sky thickened with clouds that swallowed up
moon and stars and the dragon Braun, who was as eager
for action as Edward. Of the two, Braun was the one
Draconas least trusted.

He had no idea how the young and impulsive dragon
would react. Braun had done well so far—the blasting of
the pine tree had been an inspired idea. Draconas hoped
Braun would continue to behave rationally and

circumspectly, but he couldn't count on it. Braun was being motivated by vengeance and that was a self-damning emotion, both in humans and in dragons.

As for Edward, Draconas had only one regret and that was the undeniable fact that His Grace was in no way graceful when it came to trekking through the woods. Edward made noise enough for six kings, slipping and stumbling, cursing beneath his breath, treading on dry branches that crackled and crunched beneath his boots, and once nearly upsetting himself when his foot turned on a rock.

"For all the noise you're making, we might as well shoot off one of those blasted cannons to announce we're coming," Draconas told him.

"It's all very well for you to talk," Edward returned, breathing hard. "You have eyes like a bat, apparently. I can't see a damn thing in this witch's murk."

Draconas felt a twinge of remorse. He tended to forget that humans were not blessed with his dragon's ability to see in the darkness.

"Place your toe first and roll back on the heel," Draconas suggested. "You'll find your footing more secure."

"I look like a mincing dancing master," Edward grumbled, but he did as Draconas recommended, and the two proceeded. Fortunately rain began to fall again, masking their footfalls.

They climbed to a point that brought them directly underneath the overhanging ledge on which stood the marked pine. Beyond the pine, so Braun had reported, was the cavern opening, with what appeared to be a crude road leading up to it.

The road provides the humans easy access, Draconas thought, pleased to have his theory confirmed.

They stood beneath the ledge, peering upward. The rain pattered down on them lightly, dripped off the ledge. Thunder grumbled above them. Lightning spread blue-white fire over the underbelly of the clouds.

Holding his breath, Draconas cocked his head, listened.

"What is it?" whispered Edward, tensing.

"Voices," said Draconas. "I'm going to take a look."

Catching hold of the edge, he swung himself easily up and over the ledge. He flattened himself on the rock shelf, taking care to keep hidden in the ruins of the pine tree. No ordinary human would be able to see him in the rain and the night, but who knew what a human gifted with the dragon magic might be able to do or see?

And humans were not the only beings who would be keeping watch for them.

Ahead of him, about twenty paces away, was the cavern's opening, a long and narrow slit in the mountain. A soldier sat hunched on a boulder, his head slumped to his chest. The man was cloaked and wore a steel helm, chain mail, and carried a sword. He was the only person in sight. No mad monks.

The soldier had taken refuge from the rain beneath a shelf of rock that thrust out over the cave, creating a natural portico. By day, the cavern's entrance would be concealed in the shadow of this portico, effectively hiding it from view. Draconas could have searched for years and might have never discovered it. It was the road that gave it away, and Braun would have never found that if Draconas had not told him to look for it.

A narrow strip of white rock eked out of solid gray, the road had not been carved out of the stone. The road had been ground into it, the path worn smooth by countless numbers of feet coming and going over three centuries, trailing down the mountainside. Braun followed the road from the air, reported that it disappeared into a forest along the river. The strange road apparently came from nowhere and led back there, for Braun could not any find trace of it in the lands surrounding the mountains.

Draconas turned his attention back to the voices. On first hearing, he had thought them to be right above him. He now realized that the voices were some distance away, coming from inside the cavern that was acting to amplify them. He could make out at least two distinct speakers, but, due to the echoes bouncing off the cavern walls, he could not understand what they were saying.

Under the cover of thunder, Draconas slithered off the ledge, dropped back down.

"One guard," he reported, whispering into Edward's ear. "And he's asleep."

"Any sign of the enchantment?" Edward whispered back. "Fairy dust sprinkled about the opening? Eerily glowing cobwebs strung across the entrance?"

"We won't know if the enchantment's working until we try to enter. And if it is," Draconas added coolly, "you won't find it so damn funny. For mercy's sake, keep as silent as you can!"

Draconas again leaped for the ledge, pulled himself up and over. He crouched low, listening to make certain that no one else was coming. He heard nothing, except the voices within the cavern.

The somnambulant guard slumped on the boulder. Draconas couldn't blame him for keeping careless watch. Three hundred years of these trysts and nothing had happened, ever.

"Hand me my staff," said Draconas.

Edward handed up the staff. Draconas rested it on the ground beside him, then reached for the king. Catching hold of Edward's hand, Draconas hauled him up onto the ledge.

"Quiet!" Draconas warned.

The two crouched, frozen. The voices still continued their conversation, but over that they could hear footfalls and other, stranger noises.

"That sounded like a baby's cry!" Edward breathed.

"Keep silent!" Draconas returned irritably, trying to think. He turned to the king, gripped his hand, looked him in the eye. "Whatever happens, whatever you hear or see, you must not interfere. Promise me."

"What's going on? You have to tell me."

"There's no time. Promise me," Draconas said, "or I turn back."

Edward stood frowning, glancing balefully at the dark

cavern. The footfalls and the sound of whimpering and crying grew louder. They were nearing the entrance.

"I promise," he muttered.

"There's nothing you can do," Draconas told him. "If you try to stop them, they'll fight and you'll risk harming the children. Take cover over there. Wait for my signal."

Edward did as ordered, though he was plainly not happy. Like all animals, humans had the instinctive need to protect the young of the species. Draconas should have warned the king of the possibility that there might be children involved, but he had never supposed they might arrive in the middle of a transfer.

Of all the confounded luck!

Draconas waited one more second to make certain that Edward obeyed orders. The king might be a romantic, but he had a good measure of common sense, and he did as he was told, padding softly past the slumbering guard, taking cover in a jumble of rocks near the cavern's entrance. Once Edward was safely ensconced, Draconas clambered from boulder to boulder, climbing up the outside of the cavern's wall and out onto the portico. Flattening himself on top of it, he peered over the edge.

The sleeping soldier was directly beneath him.

Three more soldiers, accoutered like the first, in steel helms and armed with swords, emerged from the cavern.

"Wake up, you lazy bastard," said one, thumping the look-out. "Lucky for you it was me and not Grald caught you snoring on watch. Else you'd be asleep permanent."

"Bah, what's to watch for? Nothin' but goats up here," said the guard with a yawn. He looked back into the cavern. "I wish those old biddies would get a move on. Can't you make 'em hurry?"

"Hurry up in there," the soldier called. "And douse that blamed torch!"

"I won't," returned a shrill female voice, sharp and indignant. "It's dark as pitch out here."

"Our way's been lit before," said another female.

"You've had moonlight before," returned the soldier.

"Well, the moon's not out, is it?"

Five women, dressed as nuns, in black habits and black wimples, emerged from the cavern. One of them carried the contested torch, blazing brightly. Four of them carried bundles of cloth that occasionally stirred or let out a cry or a whimper. At the sight, Edward gave a gasp that was audible to Draconas, but, thankfully, not to the soldiers, who were still arguing with the women.

"Grald's orders," said the soldier. "No light. You can take it up with him."

The women looked at each other.

"Put it out," said one dourly.

The soldier took the torch, doused it in a puddle. The women continued to grumble and complain that they couldn't see and they'd surely fall off the cliff.

"If I break my neck, you'll be left to care for this squalling brat," said one.

"Your eyes'll get accustomed to the dark," said the soldier. "The walk's not that far. The wagon's waiting for us in the woods."

The women began to creep along the road, shuffling their feet to feel their way.

"We'll be all night at this rate," groaned the soldier who had been asleep.

"Don't worry," returned his comrade. "Grald will soon be along and then you'll see the old crones hop lively."

"Keep your voice down," said the first nervously. "Those women have the magic, you know, and they'd just as soon turn us inside out as look at us."

"Let them try," said the other with a shrug, but he did lower his voice.

His comrade looked back around. "How long will Grald be in there with her?"

" 'Til whenever Her Worship decides to dismiss him."

"Should one of us wait for him?"

"He ordered us to guard the women. He'll meet us at the wagon. Don't worry. If trouble comes, Grald can take care of himself."

"Don't I know it," said the soldier sincerely.

As the soldier had predicted, the women soon grew used to the darkness and mended their pace. The soldiers hastened after them. Draconas could smell the dragon magic on the women, as Edward had been able to smell the thunder.

Once they were gone, the king rose from his hiding place, walked out to stand in front of the cave. Slithering down from his perch, Draconas dragged the king into the shadows.

"Nuns carrying babies out of a cave!" Edward confronted him. "And you knew they'd be here."

"At least," said Draconas, "we know that the entrance is not enchanted."

"The hell with that! What about the babies? Where are they taking them? Whose are they? What in the name of the Holy Mother is going on?"

"Come with me," said Draconas. "And for your life, make no sound."

"Damn it, Draconas—"

"Are you coming?" Draconas asked, starting toward the cavern entrance.

Edward had little choice. Muttering, he followed after.

"It's dark as death in here. Hold onto me or you'll soon lose your way," Draconas told him.

Draconas felt Edward's hand close over his arm. The king was a quick learner. He moved almost as silently as Draconas.

The narrow entrance opened up into a wide cavern with a high ceiling. They would come to pick up the children once a month, on a night with a full moon to light their way. He wondered how many babies had been taken from this dark and fearful place to what darker and more fearful fate? Hundreds? Thousands? He was glad Edward didn't know what horrors these children faced. No human possessed of that knowledge could have stood by and watched them being spirited away without doing something to try to save them.

The two voices grew louder, clearer, and he was able to determine their location. The large chamber ended. A small opening to his left led into another chamber beyond. Light emanated from this chamber, spilled out onto the floor, carrying a man's shadow with it. Draconas halted so suddenly that Edward bumped into him.

Draconas squeezed Edward's arm, warning him to be silent.

Edward squeezed back, much harder than necessary. Yes, I'll keep quiet now, that painful squeeze said, but I have plenty to say later.

Draconas smiled in the darkness. He moved closer to the stone wall, away from the light.

Both men stood still, barely breathing, listening.

The language the two voices spoke was the language of most of those living on this part of the continent, although the male voice had the dialect and accent of someone who came from farther south. The other speaker, "Her Worship," spoke with a sibilant lisp, as might be expected of a creature with a long and slender tongue flicking between sharp fangs.

"You are certain he will try the pass?"

"I am. Where else would he try?"

"I do not know, but if there is another way he will find it. He is not one to underestimate, as I think you would have learned by now."

"Your warrior women patrol the border—"

"Yes, because they spotted the monks. Another example of your incompetence."

"They let themselves be seen. You suggested it—"

"I suggested that the soldiers should be seen, to give the idea that there might be an invasion. Instead the warriors saw the monks. The women are not fools. They have been asking questions. The Mistress had to pass them off as mere travelers."

"Besides, there is the enchantment," Grald continued in sullen tones. "He tried once to cross and failed—"

"And you think that failure would deter him? He is a

dragon, Grald, not a human. I think you forget that sometimes."

"He is in human form," Grald returned. "And that makes him vulnerable."

"Not so vulnerable but that your monk botched his job."

"We had no time. We had to move fast—"

"And so do I. The old woman is frail and feeble and of no more use to me. The Mistress dies this night. Once you have started the others on their way, return in the morning to collect the body. Burn it as you did the others."

Edward dug his fingers into Draconas's arm.

I heard, damn it. Draconas jerked his arm away. *Now what the devil do we do?*

Grald was not pleased. "I am opposed to this. The woman could live many more weeks, months even. More time is needed to prepare the new—"

"The decision is mine to make," said the lisping voice. There came the sound of an enormous bulk shifting its great weight, of claws scraping against rock floors and scales rubbing against rock walls. "You have what you came for. Take care of your business and let me take care of mine."

"Very well, Maristara. You know what you're doing, I guess. I'll be in touch," said Grald.

The shadow bowed low, then started to move.

Draconas flattened himself against the wall. Beside him, he felt Edward stir, reaching for his sword. Draconas laid a restraining hand on the king's arm.

For a brief moment, Grald's shadow blotted out the light, and then he emerged into the chamber in which they were hiding.

Draconas stared. He felt Edward give a little start of amazement.

Grald was a giant of a man. He stood at least seven feet tall, with massive shoulders and arms, a chest like an oaken barrel, and thighs that were thick and muscular.

Draconas could have bathed in the cuirass the man wore over his upper torso. He wore a huge hammer strapped to his back. A broadsword clanged at his hip.

Grald stalked past them without seeing them. He was blind angry, stomping his feet and cursing beneath his breath, and looking neither to the right nor the left. Edward and Draconas kept still until they heard his huge footfalls die away in the distance.

The dragon made her departure, as well. Draconas recognized every sound, knew each for what it was—the scrape of a wing tip against the wall, the scrabble of her claws on the floor, the shuffling sound made by the long, sinuous tail dragging across stone.

The image conjured up by these sounds was so clear to him that he could not imagine how Edward would fail to realize the truth. Draconas was going to be forced to explain the unfortunate fact that they'd discovered a dragon in a kingdom that was supposed to be free of dragons and he began to swiftly cobble together a mixture of truth, half-truths, and downright lies.

Edward didn't say anything. The king was strangely silent.

Draconas plucked the king's sleeve. "We'll go out the same way we came—"

"Go?" Edward turned to him, amazed. "We're not going anywhere. We must save the Mistress."

"Keep your voice down," Draconas warned. "These caves are echo chambers."

"We must save the Mistress," Edward whispered. He pointed toward the chamber. "You heard what that Maristara woman said. She plans to slay her this night."

"Your Majesty, it's far too danger—"

"There you go again. Calling me 'Your Majesty' in that honey-coated voice. But it won't work this time, Draconas." Edward was grim and determined. "You were right when you said this quest was a holy one. God brought me here for a higher purpose than to save my kingdom from the dragon. God means me to save this woman from a terrible death."

Draconas could have told him that God had nothing to do with it. Edward had been brought here by a dragon on a ruse—a ruse that had failed, for Draconas had no intention of coming between the dragon and her prey. The Mistress was as good as dead, as far as Draconas was concerned. He would have to devise another plan. His task now was to save this hotheaded human from himself. Draconas was sorry he'd ever shown Edward that beautiful face in the topaz.

The king drew his sword, heading for the chamber where the light had been left to burn itself out.

Draconas bounded after him.

"Didn't you hear those sounds? This cavern is guarded, Edward, and the guard is no ordinary one."

"Some great beast, you mean?" Edward glanced at him with cold disdain. "A mastiff, perhaps? A wolf? A lion or a bear? Do you think I'm afraid of any of these? I must find her, Draconas. Find her and rescue her. God brought me here for this purpose. God is with me."

He better be, because I'm not, Draconas thought to himself in exasperation. Aloud he said, "How will you find her? You have no idea where *you* are, much less where she is."

Edward paused, looked upward. "You said yourself we were inside Sentinel Mountain. The monastery must be directly above us. She will be there and I will find her. God will see to it." He rested his hand on Draconas's shoulder. "You have had everything your way thus far, my friend. But not now. I must do this and nothing will stop me save death itself. If I do not return, take word to my beloved wife that I died on a holy quest."

"Oh, for the love—"

Edward clapped him on the shoulder and advanced into the chamber. He appropriated the torch that Grald had left burning, for Draconas could see the light waver, then move. He could hear the king's footfalls moving with it.

Calling down imprecations on the human's head, Draconas ran after Edward. He caught up with him just as he was exiting the second chamber and entering a third. Dragons always chamber their lairs, a defensive measure that allows them to seal off some chambers in case of attack, keep others open. Edward held the torch high, looking all around him, moving slowly. He was at least proceeding with caution, not rushing heedlessly into danger.

Coming up from behind, Draconas let himself be heard, so as not to startle him. Edward turned to regard Draconas with a warm smile.

"I knew you would come. I knew you would not fail me."

"You knew more than I did then," Draconas muttered. "Here, give me the torch if you're insistent upon this."

"I am," said Edward. "I have seen no sign of your wild beast, Draconas."

"You heard the sounds, same as I did," said Draconas.

"I heard them," said Edward, "but I don't hear them now, do you?"

"No," Draconas admitted.

Despite their immense girth, dragons are adept at silent movement. Their weight is not commensurate with their size. Dragons weigh far less than they look. Their bones are hollow, so that they can fly. Their hide is thin, which is why it is protected by scales. Because they do not have much mass, they can squeeze their bodies into impossibly small spaces and thus they build their lairs with narrow tunnels and small alcoves and cul-de-sacs.

Dragons do not appreciate being roused to action and much prefer to draw an enemy into an ambush, where the dragon may deal with him swiftly and surely. They lure any foe foolish enough to attack them deeper and deeper into their lairs, lure them to their doom.

Maristara could be doing that very thing. She might be lulling them into complacency, waiting for them to lose themselves in the labyrinth, waiting for them to come to her.

The chambers in this part of her lair were large, the tunnel easy to follow, for they were near the opening. Soon, however, as Draconas had foreseen, the chambers narrowed. The main tunnel split and branched off into other tunnels. They had entered the dragon's defensive maze and this was where she might choose to fight them, lying in wait in an alcove or curled up at the end of a cul-de-sac.

Draconas claimed the lead. He would come upon the dragon first or so he reasoned. He would allow Maristara to see him in his dragon form. Hopefully the unexpected sight of another dragon sneaking into her lair would disrupt her own plan of attack long enough to give Draconas the advantage.

Fighting humans is, for dragons, pitiably easy. One blast of fiery breath, one swipe of a mighty paw, one crunch of the powerful jaws and it is over. Fighting another dragon, however, requires thought and guile, strength and cunning. Expecting an easy time against a human, Maristara would find herself up against a much more formidable foe. In the split second of her confusion, Draconas could cast a spell that would incapacitate her and then both he and Edward would have a chance to flee. He would use the dragon's maze against her, for she could not maneuver swiftly through the narrow tunnels and they could. Draconas never lost his way underground. He would be able to guide them to safety—if all went according to plan.

Which, he realized suddenly, had not happened once since they'd started on this ill-fated venture.

10

DRACONAS HAD CONFIDENTLY ASSUMED HE'D taken everything into account when making his plans to deal with the dragon, but, apparently, he'd missed one. A major one.

No dragon.

Draconas was not lost in the labyrinthine tunnels. He was more at home in dragon mazes than he was in the streets of crowded cities. He kept to those tunnels used by the dragon, which were easy to distinguish, for she had left her mark upon the stone walls—places worn smooth by centuries of her bulky body scraping against the rock, shedding scales that glittered in the torchlight. No refuse, dragons kept their dwellings neat. He wondered absently what she did with it. Draconas carefully avoided those passages that gave no sign of her comings and goings. Those were probably laid with traps.

He listened hard to try to detect some trace of her and at first he did think he could hear the scrape of a claw or the dragging thump of her tail. The sounds were faint, however, and he couldn't be certain. He couldn't tell if the dragon was ahead of him or behind. This last hour, he'd heard nothing except the skittering of rats. He assumed the worst—Maristara had chosen her battleground and was waiting for them.

He crept grimly, stealthily on, but nothing happened. He came to several places that he himself would have deemed ideal for an ambush and he tensed, ready to meet the dragon's attack, only to encounter nothing more frightening than his own shadow, bobbing up to meet him as he rounded the corner.

"What a fearful, smothering sort of place," Edward remarked in hushed tones. "These tunnels don't seem natural to me. It looks as if they've been engineered. Are you sure you know where you're going?"

Since that was the fifth time Edward had asked that question, Draconas saw no need to answer.

He did not relax his guard. He continued to move slowly and deliberately, ignoring Edward's urgings to press forward with haste. Once, annoyed at Draconas's slow and deliberate pace, Edward had tried to surge ahead. Draconas pulled him back. The dragon was here somewhere. She had to be. There was nowhere else for her to go. Draconas began to consider the possibility that she did not know *they* were here. Either that, or she had made other arrangements for their disposal.

"We must be near the tunnel's end," Edward said suddenly. "I know this sounds odd, but I smell perfume."

"Not perfume," said Draconas, and he came to a halt. "Incense."

Incense and something more—humans. The scent of humans in a dragon's lair was something he had never before experienced. He'd noted the scent of the baby-traffickers immediately on entering, but the soldiers and the false nuns had not passed beyond the first chamber. The giant human, Grald, had advanced into the second chamber, but no farther. Draconas had not smelled humans in the labyrinthine lair until now. The human scent was strong and all-pervasive and it came from somewhere up ahead. Humans frequented this place they were about to enter. They came here often and of their own free will.

For this was not the stench of slave pens. The smell of human flesh mingled with fragrant flowers and incense and perfumed oils.

And no sign of the dragon. Draconas realized with a tightening of his gut that he hadn't seen a dragon scale in the last one hundred yards or so.

"Why are you stopping?" Edward demanded. "If that's incense you smell, then we must have reached our destination. We have to hurry if we are to save the Mistress from that assassin!"

"What the hell," Draconas muttered in reckless agreement. "We've come farther than I ever thought possible."

He broke into a run, with Edward pounding along behind. Rounding a bend in the tunnel, they came close to bashing their brains against a stone wall.

"A dead end!" exclaimed Edward in tones of bitter frustration.

"In more ways than one," Draconas said grimly.

This was the ambush. She'd caught them in a cul-de-sac. He was surprised he couldn't hear the dragon creeping up on them, but then she was old and powerful and she was cunning. Grasping his staff in two hands, he whipped about to face . . .

Nothing.

Nothing but darkness and silence.

"Damn!" said Draconas. Nerves taut, he lashed out at nothing.

Edward ran his hand along the wall. "You know what's crazy? I still smell perfume."

Draconas colored his mind gray, the same color as the rock wall that blocked their way. His mind as gray as the stone, he thrust his staff into the wall.

The butt end of the staff vanished, slid through solid rock.

"Holy Mother and all the saints of heaven preserve us!" Edward whispered, falling back a pace.

"An illusion," said Draconas, triumphant.

"I don't understand," said Edward, clearly shaken. He put out his hand tentatively. His fingers brushed cold stone. Quickly he snatched back his hand, stared at Draconas. "How do you do that?"

"You were right. We have reached the monastery." Draconas gestured at the wall. "Beyond us is a chamber filled with light. Incense-laden peat burns in an iron brazier. A marble altar stands at the far end of the room. Directly across from where we stand, another door leads out of the chamber. The symbol of an Eye is carved in the rock upon the floor."

"You are mad," said Edward, eying him askance. "I see cold, hard rock."

"You *see*! Don't see," said Draconas. "Don't listen to your eyes. They have been fooled. Listen to your other senses. You *smell* incense."

Edward stared at the wall, then shook his head. "I can't help myself. I know what I see and what I feel. I see and feel solid rock."

Draconas retrieved his staff. He took another glance at the altar room, then shrugged and turned away. "I guess this ends it. We might as well go back."

"But there must be another entrance—" Edward began.

Draconas whipped around, swinging his staff. He socked the king on the jaw, sent His Majesty tumbling through the illusory rock wall.

Lying on his back on the stone floor, Edward lay blinking at the blazing light burning in a brazier on an iron stand near the altar at the far end of the room. He stared at the blazing light, then, rubbing his bruised jaw, he sat up.

"Are you all right, Your Majesty?" came a voice.

"Draconas?" Edward asked, looking about. "Where are you?"

"On the other side of the illusion. I'll keep watch at this end. You go find the Mistress and bring her back here."

Edward stared intently at the wall. He could hear

Draconas's voice quite clearly, as if he were only arm's length away. Edward had fallen through a wall wasn't a wall and he did his best to convince himself of the illusion. But he could see the firelight gleaming off stone and if he put out his hand, he'd be able to feel the rock.

"You were the one in a hurry," Draconas reminded him impatiently. "You'd better mark the place where you entered the illusion. The opening is not very big and it is surrounded by solid rock. I can't have you bashing in your head. Here, take this with you."

A blazing torch sailed through the solid rock wall, landed on the floor in front of Edward.

"This is not possible," said Edward. "By all the laws of science, this is not possible. I'd think I was going mad, but my jaw hurts like hell."

He gave his aching jaw another rub, then removed one of his gloves and placed it at the base of the wall, near the torch.

"Can you see that?" he asked doubtfully. "Is that in the right place?"

"Your glove? I can see it. Good idea. If you need help, give a shout. Otherwise, I'll be here waiting for you."

"Why don't you come with me?" Edward asked, picking up the flaring torch.

"This is our only way out," Draconas returned. "I think it would be wise if one of us stayed to guard it."

"Ah, yes," said Edward. "Of course." But he didn't believe him.

Edward wanted to trust Draconas, for he liked and admired the man. He couldn't, however. A king who wants to be a good king should be a keen observer of his fellow men, learning to read them as a sailor reads the subtle signs of sea and sky, to know when storms are brewing or when the wind will rise or switch direction or if there are shoals on which he might run aground. Draconas's waters were calm and placid, but Edward saw secrets hidden in their depths.

All men have secrets including Edward, but he had the

feeling that the the secrets of Draconas were not the ordinary secrets of ordinary men. Draconas knew that Edward didn't trust him and, oddly, Edward understood that in some strange way, he had risen in his companion's estimation because of it.

Clapping his hand over his sword to make certain he'd not lost it in the fall, Edward walked across the room, heading for the open door that stood directly across from him. He couldn't make out what lay beyond that door, but he assumed it must be another room or a corridor. He moved rapidly, for he had wasted time back there at the wall, casting a curious glance around the room as he passed through it.

The marble altar at the far end was certainly impressive. The dragon carvings had been done by a master, seemingly, for every scale of a thousand, thousand scales had been carefully delineated. By contrast, the carving of the Eye on the floor looked rustic and crude. He noted the worn prayer rugs, arranged in a circle around the Eye, and a thrill shivered up the base of his spine.

"This is where they work the magic," Edward said to himself. "Magic that is a tool of the devil, reviled by God. Magic that fools the senses, makes us distrust ourselves. I can see why we are warned against it."

The idea was unsettling and, despite his pressing need for haste, Edward's steps slowed. He had grown up in the church and, though he considered himself a man of science, he was also a man of faith. He had no difficulty reconciling the two, as did some of his generation, for no matter how much science managed to explain, it could never provide him with the why, the how. God was always somewhere in every equation.

Edward had felt certain that God was with him on this holy quest, but now he had the unnerving feeling that he had left God waiting in the antechamber. The illusion of the wall, the stone altar, with its dragon's Eye, whose stony pupil seemed aware of him, were the stuff of dreams, and dreams were the unsavory, outlandish cavortings of the mind escaping nightly from civilization's safe prison house. Edward thought of this Mistress that he was going to save. He saw in his mind's eye the beautiful face and he remembered the stories of the priest who told tales of the pleasing shapes the Evil One could assume in order to lure man to his soul's destruction. One could roll one's eyes at that when seated safely in one's pew, but here, in the perfumed firelight, being watched by that stone Eye, his stomach shriveled and his mouth went dry.

Edward hesitated, but only for a moment. The rational, scientific part of him struck him on his mental jaw, much as Draconas had struck him on his real jaw, and knocked the terrors of the nursery out of his head. There were terrors here, but one was a murderer and, if that involved the Evil One at all, it was the evil that dwelt within men's hearts.

Swiftly, but not heedlessly, Edward passed through the open doorway and entered a corridor of rough-hewn stone. Ahead of him was a stone staircase. He took the stairs several at a time, and came to a door at the top.

This door was closed. Edward placed the torch in an iron sconce on the wall, to have both hands free, then studied the door, noting that it opened inward. He was pleased and rather surprised to find it was not locked nor barred in any way. If Draconas had been there, he could have told the king that in places where there is magic, padlocks and keys are not necessary, but Edward had no knowledge of this. He put his hand upon the handle, which was of wrought iron twisted into the shape of a dragon, and gave the door a gentle tug.

Opening it a crack, he peered out into a hallway and some part of him sighed in relief. Here was not more dream-stuff. Here was civilization: polished marble floors, wood-paneled walls, oiled rosewood and ebony furniture. Torchlight gleamed off the shimmering thread of a fine tapestry hanging on the wall directly opposite. Looking up, he met a dragon's eyes looking down at him—the painted eyes of a painted face of a painted dragon, an image in an elaborate mural.

The hallway was dark and it was empty.

Edward stepped cautiously into the shadows, keeping the door open, and wondered which way he should go.

To his right, darkness. To his left, not very far from where he was standing, faint light shone from an open door, casting a warm reflection on the cold marble.

He heard breathing—the rasping, shallow breathing of one who is either very old or very ill, and he smelled the fetid air of the sickroom. Edward listened intently, but could catch no other scent, hear no other sound. That room and the person in that room would at least be his starting point.

Reaching down to his belt, Edward removed his knife and wedged it firmly between the door and the door jamb, propping the door open. This would not only keep the door from shutting and perhaps locking, but it would also provide him with a strip of light to mark his way back.

Keeping close to the wall, he padded soft-footed down the hallway. The light's soft glow spilled into the hall, unbroken by any shadow. The labored breathing continued without pause. The night was quiet, except for a drumming sound that Edward eventually recognized as rain beating on the roof.

Nearing the room, he flattened himself against the wall and peered over his shoulder into a large room of sumptuous elegance and beauty; the walls hung with heavy cut-velvet draperies, the marble floors softened and warmed by hand-woven rugs. A writing desk—its surface bare—stood at the far end of the room. Four large, high-backed chairs were placed two and two, facing each other, in front of what was probably a window, covered over by the thick curtains. Glints of light came from all around the room, reflecting off jeweled boxes, a silver flagon, a set of gold-inlaid chalices. A dainty oil lamp, standing on a small, gilt-edged table, gave the light that had drawn him to this room and its sole occupant—an eldery woman, asleep in her bed.

She slept on her back, her mouth open, her thin body covered by a coverlet of silk stitched in gold. Fine lace was at her throat and her wrists. A locket of gold hung around her neck. Her hands lay on the silken coverlet and they were thin and bony and veined with blue. Her yellow-white hair had been neatly braided and hung down beneath the white lace cap that covered her head. A dressing gown of embroidered silk had been neatly folded and laid across the foot of the bed.

"Frail and feeble," Edward said to himself, repeating words the assassin had used.

The old woman is frail and feeble and of no more use to me. The Mistress dies this night.

Edward had thought and dreamed so long of the beautiful face in the topaz that he had not until this moment equated "frail and feeble" with the words "Mistress dies." Now, looking down at the elderly woman sleeping peacefully in her bed, he realized that they were one.

"She is the Mistress of Dragons and she is the one who is meant to die this night."

He glanced again around the room adorned with every symbol of wealth. Yet here she lay alone, abandoned. No loving daughters, no grieving sons, not even a servant to fetch her water or trim the wick of the smoking oil lamp. And here she would die alone, by violence.

Poor woman, he thought, pitying her deeply. Poor woman.

He gazed down at her, conflicted, uncertain what to do. She seemed so frail, he feared he might kill her if he lifted her. Yet he could not leave her to be brutally murdered. He listened intently to her breathing and decided that, though weak, it was not the rattling, gasping breath of the dying.

She is old and feeble, but, as the giant Grald himself had said, she might well live many more days. Edward glanced again around the empty room, filled with wealth, but devoid of comfort. Perhaps all she needed was care and attention. He would summon his own physician, a clever fellow who specialized in restorative medicines. And he would not mention his dragon to her, not until she regained her strength.

"And if she does not recover, at least she will leave this life in peace, with a priest by her side. And she will be given a holy burial," he added grimly, thinking of Grald and his instructions to burn the body.

Edward knelt down beside the bed, so that when he woke her, she would not find a man looming threateningly over her. He reached out his hand and gently touched her shoulder.

"Madame . . ." he said softly.

Her eyelids flickered, but she did not awaken. She seemed deeply sunk in sleep. He thought this odd, for the elderly tend to drift light as thistledown on sleep's surface.

Perhaps she has been drugged. Dosed with poppy-water.

He slid her flaccid arms beneath the coverlet, tucked the blanket around her as one would swaddle a babe, then lifted her out of the bed. She weighed nothing in his arms. Her head lolled against his shoulder. She gave no sign that she was aware of anything that was happening to her and he was convinced now that they had drugged her.

As he carried her to the door, the coverlet dragged behind on the floor, tangled under his boots. Fearing it would trip him, he paused to try to gather up the coverlet's ends with one hand, while still supporting the woman's frail body. He was involved in this when he heard voices.

Edward halted all movement, listened intently.

The rain thudded on the roof and, far in the distance, a rumble of thunder. Voices spoke, then came footfalls—the slap of wet sandals against a marble floor, the sounds of someone moving in haste and with purpose.

The murderer.

Edward entered the hallway, carrying his burden toward the door that he'd left slightly ajar. The elderly woman's head bumped gently on his chest. The coverlet trailed behind him.

11

MELISANDE WOKE ABRUPTLY. SITTING UP IN BED, she threw off the sheet and started to rise, only to realize that she had no idea what had awakened her. She stared around in a sleep-dazed state, suspended halfway between dreaming and waking, listening again for the sound that had roused her with a suddenness that made her heart race, her blood throb in her temples.

Her first thought was for Bellona and she reached out a hand in the darkness to touch her, to make certain she was beside her.

Bellona's breathing was deep and easy. She responded to Melisande's touch, but only as does a slumbering cat, stretching her body, then sliding back into sleep.

Melisande said to herself, "A dream," and was starting to lie back down when she heard the voice.

"Melisande! Come to me! I need you!"

"Mistress!" cried Melisande, starting up and staring around the darkened chamber.

The only person with her was Bellona, half-wakeful at Melisande's cry.

"Melis," she murmured drowsily, "what is it? Did you call me?"

"No, dear, no. I'm fine. Go back to sleep," Melisande said, drawing the blanket over Bellona's shoulders. The rain had begun again, and the night air was damp and cool.

Melisande listened, unmoving, not breathing, for the call to come again. She heard nothing, however. A dream, she said to herself. Yet the voice had been very real. She could hear it still, hear the urgent timbre, hear the panicked, desperate tone.

Fear constricted her heart, squeezed it so that for a moment she could not breathe. Her limbs went numb. Prickles stung her fingertips. She rose hastily from her bed and fumbled her way through the darkness to the door. The thought came to her that she could not go into the presence of the Mistress naked and she grabbed up the ceremonial gown she had been wearing the night before.

She was so shaken that she tried to thrust her head through the sleeve opening, and she paused a moment to calm down. She would gain nothing by haste. She draped the purple-dipped black gown over her head, settled it around her, and clasped the belt around her waist. She remembered, incongruously, Lucretta complaining of the blood marring the sheen of the gold-embroidered hem. Melisande had soaked the dress in cold water the next day, scrubbed off the blood. She slid her sandals onto her feet.

Her mind still fogged with sleep, she opened the door to their bedchamber without really knowing what she was doing and hastened out of the barracks into the quadrangle.

A steady rain continued to fall. The cool water on her face woke her thoroughly. She knew where she was and what she must do. The night was very dark and quiet, heavy with clouds and rain. The couples slept, worn out by their pleasures. In the nursery the newborn babes, product of a past Coupling Night, slept the sleep of innocence. The sisters slept and dreamed of dragons. The warriors slept and dreamt of blood, except for those who kept the watch. The sound of their footfalls were drowned in the rain.

"I am coming, Mistress," Melisande said softly.

The rain was falling so heavily that she had the feeling that the night had taken liquid form and darkness itself pelted her, its drops hard and stinging. Her robes were soon sodden and the heavy fabric clung to her body, its weight dragged at her, the wet skirts wrapping around her legs, hampering her progress. Her hair dripped water into her eyes. Tree branches, their wet leaves dangling, clutched at her.

She thrust the branches aside, splashed through the rivulets of water running along the walkways. Slipping in the mud, she hastened on through the night and the rain, feeling her way more than seeing it, and at last reached the quarters of the Mistress.

The guards were at their post. Huddled in cloaks, they bowed their heads against the rain. The sound of Melisande's footsteps roused them and they started up, raising their spears. Their grim expressions changed to startled surprise, to see Melisande, soaked and bedraggled, come running out of the darkness.

"Let me pass," she commanded, thrusting aside their spears, as she had thrust aside the wet branches.

"Is anything wrong?" one asked, alarmed.

Melisande turned back, her hand on the door.

"No one is to enter. No one." She paused, her throat constricting, then said quietly, "The death watch begins."

"Yes, Priestess," said the guards, their faces ghostly glimmers in the rain. "The Mistress's blessing be with you, Priestess."

The guards pushed open the great bronze doors. The hallway stretched before her, dark and quiet. The doors closed behind her, the guards pulling them shut gently and quietly, not wanting to disturb the hushed and fearful silence.

The thought came to Melisande, unbidden, that when

next she entered this door, she would do so as the Mistress of Dragons.

"I am not ready. It's too soon. Mistress, walk with me and grant me strength!" she prayed.

Then, straightening, she wiped her eyes of tears and rain. Lighting one of the candles that were always kept on the table by the door, she lifted up the candle in one hand and took hold of her wet skirts in the other. Swiftly, with heart-aching trepidation, she walked down the silent, dark hallway.

She wondered as she went if she had truly heard the Mistress's voice in her mind or if it had been a dream or maybe a combination of both, her dream speaking to her from her aching heart.

Reaching the end of the hall, Melisande rounded the corner and entered the hallway that led to the Mistress's room.

She halted, staring in dismay. So shocking was the sight that for a moment she was paralyzed, unable to move or think or make a sound beyond one startled gasp.

The door leading to the Mistress's room was open and, farther down the hall, the door that led to the Sanctuary was also wide open. Light flared out into the hallway and in the light she could see a man holding what looked to be a bundle of the Mistress's bedclothes. Melisande's dazed brain could not think why any thief should want to take a coverlet; then she caught a glimpse of a limp hand, dangling down from the folds of blue and green silk.

Shocked understanding gave her voice and strength.

"Mistress! Stop!" she called desperately, but, at the sound, the man bolted into the Sanctuary, carrying the Mistress with him.

The door slammed shut. The light vanished. The hall was dark, except for the flickering light coming from the Mistress's chamber.

Melisande started to run after them, but at her first step, her wet sandals slipped upon the marble floor and she fell heavily, landing on her hands and knees, bruising her knee and spraining her left wrist. Fear for the Mistress numbed the pain. Melisande scrambled to her feet and dashed frantically down the hall.

She stopped at the Mistress's chambers only long enough to make certain that she had seen what her disordered mind told her she had seen.

The Mistress was gone from her bed, as were the bedclothes. The man had carried her off. The Mistress, knowing she was in danger, had cried to Melisande to help.

"Too late!" Melisande moaned in agony. "I am too late. Bellona! I must summon the guard—"

She started to turn back toward the entryway, but her heart misgave her, and she turned again, a prey to indecision. Every second counted perhaps.

"He is a man," she faltered, quailing, "and he is armed . . . and I am armed," she said, calming herself. "Armed with the magic."

A strange sensation swept over her, one of resolve that banished all fear.

"The fool! The stair leads him to the sacred Sanctuary—a dead end for him, who would dare steal away the Mistress."

Melisande ran after them. The magic that she had only ever used in anger against dragons burned on her lips and in her belly.

12

"MISTRESS! STOP!" THE WOMAN CRIED.

In Edward's excitement, her voice was the hissing, sibilant voice he'd heard in the cave, the voice promising that this night, the Mistress would die. Edward looked back to try to see the assassin's face, but she was in shadow and he could not make out her features.

Anger swelled in him, and he would have liked to have been able to halt to confront this assassin, but his first care must be for the elderly woman he held in his arms. He would see to it that she reached safety. He would hand her over to Draconas, then he would deal with the fiend seeking to take this poor woman's life. Edward had his plans already formed. He had decided that he would remain here in this kingdom. He would capture this treacherous female alive and turn her over to the proper authorities. He would see to it that the elderly woman received proper care and attention. Finally, he would start his own investigation regarding Grald, the soldiers, and the mysterious baby smugglers.

All this he thought through in an instant, as he clattered down the stairs, heading for the firelit chamber.

He held the old woman firmly but gently, worried that he would stumble and trip over the trailing coverlet in which she was wrapped. She never stirred, but lay comatose in his arms, sunken in her drugged sleep, oblivious to the jostling and the shouting, the tramping of his feet, and the clanking rattle of his sword hitting against the rock walls.

He reached the altar room, with its white marble altar, and its strange and unholy Eye in the floor, an Eye that flickered in the firelight and seemed intent upon him.

"I have her!" Edward called to Draconas, hastening across the chamber, moving rapidly toward the wall and the place on the floor where his glove lay. "Someone is following us—"

Edward glanced down at the woman and his voice suddenly seized in his throat. She had come, all unexpectedly, to life. Her eyes were open and they were dark and filled with fire and the reflection of his face. He saw no fear in her unblinking eyes, only a strange and impassive calm that was unnerving, made his skin crawl.

"Madame," he stammered, his wits scattered, "Madame, I am not going to harm you. Please believe me—"

"Melisande," the elderly woman said, "are you here?"

"I am here, Mistress," said another voice, low and sweet and terrible.

Baffled and confused, still holding onto the elderly woman, Edward turned.

Pale beauty gleamed in the firelight. Eyes of blue flame and rain sparkled. A face of oval ivory, pure cut, chiseled smooth, touched with carnelian and rose, was drenched in water, freezing to ice. Her face. The face in the topaz. Melisande.

He stared, confounded, unable to speak or move. The young woman said nothing. The elderly woman was silent. Three hearts beat away the seconds, then, suddenly, the door slammed shut. Edward started at the sound. His nerves were unraveling.

Melisande glanced over her shoulder at the door, but then swiftly shifted her blue-flame gaze back to him.

"Release the Mistress," she commanded.

The words of explanation Edward longed to say grew tangled in smoky perfume and wet tendrils of long fair hair, conflicting thoughts of assassins and magic, insane monks and false nuns and holy quests and somewhere, long ago, the tale of a wild witch of the wood with whom, if a man fell in love, he was lost forever.

"Mistress Melisande, I mean, Madame"—his words labored to escape the tangle—"I have no intention of . . . that is . . . Your Mistress is in danger. I overheard—"

Melisande made a gesture at once so commanding and so filled with grace that it broke the threads of his thoughts, sent them drifting away like strands of cut cobweb.

"You have committed sacrilege," said Melisande, her tone dire. "You have laid your foul hands on the sacred body of our Mistress and that is an unpardonable crime for which you will surely be condemned to death."

Edward felt the hot blood suffuse his face. He looked down at the elderly woman in his arms, who had remained quiet through all this, letting her minion deal with the situation. She did not move, she did not even seem to breathe. Her eyes held him in their keeping and he was beginning to grow more and more uneasy.

He knew himself to be in the right, and yet he felt unaccountably in the wrong. He had to explain himself. He had to warn her and the Mistress that somewhere out there was an assassin. His one worry now was Draconas. Edward didn't want him interfering, and he cast a swift, sidelong glance at the wall that wasn't a wall, at his glove lying on the floor. Try as he might, he could not penetrate the illusion. He hoped Draconas saw that glance and took its meaning.

"I will release your Mistress," Edward said, temporizing, "if you give me a chance to explain myself. I assure you, I mean her no harm."

Melisande, by her raised head and tightened lips, seemed about to refuse.

It was the Mistress who spoke. "We will hear him," she said.

Melisande eyed him balefully. "Lay her upon the floor. Have a care. She is very weak."

Edward did as he was told, bending his knee to lay the elderly woman, wrapped in the silken coverlet, gently upon the stone floor of the chamber. As he did so, he placed his hand beneath her head, as when holding a baby, so as not to let her head strike the stone. He looked full into her eyes and he looked into a darkness that was darker than the last night of the last day of the end of the world. In the darkness, he saw a malevolence that was a growing, breathing, living thing, a thing that clamped onto his heart with cold, strong hands and started to squeeze it, so that he found it hard to breathe.

Shuddering, he shrank back, so horrified that he lost his balance. His leg that was supporting him slipped and he fell onto his knees. He could not take his eyes from the terrible eyes of the old woman. She held him in thrall.

"Now you will punish him, Melisande," the Mistress instructed.

He tore his gaze free of the old woman, looked to the face in the topaz, the face in his dreams.

Ice-pale, blue-fire, Melisande stretched forth her hands.

Ropes made of light, flaring purple-white, twisted from her fingers, twined around Edward's body. Grasping the rope-light, she lifted him up, and flung him against the stone wall.

Blinding pain burst behind his eyes. He tasted blood in his mouth and felt himself falling into the malevolent darkness of the old woman's eyes.

He struggled against it and heard, as he did so, Melisande's soft voice say softly and anxiously, "Mistress, are you all right? Did he harm you?"

And he heard a feeble voice reply, "All is well,

Melisande. Do not fret. You must see to our assassin. I thought I heard him move."

"I will, Mistress. He will trouble you no more."

Pale beauty stood over him.

Darkness pounced and devoured.

13

ON THE OTHER SIDE OF THE ILLUSION, DRACONAS
waited in the darkness that for him wasn't dark, because
at last he had some glimmering of the truth. He had to
act quickly, for, if he was right, he did not have much
time. He knew the illusion was still in place, for he'd seen
Edward searching for him. Poor Edward, still fooled
by it.

Other eyes, eyes more knowledgeable than Edward's,
could penetrate it, however, and those eyes must not see
him.

Moving slowly, so as not to draw unwanted attention,
he stood up, put his back against the wall. His mind filled
itself with the image of the mountain. He wrapped himself
in the bones of the mountain. He became the mountain.

The king lay very close to the illusory wall, so close
that Draconas might have reached out to touch him. He
did not touch him, not even to see if he was alive or if
he was dead. Hidden in his own illusion, Draconas
watched and waited.

Her work done, her magic cast, Melisande hastened back
to the Mistress, knelt down beside her.

The Mistress's breathing came in shallow, gargling gasps. Every breath seemed a struggle.

Melisande slid her hand beneath the pitiably thin shoulders, lifted her head, pillowed it on the bunched-up folds of the coverlet. She eased the Mistress back down.

"The floor is chill. You should not be lying here. Can you stand?"

The Mistress shook her head. "Let me . . . rest a moment."

Melisande was frightened. The Mistress looked so very ill. Taking hold of the Mistress's thin, wrinkled hand, Melisande pressed the hand to her cheek, wet with rainwater and tears of fear and self-reproach.

"Mistress, I am so sorry. I should have been there to guard you. Forgive me."

"Melisande, hush," whispered the Mistress. She took hold of the soft young hand in her thin, feeble one, caressed the hand gently, as if reveling in its youth and strength. Her gaze wandered in the direction of Edward, but she could not see him. "Is he dead?"

"Dead or unconscious," said Melisande, casting the body a brief, uncaring glance. "If he is dead, we are spared the trouble of a trial. If not, he will be brought to justice for his crime. Now, I will carry you back to your room. Then I will summon help—"

"Not yet, Melisande," gasped the Mistress, holding onto the hand more tightly, struggling to speak. "First there is something . . . you must do."

Melisande was wet and shivering, starting to feel the ill effects of the blood bane. She feared that soon she might be too weak to carry the Mistress and she dared not leave her alone with the assailant. "I will do anything you ask, Mistress, but first, let me move you to where you will be more comfortable—"

"Do you defy me, Melisande?" asked the Mistress and she seemed more sad than angry.

"No, Mistress," Melisande faltered. "I am concerned for your welfare."

"Then do as I tell you."

The Mistress fell back, gasping. Her eyes closed. She lay still a moment, her body so frail that the beating of her heart shook her entire form.

Her eyes opened, and their dimming gaze wandered past Melisande to the far end of the chamber. "Go to the altar."

Melisande glanced uneasily at the body of the assailant. He was still now, but only a moment before she thought she had heard him stir, give a muffled groan. He wasn't dead. She hadn't killed him. Any moment, he might regain consciousness.

Melisande rubbed her arms to try to ease her shivering. She was tempted to ignore the Mistress's commands, which were hardly rational at a time like this, and lift her up despite her protests and carry her to her room. She would then summon Bellona, who would know how to deal with the situation. Melisande had never wanted her lover's strength more than now.

"Melisande," said the Mistress, her feeble voice sharpening. "What I ask of you is important. Go to the altar."

All her life, Melisande had obeyed the commands of the Mistress, obeyed out of love and respect, not out of fear. She could not now disobey, especially as this command might be the Mistress's last.

Melisande kissed the Mistress's hand, laid it across her breast. She cast one final, hard look at the man. He lay still. Maybe that groan had been his last. Satisfied that for the moment, at least, he posed no threat, Melisande walked to the back of the chamber, where the marble altar stood.

The Mistress had barely strength enough to turn her head. Her eyes were the only part of her that seemed alive and they followed Melisande's every movement, a hunger burning in them. The Eye carved into the floor watched, too.

Arriving at the altar, Melisande knelt in front of it, on her blanket, where she was accustomed to kneel. She staggered as she sank down. Shock and fatigue and the blood bane were combining to weaken her. She closed her eyes, clasped her hands together tightly, and prayed a small prayer for herself, asking for strength.

"I am here at the altar, Mistress," said Melisande, keeping her voice from shaking through a great effort of will. "What is it you would have me do?"

"Ask no questions, Melisande," said the Mistress. She sounded eager, impatient. "Do exactly as I command you. Stand up and go into the alcove behind the altar."

Melisande turned to regard the Mistress in wonder. She felt vaguely uneasy, though she could not tell why. The Mistress did not sound like herself.

"Stand up," said the Mistress insistently, "and go into the alcove."

Melisande rose unsteadily, not certain she had heard right. "Only the Mistress of Dragons may enter the alcove—"

"And you will be Mistress soon, won't you, Melisande. Do as I tell you."

Troubled, Melisande did as she was bade. From when she had first entered this chamber as a novitiate ten years before, she had viewed the mysterious and shadowy alcove behind the altar as the most holy place in the world, sacred and sacrosanct, awful and wonderful. When she had dared to dream that one day she might become Mistress, she had allowed herself to dream of what it would be like to come back here, to walk up the three stairs that separated the alcove from the rest of the chamber, to move past the burning brazier, to take her place at the altar, to look out over the faces of the sisters gathered around the Eye, faces that looked to her with trust and confidence.

This was not the moment she had dreamed. There was something wrong, something ghastly. She was not the Mistress. She had no right to be here. Melisande moved slowly, reluctantly, hoping that the Mistress would change her mind and order her to halt. Her foot on the first stair, Melisande turned around.

"Mistress, please. It is not right. Let me take you back—"

"Proceed, Melisande," said the Mistress and her voice was iron-cold and iron-sharp.

Sighing deeply, trying to reassure herself that this could not be sacrilege, for the Mistress herself had ordered it and the Mistress was wise in all things, Melisande climbed the three stairs and entered the alcove.

The light of the brazier could not penetrate the shadows that had been here when the alcove was hollowed out of the rock hundreds of years ago. The shadows were cool and dark and did not threaten, but they did not welcome either. Melisande sought for the holy peace that must reside here, but she could not find it. The shadows seemed like hounds, waiting to leap on her at their master's bidding.

"Nonsense," she said to herself. "It is only a fancy of the sickness."

She was no longer shivering, but hot with fever. She turned to face the Mistress, found herself looking into the Eye. It was huge and all-encompassing, and it stared straight at her.

Melisande leaned her elbows on the altar, clasped her hands and rested her burning forehead against them. She had to be strong. If she collapsed, the Mistress would be alone and helpless.

"Mistress," said Melisande, "forgive my weakness, but I am not well. Let me go—"

"You will be well, Melisande," said the Mistress. "Well and young and strong and invincible. Open the sarcophagus."

"There is no sarcophagus, Mistress," Melisande said. Her heart ached with pity. She saw now that the Mistress had slipped into the delusional state that came sometimes to the very old. "There is only the marble altar. I am going to take you back to your room now—"

The Mistress sprang to her feet. The silken coverlet spilled from around her shoulders and lay in a gold-threaded puddle around her bare ankles. Her thin body quivered with intensity.

"You are not Mistress yet, Melisande!" she cried and there was something terrible in her tone. "Obey me."

Melisande's throat constricted. Her mouth went dry. If this was madness, it might be best to humor it, lest the Mistress would come to more harm in her unnatural excitement.

"Very well, Mistress. I will lift the lid of the . . . sarcophagus."

Melisande spread her hands upon the top of the marble altar, examined it searchingly. The altar was long and narrow and it did have the look of a tomb, though she had never noticed that until now. Perhaps that is what had put this idea into the Mistress's enfeebled mind. The top of the altar might well be a covering, for its marble rim overlapped the main part. She looked up, to find the Mistress's eyes on her.

"The lid is heavy," said the Mistress, "but if you push hard, using both hands, you can move it."

If this was madness, it spoke with the voice of reason. Queasy with a fear to which she could put no name, Melisande placed both hands upon the top of the stone altar and shoved, hard, as the Mistress had told her. The top moved.

Melisande's hands shook. Her mouth dried up, her palms were wet with sweat. She felt sick and was afraid she might pass out.

"Push harder," said the Mistress.

"No, Mistress, please," pleaded Melisande, a prey to terror.

"Open it!"

With the last of her strength, Melisande shoved. The marble lid moved, grating, grinding.

Within was darkness, deep and endless as the final darkness that closes our eyes, never to open them. Air wafted cool, but with a strange smell, not musty or dank, as of a tomb, but a horrible smell of fresh blood. Melisande gagged and would have drawn back, away from death and the smell of blood, but she could not move.

Fear gripped her, held her fast.

The marble lid slid open of its own volition. Shuddering, unwilling, but unable to help herself, Melisande looked into the tomb.

The Mistress stared back at her.

A shudder of horror drove through Melisande's body. She could not scream or make a sound. She gripped the altar for support or she would have fallen.

The Mistress lay inside the tomb. Her face was the same beloved face that Melisande had known all her life, lined with the passing of the years, but on that face was an expression of indescribable torment and agony. The smell of fresh blood came from the gaping, hideous wound in the woman's chest.

Her heart had been torn out of her body. Yet, by some power, the Mistress lived.

The eyes that stared into Melisande's were horrifyingly aware. The woman's hands were clenched to fists to endure the unending pain. The mouth gaped wide in a scream that could never be heard. She could not move. She could not cry out. She could not breathe. Yet she could not die.

How long had she lain here like this? How long had she been a prisoner in the unending darkness, a prisoner of pain and terror?

Melisande lifted her frightened gaze to the living Mistress, who was now approaching her, moving closer and closer, and Melisande knew the time had been long, very long. Years and years of agony, endless darkness, unbearable loneliness, fear.

The Mistress held in her hand a golden locket. One of Melisande's earliest memories was wanting to touch and fondle that beautiful locket.

"You are wondering what I did with her heart. Her heart is in here, Melisande," said the Mistress, moving closer. "When I open the locket, she will die."

"What are you?" Melisande cried, clinging to the tomb, life clinging to death. "Who are you?"

"I am you, Melisande," said the Mistress softly. Her hand reached out to her, to her beating heart. "Or I soon will be."

The hand of flesh withered away, became a claw—a claw glistening with scales, its talons sharp and shining.

A dragon's claw.

14

EDWARD STIRRED AND GROANED. HIS HANDS twitched. From the other side of his illusion, Draconas whispered harshly, "Keep still!"

His head aching and his wits befuddled, Edward readily obeyed the command. He pressed his cheek against the cold stone, closed his eyes to the flaring light, and willed the dizziness and nausea to pass. He listened to the two women speak casually, callously of his death. He was in danger, but he did not have the vaguest notion how or why.

He had a hazy recollection of what had happened to him, though none of it made sense. Slender, delicate fingers, from which burst forth arcing streams of radiant light that burned his flesh and clothes, sent tingling jolts through his bloodstream. He might not have believed it, but he could feel the burns on his skin.

The unreality of it made what had befallen him all the more horrible. He hoped that Draconas knew what was going on and that Draconas was devising some means of dealing with the situation. Edward's task for the moment was to remain conscious and endure the pounding ache in his head.

He whispered a prayer to God to save him and he whispered to Draconas, "What do I do?"

"Nothing, yet," was the answer. "Be still and be silent!"

Edward swallowed a bitter taste in his mouth and, despite Draconas's warning, he risked turning his head ever so slightly so that he could see and hear what was happening.

"I will do anything you ask, Mistress, but first, let's move you to where you will be more comfortable—" the young woman was saying.

Good idea! Edward urged her, grimly hopeful. Let them leave, both of them. Witches or demons or whatever they are. He gazed at her and though his vision was a little blurred, he could still see that she was very beautiful. Witches are not supposed to be beautiful, he thought in a dreamlike haze of pain. Nor are murderers. But she is very beautiful . . .

"Do you defy me, Melisande?" asked the elderly woman.

Melisande. What a lovely name, thought Edward. I wonder what it means. The name suits her. God, my head hurts! He closed his eyes to let a wave of nausea pass and slipped for a moment into the darkness and he missed some of what passed between the women.

When he opened his eyes again, Melisande was standing at the stone altar. He saw her shoving on the stone top of the altar, heard the grinding sound of stone against stone as the lid moved. She looked inside and her face went livid, as white as if someone had emptied her of blood and life. She was terrified. She could barely stand. He saw her frightened gaze go to the elderly woman, who held dangling a golden locket in her hand.

"I am you, Melisande," said the old woman, and Edward recognized the voice.

The sibilant voice, the voice in the cave. The voice of the murderer.

Edward lifted his head. His hand slid to his sword. He tensed, ready to jump to his feet.

A hand reached through the wall, closed over his wrist, its iron-band grip halting his movement.

"Wait!" ordered Draconas.

Edward jerked his arm to try to break Draconas's hold and free his wrist, but the man's grip was incredibly strong, crushing and bruising.

"I will tell you when," Draconas continued, his whisper chill and sharp. "You will save her life, but not yet. Move now, and you both die. Trust me in this, Edward."

Edward hesitated. He had no trust in Draconas, but he had less trust in himself, for his head hurt abominably and it was difficult to think.

"If you want to save her, you must do what I tell you," Draconas urged.

"I want to save her," said Edward, his gaze on Melisande.

Draconas's grip on him loosened, but Edward still felt the man's warding hold on his wrist and he smiled ruefully. *Draconas doesn't trust me any more than I trust Draconas.*

Edward settled inch by cautious inch back down to the stone floor. His precaution was needless. Both women had forgotten him, one too frightened to remember and the other too intent on her victim.

Edward waited, but he was determined not to wait long.

"He's not going to wait long," Draconas said to himself. "Can I count on him? That's the question. He's done well so far. But this—what he must face next—I'm not sure he's ready for it. I'm not sure I'm ready for it. We may all end up dead.

"I should leave," he reflected. "Once I see how Maristara manages to shift her form, I can make good my escape. It's my duty to escape, for I should carry word of this to the Parliament. The humans will die, of course, Edward and the woman, and, in fact, it would be best if they did die, here and now, for if they live, they will see what they should not see. What no human is meant to see."

His argument was logical and he should certainly act on it, but he wouldn't. He would stay and fight Maristara and save the humans for one reason—because he could not endure the thought of letting the dragon win.

He readied himself, readied his magic.

"Edward," he called softly through the illusion, "when I say the word, run to the woman, grab hold of her, and run back here, into the cave. Then keep running, both of you, and don't look behind. No matter what you hear, don't look."

Melisande crouched behind the sarcophagus, her hands gripping the stone lid for support. Mesmerized, she stared at the hand that had transformed into a glistening scaled claw, its sharp talons reaching out for her.

The Mistress's red-eyed gaze fixed on Melisande's breast, on the folds of wet, black fabric that trembled and stirred with the wild and frantic beating of her heart. In her human hand, the Mistress held the locket, moved it slowly, hypnotically back and forth, back and forth.

"Age has its advantages," said the Mistress, stealing ever closer, using her soft voice to lull her victim. "I have ruled for fifty years in this body and it has served me well. But the body grows weak and therefore so do I. I need youth, life, new blood. Your blood, Melisande. Your beating, living heart. The Mistress dies. Long live the Mistress. Except that you won't die, Melisande. You will live in that tomb, held suspended between death and life, as you live on in me. Or rather, to be more precise, I live on in you."

With a flick of her fingers, she opened the locket. There, encapsulated within was a beating heart, the heart of the elderly woman whose body lay imprisoned in the tomb. The heart was small, magically shrunken to fit inside the locket, yet it throbbed and quivered with life. Drawing near Melisande, who could not take her terror-stricken eyes from the clawed hand, the Mistress dropped the heart out of the locket, let it fall back into the bloody cavity from which it had been wrenched.

The woman gasped in agony. She gave a shuddering sigh, a sigh of relief, a sigh that welcomed death. She cast one look at Melisande, a look of pity and despair, and then she stiffened. The clenched fists uncurled. Her eyes fixed in her head. The heart ceased to beat. She lay still.

Staring, horrified, into the tomb, Melisande saw herself. She saw her own body lying there in unending torment and unbearable darkness, a prisoner year after year, aware of all around her, listening to the voices of her sisters, listening, perhaps, to Bellona's beloved voice, unable to cry out to her, unable to touch, unable to make known the truth.

The Mistress was dead and with her death died the body that the dragon had used for so many years. Maristara abandoned the useless carcass to take on her own shape and form.

The memory of Bellona jolted Melisande out of her panicked lethargy.

"If I must die," she said to herself, "I will die so that Bellona is proud of me. I will not die like this, a prisoner. I will die a warrior."

Melisande lifted her gaze from the ravaged corpse of the Mistress to the old woman she had known as the Mistress.

The old woman was changing, shifting form, shedding the body of a human, discarding human flesh as the cicada discards its dried and useless carapace. The old woman was becoming a dragon. The hands were taloned claws covered with gray-green scales. The neck elongated, stretched, writhed out of human shoulders. Wings slid out of the back and unfurled, their span filling the chamber with darkness, as their shadows blotted out the light of the flaming brazier. The legs thickened, bent inward to lift and support the shifting, shimmering, hugely growing body. The tail coiled and uncoiled, thrashing back and forth in excitement. The face of the Mistress blurred to that of a beast. The eyes gleamed red in dark green sockets, the nose jutted outward, the teeth were fangs, dark and the tongue flickered.

Melisande could not understand what was happening. Her mind refused to believe the truth of her eyes, but understanding didn't matter.

Before her was a dragon, her enemy, an enemy she had been trained to fight since she was a small girl in the nursery, studying the pictures of dragons painted on the frescoes around the monastery.

The dragon was still not completely whole, still wriggling out of the body of the human in which she had been hiding. The red eyes, fixed on Melisande's strong, young body, glistened with anticipation. The dragon lifted her taloned claw, stretched it out, reaching over the sarcophagus, over the corpse inside, intending to seize Melisande's body, dig the talons into her breast, tear out the beating heart. The golden locket flashed in the firelight.

Melisande gripped the stone lid of the tomb and with an effort born of fear and fury, she lifted up the lid and hurled it at the dragon. Then, she ran.

"Now!" said Draconas.

Edward jumped to his feet. He had been as shocked as Melisande to see the elderly woman transform herself into a dragon, but, as with Melisande, understanding didn't matter. Action mattered.

The heavy stone lid crashed into the dragon's grasping claw, crushing it. Cursing, Maristara snatched back her claw. She made a swipe at Melisande, fleeing the alcove, but missed her. Blood from the broken talon spattered over the floor and the walls. Melisande evaded the dragon, ran for the door.

"You can't escape, Melisande," said the dragon. Her massive body almost filled the chamber. Her wings brushed the ceiling, her tail dragged across the Eye on the floor, shutting it. "The door is spell-locked."

Melisande flung herself at the door with a wild cry. She

pulled at the handle, beat on it with her fists, but the door held fast. Turning, putting her back to the door, she saw, with amazement and wonder, Edward running toward her.

"This way!" he cried.

He reached out his hand to her and his hand held life.

Melisande grasped his hand and together they ran toward the wall and the place where his glove lay on the floor.

The dragon whipped around, snatched at Edward with her uninjured claw, prepared to grab the intruder and crush him to death.

Edward fell back. Shoving Melisande safely behind him, he slashed at the dragon's claw with his sword.

"Run!" Draconas cried, leaping out from the wall.

Edward sheathed his sword. Turning to Melisande, he swept her up into his arms and lunged forward. The wall loomed ahead of them. Melisande cried out, as it seemed that they must dash themselves to pieces on the sharp rock. He had no time to think or argue with his brain or his eyes or with Melisande, who flung her arm up in front of her face. He ran headlong into the stone wall, carrying Melisande with him.

The two swept through the illusion, plunging from light and noise and confusion into sudden, blinding darkness. Unable to see, fearful of smashing into a real rock wall, Edward tried desperately to slow his breakneck dash. Momentum carried him forward. He tripped on his own feet and he tumbled to the ground, Melisande beneath him. She cried out and he rolled hurriedly off her, fearful that he had crushed her.

"I am sorry, so sorry," he babbled, not knowing what he was saying. He reached out to touch her. He could not see her in the darkness, but he could feel her beside him, feel her trembling. "Are you hurt? I am so sorry . . ."

"Run!" thundered Draconas.

"I pledge you my life," said Edward softly. "I will see that no harm comes to you. Ever."

He took gentle hold of Melisande, who hesitated a

moment, then clasped her arms spasmodically around his neck. He lifted her up, and the two stood together in the darkness, pressing close, body to body. They clung to each other tightly, glad for shared warmth, glad for the feel of flesh and bone and heart beating against heart.

Holding fast to life and to each other, they fled into the labyrinthine darkness.

15

DRACONAS JUMPED THROUGH THE ILLUSION, THEN came to a halt, keeping his back to the wall, a completely useless gesture since it wasn't a wall, but it made him feel more secure. His weapons were his staff, his magic, and his wits. The staff would be useless against the dragon's might. His magic was child's magic, compared to hers. He was counting on his wits to save him.

He faced Maristara, watched her warily. Though he loathed what she had done, he was forced to pay her grudging homage. The spell the dragons had used to change him from dragon to human had taken days to cast. He could shift form easily now, once the magic had been cast, but the initial transformation from dragon form to human had been accomplished at the cost of intricate and powerful magicks. Maristara had considerably shortened the process, reduced the cost.

What a clever plan—steal a human's heart, use that and magic to steal the human's body. Draconas wondered how many wretched women had died before Maristara had managed to perfect the skill.

He'd caught her at a disadvantageous moment, caught

betwixt and between her shape as a human and her true form. Draconas could sympathize. He'd been caught that way himself on one unfortunate occasion. He likened it to a man being caught with his pants down. The man is the same man as he is his with his pants up, but certain important parts of him are exposed and vulnerable.

The dragon's head on its long sinuous neck swooped down, dipped low.

"So," Maristara said, speaking mind-to-mind, as dragons do, her red eyes probing and prodding, "you are Draconas—the walker."

He saw the word "walker" green-tinged, sneering. "Walker" was a derogatory term among dragons, meaning a dragon who walks like a human, a dragon who walks among humans.

Draconas could have returned the insult, but that would be to play her game and he had his own game to play out. He had to be patient, wait for the right moment, not act prematurely.

Maristara had known him immediately, known him for what he was. Her eyes saw the human, but her mind saw the shadow, the dragon. So all dragons saw him. What was remarkable was that she had not cast her shadow on his mind in the same way. He had not known she was a dragon until she began to transform herself. He had seen the human, but not the shadow. That made her immensely dangerous, for it meant that no dragon could detect her in her stolen human body.

He sought her mind with his, feeling her out, as a fencer feels out an opponent. She was a blur of color: the red-gold of expectation, and blazing orange with fury and outrage, cooled by a cold undercurrent of ice-blue cunning.

He could hear—over the dragon's hissing breath—the footsteps of the two humans fumbling their blind way through the pitch-dark tunnels, whipped by fear's lash. They were still too close. He had to stall for time.

Maristara could hear them, too. She could hear her new body escaping her. She wasn't concerned. They could never find their way out of her tunnels. She would chase them down, catch them at her leisure. Her concern now was Draconas. She was trying to bait him, hoping to get a reaction in order to see how he reacted, to see the colors of his mind.

Her eyes sought his, but he took care to avoid the piercing lance of her gaze. When dragons battle each other, the fight is as much mental as it is physical, each trying to lock onto the other's eyes and, from there, slice into the soul. "Fencing with the rapier eye," a dragon once termed it. Had Draconas been in dragon form, he would have thought twice about eye-fencing with Maristara, for she was ancient and adept. As it was, his puny human eyes were no match and so he sent his gaze sliding around her like quicksilver, never looking at her directly, but never taking his eyes off her.

"What a very clever walker," Maristara said.

The shift from human body to the dragon was very nearly complete. Her bulky body was too large for this chamber and that was further hampering her. She was forced to hunch her long, curved neck. Her massive head hung low. Her mane rasped against the high stone ceiling. Her wings twitched and quivered in frustration, for it is a dragon's instinct to use its vast wingspan to intimidate prey, and she couldn't do this, or risk injuring them against the rock walls of the chamber. She had to wrap her bulky tail around her hind forelegs, for there was no room for it to trail out behind her, and that further impeded her movement.

She was dragon in her outward appearance, but not yet complete. He could not smell the brimstone, nor hear the flames rumble in her belly. The fire had to kindle, the breath to cook. Yet, for all this, she was dangerous and deadly. Her teeth could cleave him in twain. Her talons could rend limb from limb. A flick of the wrist, a snap of the jaw and he'd be dead.

Her head slid closer, still talking, seeking to distract him with a kaleidoscope of whirling colors, seeking to dazzle him, make him forget himself, force him to look directly at her.

"So you know my secret. What do you think of it, Draconas? How many days of spell-casting did it take the Parliament to grant you human form? How many *minutes* does it take *me* to do the same? And so, how can you stop me? You can't, Draconas. For hundreds of years, I have been building my defenses, while you and the Parliament slumbered. Now I am too strong. You cannot defeat me. What will you do? Nothing, of course, because there is nothing to be done."

Draconas caught a whiff of brimstone. He could barely hear the footsteps of the humans.

"Your thoughts scurry around like centipedes, Draconas," Maristara continued. Her head oscillated, dipped, and swerved. Her eyes tried to catch his, but his were swift to avoid her. She was desperate to reach into his mind, as she would have reached into that woman's breast; rip out his thoughts as she had planned to rip out the heart.

She lunged, her movement so swift and unforeseen that the slashing claws sliced through Draconas's leather jerkin. A convulsive, backward leap saved him from her grasp. He landed, soft-kneed, and then, jumping into the air, he struck the cavern's stone ceiling with the butt end of his staff, sent his magic rippling through it.

The rock split and cracked. Large fissures formed. Chunks of stone shook loose and tumbled down.

Draconas turned and fled. He heard a curse from the dragon and a shattering crash, as the ceiling gave way. A tidal wave of stone, dust, dirt, and sharp fragments of rock roiled down the corridor, flooding into the hall.

Draconas ran with all his might, legs and arms and heart and adrenaline pumping, trying to outrace the cave-in. This had always been the weak point in his plan—that he might not escape his own solution.

His dragon strength gave him incredible speed, and he raced down the corridor, a step and a half ahead of the crashing rocks. Bits of stone sharp as arrowheads sliced open his flesh, and rock dust choked off his breathing.

And there ahead of him in the corridor were the humans, stopping, with true human idiocy, to stare behind them. Draconas barreled into them. Wrapping his strong arms around them, he took them down to the cavern floor, covering them with his body as the wave of debris and dust and rock broke over them.

Draconas was on his feet immediately, before the dust had settled.

"Get up!" he ordered.

Edward sat up, coughing and choking.

"Did you kill the dragon?" he gasped.

"No," said Draconas, shortly. "On your feet, both of you. We have to keep moving."

Spitting dust, Edward groped about in the darkness until he found the woman. He bent anxiously over her, took hold of her hand. She stirred, raised her head, then fell back. He lifted her gently, cradled her in his arms.

"She can't go on, Draconas. She's too weak, hurt—"

Flinging his staff to the floor, Draconas scooped up the woman's flaccid body.

"Be easy with her—" Edward said, hovering.

Draconas didn't have time to be easy. He slung the woman over his shoulder, positioned her so that he could grip her legs. Her head and arms dangled down behind.

"Hand me my staff," he ordered.

"You can't carry her like that." Edward protested, picking up the staff. "She's not—"

"I can and she is," said Draconas. He broke into a run. "Keep close. If you get lost, you're on your own. I'm not coming back for you."

Behind him, he could hear the dragon clawing and scraping at the rubble that hopefully blocked the cavern's entrance. He'd bought them time, but minutes only and these were precious few.

"Let me carry her," said Edward sternly.

"You have all you can do to carry yourself," Draconas retorted.

And, as if to prove his point, Edward fell headlong over a rock in the darkness and went sprawling. Draconas slowed his pace, listening to make certain the king was all right. Hearing muttered cursing and scrabbling, Draconas moved on.

Edward came stumbling up behind him. "When we get out of this," he said, breathing heavily, "I'm going to knock you on your ass."

"I hope you get the chance," Draconas returned. He was worried. He could no longer hear the dragon.

"What is that supposed to mean?"

Silence meant calm. Silence meant thinking, plotting, planning.

"Nothing good," Draconas said grimly.

They plunged deeper into the cavern, Edward keeping close, reaching out his hand to touch either Draconas or Melisande, reassuring himself that one was warm and breathing and that the other was near him in the stifling darkness. Draconas kept moving because he had no choice but to keep moving. It was either that or sit down and swear, which might be good for the soul but little help otherwise. He had no idea what the dragon was up to. Maristara couldn't let them escape. They knew too much. She had to stop them. The one point in their favor was that they were in her lair.

Had the humans been on their own, they would have immediately lost themselves and Maristara would have caught them. But the humans were with a dragon, who knew something about lairs, who knew that every dragon's lair had more than one exit.

Draconas moved rapidly, and Edward kept up with him, though Draconas could tell by the labored breathing, slurred speech, and faltering steps that the king could not go on much farther. When the tunnel down which they'd been running split, one branch going off to the right, the other continuing straight ahead, Draconas halted. Edward stumbled into him, steadied himself with a hand on Draconas's shoulder.

"What is it?" Edward said, with barely breath enough to ask the question. "What's wrong?"

To human eyes, both tunnels would look the same—dark and desolate. To dragon eyes and ears and nose, each was immensely different. The one that ran straight ahead was only dimly lit. Fetid air flowed from it. From the slant of the floor, it led downward, to the base of the mountain. The other tunnel had more light, there was a sniff of fresh air, and it ran straight and level.

"We're lost, aren't we?"

Edward slumped to the floor, leaned back with his head against the wall, and shut his eyes. He was nearing that dangerous stage of pain and exhaustion where he no longer cared if he lived or died.

Draconas flung the woman off his shoulder, deposited her in Edward's lap.

"I think I've found a way out. I'm going to go take a look. Try to warm her," Draconas admonished. "Put your arms around her. Hold her close."

That should restore him to life, Draconas reflected.

Melisande stirred, moaned, drew in a deep breath. She nestled nearer Edward in an instinctual need for warmth. Edward started to put his arms around her, hesitated. He didn't seem to know where to put his hands. He'd been raised a gentleman, fed on stories of knightly, chivalrous love; love that looked upon beauty from afar and did not touch; love that remained chaste and pure unto death.

"She's probably in shock," said Draconas. "What with those wet clothes and the fright she had, she might die of the cold."

"You're going to be all right, Melisande," said Edward softly, embracing her. "I'm here and I won't let anything happen to you."

As Draconas watched the two, an idea formed in his mind. The idea was strange and it was desperate, and he didn't like it. He immediately abandoned it, was sorry he'd thought of it. Yet, like an annoying song, it wouldn't go away.

"Wait here," he said unnecessarily, for neither human had strength left to go anywhere. Turning toward the light and the fresh air, he left them.

Draconas moved cautiously and warily. He could not find any sign that the dragon had been here. She'd probably not entered this tunnel since she'd built this exit hundreds of years before. Yet, she had built it, using both claws and magic. He could see the gouge marks, the scrapings on the walls, and the places where she had used her magic to blast her way through the granite, places where the rock had melted, turned glassy.

The mountain must have rumbled with her magic, Draconas thought. Shock waves would have spread throughout the valley of Seth and surrounding lands. The humans would have dismissed them as natural phenomenon— earthquakes and the like. He bet that if he looked into their histories, he would find them recorded as such.

He was close to an opening. Even the nearly useless noses of humans would have been able to smell the fresh air. The tunnel ran straight and smooth. Draconas moved silently, stealthily, listening, watchful.

And there was the opening.

The rain had stopped, but the night was wild and wind-blown. He could hear the spattering of drops shaken from the branches of the pine trees whenever a gust hit them. The moon shone. Clouds scudded over it, hiding the moon from sight, then flitting away to uncover it once more. By its light, he could see trees and he was relieved. He'd been afraid that the opening might have been bored into the side of the mountain, which meant a thousand-foot drop for those who did not have wings.

Trees meant solid ground, a ledge, a way off the mountain.

Draconas hoped to find a shallow cave or a thick stand of trees—someplace where he could safely stash the two humans, allow them to rest and recuperate before continuing their trek down the mountainside. A cave would be preferable, for he could heat it with his magic. He didn't mind camping on Maristara's mountain, so long as they weren't inside her lair. In her dragon form, she would have been able to search the mountainside and find them, but she couldn't use her dragon form. She had to continue to hide her true nature from those she had fooled for so many, many years.

She'd foiled herself.

With a feeling of well-earned satisfaction, Draconas walked out the opening.

A wall of flame erupted around him. The heat was intense and seared his skin. He flung up his arm, and then his brain took over.

The fire vanished, as did the heat.

Illusion, all illusion.

The flames might have stopped humans, though probably not for long, not if they were intelligent enough to see what Draconas had seen—that the crackling fire was feeding off rock. Maristara was slipping. She should have at least added some illusionary fuel.

Draconas started to step through the illusion, then came to a sudden halt.

A man, shapeless in black robes, stepped out from the shadows of the trees. He stared intently into the flames that flared in his dark, wild eyes. Moonlight glinted off a tonsured head.

Draconas sucked in his breath, let it out in a whistling sigh. He had once again underestimated Maristara. The illusory fire was not meant to repel. It was meant to alert.

"I know you are in there, foul hell-spawn," cried the monk. "And so does God!"

The monk raised his scrawny arms to heaven. "I call upon Him to smite—"

Draconas flung aside his staff and barreled into the monk, driving his shoulder into the man's solar plexus.

Draconas had hoped simply to disrupt the monk's

spell-casting by taking the man off his feet and knocking the breath from his body. To his astonishment, the monk crumpled at the blow. Bones cracked and snapped. Draconas felt as if he'd smashed into a bundle of dry kindling.

Repulsed, Draconas scrambled to his feet.

The monk's breath whistled oddly. Blood flowed out of his mouth. He began to writhe, his body jerked in spasms. The monk gave a gargle and died.

Draconas was sickened. He could still feel the bones snap, hear the agonized gasp as the monk's shattered ribs sliced into vital organs. Wiping a bad taste from his mouth, Draconas bent down to examine the body. The monk's bones were thin as larch needles. His head could have been that of a cadaver, it had so little flesh.

Hearing footsteps behind him, Draconas jumped to his feet, whipped around, and almost ran down Edward, who stood swaying on unsteady feet, his sword in his hand.

"Another one?" he said, staring at the dead monk.

"Where's the woman?" Draconas demanded.

Edward looked back to the cavern as if it held every treasure ever dreamt of by mankind. "In there," he said, his voice softening.

"You shouldn't have left her." Draconas shoved him aside, heading back toward the cavern.

"I heard voices and I saw the flames," Edward returned. "I thought you might need help."

"Well, I didn't," said Draconas, with a glance of disgust for the monk. "The woman is your responsibility. You wait here. I'll go fetch her—"

He felt a tap on his shoulder. Turning, he met Edward's fist, smashing into his jaw. The blow sent Draconas staggering, though it didn't knock him on his ass, as the king had promised.

"She has a name. Her name is Melisande," said Edward.

Sheathing his sword, Edward stalked back into the cavern.   Draconas waited outside, massaging his aching jaw, and thinking how much he was starting to like Edward.

It was all a damn shame, really.

16

MARISTARA WAS SHOCKED AT THE SUDDEN LOSS OF her new body, more shocked than angry, at first. Events had come crashing down on her, literally. One moment she was going to rip out a human's heart and the next the ceiling collapsed.

Draconas, the walker. The meddlesome walker.

And that youngling Braun.

They were both in this together. The son should have died along with the father. Well, all in good time.

Maristara was calm now. She had been so incensed, so infuriated at the disruption of her plans that she had almost lost her head, let rage consume her.

She had come within a snarling word of using her magic to blast apart the rock slide that blocked the cavern, going in after them, hunting them down like vermin, breathing her fire down the tunnels, poisoning them with the fumes, incinerating their miserable flesh.

She had stopped herself, just in time.

The blast would be heard and felt by everyone in the monastery and half the people in the kingdom of Seth. The sisters would be in turmoil, weeping and wailing and demanding answers, demanding leadership, crying to the Mistress for help . . .and there would be no Mistress. Only the corpse of a desiccated old woman with a gaping hole in her chest.

And a dragon.

Maristara turned away from the pile of rubble, twisting and maneuvering her body in the small, cramped Sanctuary, and mulled things over.

"Let them go for the time being, the humans and the walker." She rolled the term with hatred on her tongue. "They will not get far. I will see to that. First, there must be a new Mistress of Dragons. Whom shall I choose?"

Her mind ranged over the sisters, studying, selecting, rejecting. And then the one.

"Melisande's rival, of course," said Maristara. "Imminently suitable. Jealousy and desire cloud her vision. She will not think to question . . ."

The dragon snuffed out the fire burning in the brazier. Hunkering down in the darkness, grasping the locket in a fore claw, she fixed her eyes upon the door and, in the weak and dying voice of the former Mistress, the dragon called out softly, "Lucretta. Come to me, Lucretta. I have need of you."

Bellona woke at the sound of footsteps outside her door. When the knock came, she was halfway out of bed.

"Commander."

"Yes, what is it?" Bellona spoke softly, so as not to disturb Melisande.

"A summons from the Mistress's chambers. You are wanted. The matter is urgent."

Dawn was near. Pale, gray light illuminated the room. Bellona glanced over to see if Melisande was awake, only to find her side of the bed empty.

Bellona reached out her hand and smoothed the pillow which still had the impression of the beloved head. "So it has happened," she said to herself softly. "Poor Mistress. Yet she has lived a long life. May she join the

blessed ranks of the goddesses who watch over and protect us."

"Commander . . ."

"I'm coming," Bellona called, rising and reaching for
the soft tunic she wore beneath her armor.

"You have leave to enter. There's no trouble with the
men, is there?" she asked sharply.

A young warrior thrust open the door, walked into the
room. "No, Commander. The summons came from the
Mistress's guard."

Bellona nodded and sighed. She remembered that she'd
been going to ride out to the pass, to investigate those
strange intruders. She would put that off, of course. Melisande would have need of her here.

The Mistress is dead.

Bellona had known this time was coming. She had
thought herself prepared, but now that it was here, she
found she was deeply and profoundly saddened. She had
known no other Mistress in her lifetime. This Mistress had
presided over Bellona's birth, had watched her grow from
a harum-scarum girl-child, always getting into scrapes,
into a soldier noted for her skill and bravery. This Mistress had promoted her to her present rank. Melisande
would be Mistress, and Bellona was glad for her lover.
But, for now, there were tears for the dead.

"It is hard, isn't it, Commander," said the young warrior
softly.

"Yes, very hard." Bellona roused herself. There was
much work to be done this day, starting with escorting
the men out of the compound. They mustn't guess that
anything was amiss. "Help me on with my armor."

As the warrior buckled the ornate breastplate over the
tunic, Bellona wondered that she had slept through Melisande's departure. Bellona was a deep sleeper, but she
had trained herself to rouse at the slightest sound. There
must have been the urgent knock at the door, whispered
conversations, Melisande dressing.

"And I slept through it all," Bellona marveled, annoyed

at herself. "I should have been there for Melisande, supporting her with my prayers and my love, if nothing else."

Emerging from the barracks, Bellona came upon a group of soldiers clustered together in front of the barracks, talking in low voices. Their faces troubled, they looked immediately to Bellona. Seeing her dressed in her formal armor, they exchanged glances. Some shook their heads. Others hastily averted their faces. One brushed her hand over her eyes.

"There is no news yet," Bellona told them. "Go to your beds, get some sleep. You will need your rest."

The soldiers did as ordered, trailing off into the barracks. Usually they were jovial, rowdy as they came off duty, looking forward to a hearty meal and then sleep. This day, they were quiet, subdued.

"You will let us know, Commander?" one called after her.

Bellona waved her hand, not trusting herself to speak, and walked on.

The detail assigned to escort the men out of the monastery was already forming under Nzangia's leadership. Bellona received her salute, then beckoned her over.

"I must leave the men to you. I am summoned to the Mistress," said Bellona in an undertone.

"I know. I was there when the summons came from the Mistress's guards. Do you think . . ."

"I fear the worst," Bellona answered grimly. "Melisande was called for during the night. See to it that the men are removed from here quickly. Let no one speak to them and tell your troops to wipe those mournful looks off their faces. I do not want the men to catch any hint that anything is wrong. If they do, the news will be all over the city by midmorning. We must have time to prepare."

Nzangia nodded, fully understanding. She and her detail marched off and soon Bellona could hear them calling out in peremptory voices for the men to wake and get dressed. It was time to leave.

Bellona cast a swift glance up at the walls, to see that her soldiers were on duty and that, outwardly, all appeared normal. She noted only one infraction—two soldiers stopping to talk when they should have been attending to business. She made a mental note to reprimand them both, then hastened to the Mistress's quarters.

The walkways were wet and muddy. A tree branch, blown down during the storm, lay near the iron gong. Raindrops splattered on Bellona's helm as she walked beneath the trees. The heads of the roses, heavy with rain, drooped on their long stems, mourning the Mistress's passing.

The guards posted at the double doors leading to the Mistress's quarters came to attention as Bellona approached. Their salutes, usually snapping with energy, were slower, more solemn. They moved quietly, muting all sounds.

"Daniela, what has happened?" Bellona asked in a low voice.

"I know nothing for certain, Commander," the soldier replied softly. "This morning, when we came on duty, one of the sisters came to us to say that you must be summoned immediately."

"One of the sisters," Bellona repeated. "You do not know which one?"

"She was veiled, Commander," said the soldier. "Her face was covered."

"Then the Mistress must be dead," said Bellona.

The sisters would all wear veils in mourning for the Mistress, keep their faces hidden from sight for thirty days.

"That is what we assumed, Commander."

Poor Melisande, Bellona thought as she entered the darkened hallway. She has had all this to bear alone. How hard it must have been for her, to keep the death watch by herself, to say good-bye. She must be exhausted. And there is still the king to notify and the arrangements to be made for the people of Seth to come to the monastery to pay their homage to the new Mistress. I must see to it that Melisande gets some rest, else she will make herself ill.

At least, there will be no lying in state, no viewing of the body, no funeral.

The Mistress was so important to the safety and security of Seth that the very first Mistress of Dragons had decreed that no one should ever see the Mistress's dead body.

"It is true that the Mistress of Dragons is mortal," the very first Mistress had declared. "But she must not be seen to be mortal by those who depend on her for their very lives. They need to know that their future is secure and thus they will only ever see a living Mistress. By my decree, the body of the dead Mistress will be burned immediately after her death, with only the new Mistress presiding, and her ashes scattered over the sacred Eye in the Sanctuary."

"I always considered that a strange custom," Bellona remarked to herself, padding soft-footed down the too-quiet hall. "It seemed disrespectful to the dead. But now I understand. If the people saw the corpse of the dead Mistress, they might have doubts. They might be afraid. They might wonder if the new Mistress would be up to the task. This way, they never have a chance to doubt. A new Mistress is already at hand, already caring for them."

Bellona wondered if Melisande had performed that sad duty. The details of how and where the cremation took place were all highly secret. Only Melisande would know them and she was bound by her sacred oath never to reveal them until she herself was on her deathbed.

With subdued and pitying heart, Bellona came to the door of the Mistress's quarters. She was not surprised to find it open. Melisande would be waiting for her. She would be grieving the passing, but she would be in control of herself. Bellona had no worries on that score. A brief embrace, their tears mingling, then they would take up their new duties and move on with their lives.

Although it was now morning, a lamp still burned in the room. The heavy curtains remained closed, keeping the room in shadow. As Bellona entered, she cast a glance at the Mistress's bed.

It was empty. Bellona sighed deeply and blinked back her tears.

A woman with a white, diaphanous veil cast over her head sat at the desk. She might have been writing, for there were sheaves of paper on the desk before her, but the quill had fallen from her hand. She sat in a somber reverie, staring at nothing. She did not turn when Bellona entered, though she must have heard her footfalls, the jingle and creak of her armor.

"Mistress . . ." said Bellona softly and for all her heavy sorrow, her heart sang within her to call Melisande by her exalted new title.

The woman turned her head. Lifting her hands to her veil, she removed it.

Bellona stared in shocked astonishment.

"Lucretta! I didn't expect . . . Where is Melisande?"

Bellona was puzzled, but not overly concerned, though she did think it odd that, if Melisande required help, she should have sent for Lucretta and not one of the other sisters.

Lucretta had always been jealous of Melisande, dating back to their childhood days. Neither pretty nor charming, possessed of a hostile, cynical nature, Lucretta was one of those people who live in the belief that others are whispering bad things about them. She was tall and spare and lank. Her bony face was twisted in a perpetual scowl, as much as to say, "I know you hate me and therefore I will hate you first." Though only twenty-eight, she might have been forty. Her frowns had left their mark upon her face.

Her nickname among the soldiers was "the Prune" or sometimes "the Prude" for it was well known that she had never had a lover. She not only rejected any advances, but had acidly lectured those who dared approach her on the sins of the flesh. The only praise that could be given

Lucretta was that she was dedicated, heart and soul and body, to the Sisterhood. She had long felt that she should be Mistress. She had long resented the fact that Melisande had been the one chosen.

Lucretta did not answer Bellona's questions. She regarded Bellona with a supercilious and most unpleasant smirk. A flash of gold sparkled at her neck. She wore a locket that was sacred to the Mistress, worn only by her. A cold qualm shook Bellona.

"Where is Melisande?" she demanded, taking a step forward.

"Well you might ask, Commander," Lucretta replied haughtily, rising to her feet. "She is gone."

Her eyes, which were the same washed-out gray as her skin tone, were small and mean and gleamed with some inner pleasure. Lifting her hand, she fondled the golden locket around her neck.

"Gone?" Bellona couldn't understand the woman. "What do you mean she's gone?" A thought occurred to her. "She's attending to the cremation—"

"No, she is not," said Lucretta. "Melisande is gone from the monastery." She paused, drawing out the suspense. She was enjoying herself. "Melisande ran off with a man, her lover. He came to fetch her in the night."

"I don't believe you," said Bellona flatly.

Lucretta turned away. Reaching out her hand, she slightly parted the curtains, gazed out the window, as if she might be hunting for the errant woman. "She has been gone for many hours. Who knows where she could be by now?"

Bellona strode across the room. Her fingers itched to seize the woman by her scrawny throat and throttle her.

"Where is Melisande? What have you done to her? Tell me, by the Eye, or I will—"

"You will what, Commander?" Lucretta turned, fixed her gray, gimlet eyes on Bellona. "Lay profane hands on your Mistress?"

Bellona glared, her hands clenched to fists.

"For I *am* the Mistress of Dragons," Lucretta continued with detestable aplomb. "I was with the Mistress when she died. I performed the cremation. I scattered the ashes. Melisande abandoned her post. She abrogated her duties. She left the Mistress to die alone. She betrayed the Mistress."

Lucretta smiled sadly, her tone pity-coated. "She betrayed everyone who ever loved and trusted her."

"I don't believe you," Bellona repeated. "Melisande would never do what you accuse her of doing. She loved the Mistress. She would have given her life for her. She would have never left her to die alone."

Bellona eyed Lucretta. The woman had changed. She had never been this glib, this articulate. She had never been this commanding.

Bellona took a step closer. "You've done something to Melisande. I don't know what. Murdered her, maybe. You hated her enough for it. I'll investigate. I don't care if you *are* Mistress. And I won't be the only one. The sisters love Melisande. Everyone loves her. They detest you!"

"What they think of me is not my concern," Lucretta replied, with a lofty calm that was maddening to Bellona. "What you think of me is not my concern. Investigate, by all means. You will hurt only your beloved Melisande, not me. For I have proof."

Bellona dared not lay hands on one of the sisters, but she could intimidate and she did so, pushing forward, using her strong, muscular body to crowd the scrawny woman, shouting in her face.

"Where is Melisande?" Bellona cried. "What have you done with her?"

Lucretta did not move, did not flinch. She gazed impassively into Bellona's anger-pale eyes and quietly repeated, "I have proof. I will show you if you will get ahold of yourself. Indeed, I must show you. For I am sending you to find her and slay her."

Bellona stared at Lucretta, searched for the lie in her and could not find it. Bellona's anger burnt out, leaving her chill and numb, her mouth filled with the taste of ashes. Her heart thudded. She found it hard to breathe, to think. She stood in a stupor, her hands clenching and unclenching, trying to bring some feeling back to her fingers.

"Show me," she said in a voice dull with pain.

Wordlessly, Lucretta walked out of the Mistress's chamber. Bellona followed her, not knowing where she was bound, not caring. Her brain offered proof, her heart refuted it. She was forced to believe and yet she couldn't believe. She knew Melisande, knew her as well or better than she knew herself. Melisande *was* herself, a part of her. Dearer than friend, closer than sister. Melisande lying in her arms, warm and loving and yielding, sweet kisses in the nighttime, softness and shuddering, breathless passion. Could that have been a lie? Could she, all this time, have been feeling the hands of her male lover? In the aching climax, was it his face she saw? His name she whispered? Was that the true reason for her exhaustion this past fortnight? Had she been meeting him in the night, giving herself to him?

Her suspicions roused, Bellona looked back on their time together and suddenly certain words let drop, certain sentences left unfinished, certain deeds and actions that had been of no consequence were now fraught with sinister meaning.

All very well, logic stated, but how did her lover enter the monastery? Where did they hold their trysts? The monastery was well-guarded. No one knew that better than Bellona, who would stake her very life on the loyalty and skill of her soldiers. A glimmer of hope flickered in the howling darkness of her agony. Let Lucretta explain that, and then she would believe.

She revived enough to note that Lucretta was leading her to the Sanctuary of the Eye. The heat in the chamber was intense. The brazier had been stoked with fuel and laden with incense. Yet, beneath it, Bellona could smell the reek of blood and she very nearly gagged. She saw no signs of charring or any other indication that a body had been burned here, but the stench was unmistakable.

An urn of gold inlaid with silver stood atop the stone altar. Bellona glanced at it, then lowered her eyes in respect. Her turmoil over Melisande had caused her to forget that death had claimed the woman she had loved and honored and revered for so many years. Bellona felt ashamed and guilty and that added to her misery.

Lucretta approached the Eye carved into the floor. Turning, she looked expectantly at Bellona.

"Well?" Bellona said, challenging. "Why bring me here?"

"Look into the Eye," said Lucretta.

Bellona recoiled. "You know I am not permitted—"

"I give you dispensation. This once. Look into the Eye and see the truth. Unless"—Lucretta added, her lip curling—"you are afraid."

Bellona stood undecided. She wanted to declare angrily that she wasn't afraid, that her faith in Melisande and her love would disprove the proof, whatever that might be. Yet, she was afraid, suddenly. Very afraid. The Eye was from the goddess and could not lie and Bellona didn't want to see. Bellona wanted to hold onto her love, her faith, her pride.

"It is your duty, Commander," said the Mistress.

Not so many months ago, one of the men chosen for the coupling had managed to sneak a bottle of hard spirits into the monastery. In a drunken fit, he'd begun punching and beating the woman chosen to partner him. Going to subdue him, Bellona found out that he'd also smuggled in a knife. She saw the light flare off the blade, saw it stabbing toward her. She could not dodge the blow. She had to take it, and she had braced herself for the searing burn, twisting her body so that the knife would glance off a rib, not strike to the heart.

She knelt before the Eye.

Lucretta knelt opposite her.

"Reveal what you have seen," Lucretta commanded.

The images were fleeting and blurred, incomplete, but

telling. A man, handsome, a foreigner by his clothes, stood in this very chamber. Melisande was there, white-faced, shivering, looking frightened, near to death, but then she would be, wouldn't she? She knew the enormity of her crime. He held out his hand to Melisande, and she—wet from the rain, her black robes clinging to her body—ran to him. He swept her up in his arms and carried her . . .

The Eye closed. The images vanished, yet Bellona would see them forever.

Bellona shut her eyes, bowed her head. Her agony was like some ravening beast let loose inside her, clawing at her vitals, tearing at her, slashing and cutting. The pain of loss, of betrayal, was unendurable and if she could have willed herself to die in that moment, she would have done so.

Bellona rose to her feet and with a wrenching effort caged up the beast inside her, muzzled its howls of pain and rage.

"She met him here in the Sanctuary, that is clear enough," Bellona said with cold and terrible calm. Her gaze fixed on Lucretta. "But how did he get in without anyone seeing him? And where did they go?"

Lucretta stood up, her lank body awkward and ungraceful. Folding her hands over her thin stomach, she pursed her lips.

"The Mistress of Dragons is given knowledge that others are not. I know how he entered and I know how they both escaped. You do not need such information—"

"I do if I'm going to go after them," Bellona returned, knife-edged.

"No, you do not!" said Lucretta. Her gaze lifted, met Bellona's. "I'll show you where to pick up their trail. Come." She reached out her thin and bony hand, intending to place her cold fingers on Bellona's. "We will return to my chambers. I have there a map—"

Bellona shifted her feet, avoided the touch.

"Please proceed, Mistress. I will follow."

Lucretta did so, walking from the sacred chamber with what majesty her spare frame and shuffling gait permitted. Bellona followed, the ravening beast quiet in his cage.

To keep it silent, to keep it from tearing her apart, she began to feed it hatred.

17

BY THE TIME MORNING'S GRAY LIGHT SPREAD OVER the sky, washing out the stars and reducing the shining, globular moon to a pale wafer, flat and insubstantial, Draconas had his two humans safely ensconced in a shallow depression he had found on a cliff side.

Melisande sank to the floor. Sick with the shock and the lingering horror of the dragon's attack and the terrible thought that she might now be lying in that bloodstained tomb, she could think of nothing but those hands clenched to fists of agony, that mouth opened in its silent scream of pain, the dragon's claw, the golden locket.

She did not know where she was, could not have said how she came to be here. The flight through the darkness was unreal. These men who were with her were strange and frightening. They had saved her life, but why? What had they come for? Their presence didn't make sense, it seemed sinister.

She had never been around men much, just those who came to service the cows, and she had always been disgusted by their largeness and their grasping hands and the naked lust in their eyes. Crawling into a corner of the small cave, she sat with her back against the wall, her arms clasped about her, watching the two men warily.

"We should build a fire," said Edward. "Look at her. She's shivering."

His gaze on her was anxious and worried. He was a comely man, she had to admit. His hazel eyes, with their flecks of sunlight, radiated with admiration for her and that warmed her, in spite of herself, and seemed to steal away the horror of the night. He had fought the dragon for her. He appeared open and honest, yet how had he come to be there?

"Too dangerous," said Draconas.

Dark-eyed and taciturn, saturnine—this man hardly looked at her at all and, on those rare occasions when she caught him regarding her, the expression in his eyes was of cool appraisement, as if considering how to be make use of her.

I have to get away, Melisande resolved. *Yes, Edward, you are very handsome and very charming, but I don't trust you. And I certainly don't trust your friend. If you think I owe you something for saving me, you are mistaken. I owe you nothing. I owe my people everything. I owe them the truth. I have to return to them, tell them, warn them.*

You are tired, she told the two men silently. *You will sleep and when you do, I will leave.*

She had to put them off their guard. Make them think she was weak and exhausted, which should be easy, she thought with a bleak sigh. She drew her knees up, laid her arms on her knees, her head on her arms. She closed her eyes, shut out the sight of them.

Edward seated himself, easing himself to the ground with a stifled groan.

"Is she all right?" he asked in concern. "She looks so . . . ill."

"She'll be fine," said Draconas absently, preoccupied with his own problems. "She's young and strong. She just needs rest."

Edward nodded. He had a few problems of his own.

"You should get some sleep," Draconas advised. "I'll go fetch the horses."

"You said it was too dangerous to build a fire. Isn't it more dangerous to go traipsing about after the horses?"

"I'll manage," said Draconas. "I have to. Or do you plan to walk all the way back to Ramsgate carrying her in your arms?"

Edward flushed. His head throbbed. He felt sick and dizzy and angry, rightfully angry. He'd been used, lied to, and it was time to stop. "Answer me this, Draconas. You brought me here to fetch this Mistress, who was supposed to drive away the dragon that threatens my kingdom. And what do we find here—a dragon! And it seems to me you weren't at all surprised—"

"But we did!" said Melisande, lifting her head. The blue flame had died in her eyes, leaving them just blue, a shadowed blue. "We did keep away the dragons. We fought them and killed them. All but—" Her lips trembled. She shuddered and clasped her arms around her legs, holding onto herself to keep from shattering.

"Yes, Melisande, you killed them," said Draconas, his tone mild, even. "And who taught you the dragon-killing magic? Your Mistress—a dragon."

Melisande raised her head slightly, cast him a furtive glance. He was not looking at her. He stared out of the shelter, into the dawning, into the birdsong and the smell of crushed pine needles and the wind sighing gladly now that the storm had passed.

"You weren't protecting your kingdom, Melisande," Draconas continued. "You were protecting your dragon."

Melisande didn't answer. She didn't stir. She hoped they would think she had fallen asleep. Her thoughts were a quagmire. She tried wading through them, but she couldn't lift one thought out of the horrifying muck without feeling herself being dragged down deeper by another. She needed time to think, to sort all this out.

"I think she's asleep," said Edward softly.

"You should be, too," said Draconas, standing up and

stretching. "I'm going to go get the horses. You'll be safe enough here, while I'm gone. They won't have the search parties out yet. They'll have to get organized."

Edward flicked Draconas a glance. "Sleep's the worst thing you can do with a head injury. I've heard Gunderson speak of men with cracked skulls who went to sleep and never woke." He paused, added quietly, as Draconas was starting to leave, "You weren't surprised to see the dragon, were you? In fact, I think you expected it."

"Oh, I was surprised, all right," Draconas said. "This quest of yours has been nothing but one surprise after another."

He walked off. Edward wanted to rise up in anger and shout, "Don't you walk out on me, sir! I have more to say to you!" but he was too tired, too hurt.

Let him go, he thought, and he didn't much care if he came back.

Edward chivalrously chose to rest as far from Melisande as their small shelter permitted, which wasn't very far. He laid down, his gaze fixed on her. He fully intended to keep watch, but his eyes closed, in spite of himself. He gave a deep sigh and slipped into a fitful and pain-racked slumber.

Draconas left the cave, walked some distance, giving them both time to lose themselves in sleep. He did intend to go fetch the horses, but not yet. He flexed his muscles, rubbed away the few sore spots and bruises. He was tired, but not exhausted. He could go for several days without sleep. What he required now was food. Not planning to make a long stay of it, they'd left all their supplies in their saddlebags.

And there was Braun. Draconas had yet to make his report. The dragon would be waiting impatiently to hear what had happened. He would have to keep waiting. Draconas wanted to sort things out in his own mind first.

After half an hour, he padded quietly back to the cave to look at his charges.

Both were asleep. Edward lay on his back, one arm

over his chest. He muttered and grimaced. He was still in pain. Melisande lay on her side, her legs drawn into her body, her arm over her face, still trying to hide. She hadn't meant to fall asleep, of course. She'd been planning to slip away, try to go back to her people.

"Courageous," he told her silently, leaning over her. "But foolish."

Certain that they were deeply slumbering and would not waken at his touch, Draconas set about doing what he could to cure their hurts. Maristara couldn't let them escape, not with what they knew. She'd send someone after them, if she didn't come herself. These two had to be fit to travel.

Draconas had the power to heal himself, as do all dragons, who use a combination of magic and mental discipline to reverse the effects of all but the most critical injuries. Dragon-magic spreads warmth throughout the body, alleviating shock. Dragons can slow their heartbeat to stop bleeding, both internal and external. They can send themselves into a deep, healing stasis, allowing their bodies to regenerate and repair injured organs, broken bones, snapped tendons. Draconas could do this to himself, and he had done so in the past. Humans were so very reckless, so careless of their own well-being. Life lived among them was fraught with peril.

Draconas could not heal humans as he could heal himself. He could not cause their organs to regenerate, for example, but he could reduce shock and slow racing hearts or speed up failing ones. He could cauterize wounds by touch, leaving scars, but removing infection. He could mend minor breaks. He supposed by a strict reading of dragon law, he was meddling in their lives by healing them, but he generally found ways to justify it. And he was careful to never let them know that he had helped them. Fortunately, most humans subscribed to the belief that either sleep or strong spirits or a combination of both could cure almost any ill.

Draconas placed practiced hands on the bruised and

ugly gash in Edward's head, let his magic flow into the human, deepened his slumbers. The lines of pain smoothed from the king's face. Edward relaxed, his breathing grew more even. Draconas poked and prodded, found no other injuries. He moved on to his next patient.

Melisande's injuries were superficial—scrapes and cuts and bruises, nothing more. She had taken the worst wound in her soul. Draconas could tend to her body, but the other would have to heal on its own or not, as the case may be. He could only keep her warm and trust that the intelligence and courage she had exhibited in battling the dragon would aid her in continuing the fight.

His task done, he left them, went outside the cave, and summoned Braun.

"This is terrible," said the dragon grimly. "Far worse than anything we imagined. I cannot believe it."

The two dragons spoke mind to mind. The day being clear and cloudless, Braun did not like to fly where Maristara might see him. He had taken refuge on the top of another mountain, as close as he could come to the Sentinel peak. Looking into Braun's mind, Draconas saw a miasma of ugly colors—vibrant shock mixing with disgust and revulsion; anger mingling with dismay and, running through all, a thin, red trickle of fear.

Draconas probed deeply, and was at last satisfied. The young dragon's emotions were real, not manufactured. Draconas had nursed a few suspicions about Braun. Patricide was not unheard of among dragons. Theirs was a bloody history, especially in that time when the planet was new, long before humans walked upright on it. Maristara's partner was a male. Perhaps that partner was her grandson.

Draconas was glad to know that his suspicions were unfounded. Braun was young. He had not yet mastered the art of hiding his emotions.

"If word of what is happening in Seth leaks out, if other humans discover that dragons are stealing their babies and raising them to a life of torment and torture, they will be enraged. Their governments will send out armies to hunt us down. The slaughter, the killing will be incalculable."

He meant the slaughter of humans, but dragons would die, too. That was inevitable, especially since human ingenuity seemed to delight in inventing new and better ways to kill.

"What can Maristara and her fiend of a partner be thinking?" Braun demanded angrily. "Can't they see the danger?"

"They see it," said Draconas. "They want it."

A vibrant burst of outrage, then cool calm spread through the dragon's mind.

"Of course," said Braun. "How stupid of me! Turmoil and chaos work well for them. They mean to destabilize human society, then send out these false monks, gifted with the dragon magic, to take control."

"They seize a kingdom here, a nation there," Draconas remarked. "They have one kingdom that we know of. My guess is that they have one other—the place where they take the children. You didn't happen to see where that wagon of babies went?"

"They drove the wagon into the forest that borders the river. From there, they took to boats, and I lost them. I flew up and down the river, but saw no trace of them."

"The riverbank is thick with trees. They could have left the boats at any place along the shore, struck out overland. We'll never find them. It's like trying to track weasels."

"My father found them," Braun said. "That is why they killed him."

"He knew too much," Draconas agreed. "And now so do we. You had best be careful, my friend. Be careful what you say and who hears it."

"I will have to take this to Parliament—"

"No!" Draconas admonished sharply. "Tell Anora, no one else."

Braun was silent, his mind gray, subdued. "Can we trust her, do you think?"

"We have to," said Draconas flatly, adding after some thought, "yes, I think we can."

"How can you be so sure? At this point, I don't feel I know anything for certain," Braun returned.

"These monks practice male dragon magic—battle magic. The spell that first monk cast at me was taught to him by a male dragon. The human females, like those who attacked you, are taught only defensive magic. It's actually quite clever of Maristara and her partner, to divide it up like that. That way, they don't make any one human too powerful."

"Then you think there are only two of them involved?"

"That I don't know. I hope there are only two of them," Draconas said tersely. "If there are more . . ." He left that hanging. "You must impress upon Anora that she cannot tell anyone. She won't like that. She will want to take it to Parliament and that is the one thing she must not do. Our one advantage over our foes is that they don't know precisely what we know. I intend to keep it that way. Anora has to decide what is to be done on her own."

"What *is* to be done?" Braun demanded, frustrated and helpless. "I suppose we could attack this wretched human kingdom, destroy it, burn it to the ground and then bury what is left so that no one can ever find it."

"And what would you have accomplished, besides killing a few thousand humans? Maristara would simply hide out in her lair until we had gone, then fly off to find another kingdom. You would fail to catch her partner, for we have no idea where or who he is. The humans in this area would be in an uproar. Word that hundreds of dragons have wiped out a human kingdom would spread throughout the continent. As you said, their governments would send armies after us and we'd end up throwing ourselves into the very pit we are trying to avoid."

"At the very least," Draconas added, "we should make Maristara exert a little effort to kill us."

"I'm glad you find this amusing," Braun said coldly.

"Oh, I do. I've been laughing heartily ever since that monk knocked me half-senseless."

Draconas sat brooding, absorbed in his thoughts.

"Look at it another way," Braun said suddenly. "If you were Maristara, what would you do now?"

"Do?" Draconas shrugged. "Not much. Why should I? I will try to slay these two humans, of course. They know the truth about me and they might manage to sneak back into Seth and ruin everything I've accomplished."

He fell silent, his watchful gaze roving over the hillside and into the skies. He could see Braun with the rising of the sun—a graceful, winged figure perched high on the mountain peak, silhouetted against a smear of white, wispy cloud.

"You have a plan," said the dragon. "I see it in your mind. It is a good one."

"No, it's not," said Draconas, irritated at himself. He had not meant his plan for sharing. He'd thought he'd buried it deep, but apparently he'd missed. "There are too many variables. And it would be twenty years in the making."

"You talk like a human," said Braun disparagingly. "What are twenty years to us? An eye-blink, nothing more."

"It goes against all our precepts. No, it's wrong," said Draconas shortly. "We can't consider it."

"What about those human babies you saw them stealing? What terrible torment do they face at the hands of these monsters? What about the wretched human female kept horribly alive in that tomb? How many humans have died because of Maristara? How many more will die if humans and dragons go to war?" Braun demanded.

"I know, damn it!" Draconas returned. "You don't have to lecture me."

"I will tell your plan to Anora," said Braun. "I think she will approve it. Even if we decide to take other action in the meantime, this will be an excellent fallback for us."

"Remind her that we are talking about human lives here," said Draconas.

"I will," Braun returned gently. "Many thousands of them."

That hadn't been what Draconas meant and he was about to say so, when Braun interrupted.

"There's movement on the ground."

"Troops?" Draconas asked.

"Yes, coming out of the pass."

"Heading in which direction?"

"Your direction," said Braun.

A dragon's lair to the dragon is like a cobweb to the spider. The spider feels every quiver of each silken strand. The dragon knows what happens in every tunnel. She would have felt the heat of her illusory fire, heard the death cry of that wretched monk. Maristara knew where to go looking for them, if not where to find them.

"How many?"

"Thirty."

"More of those crazed monks?"

"Soldiers. I see the gleam of their armor."

"How long before they get near here?"

"They are on horseback and moving fast now, for they're on a road. They'll soon have to leave it, enter a rocky defile. That will slow them considerably. I say you have a couple of hours yet before they come anywhere near you. Can you deal with them?"

"Yes, they're actually going to help me. One of my humans is not being very cooperative."

The dragon lifted his wings, sprang into the air, and soared upward on the thermals. "Then, if you do not require my help, I will go make my report to Anora. I hope to be back soon."

"Take your time," Draconas returned. "We have time, it seems. All the time in the world."

"An eye-blink," Braun said.

The dragon flew away, heading south. Draconas watched him depart. He cast an illusion on the shelter, making the depression blend into the mountainside.

"That should keep them safe for a little while," he remarked to himself. "An eye-blink."

He went off to find the horses.

18

DRACONAS STOOD OUTSIDE THE SHELTER, HIDDEN
in a stand of aspen trees. On the hillside opposite him,
across a deep ravine, helms and armor and spears gleamed
with the bright polish of the noon sun. Draconas watched
the warriors wending their way steadily in his direction.
His dragon eyes picked out details. All the warriors were
female. No mad monks among them. Each was armed
with bow and arrows, as well as spears. They carried water, but no other supplies. They expected the chase to be
a short one, their quarry easily captured.

No, not captured, Draconas amended. Killed.

He hunkered down amidst the aspens. He was considering the oddity of an army of all-female warriors. Very
rarely had that happened in human history, but he could
see how it made sense for Maristara. He had just about
decided that the warriors were close enough that he should
wake his humans, when he saw that one of them was
already awake.

Melisande stood in the entrance to the cavern, poised
to make her escape. She would not rush out heedlessly.
She would take a good look around her first, he decided,

and that's what she did. Blinking in the bright sunshine, she shaded her eyes, waited until she could see before proceeding. She ventured out another step or two, then sent a piercing gaze around the area. She crept out several more steps, looked to the mountain peaks, searched the sky, then her gaze again swept her immediate surroundings. She nodded slightly, satisfied, and slipped stealthily away from the cavern, heading back in the direction they'd taken to get here.

"I wouldn't do that, if I were you," said Draconas calmly.

Melisande gasped and started. She stood frozen for a moment, trying to calm her racing heart, then turned slowly toward the sound of his voice. He rose up out of the shadows, walked toward her.

Recovering quickly from her shock, she had her story ready.

"I seek some privacy, sir," she said, raising her chin. "To make my morning ablutions."

Draconas gave a nod back to the bushes where he'd been stationed. "Right in there. Safe and secure."

Melisande's clothes had dried a little during the night, but the heavy fabric was still damp and she shivered in the shade. Her hair hung around her shoulders, the curling strands matted and tangled. A few curls straggled over her face. She brushed them back. She glanced at the bushes and a soft flush mantled her cheeks.

"That is much too close—"

"Sorry, but I can't let you go wandering off."

Melisande's flush deepened. She straightened, regarded him with an imperious air. "Am I your prisoner then?"

"That's not the way to talk to someone who has just saved your life, Melisande. I've been keeping watch, all this time, while you slept. What did you think? That the dragon would simply let you walk away? After what you saw?"

The blood drained from her face. Pressing her lips together tightly, she clasped her arms across her breast. She turned away from him.

"Where were you planning to go?" he asked.

Melisande turned her head. Her blue eyes were the only color in her pale face.

"Back to my people," she said. "To tell them the truth." She turned again, came walking toward him. "You have to let me go." She reached out her hand to him, as if her argument were something physical she could hold in her palm. "I have to tell Bellona and the others. My god!" Her fingers curled in upon themselves. "A dragon! Our Mistress—a dragon! And the poor woman. Buried alive in the darkness, left to suffer horribly for years. The golden locket . . ."

She faltered, paused to regain control, then continued in a steady voice, "So you see, you have to let me return. The entrance to the cave must be near. I remember that we didn't walk very far."

Draconas caught hold of her by the wrists, jerked her toward him, forced her to look at him, to take a good, long look.

She gasped and struggled in his grasp. He saw fear in her eyes, and for a moment he was worried. Did she see him for what he was? She had the dragon magic. Could she see him in his true form?

"Let go of me!" she said, dragging backward. "You're hurting me."

No, Draconas realized. She is afraid of me because I am a man. He felt her body quiver and tense and he guessed then that she was a virgin when it came to men. If she knew love, it was from women. Female warriors. Warriors who guarded the priestesses and kept them away from men because . . . ?

Because the dragon must have some means of controlling the breeding of babies who possessed the dragon magic. Maristara could not allow these gifted women to marry and raise families. She had to keep them around in order to reap the bountiful harvest.

"If you went back, you would not live long enough to tell anyone," said Draconas. "The dragon would see to that."

He released her and she stumbled backward. Rubbing her wrists, Melisande moved out of reach. She didn't flee. She hadn't given up her cause. Her voice hardened as she talked, firmed with resolve.

"You don't frighten me, sir. Now that I know what the Mistress is, I can deal with her. I have been raised all my life to battle dragons."

Her courage impressed him. He rewarded her by falling back a step, removing himself as a threat. He cast a glance over his shoulder at the thin line of warriors, trailing down the mountainside.

Melisande drew in a deep breath. She clasped her hands together, her fingers twining.

"Why did you come?" she demanded abruptly. "Are you assassins?"

Draconas smiled, amused. "I admit that I'm not much to look at, Mistress, but does Edward seem like an assassin to you? Or act like one?"

Melisande glanced back into the cave. A band of sunlight had fallen across Edward's face. He was interestingly pale, with enough dried blood remaining from his wound to remind her what he had suffered on her account. He slept with his hand on his weapon, ready at a moment to wake to defend her. She recalled his bravery and his gallantry, and she could not help but be remorseful, touched, intrigued.

"No, he does not look like an assassin," she admitted. "But then why did you come?"

"You heard what he said last night. We came seeking the Mistress of Dragons. We wanted an audience with her. His Majesty is in dire need. A marauding dragon has been laying waste to his kingdom. He was hoping to persuade the Mistress to come work her magic, drive it away."

Melisande's eyes widened. "If that is true, then you

went about obtaining your audience in a very strange way."

"You must admit that your people are not very hospitable to strangers," Draconas remarked. "We came in the back door, but we did mean to go around to the front."

"And what made you change your mind?"

"We overheard a plot to kill the Mistress," said Draconas. "We didn't know it at the time, but what we heard was the dragon talking."

Melisande caught her breath. She glanced back at Edward. "So he came to—"

"—rescue your Mistress. Instead, he most inconveniently rescued the dragon."

"Oh!" Melisande gave a gurgling laugh. She clapped her hand to her mouth, choking back her laughter. "It's not funny. It's horrible. I must be hysterical."

She was silent a moment, pondering. "You mentioned this kingdom—"

"He is a king. King Edward of Idlyswylde. His realm is not far from here. Centuries ago, there was trade between your two kingdoms."

"Will he be all right?" she asked at length, seeming ashamed of having thought ill of him.

"He will have a scar on his head, but I doubt if he'll mind. It will remind him of you."

The flush returned to her cheeks and with it a wan smile that didn't last long. She had been momentarily distracted, but she had not lost sight of her true goal.

"You must thank His Majesty for me when he wakes. And now I must leave you. I must return to my people, do what I can to remove this threat or at least tell them so that we may all fight against the dragon. If you will show me the way back into the cavern—"

Draconas shook his head.

"So I am your prisoner," Melisande said angrily. "Just because you saved my life does not mean that you own me! I am High Priestess. I have a duty—"

"Come over here," said Draconas, gesturing.

Melisande remained unmoving, regarded him warily, defiantly. She put her hands behind her back.

"Come here," he repeated. "I want to show you something. Don't worry. I won't touch you again."

Reluctantly, unwilling, she walked over to stand near him, keeping herself at arm's length. He pointed. "Look there, along that narrow ridge."

The warriors were much closer now, moving faster than he'd anticipated. They must have found an easier route down that defile. The mounted troop was almost directly opposite where he and Melisande stood hidden in the aspen grove, separated from them by the ravine.

Yesterday's rains had sent a torrent of water through the narrow cut, to judge by the high water mark on the rocks and the smooth, wet grass, flattened by the current. The flash flood had been brief. Most of the water had already receded, but the ravine was muddy and filled with debris—boulders and tree limbs, an uprooted tree, water-soaked logs.

The warriors edged their way down into the ravine, moving rapidly but carefully, the leader dividing her attention between guiding her horse's footing and scanning the area ahead, selecting the best route. She knew where she was going, that much was certain. She never hesitated, but forged ahead with her own determined resolve.

"They're closer than I thought," Draconas remarked. "Though they'll have some trouble wading through that mess in the ravine. We need to think about escaping them."

He glanced at Melisande to see her reaction. Her lips parted, as though she had been going to speak, but the words failed her. Her eyes were wide and shocked and staring.

"Warriors of Seth, if I'm not mistaken," said Draconas. "They came down from the pass. Probably for the first time in three hundred years they've set foot across the border. They've been ordered to come after you, Melisande."

"Ordered?" Her lips shaped the words, but she could not speak them. She seemed stupefied, struck dumb.

"Orders given by the Mistress of Dragons. The new Mistress. Seth couldn't go long without a Mistress, you know. You escaped, Melisande, but another poor woman wasn't so lucky."

Melisande stared at the warriors, her eyes shimmering. She shivered and clasped her arms around herself, but she never took her gaze from the women moving inexorably closer.

"The Mistress is dead," Draconas continued, hoping to impress upon her the fact that she was in danger. "Long live the Mistress. She's ordered them to hunt you down and kill you. She can't take a chance on you coming back alive. She probably told them—"

Melisande sprang out of the shadows of the trees, waving her arms and shouting.

"Bellona!" she cried. "Bellona! I am here!"

Her shout echoed through the ravine, bounced off the canyon walls. She began running down the hillside.

Caught off guard, flat-footed, Draconas cursed himself for being an idiot. *I have to tell Bellona,* Melisande had said earlier, and her voice had lingered over the name as if it were a honey-dipped almond, sweet in her mouth.

"What's going on?" Edward cried, emerging from the cave, his naked sword in his hand. "I heard voices. Where's Melisande?"

"Stay there!" Draconas bellowed, and dashed off.

Six hundred years among humans, and they continued to astonish him with their stupidity. For, of course, instead of obeying his orders and remaining in the safety of the cave, Edward came crashing along after him.

"Melisande!" he shouted desperately. "Come back!"

She was some distance below them, scrambling frantically among the rocks and crags and trees, making her way down the hillside more by luck and instinct than skill. She halted abruptly, brought up short on a rock shelf that jutted out over the ravine. The drop below was considerable. Searching for some way off the shelf, she did not see the soldiers draw their bows and nock the arrows. She would hear the order to fire, but that would be the next to the last sound she would hear. The last would be the vicious humming buzz of the arrow and the wet thunk as it thudded into her breast.

Draconas cursed all humans roundly. She didn't have to die. A magic spell had already formed itself in his mind. He could use his magic to set fire to every single arrow, burn them to ashes. But if Melisande did not know who he was now, she would know or be able to guess then. She would recognize the use of dragon magic.

He thought of the plan, his plan, and of what would happen to Melisande if Anora decided to proceed with it. Perhaps it would be best if she died, here and now, at the hands of humans. Anora could not blame him . . .

Draconas opened his hand, let the magic trickle out of it, as so much sand.

Edward careened off boulders, shoved himself off trees, ran headlong down the cliff face.

"Look out!" he shouted. "Melisande, take cover!"

Melisande lifted her head. She saw the warriors lifting their bows. She saw the arrows aimed at her and she held out her hands.

"Bellona!" she cried, pleading.

"Fire!" called the commander's voice, cold and proud and clear.

Edward leapt onto the boulder beside Melisande. Catching her around the waist, he flung her into a pile of soggy brush and dead leaves washed up along the bank. He jumped after her, as arrows pierced the air where she had been standing.

They both landed in a heap. Edward scrambled to his feet, pulling Melisande up with him. Draconas hastened to meet them. He seized hold of her arm—limp and unresisting—and hauled her up the bank, as Edward pushed her from below.

"Fire!" came the order again.

Was it his imagination or did that voice sound relieved? And was it also his imagination or were those women terrible archers? Draconas flattened himself on his belly, dragging Melisande down beside him. Edward shielded her with his body. Arrows clattered all around them, striking the rocks or sticking in the mud or falling among the trees.

Immediately, they were up. Grabbing hold of Melisande, who lay crushed and half-stunned, Draconas dragged her up the hillside. By Edward's heavy breathing and swearing, the king had also escaped injury.

They scrambled up the hill, slipping and falling, rising and running. Melisande moved in a benumbed state, not seeming to care what happened to her.

Halfway up the hill, she startled him, therefore, by coming to a sudden halt. Shaking off Draconas's hand, ignoring Edward's frantic protests, she stood on the hillside, turned to look back at the warriors, who were once again on the move, galloping down into the ravine, coming after her.

"I told you," Draconas grunted. "She means to kill you."

Two tears welled up in Melisande's eyes and slid down her cheeks, plowing small furrows through the muck and mud on her face.

Turning away, she shoved aside his hand, refused his help. She climbed on her own.

19

TIME IS ON OUR SIDE, OR SO EDWARD CALCULATED. The warriors would have to cross the ravine and that would cost them time, for not only would they have to find a way through the uprooted trees and branches left after the flood, they would have to wade through oozing mud that sucked at the horses' hooves. Then the warriors would have to ride up the other side, which was steep and treacherous, as Edward could attest.

"You look after Melisande," Draconas ordered, when they reached the horses. "I'll take the lead."

This was one order Edward was happy to obey and, after an anxious query to ascertain if she had suffered any hurt—a query she did not answer, or even seem to hear—he lifted Melisande onto the horse he had brought as a gift for the Mistress. A bit belatedly, he asked her if she could ride.

"Yes," she said, but she did not look at him when she answered. She stared straight ahead. Her hands grasped the reins only after he thrust them into her chill fingers.

He mounted his own horse swiftly, looked back worriedly at her.

"It will be all right," he told her.

She sat on her horse, said nothing.

He rode over to her, clasped his hand over hers. She flinched at his touch, but she looked at him, was aware of him, and she did not withdraw her hand.

"You have to live," he said to her. "You are the only one who can save them."

She gazed at him long and he saw a flicker of life stir in the empty blue eyes.

Draconas came galloping up. "You two can play patty-cake later!" he said with an irate glance at their clasped hands.

Edward snatched his away hurriedly. Melisande took hold of the reins, sat up straight in the saddle, and urged the horse forward, falling in behind Draconas. Edward brought up the rear.

He had no idea where they were. He followed Draconas, who seemed to know exactly where he was going and Edward did not question. Draconas appeared intent upon saving Melisande's life, protecting her from harm, and Edward would have given his trust to the Devil himself, if that foul demon king had promised to save Melisande.

Edward divided his time watching for the warriors behind and keeping watch on Melisande ahead. She did not once look back, and he thought that a bad sign. She rode with a drooping head, abstracted, absorbed in her sorrow, letting the horse go where it would. Fortunately, the horse was accustomed to following its fellows and made no difficulty. Edward rode up closer, just to make sure.

He was worried about her, and he would have liked to have stopped somewhere, build a fire, warm her, dry her, find her meat and drink, for she had been as cold to his touch as a corpse. They dared not stop. They had to keep riding. Every so often, an arrow would rattle through the branches or thud into a tree trunk, reminding them that death traveled behind.

They spent the next few hours endeavoring to throw

off pursuit. They rode up hill and down. They doubled back on their trail, ducked into gullies, galloped unexpectedly out of cul-de-sacs. Sometimes Edward would think that they had lost the soldiers, but just when he started to breathe a little easier, he heard hoofbeats drumming behind.

The sun was midway between noon and evening, the hottest part of the day. The horses' flanks heaved, their bodies gleamed with sweat. Their eyes were wide and wild and saliva dripped from their mouths. Edward was not in much better shape than the beasts. Waking that morning, he'd been amazed to find out how much better he felt. But then, as everyone knew, a good sleep cured most ills. Heat, tension, and fatigue brought back the dull, pounding ache in his head. He was stiff and sore from the hard riding, and he could not imagine how difficult this must be for Melisande, who rode with her skirts hitched up over her knees.

She said no word of complaint, however. She said no word of any kind. She did what they told her, went where they told her in silence. Edward was just thinking that this nightmare journey must go on and on forever, and then cooling shadows washed over him, refreshed and revived him.

They left the barren mountain trail behind, entered a forest thick with oak and linden, poplar and pine and sighing willow trees.

A breeze stirred the leaves. The air temperature dropped. The smell of water came to both men and horses. Galloping up a slight rise, they topped it, and there before them was the river, swift-flowing, wide, dark, and deep.

"The Aston," said Edward, reining in his horse. He cast a grim glance at Draconas. "We're trapped. There's no ford here. We can't cross. The warriors will catch us now, for certain. You've brought us the wrong way!"

"On the contrary," Draconas returned, swinging himself out of the saddle. "This is what I've been searching for. Look there."

He pointed to a trail, a narrow strip of dirt worn into the grass and weeds and marked with countless hoofprints of deer and elk, crisscrossed by the paw prints of wolf and fox and mountain lion and, here and there, the deep gouges made by a bear's claws. Draconas pointed again, not to the trail this time, but on either side of it. Edward looked down. At first he saw nothing, then the tracks leapt out at him, so that he wondered if he'd gone stupid or blind or both to have missed them.

Two faint ruts ran on either side of the muddy track.

"Wagon wheels," said Edward.

"Wait here," Draconas said. He tromped along the wheel ruts, following their trail, and vanished into a thicket. He was gone some time.

Edward had no idea what Draconas was looking for or what this had to do with them. He glanced anxiously behind them. He hadn't heard the hoofbeats for some time, but he'd been fooled by that too often now to take much hope in it. He looked over at Melisande.

"Are you all right?" he asked.

"I'm thirsty," she said, not looking at him.

"We've come to the right place for that, seemingly," he replied, trying to win a smile.

There came a noise of rustling branches directly behind them. Edward turned swiftly, his hand on his sword, but it was only Draconas, emerging out of the thicket.

"I've found the wagon," he reported, looking pleased with himself.

"That's interesting," Edward remarked caustically. "I don't see—"

"And three boats," Draconas reported. He turned and pointed. "They're over there. Drawn up on the bank, covered by a tarp."

Edward gazed out at the swift-flowing river and he suddenly understood. He eased himself down out of the saddle, then went to help Melisande. She tried to dismount herself, but she was stiff from the long ride and she half-slid, half-tumbled into his arms.

Gasping in pain, she bit back a cry, nearly falling as she tried to stand. Her clothes were disheveled, her skirts up around her thighs. She shook her skirts down, but not before he had caught a glimpse of bare flesh, saw that the skin on her legs was rubbed raw from the constant jolting movement. He also saw that her legs were shapely, well-formed, with small, delicate ankles and feet.

"You should walk around, if you can," Edward said in some confusion. "Restore the circulation. I'll see to the horses."

Melisande nodded and limped slowly toward the thick trees, her lips pressed tightly over the pain.

"What about the warriors?" Edward asked Draconas, who was removing his saddle and bridle.

"I think we've lost them," said Draconas. "But only for the time being. That leader of theirs has the tenacity of a bull baiter. She'll track us down unless we throw her off the trail permanently. The boats are sound. Though taking to the river will mean leaving behind the horses."

"That is nothing," said Edward, his gaze following Melisande. "She cannot ride any farther. It's a wonder she made it this long." He paused, frowning. "Do you think we should let her go off alone?"

"I don't believe she'd appreciate our company," said Draconas dryly.

"Oh," said Edward in embarrassed understanding.

He turned his back on the amused Draconas and began to unsaddle his horse, talking to relieve his tension.

"Probably those warriors will find the horses."

"Better the horses than us," said Draconas. Walking down to the river, he cupped his hands, scooped up water to slake his thirst.

Edward flung the saddle onto the ground. "How did you know that you'd find boats here? And the wagon? And how did you even know where 'here' was? I've been lost ever since we left the cave."

"Just doing my job," Draconas replied. "What you're paying me for. As for the wagon"—he raised his head, gazed down the river—"they had to have some way to transport the babies."

"Babies?" Edward was confused. "What—Oh! Lord bless and keep me. I'd completely forgotten! The babies from the cave."

He could not believe that it was only last night that they'd come across the baby smugglers. It seemed a year of nights to Edward.

"Yes, I suppose that makes sense. But how did you know they would travel by river? How did you know you'd find boats?"

"A lucky guess," said Draconas offhandedly. Standing up, he cocked his head, listening.

"Hear anything?" Edward asked.

Draconas shook his head. "No, I think this time we've lost them. Their commander's good, whoever she is."

"And yet, she is a woman," said Edward. "I know that history speaks of female warriors in ancient times, but . . . it seems very strange to me. Against God's wishes."

"Men take life and women give it, is that it?" Draconas asked.

Before Edward could respond, Melisande came limping back out of the thicket, and he forgot everything in his concern for her. Leaving Draconas to finish with the horses, Edward went to speak to her.

"You will be glad to hear we are not going to ride anymore. Draconas has found a boat. We will take to the river. How are you feeling? Any better?"

She had regained some color in her pallid cheeks. She still limped, but her walk was stronger. She looked past Edward at the river, running high and fast due to last night's rainstorms. The surface of the dark green water was littered with flotsam the river had caught up in its passing: tree snags, bundles of sticks from an old beaver dam, a log covered with green lichen. The current carried it all swiftly downstream, into the shadows of the willow trees overhanging the riverbanks.

Edward saw the river in her eyes and he knew her

thoughts, knew them as well as if she'd spoken them aloud.

"So too are you caught up in the swift current," he said. "Swept downstream to an unknown fate. You are not alone, Melisande," he added earnestly. "Never think you are alone." He glanced out at the river that ran so very fast and broad and deep and the end of it nowhere in sight. "Wherever the water takes us, it will take us together. So I do swear, upon my honor."

Her blue eyes held the river in them for long moments, then their gaze shifted and Edward saw himself reflected in them. He touched her hand and this time, she did not flinch. Fingers brushed his and they were frightfully cold. He curled his fingers over hers and felt her skin start to warm.

A horn call pierced the air. High-pitched, thin and wailing as a wraith's dismal cry, the call spooked the horses and raised the hair on Edward's neck. Melisande's hand clutched his spasmodically, and the two stood immobilized until long after the horrid sound had ceased.

"What was that?" Edward gasped.

"Bellona," Melisande said in a low voice. "The call is meant for me. She is telling me that I cannot escape my fate."

"Nonsense—" Edward began.

She pulled away from him.

"You heard that horn call?" she asked Draconas.

"The dead heard that horn call, Melisande," he replied.

"I am a danger to you," she went on, not heeding him, talking rapidly. "To both you gentlemen. You should leave me here. Bellona will not come after you. She wants only me."

"Absolutely not!" Edward said angrily.

"I thank you for what you have tried to do for me, Your Majesty," Melisande said gently, "but it is of no use. I know Bellona. She will not rest until she has . . ." Her voice faltered, but she rallied and continued on calmly, "until she has found me. You risk your life for me, Sire, a perfect stranger, and that is not right. You should live to return to your kingdom, your people."

"I wish I could claim that His Majesty was completely disinterested," said Draconas coolly. "But he's not. He has a stake in your welfare. As I told you this morning, His Majesty came to Seth for—"

"That's enough, Draconas," Edward interrupted, the hot blood mounting to his face. He looked back on his "quest" as a silly, schoolboy adventure, a journey into a minstrel's tale, not meant to be taken seriously. He realized now how wrong he had been in everything he had done and he was bitterly ashamed of himself. He could not let her die because he had been a thoughtless fool.

"Believe me, Melisande, when I tell you that I never meant for matters to happen the way they did. I intended to come before your Mistress, dressed in my finest, with gifts precious and valuable, as befit a queen. I meant to bend my knee before her and ask her, humbly, to do me the favor—the very great favor—of traveling to my kingdom to rid it of the dragon who has brought upon us so much misery and destruction. Nothing has turned out as I planned and it is my fault. I knew I was doing wrong to sneak into the monastery like that. I was playing at being a hero."

Draconas stood at his elbow, plucking at his sleeve. "Your Majesty, that horn call was very near. We don't have time for this."

"Yes, we do," said Edward sharply. He drew in a deep breath, never taking his eyes from Melisande. "I have need of you. I'll not deny it. I am responsible for the lives of my people. I am pledged to God to give my life to save them, to place myself between them and danger. And I am helpless before this dragon. You have been raised to fight dragons with your magic. Come to my kingdom. Use your magic to save my people. I can never in my life repay you, but I will try, all the rest of my days."

"But what of *my* people?" Melisande asked. "I cannot abandon them, now that I know the truth."

"You will come back to Seth," Edward promised. "And I will come with you. We will come back with an army and you shall ride at its head."

Melisande was obviously much impressed with him, but still she hesitated. Perhaps she still did not trust him. The horn blast sounded again, much nearer. She cast a despairing glance in the direction of the sound.

"And if I do not choose to go with you?"

"Then I will stay with you until the warriors find us. I will stay here and tell them the truth about the dragon—"

Melisande shook her head. "They won't believe you."

"Then I will tell them to take my life," Edward said proudly, "for I am the one at fault. And I will beg them to spare yours, for you are innocent."

She gazed intently at him, trying to see into his heart and beyond, to his soul.

He faced her confidently, steadfast in the knowledge that, if she chose, he would do what he promised.

"I believe you would do that," she said at last in a kind of wonder. "Why? I am a stranger."

"Because I brought you to this," Edward answered simply. "The responsibility is my own and I accept it."

A faint blush mantled her cheeks. Her breast rose with a quick, indrawn breath. Her clasped hands trembled. Edward saw admiration in her eyes and something warmer, softer, and his blood tingled through his body, prickled in his fingertips and rushed from his brain to swell his heart, so that he was giddy and light-headed.

"Will you come with me, Melisande?" he asked. "Or will we stay to face death together?"

Melisande turned her head, gazed upstream, to where the eerie echoes of the horn call seemed to linger in the air. She bowed her head, gave herself to swift-flowing fate.

"I will come with you."

*   *   *

"You're very persuasive," Draconas remarked, as he and the king hastened down the bank toward the boats. "No wonder your people love you."

"I meant what I said," Edward returned coldly. "And keep your voice down."

He glanced at Melisande, walking slowly behind, her arms folded across her breast, her head bowed in thought.

"How close do you think those soldiers are?" Edward asked, abruptly changing the subject. He was still angry at Draconas, but this was no time to start a fight.

Draconas flicked him a sidelong glance and came as near to smiling as he ever did. "Close enough so that we should not dawdle. Help me haul out the boats."

"We don't need both of them," Edward protested, eyeing the boats. "They'll seat eight people, at least. One will do for us and our supplies with room to spare."

"True," said Draconas, "but I don't want to provide that commander with the means of coming after us."

He and Edward dragged off the tarp that covered the boats, carried them one by one out from under their makeshift shelter of tree limbs.

"There were at least six boats here," said Draconas, indicating indentions in the wet ground. "The baby-smugglers took three of them, left three behind."

They hauled one boat to the water, loaded it with their supplies—food, blankets, water skins. Edward helped Melisande into the boat. She eyed it warily, entered it with trepidation. She had never before been on the water. Using his staff, Draconas staved in the bottom of the other two.

The boat came equipped with a pair of oars set in oar-locks. Draconas volunteered to handle the oars. Melisande sat in the prow, wrapped in a horse blanket for warmth. She stared nervously at the water rolling past the gunwale. Blanching at the rocking motion of the boat in the current, she clutched the benchlike seat with both hands.

Climbing over Draconas to reach the stern, Edward

bent down to say in passing, "Which way do you think those baby-snatchers went?"

"Downstream," said Draconas.

"The same route we're taking."

Draconas nodded absently, absorbed in testing the movement of the oars in the oarlocks.

"Is that wise? Suppose we run into them?"

"We won't," said Draconas.

"How do you know?"

Draconas shrugged. He tested the oars, first one, then the other.

Edward bent close, his breath hot on Draconas's cheek. "I wish just once you'd tell me what you know and how you know it!"

Draconas looked up at him. "No, you don't, Your Majesty. And now, we'd best be getting under way."

Edward opened his mouth, snapped it shut again. He made his way to the stern, cast off the lines. The river carried the boat rapidly away from shore. A few strong pulls by Draconas on the oars steered them away from the bank and dangerous tree roots and snags.

Edward was wondering what Draconas had meant by that enigmatic statement and trying to decide if he should have it out with the man, when he heard hoofbeats on the shore. He turned around, stared back into the trees, expecting at every moment to hear the deadly hum of arrows. He saw, receding in the distance, the horses grazing calmly on the grass near the riverbank. No sight of the female warriors.

Women warriors. He'd never seen women like that, women with hard-muscled bodies and scars roping their arms and legs. Women racing toward an enemy with the fire of death in their eyes. Feminine hands wielding spears and bow and arrows instead of tapestry needles. Half-naked, all of them. He pictured them riding toward him, bodies gleaming in the sunlight. Half-naked and not ashamed, their thoughts focused on their duty. He saw again the curve of a breast as one drew back the bowstring, saw the play of muscle in the arm, and the tightening of the taut, bare abdomen.

They were beautiful in a disturbing, unsettling way. He didn't like thinking about them, yet he couldn't help himself.

Melisande. His thoughts did not return to her, for they had never truly left her. The images of the warrior women were so much flotsam, floating on the surface. Melisande was the murmur of the river, ever with him.

"Go ahead and sleep," Edward told her. "You're safe, for the moment."

Melisande was too exhausted to argue. Wrapping herself in the blanket, she curled up on the bench, and, despite her awkward and uncomfortable position, the rocking of the boat lulled her into slumber.

The boat drifted in and out of the shadows of the trees.

The sun's rays touched her hair, caused it to shimmer with a golden radiance. Her face, in the shadows, was pale and sad. Her sorrow and her beauty touched something deep within him.

Edward watched her, and he felt empowered, the guardian of her sleep. Her champion.

"I am responsible for her," he reminded himself. "She trusts me. She has given herself into my care. I must cherish her."

Cherish.

The word brought to him, unbidden and most unwelcome, the memory of his wedding vows. Those brought to him the memory of his wife.

Ermintrude's face with its cheerful smile and flashing dimples opened up the door of his conscience and peeped in at him.

He slammed the door shut with haste and stood with his back against it, guilty and ashamed.

20

FROM THE TIME THEY WERE CHILDREN, BELLONA
had loved Melisande. She had been a beautiful child—
golden-haired, fair-skinned, her blue eyes possessing a
wisdom not usually seen in children, as if she had been
born knowing humanity's secrets. It was not her beauty
that had attracted Bellona, though the older girl had loved
to watch the little child with hair like sunshine play about
the courtyard. The same qualities in Melisande that had
brought her to the notice of the Mistress, brought her to
the notice of Bellona. At six years old, Melisande had led
the games of the other girls. Her quick intelligence had
impressed her teachers. She was strongly gifted with the
blood bane magic—a skill that Bellona lacked and one
that she secretly mourned.

Slated to be a warrior, Bellona had been marked by her
superiors as one who would advance in rank and power.
Dark-eyed, dark-haired, her spirit reposed in darkness.
She said little, opened her heart to no one, watched, ob-
served, taking part only in those activities that tested her
body, enhanced her physical strength.

As the two girls grew older, Melisande, sensitive to the

slightest touch, felt those dark eyes often upon her and she found in the quiet, strong Bellona a place of rest, a place of ease.

The dragon encouraged love between the women warriors and her priestesses. Thus she kept them both bound to the monastery, bound to each other, bound to her. Neither knew this, of course, and it would not have made much difference if they had.

Bellona remembered the first time she had made her love known to Melisande. The memory came to her as a torment, as she was riding her horse along the cliff's edge, seeking out Melisande, with orders to slay her. Bellona used the memory to spur herself on, jabbed it repeatedly into her flesh until the blood ran. The pain was searing, but it was easier to bear than the pain of loss that left her empty and aching.

Melisande was sixteen, Bellona eighteen. Bellona was off-duty that night, a Coupling Night. She and Melisande sat in the darkness beneath the trees, eavesdropping on the warriors' talk, exchanging jokes about the "cows" and the "bulls."

Had Bellona been with her warriors, she would have been the first to laugh. Sitting with Melisande, Bellona wondered uneasily how much she understood. She suddenly found the jokes crude and embarrassing, and she wished the warriors would shut up. A young virgin priestess should not hear such things.

Bellona was just about to suggest that they find someplace quieter, when Melisande gave a little gasp of pain.

"A bee stung me," she said in shocked and aggrieved tones. "Look at that." She held her arm to the light of the fires burning on the walls.

Bellona could see the reddening bump on the smooth, white skin. "I think the stinger's still inside."

"It might become infected," said Melisande calmly. "You must suck it out. I would, but I can't reach it."

Something in her voice made Bellona look up with a quickening of her heartbeat.

"You should go to the healer, Priestess—" Bellona said, feeling her blood pulse in her veins.

"There's no time," said Melisande. "The infection might be spreading. Quick, Bellona. Save me."

She held out her arm, so white and soft and fragrant with night's perfume.

Bellona put her lips on the warm flesh, felt Melisande trembling. Bellona drew back.

"I'm sorry!" she gasped, drawing away.

"You should be," said Melisande, drawing her back, drawing her close, pulling her down beside her, crushing the sweet and fragrant grass. "For making me wait so long. I have always, always loved you . . ."

"Commander! I see them!" one of the women cried, jolting Bellona out of her honey-stung memories.

Upbraiding herself for her inattentiveness, Bellona looked again upon the searing reality of day.

She saw Melisande running down a hillside, waving her arms.

"Bellona!" she cried and the note of love in her voice tore Bellona's heart and drained it of blood, drained it of life.

It's all a mistake! The Mistress misunderstood. Melisande will explain.

The words were on Bellona's lips for the warriors to hold their fire, when she heard another voice, a man's voice. Looking up to the top of the cliff, she saw him, the lover.

Bellona gave the command to fire, but she was glad, in her blood-drained heart, that her highly skilled archers were unusually inept this day.

The warriors rode after the fugitives, Bellona urging them on. None of them had never been on the southern slope of the mountain before now. Few had ever left the valley.

The warriors were expert trackers, however, and the three they were chasing could not help but leave the marks of their passing. They never managed to catch up to them, however.

Bellona was acid-tongued and merciless in pushing her troops, who held their own tongues and kept silent, for all of them knew the reason why.

They followed the tracks of the three horses to the river and, at first, Bellona's heart leapt, for she was certain that here she must catch them, for there was no longer anywhere they could run. They found the three horses and their saddles and bridles, but no sign of the fugitives. Footprints—belonging to two pairs of boots and one pair of sandals—led into the water and did not come back. On the shore were two boats, both with their hulls staved in.

Bellona stared downstream, tried to estimate how far ahead they were, how much distance they might have covered. Her lack of knowledge of the geography of this part of the country hampered her thinking. She turned over plans in her mind, then she issued orders.

"I need the swiftest rider to go to the monastery. Bring back a map of this area, one that has the major cities marked on it." For that's where he will take her, she added silently. "A city, where they can lose themselves in the multitudes."

"The rest of you," she continued aloud, "start making repairs to that boat. I saw a wagon in the trees. Use some of the planking from it to patch those holes."

The women exchanged glances, then all of them looked to Nzangia.

"Commander," she began hesitantly.

"I gave an order," Bellona said sharply. "Why are you standing about?"

"Commander, the horses are spent. They will have to rest. As for repairing the boat, I, for one, know nothing about boats or how they are put together."

"It would take a Boatwright to fix it, Commander," said another.

"Then bring me a Boatwright," shouted Bellona. Her hands clenched to fists. "Bring me somebody who can do something beyond standing there gawking at me like a bunch of sorry peasants!"

The women were silent, uncomfortable.

"You, Drusilla," said Nzangia at last, "you are the best rider. Do as the commander orders."

Drusilla cast Nzangia a questioning glance.

Nzangia gave a small shrug, rolled her eyes in the direction of Bellona.

Drusilla nodded. Jumping on her horse, she galloped off, heading back toward the mountain.

Bellona turned her back on them. She stared at the boat, squatted down beside it, pretended to examine it. She had no more idea how to fix it than did her warriors, but looking at it meant she didn't have to look at them. She was acutely aware of their eyes on her.

"We're going to be here awhile, so we might as well make camp," said Nzangia abruptly. "Unsaddle the horses, rub them down, and let them graze."

She continued to issue orders, posting guards, sending out hunters. The women dispersed, glad to have something to do. The tension eased. Nzangia hung about, eyeing Bellona, evidently wanting to talk.

Bellona avoided her.

If the boat can't be repaired, she thought, we'll have to proceed downstream on foot.

That brought to mind the wagon. Strange, to find a wagon here, so far from anywhere.

She rose from the boat, walked over to look at the wagon, glad for another excuse for evading Nzangia. Bellona was mildly surprised to see that the wagon had been recently used. The wooden wheels were caked with mud and wet grass, still damp from last night's rain.

She had it settled in her mind that the wagon had been abandoned by some farmer, but she found on examination that the wagon had been built to carry people, not turnips. Two bench seats ran the length of the wagon bed on either side. A wicker frame had been added to protect the passengers, keep them from tumbling out. Looking into the wagon bed, she found caked mud from wet boots smeared over the floorboards.

She stared at the wagon, frowning. Something was not right with this vehicle . . . and then she had it.

There was no seat for the driver.

No driver because there was no horse.

The wagon was pulled by people.

She looked back at the river. Easy enough to transport people by boat. Transporting dray horses would be far more difficult. What were these people doing here so near Seth? What cargo were they hauling?

It would be different if there were any cities or towns or villages about but there were none. She'd had a clear view of the surrounding countryside as they rode down the mountain and there was no sign of civilization for miles and miles, from here to the horizon.

This must have something to do with Melisande, for the lover had brought her here. His boat had carried her away. What had the wagon to do with it?

Bellona climbed inside the wagon bed, poked about. She peered under the bench. A scrap of soiled, damp cloth lay crumpled on the floorboards. Bellona picked it up, shook it out. She stared at the narrow cotton band, thinking it looked familiar, but she could not immediately place it.

The stench hit her. She wrinkled her nose, then sniffed again, and she knew what this was—a baby's swaddling band.

Bellona was completely baffled. She could make nothing of this mystery. She started to toss away the scrap of cloth then, on impulse, she thrust it into her belt. She would ask the Mistress.

Asking the Mistress meant asking Lucretta. Bellona looked forward to a lifetime of asking Lucretta, of being ordered about by Lucretta, of the monastery being run by that embittered, dour female. A lifetime of praying to Lucretta.

Bellona could feel Nzangia's eyes boring holes through her armor, and she half-turned, glanced over her shoulder at her second.

"I'm going to scout upstream," Bellona said. "You wait here."

She turned her back, walked rapidly away. She walked until she was out of sight of her troops, out of earshot.

"A lifetime of going to an empty bed at night," Bellona whispered. "A lifetime of waking to empty hours by day."

Alone, she gave way to the pain. She curled in on herself, hands clutching at an unseen wound, her nails tearing her flesh. A shudder wrenched her body and she sank to her knees, rocking back and forth in agony.

She grew calmer at last. The frenzy of grief subsided and it was then that she saw another boat. Swallowing her tears, she sat back on her heels. The boat was a small one, hidden deep in the bracken some distance apart from the two that the lover had wrecked.

She very nearly thanked the Mistress for this miracle, then, remembering that she would be thanking Lucretta, Bellona kept her mouth shut.

The warriors returned from their hunt with a deer. As night fell, the smell of roasting meat filled the air. On another occasion, the women would have enjoyed themselves, for this was a rare adventure. The nature of their mission and the dark demeanor of their commander cast a pall over them.

Bellona returned to camp, determined to act as if all were normal. She joined her troops in the meal and made an attempt to eat, but her stomach roiled at the first taste of the meat, and she handed her share to Nzangia. Bellona tried to discuss the day's events, as she would have under other circumstances, but no one knew what to say.

She engaged in a desperate conversation with Nzangia about how the women needed more training in fighting on horseback. Eventually the subject was exhausted and Bellona did not start another. She lapsed into silence. Sitting on the ground, her knees hunched, she stared into the flames.

The rest of the evening passed in silence. The women lounged around the fire, chewing on the deer meat, which was burnt black on the outside and raw on the inside, and tried to avoid looking at Bellona's pain-ravaged face.

"Commander!" One of the scouts came into camp on the run. "Riders coming. This way."

Bellona leaped to her feet, glad to have something to do. The warriors grabbed their weapons and flaming brands, arraying themselves in battle formation.

Drusilla rode into camp. Her face was taut, her expression strained. She said nothing, but her look said everything. Sliding off her horse, she stood at attention and called out, "One comes, Commander. The Mistress of Dragons."

Lucretta rode into camp.

The warriors sank to their knees. Bellona bent her knee, then went to meet the Mistress, who gestured for the others to rise. Holding the flaming brands high, the warriors gathered around the Mistress, forming a circle of smoky fire.

Lucretta did not like riding. She did not like horses, and the horse knew it, for the animal was restless and skittery. Bellona glanced for some clue to Drusilla.

"I never reached the monastery. She was on her way down here," she reported in a low voice. "I don't know how she knew where to find us . . ."

"Mistress!" Bellona said, troubled. "Why have you come? There was no need—"

"What is this nonsense about a boat?" the Mistress demanded.

"We followed the three fugitives here, Mistress," said Bellona. "They took to the water." She made a vague gesture. "There is a wagon over there and some boats.

I'm not sure why or what the boats were used for, but they—"

"I am not interested in boats or wagons. Your warriors fired arrows at Melisande and missed," said Lucretta. "Many times."

"That is true, Mistress," Bellona replied. "We had bad luck this day."

"Bad luck, is it? I wonder if you were really trying to hit your target?" Her gaze swept over the assembled troops. "It seems strange to me that such talented marksmen—as I have seen them exhibit their skill on the archery range—should bungle this simple task so badly."

"I can assure the Mistress that every warrior did her duty," Bellona returned with rising anger. "To intimate otherwise is to question our honor—"

"It is not *their* honor I question," said Lucretta, leaning over the pommel. "After all, they were just obeying orders. It is *your* honor I question, Bellona. You loved the little whore and you could not bear to see her die—"

Her fists clenched, Bellona sprang at Lucretta.

"Bellona!" Nzangia cried in low, urgent tones. Her strong fingers dug into Bellona's muscular arms, dragged her back, "This is insane. Think what you're doing! She is the Mistress!"

"She cannot speak to me like that!" Bellona raved, fighting to free herself.

Two more warriors joined Nzangia and between them they managed to wrestle Bellona to the ground. Only when she was flat on her belly, her face in the mud and Nzangia's knee in her back, did Bellona cease to struggle. Her straining muscles relaxed. Her body went limp. She closed her eyes.

The change was so sudden and unexpected that Nzangia fearfully put her hand to Bellona's neck to feel her pulse.

"I'm still alive," muttered Bellona, spitting mud. "Sadly."

"Don't say that, Commander," whispered Nzangia

fiercely, helping her to her feet. "Never say that."

Lucretta straightened herself in the saddle, gazed down at them imperiously. "You are hereby relieved of your command, Bellona. Nzangia, I name you commander. Place this woman under arrest. Tie her up. She will be taken back for trial."

"Mistress—" Nzangia started to protest.

"Obey me!" Lucretta said coldly. "Or I will find someone who will."

"I'm sorry, Commander," Nzangia said softly, binding Bellona's wrists and arms with bowstrings.

"It's not your fault," Bellona said quietly.

"This is just temporary. The Mistress will have second thoughts. I'll talk to her . . ."

"Don't bother," said Bellona. "She hates me, as she hated Melisande. It's better this way. Truly it is."

Lucretta was trying to dismount and not making a very good job of it. In swinging her long, bony leg over the saddle pommel, she got tangled in her robes. The horse rolled its eyes and swiveled its head around, seemed likely to nip, at which point several of the women ran to assist. Bellona wiggled her hands to test the tightness of her bindings.

Lucretta wisely allowed the women to help her out of the saddle. Once on the ground, she staggered a little, then managed to stand upright.

"Order your warriors to their beds, Commander. We will be up and riding before the dawn. I want to be back at the monastery by first light."

"The monastery?" Nzangia stared. "Begging your pardon, Mistress, but aren't we going to keep after the fugitives?"

"We return to Seth tomorrow," Lucretta reiterated, her voice grating. "As for the whore, her guilty conscience will be her punishment, since she has escaped ours."

Bellona could not believe what she was hearing and neither could Nzangia, who ventured one more protest. "Mistress, at least allow me to take a patrol downriver—"

Lucretta's eyes flared. "Listen to me, all of you. Our
late Mistress was a good woman. None better. But she
was old and frail and, due to her frailty, she let certain
things slip. When I give a command, I expect obedience,
not arguments. Is that understood? Commander?"

The warriors were silent, grave. One and all, they had
loved the late Mistress, loved and respected her. Yet, perhaps this new Mistress was right. Perhaps discipline had
lapsed. Certainly, it must have, if their High Priestess
could have smuggled her lover into the Sanctuary, as was
being rumored. Perhaps it was time for a change. None
of them liked Lucretta, but they were starting to regard
her with respect.

"Yes, Mistress. Forgive me, Mistress," said Nzangia.

"Good," said Lucretta, her complacency returned. "As
for the morrow, we are needed in Seth. His Majesty will
be making the public announcement of the Mistress's
death and that means that, by custom, the funeral must be
held within the week. Thousands will be coming to the
monastery to pay their respects. Your warriors will be
needed to control the crowds, for the work of our priestesses must be disrupted as little as possible. We dare not
relax our vigilance against the dragons, who might seize
upon what they perceive to be a time of weakness to attack us."

Nzangia bowed her obedience.

"That is settled then." Lucretta glanced around. "One
of you—prepare me a bed."

The warriors looked at each other in some dismay.
They were accustomed, when on patrol, to wrapping
themselves in horse blankets and sleeping on the wet and
muddy riverbank. This would never do for the Mistress
of Dragons, however.

"Suggest that she sleep in the wagon," said Bellona in
a harsh whisper.

"Mistress," said Nzangia, relieved, "we found a wagon
hidden in the trees. We can make you a bed—"

"What did you say?" Lucretta demanded sharply.

"A wagon, Mistress," said Nzangia. Thinking to help her commander, she added, "It was Bellona's idea. She suggested that since the ground is wet, you could sleep in the wagon. You would find it more—"

"I will hear no more of Bellona's 'suggestions,'" cried Lucretta shrilly. "Gag her mouth and bind her to that tree. I will sleep on the ground with the rest of you."

Turning her back, the Mistress stalked off toward the fire, where she stood stiffly upright, warming her hands at the glimmering coals.

The warriors made their preparations for sleep. They banked the fire and cobbled together a makeshift bed for the Mistress, carefully choosing the driest ground, going over it assiduously to remove any stones or sticks, then laying down blankets for her repose.

The warriors kept food ready for those returning from guard duty. They ate quickly and silently, glancing askance at the Mistress, who lay in state upon the blankets, her body stretched out flat on her back, her hands folded over her stomach. Awed, none of the warriors dared to make their beds near her.

Nzangia crouched beside Bellona, a strip of cloth in her hands.

"Strange about the wagon, don't you think?" Bellona asked in a soft voice, her gaze fixed on the Mistress. "She would have been far more comfortable in it."

"It all seems strange, as if I were in a dream," said Nzangia. "Though I do think the Mistress is right. We have been letting some things slide."

She lifted the gag to tie it around Bellona's mouth.

Bellona raised her bound hands, halted her. "Bring me a blanket."

"Yes, of course—"

"—with a knife wrapped inside."

Nzangia flinched, almost dropped the gag.

"You're not thinking straight, Commander—"

"Nzangia, I'm not going to slit my wrists," Bellona interrupted impatiently. "I'm going after Melisande. I'm going to bring her back to stand trial, to answer for her crimes."

Nzangia stared, then glanced askance at the Mistress. "I don't know, Bellona—"

"Lucretta impugned my honor, Nzangia. And yours. And theirs." Bellona gestured to the warriors, who had gone to their beds in silence, without any of the usual gibes and light-hearted banter. "I will carry that shame to my grave."

Nzangia hesitated.

"You will not get into trouble," Bellona persisted. "I will make it look as if I drowned myself in the river. I have to do this, Nzangia. I have to! You love Drusilla," she added, her voice faltering. "You understand."

Nzangia tied the gag around Bellona's mouth with sharp efficiency, then stood up. She gazed down at her former commander, then, turning on her heel, she walked away. Bellona kept her in sight for as long as possible, lost sight of her when she entered the forest. Nzangia would be making the rounds, checking on the guards, making certain they were at their posts, none of them fallen asleep.

Bellona could do nothing more. She leaned back wearily against the tree. She had no idea whether Nzangia would do as she wanted or not. Hopefully what she had said had made an impression, but Bellona did not know. Nzangia had been startled at first by her sudden rise to power, but she had always been ambitious and she was quickly adapting, fitting into her new role with ease. She and Lucretta would get along well. Nzangia would see to that.

"If nothing else, Nzangia will be glad to be rid of me," Bellona said to herself. "And so might Lucretta. She was so odd about the wagon. Not the least curious about it. She should be. It's close to the borders of the kingdom. Too close. Not that it matters. Nothing matters, except Melisande. I will bring her back to face her crimes. I will prove to Nzangia, prove to Lucretta that I am bound by honor and my oath, that I did not let Melisande deliberately escape me.

"I will prove it to them all," she vowed, but she knew in her heart that she was proving it to only one—herself.

The night was clear and cool. The river caught the light of the stars, carried the silvery gleam upon its smooth surface.

Bellona wiggled her wrists again. Her warriors had done their job well, as she would have expected them to do. The bowstrings were tied tight, bit into her flesh. She shifted position. After all, Nzangia had forgotten to bind her to the tree. Bellona leaned back against the trunk, closed her eyes against the silver-gilded dark ripples gliding downstream. Melisande was there, gliding on top of them, silver-gilded, and Bellona was beneath, in the cold darkness, swept under, swept away . . .

"Bellona!" Nzangia whispered in her ear. A hand shook her shoulder.

Bellona woke with a start, never having meant to fall asleep.

Nzangia held a folded blanket in her hands. Carefully, she unwrapped it, spread it around Bellona's shoulders, draped it over her bound hands and feet.

A hunting knife fell into Bellona's lap. She grasped the hilt gratefully.

"Thank you," she said gruffly.

"Good luck," Nzangia said and walked back into the darkness.

Bellona held the knife fast, finding comfort in the feel of the cold, sharp iron. She settled down to wait until the dead of night, when all were drowned deep in slumber.

"Commander!" Drusilla cried, coming to shake Nzangia awake. "Come quickly."

"What is it?" Nzangia demanded, rising up on the instant.

Drusilla led her to river's edge, pointed at Bellona's

armor, which lay stacked neatly on the bank. She showed her the footprints that led into the water.

"She has drowned herself," said Drusilla.

The women stood gathered together on the bank. Their faces expressed both their sorrow and their approval. One of the women hastily gathered up the severed bowstrings, flung them into the water.

"I will tell the Mistress," said Nzangia.

Lucretta heard the news without emotion, without reaction of any sort. She threw off her blanket. Stiff and sore from yesterday's ride and from sleeping all night on the hard ground, she grimaced as she tried to stand, held out her hand for Nzangia to aid her.

"I will see this for myself," said Lucretta.

"Mistress," said Nzangia, her gaze fixed on the shifting shadows beneath the trees, "you wanted to make an early start. We have much to do back at the monastery and there is nothing more we can do here. What's done is done, and for the best, I think."

Lucretta cast Nzangia a shrewd glance.

Nzangia met her glance and held it.

An understanding passed between them.

"A good suggestion, Commander," said Lucretta with unaccustomed mildness. "We will start at once."

"As you command, Mistress," said Nzangia humbly.

21

THE FUGITIVES WERE ALSO UP WITH THE DAWN. A
soft fog covered the river, but the mists soon burned off
with the rising of the sun. The water sparkled, the poplar
leaves shimmered. Melisande returned from her morning
ablutions smelling of mint, which she had crushed beneath
her feet.

Their sleep had done them good. Everyone seemed in
better spirits and Melisande was able to eat some of the
last of the dried venison, which Edward had saved for
her.

Her spirits dimmed a little, as she climbed into the boat.
Looking downstream, she had a clear view of the mountain peak on which the monastery was built. Her eyes
grew shadowed, her face drawn and troubled.

The river's swift, sun-dappled water bore them rapidly
downstream. The three were silent at the beginning of the
journey. Two of them were thinking thoughts of the other,
wondering secretly if the other was thinking thoughts of
them. Draconas's thoughts, on the other hand, left the
boat, ranged far down the river.

He found boats much preferable to horses. The current

carried them along at a rapid pace. He did not have much work at the oars, beyond correcting their direction now and again, and he followed in his mind the journey of those babies that had been spirited away from the kingdom of Seth. He guessed that those same mad monks, driven insane by mistreatment and the dragon magic that burned in their blood like plague's fever, had begun life in the very same way. Male babies, smuggled out of Seth, given to Maristara's dragon partner. And this had been going on for hundreds of years.

Edward's hazel eyes were fixed on Melisande, wrapped in the blanket, staring into the water that slid away beneath her. His thoughts were mostly of her, but sometimes Ermintrude intruded and then he would shift his eyes away from Melisande, stubbornly fix them on the tree-lined bank.

Melisande had nothing to do but think. Her life had altered so suddenly, so abruptly, that she stared at herself in confused dismay, as she had once stared at a mosaic in the making, trying to see in the random pieces of sharp-edged tiles a picture, a pattern. Just as she felt she might be starting to understand, she shoved the tiles away from her, left them in a jumble, and turned her thoughts to Edward.

She had mistaken him. He was not like other men she had known. She looked at him, whenever he was not looking at her, letting her eyes linger on his countenance, finding some solace in her pain by tracing the lines of his face or watching his hands.

Then came the tense moment when he looked suddenly at her and she could not look away. Their eyes met. She shifted her gaze swiftly to the willow trees. Edward decided that it was time for conversation.

"Draconas—you said when we made camp last night that the warriors wouldn't come after us."

"And I was right, wasn't I?" Draconas leaned on the oars.

"Yes, but how did you know?"

"We're traveling the same route as the boats carrying the smugglers," Draconas replied. "If the warriors came after us, there is the possibility they might stumble across the babies. They would recognize the children and start asking questions. The dragon can't risk that."

"What babies?" Melisande asked. "What are you talking about?"

Edward was silent, soundly kicking himself. He hadn't meant to bring this up. He hadn't wanted to add to her worries. He glared pointedly at Draconas, urging him to make some innocuous response, turn the subject. Draconas, of course, ignored him.

"The male babies born to the women in the monastery," Draconas answered. "The ones the Mistress sends away every month. What happens to them?"

"They are given to good people in the kingdom, people who cannot have children or—"

Melisande fell silent. She stared at him, amazed, and suddenly afraid.

"How did you know?" she demanded. "How did you know about the babies?"

"When we entered the cave, we came upon some old women dressed all in black, carrying babies out of the cave. We overheard the dragon discussing them. The dragon is selling those babies into slavery."

"I don't believe it," said Melisande, clutching the gunwale with her hands so tightly that the knuckles were chalk white. "The babies are given to good homes."

"Did you ever meet any of these children later in their lives?" Draconas asked. "Did any ever come back to visit their true mothers?"

"They are not permitted to do so."

Draconas smiled, twitched an eyebrow. "And that didn't seem strange to you? Didn't you ever wonder about them?"

Melisande had often wondered. She had wondered about the babies. She had wondered more about her father. She had never told anyone that, not even Bellona.

Every month, at Coupling Night, she would look over the long rows of men and wonder if he was among them. What was he like? Was he a noble lord? Humble peasant? A musician? Did his hands gently brush harp strings or grasp the blacksmith's hammer?

"The children are a gift," said Melisande, speaking the words the Mistress had spoken. "A sacred gift, a divine gift. Those who receive these children are specially singled out for this blessing. They agree, when they accept it, never to reveal to the child or to any other that the boy is not their own. To do so would anger the Mistress . . ." Her voice trailed off. She remembered angering the Mistress.

"But you still wonder, don't you?" Draconas said. "Secrets are hard to keep. People whisper. People gossip. Everyone claims to know some family who has received a 'monastery child.' But it is always the friend of a friend. Isn't that how it goes?"

To believe him was to believe something monstrous. The babies—neat, small bundles of cloth, tiny fists, rosebud mouths, wondering eyes. Taken away by stealth, by night. No one knew how or where they went, only the Mistress. No one knew a "montastery child." Only the Mistress.

"I am a fool," said Melisande softly.

"You were duped," Edward told her. "You are not to blame. You couldn't have known."

"Couldn't I?" Melisande stared out over the water, at the willows trailing their weeping boughs into the river, at the water bearing them forward, sliding away behind. "I could not sleep last night for thinking of the dragon's victim, trapped in the sarcophagus, trapped in the darkness, in endless pain, alone and forgotten, with no hope left to her except one—the hope of death. And we were there with her in the same room, so close to her that we could have touched her. Proud, complacent, we worked our magic. Perhaps she heard our voices. Perhaps she cried out. Perhaps I heard her!"

Her hands let loose the gunwale, twisted together. "Once, I thought I did hear a voice, a cry. I told myself I was hearing things, but maybe it was her, desperate for help, and I turned away. I did not want to disturb the beautiful tranquility of my life. And the babies," she continued on relentlessly. "I should have known. Now that I look back, it is so obvious. I never met a monastery child! Why didn't I ever question what happened to them?"

Lifting her head, she looked at Edward. "Why did you choose our kingdom? Did you know a dragon was secretly running it?"

"Did we, Draconas?" asked Edward.

The question came so suddenly that Draconas very nearly answered with the truth and he had to shift the words about on his tongue, like divesting himself of a cherry pit.

"I chose your kingdom because your people were known to fight off dragons," he said, carefully picking his words. "For hundreds of years, your kingdom was safe from them."

"We thought they were coming to harm us," said Melisande, her voice soft. "But now I wonder if they were attacking us, as the Mistress claimed, or if they were trying to save us."

"I don't suppose we'll ever know," Draconas remarked.

"I don't suppose we will." Melisande sighed deeply. "Tell me something about this dragon that is attacking your kingdom, Your Majesty."

Edward told his tale. Melisande listened with quiet gravity.

Draconas, seated between the two, rowed the boat down the river.

Their journey continued through the morning and into afternoon, idyllic, undisturbed. Having exhausted the subject of the dragon, Edward and Melisande found nothing else to talk about. They tried discussing fish, having seen one jump, but that didn't last long, nor did an attempt at ornithology. What each truly wanted to say could not very well be said at opposite ends of a boat with Draconas in the middle.

The river's current slowed, but they barely noticed. Draconas's strong arms propelled the boat through the water. He refused to let Edward spell him at the oars, saying that he enjoyed the exercise.

The Aston river was known to have a great many tributaries, contributing to the main body, from small creeks that sprang up from beneath the ground or drizzled down out of the cliffs to larger streams that entered the river only after they had explored other, distant lands. The Aston was a branching river, too, extending many arms into the surrounding countryside, unable to keep its hands to itself.

That afternoon, they came upon a tall edifice of red rock, jutting up out of the earth, that split the river into two of these branches. One, the smaller of the two, veered off westward. The other, the main body of the river, continued to flow south. Draconas slowed the boat's progress, as he considered which fork to take. Logic dictated that they proceed southward, for Ramsgate-upon-the-Aston lay in that direction. The wind, blowing from the east, and the river's current took them closer to the western fork. He was going to have to do some work to head them the right way and he was bending to the oars when he sensed the magic.

Dragon magic, faint as a trace of perfume lingering on the air long after the wearer has departed, yet unmistakable. And it came from the west.

Looking down that western branch, Draconas saw blue water slicing through sheer red rock walls, their vast height blotting out the sunlight.

In his mind's eye, Draconas could see that boatload of black-garbed women, holding mewling babies, guarded by soldiers and the enormous Grald, sailing down between those red rock walls. He hadn't noticed that any of the humans were particularly strong in dragon magic. But then, the dragon's own magic had been so over-whelmingly powerful that it might have masked the weaker magic of the others.

Sensing the magic like this was odd. Damn odd.

He lifted his oars from the water, let the current carry them. "I'm taking the western fork," he told Edward.

"But my kingdom lies to the south," Edward protested.

"We can always come back," Draconas told him.

Edward looked at him sharply. "What is it? What's going on? Why do you want to go that direction?"

"I thought I caught a glimpse of another boat," Draconas replied. "Down there."

"You think it's the boat carrying the children."

"I think it's likely."

"But they would be much farther ahead of us. They had a head start—"

"Not that much," Draconas argued. "They could not sail the river by night. They launched in the morning, only a few hours before we came. And, remember, they are ferrying women and small babies. They might have had to stop for any number of reasons."

"If there's any chance he's right," Melisande struck in, "we should go after them. I want to know the truth."

Edward had no more arguments, after that. Draconas propelled the boat in amongst the shadows of the high rock walls.

The temperature dropped precipitously. Melisande clasped her hands around her arms and Edward's expression darkened. The current grew swifter as the river narrowed to fit within the walls. The sense of dragon magic strengthened and it was not long before Draconas found the source—a gaping hole in the canyon wall, forming either a cavern or a tunnel that lay half-submerged beneath the waterline.

He stared hard into the sunken cave as they sailed past, trying to see what was causing the magic. The darkness was absolute. He could see nothing, yet he was convinced that the smugglers had come this way and that they had entered the cave.

"There's a dragon feel about that place," said Melisande, shuddering.

Startled, Draconas turned to look at her. Her face pale, tense, and strained, she gazed, wide-eyed, into the cavern.

So she feels it, too, he thought. Though she probably doesn't understand it. She is so accustomed to being around the dragon magic that she doesn't notice it until she is away from it. Now she is sensitive to it, though she can't quite place it.

"I don't know about a dragon feel, but it has an evil feel to it," Edward stated. "Probably a smuggler's den. Do you think they went in there?"

"Maybe," Draconas temporized.

Edward cast another glance at the sunken cave as they floated past. "I wouldn't relish the thought of going in there after—"

Movement caught his eye. Lifting his head, he stared upward. "Blessed Mother of God save us! Speak of the demon and there he is!"

Draconas did not look up. He knew full well what he would see—Braun, flying in lazy circles, high above the red rock cliffs.

"That is what I felt!" Melisande cried, staring up at the dragon. "I couldn't understand. . . . Will the dragon attack us?"

"No," said Draconas shortly.

"How can you be so sure?" she asked, astonished at the certainty with which he spoke.

"The canyon walls protect us. It's too narrow. The dragon would risk injuring his wings. There, you see, he's flying off."

And good riddance, Draconas thought. He didn't want to meet with Braun. He guessed that the dragon's appearance meant that Anora had decided to go along with Draconas's plan.

Speaking to his thoughts, Braun's mind touched his.

"There's an ideal place to camp not far from where you are now," the dragon reported. "The gorge comes to an end and there's a thick stand of trees on the north side of the bank, not far from that cavern you're thinking of investigating. I'll meet with you after dark. Make certain we won't be disturbed."

"I'm having second thoughts about this," Draconas told him.

"I know you are," said Braun. "And I'm here to dispel them."

22

DRACONAS MADE CAMP IN THE LATE AFTERNOON at the location the dragon had suggested. As he helped Edward drag the boat onto the shore, Draconas felt a sudden strong temptation to urge the king to take Melisande and the boat and travel far downriver, to keep going and never stop until they reached the sea.

Draconas did not give way to the temptation, of course. The hard practicality of his nature kept him from doing anything so wildly foolish and romantic. For one, he knew that no matter how many rivers she sailed or how many oceans she crossed, the woman with the dragon magic, burning like a sickness in her blood, could never escape the reach of Maristara. For two, he knew that even if he rid himself of the humans, he could not rid himself of the problem.

He helped pull the boat onto the shore and covered it over with bracken and tree limbs, to hide it from sight. They were downstream from the red rock cliffs, an extravagance taken by the river at just that one point and then abandoned, seemingly, for the shore on which they stood and the shore that lay opposite were tree-lined, mundane, and ordinary. The river that had rushed frantically through the cliffs slowed its pace, went back to drifting and murmuring.

The setting sun shone glittering yellow through the leaves on the trees of the far shore. The water and the sky were the same gray-blue. Melisande had not spoken since they'd come across that dragon-tainted cavern. She sat on the roots of a willow tree, gazing unseeing into the water, twining the leaves absently in her hands.

Edward, restless and antsy, paced up and down the beach. Taking pity on him, Draconas reminded the king that their supplies were running low, suggested he might do some fishing. After one long, yearning look at Melisande, who didn't notice, Edward muttered something and plunged into the forest.

When he had gone, Melisande gave a deep sigh. "The dragon told them something awful about me, didn't she?" she asked. One by one, she plucked the leaves off the bough, tossed them into the water.

"What was that, Priestess?" Draconas asked. He hadn't been listening. He'd been thinking of fresh meat, his one weakness. He could not go long without craving it.

"The dragon must have told Bell— . . . told the warriors that I did something terrible, to make them want to kill me. I was just wondering what she said to Bell—to them."

"Probably that you ran off with your lover," Draconas replied off-handedly, his mind on a roasted haunch.

He glanced at her and was immediately sorry he'd said that. Her face had drained off all color, so that her skin was waxen white. She said nothing, but sat staring out across the sluggishly rolling river, her hands fallen limp and lifeless.

"Yes," she murmured, her tone low and sad. "That is probably what she told Bell—them."

The sky was now streaked with red and orange and purple, the last fling of the dying sun. Her gaze went upriver, to the red rocks. She looked long and searchingly, waiting. Not with hope. With the lack of it.

Waiting for her lover, Draconas realized. Waiting for her to come. She won't be deterred, that lover. No matter what the dragon says. She'll come after her and Melisande knows it. She also knows that when the lover finds her, she'll kill her.

Her gaze shifted abruptly to him and there was some of the sun's flame in it.

"You know so much about us, about our kingdom. You knew about the babies. Edward says that you knew or at least suspected there was a dragon in the mountain before you even entered."

Draconas noted that she had called him "Edward." He shrugged. "I'm a dragon hunter. People pay me to know about dragons."

"Then I have a question," said Melisande. "Can all dragons turn into humans?" She made a gesture with her hand. "Could Edward be a dragon? Or you?"

"I haven't ripped out anyone's heart lately, if that's what you're asking," said Draconas.

She looked away, back to the sky. The reds and pinks had deepened all to purple, deepening to black. The evening star appeared, intent on hurrying away the day.

Melisande rose suddenly, rubbing her arms. "I wish His Majesty would return," she said, unconscious that she had used his name before. "I have a feeling that dragon is still about."

"I'll go find him," offered Draconas, and he walked away, shaking his head.

Dangerous, these dragon-tainted humans. Very dangerous.

Draconas found Edward fashioning a snare. They ate rabbit that night. Although Melisande protested at first that she was not hungry, the smell of the rabbit, roasting on a stick over the fire, proved irresistible.

Afterward, they sat in silence. Edward watched the

night deepen over the river. Melisande's gaze turned often upstream. She was still waiting.

Draconas offered to keep watch. Edward argued politely, but eventually gave way, with the understanding that Draconas was to wake him halfway through the night. Draconas promised and it was a promise he meant to keep. He had not slept for two nights running and he was starting to feel the need. His meeting with Braun shouldn't take all that long, since there would be very little conversation. Mostly the dragon would do the talking with Draconas listening and replying "yes" at the proper intervals.

I'll have my say, though, Draconas promised himself. I'll make certain they knew how I feel about this plan.

Which led him to wonder, how did he feel about it?

He couldn't come up with an answer. He thought he'd been opposed to it, but after his conversation about dragons with Melisande, he wasn't sure anymore.

Edward chose the best place for Melisande to make her bed, gave her the best horse blanket. He selected a place for himself a decorous distance away. Draconas almost asked Edward if he was going to place a sword between them, as did the chivalric knights of old, but guessed from the expression on the king's face that he would not see the humor in that.

Once the humans had wrapped themselves in their blankets and lain down, with their backs turned conspicuously and uneasily toward each other, Draconas cast his magic over them, like covering them with yet another blanket. Both of them relaxed, rolled over, fell into a deep slumber. He then went off to meet Braun, looking for someplace where they could talk undisturbed and Draconas could still keep an eye on his charges.

The lover was out there, and Melisande knew she would find her.

Just one more damn thing to worry about.

*   *   *

Melisande was right. Bellona was close to finding them. If Draconas had known how close, he might not have left his humans at all that night.

The boat she'd discovered was smaller than the others, had probably been used to ferry supplies, for there was a fine sifting of ground corn meal all over the bottom and a rope tied through a metal hook at the stern. Bellona traveled as far as she could in the darkness of that first night, hoping to put as much distance between herself and the warriors as possible. At length, after a collision with a tree branch nearly staved in the side of the boat, she made camp. She slept fitfully, often waking to think she heard Melisande's voice, calling her.

Rising with the dawn, Bellona set out downstream. Her boat was lighter and she traveled faster. She would have quickly caught up with them, but at the point where the red rock cliff broke the river in two, she chose to take the southern route, not the one to the west.

Bellona considered both, but she did not like the feel of that western branch of the river. Imperfect as her knowledge of the land outside of Seth was, she did recall hearing old tales about others kingdoms that lay to the south. Melisande was not that far ahead of her. Like her, the trio would not have been able to travel at night. She was certain that she must catch them, and she kept sharp watch along the banks.

Time passed. The sun set in glory, in reds and purples. The trees cast long shadows over her and over her heart. She had taken the wrong branch. She knew with bitter certainty that they had gone westward.

She had all that way to go back, upriver.

Bellona slammed her hand into the seat with such force that she bruised her palm. She considered going farther that night, but she was bone-tired. Her arms ached with the unaccustomed exertion and she feared she might miss some sign of them in the darkness. Reluctantly, she made camp.

She got little sleep that night. Her heart, gnawed raw by jealousy, kept waking her with its pain.

Braun directed Draconas to a location farther down the beach, where the dragon had found a large patch of open ground near the water. Draconas's boots crunched in the sand. To his eyes, the dragon shimmered in the darkness with the warmth of the living against a backdrop of stone—the bare-bone skeleton of the world.

The dragon was brisk, businesslike. He skipped all pleasantries, came right to the matter at hand.

"Anora approves of your plan. Indeed, she was immensely impressed and praised you highly. She sends this, as you requested."

He handed over a small bottle encrusted with jewels. Dragons are fond of pretty things. Draconas recognized the work as Middle Eastern. He thrust the bottle inside the breast of his leather jacket.

"I didn't request it," he said.

"Yes, you did," said Braun. "Oh, maybe not in so many words, but I could see it at the back of your mind. The formula is an ancient one. According to Anora, it was developed during the days of antiquity when we were assisting the humans in their desperate struggle for survival. All those predators, you know, and they are so fragile. Strong-willed, but fragile. At first our ancestors hoped that the humans would grow scales, but—well, never mind all that. You don't need the full recital. Bad enough I had to sit through it. Suffice it to say that this potion will do what is needful—make the male desirous, the female receptive, and it will ensure that she will conceive, so that one coupling will be all that is necessary."

"Waste not, want not," muttered Draconas. "The female has a name, by the way. Her name is Melisande."

He didn't know why he'd said that, except that he felt out-of-sorts.

"She'll recognize the potion," Draconas continued. "It's

undoubtedly the same one that Maristara uses on her humans."

"Then we know it works," said Braun. "We've seen the proof. Anora says that the child born of this union will be very powerful in dragon magic. The mother is immensely gifted. I felt her from a great distance."

"And if it is a boy, we'll have added one more mad monk to the world."

"On the contrary, Draconas, for we will be there to see that the boy is properly taught. Your orders are to bring the woman to Anora, who will care for her and her son."

"So they're to be prisoners," said Draconas.

"They will be given the best of everything," Braun assured him. "Whatever they desire shall be theirs for the asking."

"Still prisoners," said Draconas. "Like the people of Seth. They have everything they want."

Braun bit off an exasperated sigh. He was trying very hard to maintain his composure. Draconas wasn't making it easy.

"You know as well as I do that this woman cannot be allowed to wander about the world freely. Nor can her child. The boy must be properly trained."

"So he can grow up to fight dragons. How can you be so certain it will be a male?"

"This king you chose has fathered two sons already. But if not a male, a female will do, though it would not be as desirable."

"And since you have Melisande as a prisoner, you could always try your hand at breeding more," Draconas said acidly. "It works quite well for Maristara."

Braun's mane rustled, his scales clicked, his tail twitched. He dug his claws into the sand.

"Must I again remind you of the lives at stake?"

No, said Draconas silently, you mustn't. I know. Damn it, I know. He reached into his jerkin, touched the potion bottle, felt the jewels, cold and hard and sharp-edged.

"So what is your plan for this boy?" Draconas asked,

his mind's colors conciliatory. "I assume that once he's grown, he's meant to kill Maristara and her cohort and deal with the mad monks and the baby smugglers and all the rest. I just wondered how you planned to carry this off?"

"We have some ideas," said Braun, his own colors simmering, vague.

Draconas stood staring out at the river sliding past him. The stars shone in the water, but the river couldn't catch them. "You don't know, do you? And neither does Anora."

"We have twenty years to discuss the matter," said Braun.

Draconas snorted. "You're stalling. Just as you've done all along. What's another twenty years added onto three hundred? You've made the decision not to decide. You're doing nothing."

"We are doing something—" Braun began.

"Exactly what Maristara is doing," Draconas cut in. "Manipulating humans, using them to our own ends, never mind that we may be destroying their lives."

"A few lives, to save many. And humans are so careless of their lives, Draconas. They waste them as if they were of no more value than this sand beneath my claws."

The colors of Braun's mind were like jewels in Draconas's hand—hard, jagged, sharp-edged.

"You have no choice, Draconas. Anora has commanded that you proceed. I will return in a week or so to hear your report and to assist you in bringing the female to Anora. I would come sooner, but a special session of the Parliament has been convened to discuss the matter."

"You know that someone in Parliament is reporting back to Maristara—"

"Rest assured, we will not reveal all we know. Anora thinks that it would seem strange to Maristara if we did not call a special session and that she would start to suspect something. Do not worry, Draconas. You know

Anora. She is a master at controlling her thoughts. They will see only what she wants them to see."

Braun spread his wings, prepared to depart. "I am glad you agreed to go along with this. I know you have doubts. 'Draconas has a dragon's soul,' Anora says, 'but his heart is human.' Rest assured, you are doing the right thing."

Anora was always saying that. He'd lost count of the number of times he'd heard it. Still, she would always add that he was the best walker there had ever been.

"And what do I tell this king whose kingdom is being ravaged by an evil dragon?" Draconas asked, as Braun lifted up into the air, his wing tips brushing the treetops.

"Tell His Majesty that the coming of the Mistress of Dragons so terrified the great beast that he fled at the prospect," Braun returned, chuckling.

The dragon soared into the sky. The light of the moon glanced off this scales, so that for an instant he was all glittering silver, and then he wheeled, rising ever upward, and he was an absence of stars, and he was gone.

Draconas walked slowly back toward the campsite. He was suddenly so tired that he could barely move. His body would accede to the demands he made on it only up to a certain point, and then it would assert its own will, which he had best consider, or be prepared to face the consequences.

He still had to deal with two more matters before he could sleep. Leaving the shoreline, he plunged into the woods, searching for a shelter for the humans. He needed a place that was close to shore, but not too close. A place that was secluded, yet easily found.

A fallen oak tree proved ideal. The oak lay propped at an angle, forming a natural lean-to. Wild grapevines had grown over it, covering the oak with broad green leaves that formed a tarplike roof. A few blankets, spread beneath the tree, and his humans would have a very cozy bower.

Draconas marked a trail to the oak on his way back to camp.

On his return, he found Melisande and Edward both deep in sleep. Melisande slept on her back, her face to the moonlight, her arms widespread. Edward maintained his discipline, even in his sleep, for he slept on his side, his back to her, his face turned resolutely away.

Draconas brought out the potion. He picked up the water skin, removed the stopper. He used his teeth to pull out the cork of the potion bottle. Holding both objects in his hands, he stared at them, irresolute.

The faces of all the humans he had known looked back at him.

So many, he thought, gazing down the long, long row. So many and where have they gone? All he had were memories: a face, the sound of laughter, the lifting of a hand in farewell. All of them, bidding farewell and turning away, to vanish in the dust. To become the dust.

Two more. Two more to join that long line. Six hundred years from now, he would look back and he might see a face, the flash of a smile, the lifted hand.

Or he might see only the dust.

He poured the potion into the water skin, replaced the stopper. He cast a circle of enchantment over the camp, so that they could sleep undisturbed, then spread his blanket and laid down in its center.

In his dreams, he was always a dragon. He never dreamed of himself in his human body. As he was drifting into sleep, he extended his wings over them, his dragon soul keeping watch, while his human heart slept.

23

DRACONAS WOKE TO BRIGHT SUNLIGHT SHINING full in his eyes, and the sound of splashing. He propped himself up on one elbow, watched Edward scoop a fish out of the water with his bare hands and fling it up onto the bank. Several fish lay there already, flopping about, gasping.

"I'm impressed," said Draconas.

"It's a trick I learned as a boy," Edward said. "My father taught me."

He made a dart, a dive, and another fish flew through the air, scales gleaming.

"I think that should be enough for breakfast," he commented, wading out of the water.

Shaking his arms, shivering in the cool morning air, he toweled himself with his blanket, pulled his shirt on over his head.

"I thought you were going to sleep the day away," he added, grinning at Draconas. "Now that I caught the fish, you can cook them. That's your punishment for not waking me for my turn at watch."

Draconas glanced at the water skin, saw that it had been

moved. The sand beneath the stopper was damp.

"Where is Melisande?" he asked, looking around and not finding her.

"She wanted to bathe. I rigged her up a screen." Edward gestured to a blanket, draped over a tree limb. "She's in the water downstream."

Draconas heard the sounds of humming from behind it. He seemed to vaguely recognize the tune, then remembered it as one of Edward's songs.

> But winter's gone and spring is going
> And by thine own fireside I've been,
> And told thee dear, with garments flowing
> I met thee when the spring was green . . .

Her voice was low and sweet. Draconas went to the shore, plunged his hands into the river, vigorously scrubbed his face and laved cold water on the back of his neck. He found Edward standing idle, a wriggling fish in his hands. He was staring at the blanket, listening breathlessly to the song.

"So, what are the plans for today?" Edward asked, starting guiltily. He added the fish to his catch. "Are we going to continue to hunt for baby smugglers?"

"I plan to go have a look at that sunken cave we passed."

"Good," said Edward. "I'll come with you."

"You're a pretty sort of knight-errant," said Draconas. "Who's going to guard Melisande with both of us gone?"

A slow flush mounted in Edward's cheeks. He threw down one fish, picked up another, then dropped it back to the sand.

"Then you stay with her, Draconas. Let me go investigate the cave."

"Out of the question. I know what I'm looking for. You're not yet recovered from your wounds. You both could use the rest. I found a shelter in the woods yesterday, while I was out hunting. A sort of natural lean-to made by a fallen oak tree. You can sleep, cook your fish . . ."

"It's just that I don't think I should be alone . . . I don't trust . . ." He paused, changed the subject. "How far do you think we are from home?"

Home. Wife.

Draconas liked Ermintrude, liked her cheerful practicality, liked her concern for her husband. He remembered her tears, and how close a single tear had come to falling on him, revealing him for what he was. He glanced again at the water skin, wondered if she'd drunk from it. He guessed, by the song, that they were both under the potion's influence.

Melisande came out from behind the screen, her hair sleek and shining from the river water. Lacking a comb, she dragged her fingers through it and it fell in lazy, wet curls around her shoulders and down her back. Edward gazed at her dumbly, with such naked love and longing in his eyes that he did not have to speak it. She looked at him, only at him, and smiled.

"We're a long way from home," said Draconas. He waved his hand. "The shelter's in there among the trees. I marked the trail. You shouldn't have any trouble finding it."

Turning, he began walking up the beach, in the direction of the sunken cave.

"But don't you want breakfast?" Edward asked, startled at this sudden departure.

"You can have my share," said Draconas. "Don't look for me before nightfall."

"Draconas," Edward called to his back. "What's going on? What's the matter with you?"

Draconas kept walking.

"Draconas?" That was Melisande. "Be careful."

He didn't turn around. He kept walking, and soon they were both out of earshot. He entered into the forest and they were out of sight.

Resolutely, he put them out of mind.

*   *   *

"Where is he going?" Melisande asked.

"Off to investigate that cave," said Edward.

Melisande was troubled. "He shouldn't have gone alone. That is a terrible place. I feel it." She rested her hand on Edward's arm. "You should go after him. Stop him."

Edward looked down at her hand, which was slender, with narrow, tapering fingers and short, rounded, pink-tinged nails. He felt her touch through the fabric of his wet shirt, felt it warm against his cold skin. His desire was a physical pain, and he wrenched his arm away. Turning abruptly, he scooped up the fish, began tossing them in the water.

"It wouldn't do any good," he said, his voice muffled. "I already offered to go. He said I should stay here with you. He's right, of course."

"What are you doing with the fish?"

"Throwing them back. I can't stand to see them flopping about. If you're hungry, I'll try to find something else—"

"I'm not hungry," she said.

Edward washed the fish slime off his hands, watched the fish swim away.

"I'm not either," he said.

He felt her close behind him, not touching, but close. He couldn't stay here, rooted to the spot. He had to turn around. He had to face her. He had to face his pain and deal with it.

He steeled himself.

"We should go find that shelter," he said briskly, turning.

He looked into her eyes, bluer than the river or the sky. A wave of desire surged out of him. He saw, in her eyes, the wave catch her up and carry her back to him, carry her into his arms.

They did not kiss. They stood there on the beach, in the morning sunlight, clasped in each other's arms, feeling warmth and softness and the beating of their two hearts.

"Loving you breaks every vow I ever took," Edward told her silently. "It breaks the laws of my land and the laws of my church. Yet loving you seems to me the only truth in a life of falsehoods."

"I don't love you," Melisande told him silently. Her head bent, eyes lowered, she crowded close to him. "But I need you. I need your hands to tell me that my flesh is warm. I need your lips to assure me that I am not shut up in that dark tomb. Love me. Bring me back to life."

"We should go find this shelter," said Edward aloud, his voice husky with his passion.

He said they should go, but he did not move. He smoothed back a wet, dangling curl and looked into her face which was so beautiful and into her eyes, where he saw himself.

"Yes," she said. "We should find the shelter."

Arms linked, holding fast to each other, they started to walk up the beach toward the woods, where Draconas had told them they could find the trail. Halfway there, Melisande stopped.

"We should take the water skin," she said. "If we're going to be there all day."

Edward agreed and, parting from her reluctantly, hastened back to retrieve it. He lifted it, slung it over his shoulder.

"I noticed," she said, slipping into his arms again as he returned, "that the water tasted different this morning. There was a sweetness to it."

"Yes," he agreed. "It tasted sweet."

24

DRACONAS HAD HOPED THAT HE COULD APPROACH the cave by land, but discovered that he could not get close to it. The red rock cliff was sheer, with nary a hand- or foothold in sight. The only way to access the cave was by water. He stripped down to his breeches, took off his boots, and dove into the river. The water was cold and he gasped reflexively at the shock. Dragons are clumsy swimmers, having no liking for it, avoiding water when they can. What he lacked in skill, he made up for in strength. Kicking and blowing, he doggedly thrashed up-river to the cavern's entrance.

The cold wasn't so bad, once he got used to it. Treading water, he peered inside the cave. The feel, the scent, the taste of dragon magic was all-pervasive, touched all his senses. Draconas was perplexed. He'd never experienced anything similar.

But then, he reminded himself, he'd never experienced insane monks before, either.

He swam inside, paddling with his arms and legs, taking care not to break the surface, so as not to make any sound. Gentle ripples marking his passing washed up on the rock walls on either side of him.

This section of the cavern had a low, arched ceiling. If he'd been in a boat, he would have had to duck as the boat passed through. If the gigantic Grald came this way, he must have had to bend almost double.

Draconas soon left daylight behind. The passageway was not completely dark, however, for it opened into a much larger chamber, illuminated by an eerie, soft, orange-brown glow, reminiscent of twilight. He halted before swimming into the twilit grotto. Moving his legs to keep himself afloat, he found a rock that jutted out into the dark water and latched onto it, intending to take a good look around.

The grotto was larger than the passageway. A tall man could stand to his full height here. A hole bored though the rock wall permitted a glimpse of blue sky and accounted for the diffused light. The hole was smooth. He doubted if it was a natural formation.

The river flowed through the grotto, and he guessed that this wasn't a cavern so much as a large tunnel. That was why he had found no sign of the baby smugglers. They had entered this passageway. The river carried them through the tunnel and out the other side. Follow this branch of the river and it might eventually lead him to Maristara's human baby farm.

As Edward had said, the grotto was an ideal hideout for smugglers. The river's flow had worn smooth the rock on either side of the waterway to form a natural landing site. Draconas could see evidence that people had camped here—charred spots on the rock ledge where they'd lit fires, a few gnawed bones, a length of discarded rope with a frayed end.

Beyond the campsite, a blank stone wall curved up to meet the ceiling. The chamber was empty. If the baby smugglers had been here, they'd left days before.

Draconas shoved himself off from the rock, entering the grotto, the twilight. He pushed himself through the water, not swimming so much as shoving the river impatiently aside. The shadows deepened as he neared the bank, so that he found it hard to see. He blamed the murky water and he blinked repeatedly to clear the water from his eyes. Reaching the ledge, he placed his hands on it, intending to use it to leverage himself up out of the water.

Strong hands grabbed hold of his wrists.

Draconas gasped in shock, reacted instinctively. Grabbing the hands that had grabbed him, Draconas tried to pull the person who had ahold of him into the water.

Draconas might as well have tried to pull down the mountain. The person didn't budge. His grip on Draconas tightened.

Looking up, Draconas saw Grald standing over him.

Much as Edward had flung the fish out of the water onto the bank, Grald lifted Draconas out of the water and flung him, hard, onto the stone floor.

Draconas groaned and gasped, arched his back, grimacing, feigning pain, feigning shock, all the while watching Grald.

The big man came closer. Draconas tensed, figuring to aim a powerful kick at Grald's kneecap, hoping to break it.

Grald foiled him by kneeling down beside him. Taking hold of his chin in a hand that could have engulfed his head, Grald turned Draconas's face to the light.

"I'm disappointed. They told me you were smart. Yet you swam right into my trap. Haven't you figured things out yet, Draconas?"

Grald tightened his grip. His fingers dug into Draconas's jaw, wrenching it, nearly dislocating it. The pain was excruciating. Grald jerked Draconas's head.

"Now do you see?" Grald asked, and he looked directly into Draconas's eyes.

Burning white light shot through Draconas's brain, illuminating every part of it. He tried to hide. His ideas, his plans, his thoughts skittered about like frightened mice, diving into every crevice and cranny. The probing, seeking, relentless light burrowed and probed, caught and dragged each one out, devoured them all.

One poor thought remained, shriveled, hiding from the blazing light.

Grald was a dragon. An elder dragon, powerful, ruthless, cunning.

Held fast in the dragon's powerful grip, Draconas could not move his head or tear away his gaze. His arms were free, however, and he felt surreptitiously about, seeking a weapon. His fingers brushed against a rock, closed over it.

Draconas slammed the rock into the side of Grald's head.

The blow would have crushed a human's skull. Grald grunted and tottered back on his heels. The blow stunned him enough that he loosened his grip on Draconas, who managed to wrench free. He staggered to his feet, still clutching the rock.

Blood trailed down the side of Grald's face. He gave his head a shake, as a dog shakes off water, and then rose ponderously.

Draconas had been lured into this trap for one purpose—to penetrate his mind, find out what he knew and, more importantly, what he planned to do with his knowledge. Grald had accomplished his purpose and there was nothing Draconas could do about it. Grald saw everything, knew everything. He knew about Braun, knew about the plan, knew about Anora and the potion she had sent, knew about Edward and Melisande.

Grald could put an end to the threat with the simple expediency of killing everyone involved—Draconas, Edward, Melisande, Braun, and possibly even Anora, if the dragon could arrange it so that the other members of Parliament did not suspect.

Yet Grald had not escaped from this encounter unscathed. Much like emptying the contents of a cask of wine into a jug, Grald had been forced to open a part of his mind in order to receive the mind of Draconas.

And Draconas had seen something fascinating. Unlike Draconas, whose dragon form was human and his human mind dragon, Grald had two minds—the mind of a human *and* the mind of the dragon. The two were not compatible.

The dragon's mind was the stronger, more powerful of the two. It had, in fact, completely consumed the human's, so that very little of the true Grald still remained. Still, the human mind remained, covering the dragon's like cheesecloth. The dragon's thoughts had to be strained through it. Which meant that Grald would be slow to react.

Draconas brought his magic to hand. No use hiding his skills now. Grald had seen everything. He knew how Draconas fought, knew all his stratagems, knew his secret ploys and talents. Draconas readied a powerful magical spell, the spell he would customarily cast in these instances—a concussive blast of magical energy intended to knock the victim senseless, quickly incapacitate him.

Grald could see the colors of the spell forming in Draconas's mind and Grald raised his hands, making ready a counterspell to block the blow. He would have another spell—a lethal spell—to follow.

Dropping his spell at the last second, Draconas turned and ran like a rabbit.

Caught flat-footed, Grald tried to halt his own magic. The dragon mind could have swiftly reversed the spell, but the human mind was slow to react and the spell proceeded to its conclusion. An enormous shield of energy, designed to deflect Draconas's attack, appeared in front of Grald. So long as the shield was raised, the dragon could not use his own magic. The shield acted to block all spells—his own and the enemy's.

Grald would have to take time to lower the shield. He would have to rethink the spell he was intending to cast, come up with another, and all that would have to be strained through the cheesecloth of the human's mind. The process would take seconds only, but those few seconds were precious to Draconas.

Head down, legs pumping, he raced for the dark water.

Grald chose to abandon all magic, fling down shield

and spear, and go after his victim with his bare hands, utilize the strength of the human body he had chosen.

Draconas heard heavy feet pounding behind him and he cursed the dragon's cunning.

Grald's long legs ate up the space that separated them. Draconas reached the bank, but before he could jump, Grald lunged, caught him in the midriff, and carried him into the river.

Dark water closed over Draconas. Grald shifted his hold on him. His huge hands held Draconas underwater, trying to drown him. Grald was not able to get a good grip on wet and slippery human flesh, and Draconas managed to wriggle free. He swam desperately for the exit.

If he could have stayed beneath the water, he might have escaped, but after only moments, his lungs began to burn. He fought on, until he was desperate for air. Pulling himself upward with powerful strokes of his arms, he broke through the surface with a gasp.

Strong hands caught hold of him beneath his armpits and lifted him out of the water. Grald hurled Draconas up against the rock wall.

White, jagged pain lanced through Draconas. Bones cracked. Blood mingled with the water in his eyes, in his mouth. He fought and struggled to escape the man's grip, but the man's hands were like iron bands. Desperate, Draconas latched onto Grald's head, thrust his thumbs into Grald's eyes.

Grald gave a bellow and flung Draconas away from him.

Draconas sank beneath the dark water. Drawing breath was agony. Movement of any kind was agony.

Draconas could feel Grald thrashing about in the water, searching with those huge hands, trying to find him. Grald's dragon brain reached out, as well, searching for the colors of Draconas's mind.

Draconas let those colors fade, grow dim and dusky: *How blissful to sink beneath the dark and still water, let it close over my head, seep into my lungs, ease the burn-*

ing, ease the pain, ease the guilt . . . easeful, easy death . . .

He let Grald see those thoughts. Let Grald think he was dying. Draconas just had to make certain the thought didn't become reality.

Grald floundered about in the water for long moments. Thinking each time he'd caught sight of his foe, Grald lunged here and he lunged there, waggling his hands and kicking out with his feet.

"You've lost him," said Maristara, appearing suddenly in Grald's mind. "Let him go."

The two communed mind to mind, as dragons are accustomed to doing, but with the problem that their two human minds continually intruded. Grald hauled his massive human body out of the river, shook himself.

"He's gone, mind and body both," said Grald sullenly. "I think he drowned."

"That was easy," returned Maristara. "Too easy."

"You didn't have to fight him," Grald muttered, wincing as he put his hand to the bruised and bloody gash on his temple. "You think he's still alive?"

"Of course."

"Very well." Grald grunted. "I'll go after him."

"Not yet. We have more urgent matters."

"The human female, you mean. The one with the dragon magic. I saw his plan. I know where the humans are hiding. I'll kill them first, then—"

"Kill the male," Maristara interrupted. "But not the female. I have a better idea. You have long been complaining that the dragon magic in the blood of the human males was growing tainted."

"I think that's why we're turning out raving madmen," said Grald.

"It has been a long time since we've had a fresh infusion of dragon blood," Maristara admitted. "Not since the early days in the monastery, with those very first women. If you're right about the blood becoming tainted—and

I'm not saying you are, mind you. My women are stronger in magic than ever—you could try an experiment with this human. Draconas has done all the preparation for us. It would be a pity to let that go to waste."

"Yes, you're right." Grald chuckled. "A good idea."

"Once you have done what is necessary, bring her back to me. I'll keep her prisoner until the babe is born, then we'll get rid of her."

"What about Draconas?" Grald asked. His human mind bore a grudge.

"First things first," said Maristara.

Draconas kept submerged underwater, taking no chances. This proved difficult, for   could not use his left arm. He used his good right arm to propel himself along until he saw shafts of sunlight slicing down through the water and realized that he was out of the cavern. He was vaguely surprised to find the sun shining. It seemed to him that darkness must have consumed the whole world.

He kicked his legs, propelled himself up to the surface, and looked about swiftly for Grald.

No sign of him and that was not good.

He struggled toward the shore. The current helped, and he washed up against the long, gnarled roots of a tree. Draconas dragged himself out of the river. He crawled a few feet, then collapsed onto the warm sand.

Breathing was like inhaling fire. He had a broken rib, maybe several. His left arm was crushed and useless, the jagged edges of the bone sticking out through purple, inflamed skin. He retched, vomited river water, and sank back, weak and shivering from cold, from shock.

The river rose, washed over his head, pulled him into the dark water. . . .

Draconas woke with a shuddering gasp. He stared at the sky. He had no idea how long he'd been unconscious. Some time, apparently, for the sunlight was fading. Either that or he was losing his eyesight. He shook so with the cold that his chattering teeth had bitten through his tongue. He tasted blood in his mouth.

He could heal himself, but he had to remain conscious to work the magic. He had to be able to think of the spell, but pain stirred all the colors into a blob of black.

Edward and Melisande. I revealed them to Grald. I told our plans to Grald. He knows where they are hiding.

A clever trap. So very clever. I met Maristara's cohort. I spoke to him, fought him, and I have no idea who he is. He never revealed his true form. I might sit next to him at the next session of Parliament and never have a clue.

I have failed. I've failed Edward and Melisande. They are probably dead by now, or will be shortly. I can do nothing to save them. I got them into this, and I got them killed.

Anger, bitter as bile, rose in him. Anger so hot and black that it came near to choking him. He was angry at them all, at Maristara, at Braun and Anora, at himself. *What right had we to get involved? Any of us? Ever?* Even those long-ago dragons who gently lifted the humans out of the mud of creation. They did not do that out of altruism, but only out of curiosity.

"Let us conduct an experiment," they said. "Let us see how this very clever species turns out."

The anger strengthened him, acted as a stick to clamp in his teeth as he sought out the magic he needed. He seized hold of it and sent it flowing through his shivering body. The magic flooded him with warmth, numbed the pain.

He lurched to his feet, took stock of his situation. He was not thoroughly healed. The process required at least a day of uninterrupted sleep and he didn't have time. His head ached, but it was only an ache, not brutal, skull-bashing pain. Breathing hurt him, for his ribs were being held together only by the baling wire of his magic. The same was true of his broken arm. He could move it and wiggle his fingers and that was about the best that could be said for it.

He looked around to get his bearings, to try to locate landmarks, for he had no idea where he'd washed up. The river was silky gray with the coming of evening, smooth and tranquil, for no wind blew. It rolled along, singing softly to itself. He stared along its bank, up and down. He stared out over the water. He could not find anything that looked familiar and he was puzzled. He hadn't drifted that far.

He lifted his head, looked up at the sky, into the luminous sunset.

The sun was setting behind him.

Draconas swore a bitter oath and smashed the fist of his good hand into the trunk of a cottonwood tree.

He was on the wrong side of the river.

He was on the western shore. Edward and Melisande were on the east.

And so was Grald.

25

EDWARD AND MELISANDE FOUND THE FALLEN OAK more by instinct and good fortune than because either of them was paying attention to the trail Draconas had so carefully marked. Their arms entwined, they walked in tandem, his strides matching hers.

They did not speak of the future. The future did not exist here in the wilderness, out of sight of any signs of man or his handiwork. They were the only two in existence. The world had been created just for them. They had no past, for they were just this moment newly born. They had no future, for neither wanted to think of that. They had only to live and breathe and love.

Edward did feel, for a moment, the odd sensation of standing apart from himself. Edward gazing at Edward in bleak dismay. He could see himself reaching out a hand to stop himself, to seize hold of himself and drag himself away. At the last moment, the hand fell to his side. He bade himself go on. This was what love was, what it was meant to be. He glanced back, but he could no longer see himself and he was glad, for he wanted to see only her, his beloved.

Melisande had no such vision of herself. She was living moment to moment, breath to breath, heartbeat to heartbeat. She was hiding from the past with its wrenching pain and its horror. Everyone she had ever loved had betrayed her, and so she ran away from them, ran until she could no longer hear their voices or see their faces. There was only his face and his hands and his love and reassurance that she was alive and breathing and beloved.

Arriving at the fallen oak, they were both suddenly shy and hesitant. Anticipation quickened the pulse, set the blood burning, but they were strangers to each other and although they knew where it must naturally end and looked forward with aching desire to that ending, neither knew how to begin.

"You must be thirsty," said Edward, grasping at the only action he could take that seemed innocent of design. He removed the water skin, which he was carrying slung over his shoulder and, pulling out the stopper, he offered it to her.

She put her lips over the opening and there was something so sensual in that movement that his heart lurched and his hand jerked. He sloshed water in her face, spilled it down the bodice of her gown.

He was appalled, frantically apologetic. She laughed and looked into his eyes. Laughter died. Their lips touched, the first kiss searching and tentative and then passion swept them up and carried them down onto the soft leaves in the cool, sweet-smelling shadow of the fallen oak tree.

They loved and they slept, wrapped in each other's arms, and woke to love again, finding new and better joy every time as each body yielded to the other's touch and each delighted in discovering new ways to bring pleasure to the other. The day had no end as it had no beginning. The sun seemed to revolve in a small tight circle above them, going round and round. They did not hunger, but their thirst was insatiable and they soon drained the water skin.

They languished in each other's arms, not talking, as lovers usually do, for all they had to talk about was the past and that brought him only guilt and her only terror. Silence, uneasy and uncomfortable, replaced passion, and the sun sank all in an instant, plunging into the river, its fire drowned. He noticed suddenly that it was growing dark and she began to feel chill.

He sat up, wiped his mouth. The water was sweet on the tongue, but it left a bitter aftertaste. He looked out into the shadows and wondered bleakly where they went from here.

"I hear something," she said. "Footsteps."

He heard it, too, sticks breaking and cracking beneath booted feet.

"It must be Draconas," said Edward. He glanced about for his forgotten clothes, found them strewn all over, beneath the log and out beyond. "Although he usually doesn't make so much noise as that."

The thought came to him that Draconas knew what they were about and was giving them fair warning of his approach. Edward handed Melisande her gown to cover her nakedness. He did not look at her as he did so.

Noting that he kept his eyes averted, Melisande was embarrassed and ashamed. She fumbled with her gown, sliding it over her head, then realizing she had put it on inside out. Sighing, shivering, she drew it off, to put it right.

"You stay here. I'll go get rid of him," Edward said, lacing up his pants.

He was eager to leave her and he hated himself for it, for everything. The memory of their bliss came back to him and he was filled with remorse.

"Melisande—"

She turned her head away. "Please go," she said. "I don't want to see Draconas. I don't want to see anyone. Not for a little while. Please, just go."

He did as she asked. Stepping out from under the fallen oak, he saw that night was coming, its shadows passed along from tree limb to tree limb, like damp sheets taken out from the river, to be wrung out and flung over him, draping him in a smothering future.

He was heartsick, overwhelmed, and confused. He had a wife, he had children, he had a kingdom. He had his God, who had proclaimed what he had done a mortal sin.

Edward picked up his shirt, stood plucking at a frayed sleeve cuff. The crashing footfalls were drawing nearer and he was suddenly angry at Draconas, for making it so very obvious that he had known all along that Edward would fall to temptation. Throwing the shirt onto the ground, Edward stalked out of the clearing. He would take Draconas by the arm and lead him back to camp and there they would have it out. He would bloody that supercilious smirk the man sometimes wore, as if he were the only person in the world who knew the truth.

A man emerged from the shadows. He was taller than he should be, taller than Draconas, and more massive. The lambent light of the setting sun touched upon the brutal face of Grald.

The man's eyes, shadowed beneath an overhanging forehead, sought out the fallen oak. His mouth leered. Edward understood nothing and everything, all in an instant. He reached for his sword, but it did not hang at his side. He'd left it behind, on the beach.

Edward lunged, hoping to catch the man by surprise, knock the breath from his body, and carry him to the ground.

Grald watched with some amusement. He jerked his leg up and his bent knee struck Edward in the face.

The jarring blow snapped his head back, broke his nose, and smashed in teeth. Pain burst inside him, pain and fear for Melisande. Bleeding from the mouth and nose, his head ringing, he tried to rise.

Grald's booted foot struck him in the ribs. Edward doubled over in agony and Grald slammed his foot into his face.

White light burst in Edward's head, light white and pure and accusing as the face of God.

Then God's face turned away.

Melisande heard Edward's cry and she shrank back into the darkness, her dress clasped against her bosom. She heard another cry, then Edward's voice, moaning, and then horrible sounds, as of something hard thudding repeatedly against unresisting flesh.

The moaning stopped, horribly.

Sounds of footsteps, coming in her direction.

She tried to scream, but terror swelled her throat.

The footsteps stopped. She was dimly aware of a huge, hulking presence that dropped down to all fours and peered into the bower at her.

A man's face, twisted into a bestial expression of lechery, peered at her.

She shrank farther back into the darkness, as though it could save her. A hand—huge and wet and covered in thick black hair—reached into the darkness and seized hold of her by the foot, dragged her, kicking and struggling, out from beneath the tree.

She fought and kicked and bent and twisted her body, trying to escape. The man pinned her to the ground, laughed at her. He dropped down on top of her, seemed to enjoy feeling her squirm beneath him.

The dragon who ruled the human body of Grald knew no lust. This was business and he wanted it done. But the human body he had taken over enjoyed his victim's futile struggles. They were necessary to him, aroused him, and so the dragon permitted the man to take his pleasure.

The man shoved Melisande's legs apart with his knees, thrashed around until he positioned himself, then drove inside her.

She cried out in pain. Tears burned in her eyes and spilled down her cheeks. He put one hand over her mouth, stopping her screams. Her tears splashed on his flesh.

At the moment of climax, his thrust nearly tore her

apart. Opening her eyes, writhing in agony, she saw black wings spread over her. A dragon's head leered down at her. Saliva dripped from its jaws, as its clawed feet dug into her flesh and its hot seed shot into her body.

26

TRAPPED ON THE OTHER SIDE OF THE RIVER, DRA-
conas sucked on the bruised and bloody knuckles of his
hand where he'd smashed it into the tree trunk and mulled
over what to do. He had to face the bitter fact that he
could not save Melisande and Edward. Too much time
had passed. The sun was setting, the river had gone pearl
gray in the dying half-light.

Grald was not one to let grass grow under his hulkish
feet. He knew precisely where to find them and he would
have gone to kill them at once. They were dead by now.
And, after all, what did it matter? They were only humans.

Draconas stared in frustration at the river. He could
plunge into that chill water, expend what was left of his
energy trying to swim against the current, only to end up
miles farther downstream. Always assuming he didn't
drown first.

Or he could change into his dragon form, take wing,
and fly over the water. He had the ability to do that, but
he would be breaking the law.

By a decree of the Parliament of Dragons, made centuries ago, a dragon who becomes a "walker" is barred

from returning to his dragon form without asking for and receiving permission from Parliament. He is permitted to forego this permission only if his own life is at stake and then only if he can manage the transformation without humans being present.

As to the dragon shifting into his true form to save a human's life, that was absolutely prohibited. The dragons cared about humans and were interested in their welfare, but humans were so numerous that the loss of a few here and there could hardly make a difference. Weigh that against the possibility that humans might discover that dragons walked among them and there was no contest.

Draconas stood on the edge of the river, watching the darkness deepen around him. His recently mended arm pained him. He could barely move his hand. His head throbbed.

He gave the law a moment's thought, gave his probable punishment another moment's thought.

"Screw it," he said.

His dragon's form was always present, always in attendance. It spread its wings over him as humans fondly believe guardian angels hover over them. Though he could not see it, he was ever conscious of it.

He closed his eyes and lifted his head, raised his arms to the unseen wings and the glittering scaled body. He was never certain in these moments if the human body flowed into the dragon or the dragon's body flowed into the human.

It didn't matter. Flesh and spirit became one. His human pains eased and disappeared. He was once again the creature of his dreams. His earthbound bonds cut loose, Draconas inhaled the night air, drew it deep into massive lungs. He felt the fire burn in his belly. He felt muscle and tendon respond to his commands, felt scales ripple. He spread his wings and took flight over the river.

From his vantage point high above the treetops, Draconas gazed down upon the beach where they had made camp.

He found the boat, right where they had left it. He saw, glinting in the starlight, Edward's sword, forgotten.

Draconas started to veer off in the direction of the fallen oak, when he noted that instead of one boat drawn up along the shore, there were two.

Grald, he thought, and fierce joy filled his heart. This time we will meet dragon-to-dragon.

Draconas plotted his attack, a magical attack, one that would severely damage the human form in which Grald was hiding. Only by changing form, by reverting back into a dragon, could Grald escape him. And when he became a dragon, Draconas would know his identity.

If it is the last thing I do, Draconas vowed, if it's my last dying thought, I will send to Braun the name of the enemy.

Circling above, Draconas watched and waited for his foe. Grald soon appeared, as if summoned by vengeful thoughts, walking out of the forest onto the beach.

Draconas glided down, taking his time, making no sudden movement or sound that might startle the brutish human into lifting his head, looking into the sky, where he would see a red-orange dragon, scales glimmering like embers in the starlight.

Draconas readied the magic in his mind. A net as fine as cobweb, spun of energy. Crackling and sparking, the net would cover Grald in silken strands of jolting thunderbolts. He would have only an instant to change his form or his human body would die and then he would have no choice. He'd be caught in transition, like Maristara had been. He'd be weak and vulnerable.

Spiraling lower, the magic tasting sweet on his tongue, Draconas was about to release the net. He flew closer and instantly arrested the magic, halted the spell.

Grald was not alone. He carried Melisande in his arms. She was either dead or unconscious, for her head lolled, her arms hung limp.

Why was Grald carrying off Melisande? Draconas could think of two reasons. Either she was dead, and he was disposing of the corpse, which seemed unlikely. Or she was alive and he was carrying her off for some purpose, some reason.

Draconas knew then what had happened. Grald had seen the plan—to have Edward impregnate Melisande, so that she would bear a child in whose blood ran the dragon magic.

He's carrying her to Maristara, as I was supposed to carry her to Anora.

Draconas wasn't certain what to do. He could not attack Grald now, not without killing Melisande. But might that not be best? Wouldn't death be preferable to what she faced in life? No matter which side in this terrible battle had hold of her, she would be a prisoner, forced to bear a child who would then be taken away from her, a child born for one reason only and that reason was destruction.

If Melisande died here and now, her death would force Anora to take immediate action against Maristara, instead of spending twenty years having fun raising this human and debating endlessly what they were to do with him once he was raised. In his present dark mood, Draconas had just about decided that Melisande should die, that she would want to die, when he caught sight of a another person on that beach.

She was not wearing her armor, but Draconas recognized her—Bellona, the female warrior who had been commander of the troops sent to slay Melisande. He knew her by the fluid play of muscle and sinew, knew her by the skill and stealth she was using to stalk her victim.

But who was her victim? Grald or Melisande? Or both?

Not that it mattered to Draconas. His plan was ruined. He could only wait and watch and perhaps salvage something out of the wreckage.

"Humans," he muttered, exasperated.

Bellona had spent the morning traveling upriver. The muscles in her arms cramped and ached from the rowing. Her hands were blistered, palms rubbed raw. She kept on, searching along the river bank for some sign of the three she was hunting. She passed by the sunken cavern. All was still and quiet within, for it was late afternoon by the time she reached it and the battle between Draconas and Grald had ended. Draconas lay unconscious on the bank some distance downstream. Grald was on his way to find Melisande.

Bellona looked closely at the cavern, her first thought that it would make an excellent hiding place for the fugitives. She did not like the feel of it, however, and she kept on going. Instinct told her Melisande was not there.

Farther down the river, she let the boat drift slowly with the current, as her eyes swept the bank.

Sunlight glinted off metal. Her heart beating fast, Bellona rowed nearer the shore.

The gleam of light came from the hilt of a sword, lying in its scabbard near the charred remnants of a campfire. Drawn up on the bank was a boat identical to the other boats she'd found. Bellona scanned the shore, but saw no signs of them. They'd spent the night here. She could see crumpled blankets lying on the sand, another blanket draped over a tree branch. They had spent the night and they had not left yet.

Her blood pulsed in her ears. Her heart beat so that it interfered with her breathing. It was a relief to jump into the cold water, let it cool her fevered skin. Wading through the water, she dragged the boat up onto the shore.

Twilight's shadows were thick among the trees, but the lambent light gilding the river illuminated the shore. A multitude of footprints in the sand confirmed the fact that people had walked this beach not long ago. She easily picked out Melisande's footprints. Bellona cursed the waning light. She could not track them in the dark.

But there was no need to track them, she realized. Wherever they had gone, they would return to camp by nightfall. She had only to wait for them. She headed for the tree line, planning to hide herself.

A woman's screams, heart-wrenching and agonized, came from the woods.

Bellona froze, listening. She recognized that beloved voice and she jerked her head around, stared into the woods, into the direction of that terrible sound.

The screams came again and again, and then suddenly ceased, as if choked off.

Bellona started running in the direction of the screams, but her way was hampered by thick brush and darkness. She was forced to slow her pace, her heart beating, this time with fear.

She could not find a way through the trees. Frustrated and desperate, she drew her sword, began to hack at the tangled branches. The sounds of movement in the woods caused her to halt. The sounds were drawing near her. Bellona had only to stay where she was and the person would come to her.

Bellona crouched down in the shadows. She had a good vantage point of the woods and the beach. The sounds were off to her right. The footfalls had purpose in them, a destination. One man, the lover. Whatever he had done to Melisande, he would pay for it.

She forced herself to wait quietly, patiently, as she had taught her warriors to wait in ambush.

The man passed quite close to her. Bellona stared at him in wonder. This man was not the lover nor yet his partner. This man was huge as a bear, clumsy and lumbering. Whoever he was, it was Melisande he held in his arms. Bellona could not see her clearly, for the shadows of the night, but she recognized the golden hair. Melisande's body hung limp and lifeless in the brute's arms.

Bellona had no idea what had happened or who this man was or how he came to be here or what had become of the other two men. She had no care for any of that. Slowly, stealthily, she raised herself up on the balls of her feet. She already held her sword in her hand.

The man lumbered onto the beach. He paused a moment to take stock of the situation. Spotting her boat, which she had not bothered to hide, he gave a grunt of satisfaction and began to walk toward it.

Sword in hand, Bellona crept out from under the cover of the trees. Running lightly, she crossed the beach, coming up behind him.

He did not hear her. He kept walking, his attention fixed on the boat. Stealthily, trying to still even the beating of her heart, Bellona raised her sword and ran for her victim.

She aimed a blow at his skull, intending to cleave through it. She could not worry about making noise now. She hoped to strike swiftly, before he could react. Her boots crunched in the sand and he heard her. The muscles in his broad back stiffened. His head started to turn. It didn't matter now. He could do nothing, hampered as he was by the burden in his arms.

Bellona raised her voice in a battle cry and with all her strength struck a killing blow at his head.

The sword burst asunder, driving splinters of metal into her hands and arms, as the blast hurled her flat on her back in the sand. Bleeding and dazed, uncertain what had happened, Bellona looked up to see the gigantic man standing over her.

Casually, as though tossing down a bit of refuse, he dropped Melisande onto the ground. She landed in a heap, crumpled, broken, making no sound.

Bellona knew then that Melisande was dead. Tears burned in her throat, stung her eyes.

The man drew a dagger he had thrust into his boot. She watched, uncaring. Let him end this pain, she thought. She averted her head.

A screech sounded high above. The screech was loud, ear-splitting, and though it was bestial, it held in it a note of warning that even Bellona could understand.

The man halted his stroke, stared upward. His mouth twisted in a snarl. The screech wakened Melisande, who stirred and moaned.

New life surged through Bellona. Seeing the man

preoccupied, she grasped his hand that held the dagger, sank her teeth into his flesh. His blood flowed in her mouth. Her tears fell on his skin.

Bellona heard the roar and it had a human sound, though it came from the throat of a dragon. The human wrung his injured hand and snarled his fury. The dragon, gleaming blue-black in the starlight, glared balefully into the heavens and snarled his rage. In her horrified sight, human and dragon were one and the same, yet they were detached, as a man and his shadow.

Appalled, . Bellona could not move. The screech sounded again, piercing and ominous. A shudder went through Bellona and she looked up into the heavens.

Circling above her, wings brushing the stars, was another dragon, his scales red as flame. His neck outstretched, his claws lowered, the red dragon came swooping down on the blue dragon like a hawk stooping on his prey.

The man flung the dagger into the sand and began to run toward the river. He reached it seconds before the dragon struck. He plunged into the dark water and disappeared.

The dragon swept over Bellona with a rush of air that swept up the sand in a blinding whirlwind. Bellona flung her arm over her face. Sand whipped around her, stinging her eyes, blasting her flesh. She lay stunned long moments, then lifted her head, blinking away the sand.

The stars shone, cold and sharp, silvering the scudding clouds.

The dragon—both dragons—were gone.

Bellona crawled on her hands and knees to Melisande. She sank down wearily beside her, as at journey's end. If death was to come, it would find them together.

27

MELISANDE LAY ON HER BACK, WHERE THE MAN had dropped her, her body half-twisted in her fall. Her face was bruised and battered. Her lips split and bleeding. She was half-dressed, as though she had been in the act of dressing when she was attacked. Her skirts were wet and Bellona knew that the wetness was Melisande's blood.

A tremor of pity and rage shook Bellona. She put her hand on Melisande's wrist, felt for a pulse, and found it. The heart beat weakly, but it beat.

At the touch, Melisande's eyes flared open. Her lips parted in a scream, her body tensed.

"Hush, Melisande, no, you are safe," said Bellona softly, stroking back the blood-crusted hair from Melisande's face.

Melisande stared at Bellona wildly at first, then she recognized her.

"Where is . . . is he?" She shook with terror.

"He's gone, Melisande," said Bellona, though she didn't say how or where.

Melisande didn't understand. The shadows of pain and

horror hovered around her, too thick and close for her to see beyond them. All she saw was the face of her beloved.

"Bellona," she mumbled through lips so swollen she could barely be understood. "I know I must die. I accept that." Her eyes closed. Tears slid beneath the lids, mingled with the blood on her face. "I welcome it . . ."

"No, Melis," Bellona said, not knowing what she was saying, her heart speaking for her. She grasped her lover's hand, held it to her lips. "You won't die. I won't let you. Don't talk. Just rest. I'll bring you some water."

"Don't leave me!" Melisande cried. She clutched at her hand.

"I won't, I won't," said Bellona soothingly, and Melisande relaxed. Her eyes closed, then opened again. She looked around.

"Edward! I heard him cry out, but it was too late." Melisande shuddered. "I saw him lying on the ground. His head . . . I think he killed him."

Bellona's lips tightened. "Edward? Your lover?"

Melisande gazed up at her steadily. "I betrayed you. No"—she paused—"I betrayed us. Our love. I'm sorry. So sorry. I never meant . . ."

She drew in a breath, let it out in a sigh. "I don't expect you to forgive me. I can't forgive myself. It will be a relief to me to die. Believe that and do not feel guilty for what you must do. I'm glad it's you, Bellona. Not any of the others."

"Melisande, don't talk about that now. Don't talk about anything. You must rest—"

"My rest will come soon enough," said Melisande with a sad smile. "I need to talk now. I have to talk, Bellona. I have to tell you the truth about the Mistress. You must find a way to warn our people, put an end to the monster who holds them in thrall."

Melisande began to tell the tale of that terrible night, starting with the rain falling and the voice that drove her from Bellona's bed, the call to come to the Mistress's chamber.

Bellona listened, at first skeptical, then amazed, then horrified. As Melisande went on, telling about Edward and how he had saved her from the dragon, Bellona saw again the vision that Lucretta had shown in the Eye—Melisande's face and the face of the man, and suddenly she saw them clearly, not through a cloud of jealous rage. Their expressions were not of joy, as of lovers meeting, but fear, as of two terrified people coming together to flee certain death.

She saw again the image of the dragon, hovering about Grald, and from that moment, Bellona began to believe. Her belief strengthened as Melisande told her what she had learned about the male babies, stolen away, sent into slavery. Bellona remembered the wagon and the bit of cloth she'd found in it, swaddling cloth. She remembered Lucretta, the change in the woman, the unaccountable change . . .

Melisande finished her story. She did not speak of Edward or their day of rapture. She did not speak of the twilight of pain and blood. Night deepened around her and around Bellona. No wind blew to rustle the trees. No animal stirred. The river flowed quietly past them, seemed to have forgotten how to sing. Or perhaps it was eavesdropping, as was Draconas, gliding unseen among the clouds, high above.

"You must think I'm mad," said Melisande at last.

"I did, at first, when you started telling about the dragon," Bellona admitted. "But I don't think that now."

Reaching into her belt, she fished out the piece of cloth she had put there. "I found this in the wagon. I saved it. I don't know why. I think I meant to ask Lucretta—" She broke off, shook her head. "Poor Lucretta. I never liked her. But she didn't deserve that."

"You have to go back," said Melisande, her grip on Bellona's hand tightening. "Promise me you will find a way to free Lucretta from the living death she is forced to endure. Promise me you will free our people from the dragon."

"We will go back to Seth together, Melis. We will destroy this monster together."

Melisande closed her eyes, shook her head.

Bellona was frightened. It was not like Melisande to give up.

"This is my fault, Melisande," said Bellona, faltering. "If I had loved you as I should have loved you, I would have had faith in you. I would have realized that even if you had found another lover, you would have never abandoned your responsibilities. When Lucretta showed me the two of you together, I knew there was something wrong, but I didn't question it. I saw what I wanted to see. If anyone pleads for forgiveness, it should be me."

She bent down, kissed Melisande tenderly.

"Forgive me for my lack of faith." Bellona hesitated, then steeled herself. "Do you want me to go look for the king or that Draconas?"

"No," said Melisande. "They are both dead. I am certain of it. They died trying to save me, Bellona. I heard Edward cry out and then . . . then . . ."

Melisande slid her arms around Bellona's neck and clung to her. She wanted to tell Bellona about the rape, about the agonizing pain, and the horrifying image of the dragon, squatting over her. She couldn't. Speaking of it would make it all the more real.

"Do you know where his kingdom is?" Bellona asked gently.

Melisande nodded. "South of here. Down the river somewhere."

"We will travel there and tell his people where to find the bodies."

"I love you, Bellona," Melisande whispered. "I will always love you. I hope you can forgive me."

"If you forgive me, our sins will cancel each other out," said Bellona. "And now let us leave this place of sorrow."

Lifting Melisande in her arms, Bellona carried her to the boat. She wrapped her in a blanket, gave her cool water to drink, bathed her maltreated face and hands, and waited patiently beside her until she sank at last into a deep, exhausted sleep.

Though weary herself, Bellona pushed the boat out into the river, climbed inside, and, guided by the moonlight, glided down the silver-tipped river.

Draconas should have stopped them. He should have swooped down, frightened the wits out of the female warrior, seized Melisande, and carried her away to Anora, as he'd been ordered to do.

He disobeyed. He allowed the boat to sail away. He did not follow it, nor did he watch to see where it went. He let it glide into the darkness and disappear.

He would be in trouble over this. He'd bungled it, he admitted that. What was the worst Anora could do? Take his "humanity" away from him? Draconas growled deep in his throat. She could have it.

Draconas sought to find any hint that Grald was still lurking about. He detected nothing of him. Grald had not made away with the prize, but he'd done what he set out to do. Draconas was sure of that.

Which left only Edward. Draconas floated down through the darkness. He did not doubt that Edward was dead. He would retrieve the body, take it back to Ermintrude. He'd have to concoct some story, of course, but that would be easy. He would tell the tale of how Edward had fought the dragon that had plagued his kingdom, how he'd gone up against the beast and how, though mortally wounded, he'd slain it.

Ermintrude would grieve, but she would be proud. Her sons would grow up idolizing their father. Edward would probably be canonized a saint, like that other supposed dragon-slayer. Not the best outcome, but not the worst, either.

Draconas landed on the beach. He let go of the dragon form with a sigh, felt it drift out of him as the soul drifts out of the body upon death, leaving only heavy, lifeless flesh and bone. It would take him time to once more adjust to his human body, to get used to feeling cramped, confined, and earthbound. He took a few tottering steps and nearly fell over Edward.

The king lay facedown on the beach, his hand over the hilt of his sword as if he'd made a desperate effort to retrieve it. Draconas couldn't understand how he could have missed seeing him, except that he'd been preoccupied with watching Bellona and Melisande.

"It only goes to show what happens when you let yourself get involved," he muttered.

Draconas rolled the king over onto his back, to make certain he was dead.

Edward groaned and opened one eye. The other was swollen shut. His face was a mess of blood and crushed bone.

"Melisande?" he whispered.

Draconas shook his head.

Edward made a moaning sound. His eyes closed. He fell back, unconscious.

Draconas smiled, relieved to have found the king alive, though he knew he shouldn't be. Edward dead was a saint. Edward alive seriously complicated matters. The devil take it. They'd sort this out together.

Draconas bloodied himself up, concocted his own story, then tended to the wounded king.

Draconas built a roaring fire to warm him. Building a fire was risky, for there was the possibility that Grald was still about, but Draconas guessed that Grald would not linger in this location. He would not chance a second meeting.

Despite Draconas's healing ministrations, Edward spent a restless night. He gabbled and writhed in his sleep, muttering to himself and once woke with a wild cry, staring at Draconas with terror-filled eyes. Draconas soothed him. Edward looked about in dream-drugged bewilderment, then sank back down into his tormented sleep. Finally, in the early hours of the morning, Draconas was gratified to see Edward relax and sink into deep and restful sleep.

Edward woke around noontime. He stared around blearily, then memory returned. Thrusting aside Draconas's restraining hand, he staggered to his feet. "Melisande! Where is she? I have to find her!"

"You're in no shape to find anyone," Draconas admonished. "Besides, she's gone."

Edward blanched. "Not . . . not dead . . ."

Draconas shook his head. "She's alive and safe. I'll tell you what happened, if you'll sit down. I spent the night saving your life and I don't want all my effort to go to waste."

"She's not dead," Edward repeated. "You're not just saying that. I saw . . . I saw blood . . ."

"She's not dead. The warrior woman followed us. She found Melisande and took her away in her boat."

Edward stared, appalled. "*She* took her! The one who shot arrows at her! We have to go after them. She'll kill her!"

"No, she won't," said Draconas. "Are you going to sit down?"

Edward hesitated, staring out at the sun-dappled river that had taken her away. Dejectedly, he slumped back down.

"So this warrior found her. Why are you so sure she won't kill her?"

"Because she saved her life. Grald—"

"Grald!" Edward was perplexed. "That brute we saw in the dragon's cave? The one who stole the babies? What does he have to do with this?"

"Don't you remember?"

"I don't remember anything," Edward said bitterly. "I heard footsteps crashing through the trees. I thought it was you and . . ." He paused, grimacing, trying to think. He winced with the pain. "Nothing. The next thing I knew, I woke up to darkness and burning pain in my head. I called out to Melisande, but she didn't answer."

"Grald attacked you," said Draconas. "He meant to kill you. You're lucky he didn't."

"Melisande . . . You said she wasn't dead. Did Grald? . . . Oh, God, did he . . ." Edward couldn't say the words.

"I don't know," Draconas said somberly. "I think so."

"But how did he find her? How did he know about her? Unless the dragon told him . . ."

Draconas nodded sagely. "That's my guess."

"Oh, God!" Edward cried. He clasped his head in his hands. "I knew something terrible had happened to her. I found her chemise torn and stained with blood . . . I knew then . . . I guessed."

He lifted his face, tear-streaked yet hard-set, resolved. "Grald. It was him? You are certain?"

"I saw him. He came out of the forest carrying Melisande in his arms. The warrior woman attacked him. He dropped Melisande and took to his heels."

"What were you doing all this time?" Edward demanded angrily. "Enjoying the show?"

"I was shoving the broken ends of bone back under the skin," Draconas returned, raising his arm, which he'd wrapped in a crude sling. "And vomiting up river water. I ran into Grald myself."

"How did you run into Grald?"

"He set a trap for me in that cavern and I walked right into it, witless as a newborn babe."

"Melisande said the place had a bad feel about it," Edward said softly.

"I should have listened to her," said Draconas.

Edward eyed him. "I have a lot of questions. At least I think I do. My head hurts so, it's hard to think. How did he find us?"

"We were careless," said Draconas bluntly. "We built a fire last night, left the boat in plain sight, for anyone to see, not to mention blankets strewn about the beach. Once he found our camp, he had only to follow our trail."

Edward frowned, puzzled this through. "But if he was after her, why set a trap for you?"

"It wasn't for me," Draconas said. "It was for her, for Melisande. He hoped to lure her into the cavern. He didn't expect me and he was not pleased to see me, I can tell you." Draconas grimaced. "When he thought he'd taken care of me, he came looking for her."

Edward mulled this over. "That makes sense," he admitted. He cast Draconas a glance, gave a rueful smile. "I'm sorry I suspected you."

He was silent long moments, his face drawn with pain. "Did Melisande go with that warrior woman willingly?" he asked, not looking at Draconas.

"She went willingly."

Edward started to say something, then closed his lips on the words. He stared bleakly at the river.

"She thought you were dead, Edward," Draconas said in answer to that unspoken, heartbroken question. "She told Bellona how you fought Grald in her defense. Melisande honors you for that."

"I pray I meet that Grald someday," said Edward.

"I pray for that, too," Draconas agreed. "And I'm not a praying man."

The two were silent; Edward gazing at the river, Draconas waiting for what must come next.

"I don't know what got into me," Edward said at last. "I should have never touched her. She was so beautiful and the sun was so warm and it seemed that there were only the two of us in a world that had been made with us in mind . . ."

"You are human," said Draconas.

Edward sighed. Resting his arms on his knees, he let his head slump forward. "Meaning I'm weak."

"No," said Draconas. "Meaning that she was beautiful and the sun was warm and there were only the two of you in the world."

Edward lifted his head, smiled wanly. "Well, no matter. It's over and done with and she is gone and I have failed. I have failed everyone who ever trusted in me. I failed Melisande. I failed my people—that cursed dragon will still be there when I return. I failed my wife. Poor Ermintrude. How can I ever look at her again?"

Draconas could have answered that Edward had not failed on at least one score. He would return home to find that the evil dragon was no longer a threat. Draconas wasn't supposed to know that, though, and so he kept silent. There was nothing he could say to comfort the king. He waited for what was to come and in the next moment, it came.

"There's one person I won't fail," Edward said.

"Let it go, Edward," Draconas told him.

"You don't know what I mean—"

"Yes, I do. Let it go. It won't help either of you. It will just cause more sorrow—for you and for her."

Edward slowly shook his head. "No, I can't let it go. If she is with child, then the child is mine and I must—"

"The child might not be yours," said Draconas brutally. "Not if Grald—"

Edward rose unsteadily to his feet. Fists clenched, hazel eyes ablaze, he stared down at Draconas.

"Do you think that matters to me? If you truly believe that I am the type of man who would take my pleasure and abandon her, then I will meet you on the field of honor to settle this any way you want."

"No, I don't think you're that kind of man," Draconas said, adding inwardly, I wish you were.

Edward wavered, but he remained standing.

"You have to find her. You're the only one I can send. The only one she would trust. I don't want anything from her. You can assure her of that. If she is with child, I want to take care of her and the baby. That's all. Whatever I can do for them. Will you find her and tell her that, Draconas?"

You should have died, Draconas said to him silently. The time will come when you're going to wish you had. But if you're willing to accept your responsibility in this, then I guess I'm willing to accept mine.

"I'll do what I can," said Draconas, adding in warning tones, "but it won't be easy."

On you, or any of us.

28

THE RIVER BORE EDWARD HOME TO HIS WIFE, HIS kingdom, and a hero's lauding. He was bewildered and perplexed by this, but it appeared that the dragon had not been sighted in a fortnight and the people gave their king the credit for driving off the beast. Edward tried to protest that he'd had nothing to do with it, but, as Gunderson told him, the people needed a hero and it was right and proper that they look for that in their ruler.

So Edward kept silent and received graciously the accolades he knew in his heart he had not earned, no matter what Gunderson might tell him to the contrary. Edward talked little about his adventures, much to the bitter disappointment of his young sons, who wanted to hear all the gruesome details—how the dragon had roared when their father had cut off its head and how much blood there had been. Edward told them gently that he did not want to speak of it and their mother told them sharply to leave their father alone.

This his sons did, mainly because their father had developed a disconcerting habit of hugging them close every time he saw them. They bore this as long as they could,

then Wilhelm took his father aside one day to tell him
that the stable boys were snickering at him, calling him
"a baby" and would his father please be less demonstra-
tive of his affection in public.

Edward, smiling fondly, promised he would and was
true to his word, settling after that for a manly clap on
the back.

Edward told the truth of what had happened only to
Gunderson, who listened in wondering amazement. He
said little, but he pressed his king's hand with deep affection and pitied him from the depths of his heart. He
agreed that Edward had done the right thing in asking
Draconas to seek out the woman.

Edward did not tell Ermintrude the truth. He had been
going to, prepared to unburden himself, but Gunderson
earnestly counseled otherwise. Was it right to inflict pain
on his wife, just to relieve his own guilty conscience? Far
better to suffer his guilt alone and in silence than to burden her. Edward saw the wisdom of this, though his silence only added weight to the burden, for he and
Ermintrude had always agreed that there would be no secrets between them.

Ermintrude knew something had happened to change
her husband, and her wife's heart suspected the truth. He
had sometimes been brusque with people, especially pe-
titioners. Now he was kinder, more understanding, listened to their problems with exemplary patience. He
abandoned his scientific studies, gave away his astrolabe
and his books and star charts, filled his office with texts
on kingship and statecraft, on law and governing. He
laughed less frequently, and she often caught him standing
at the window, staring out at the river with a sad and
wistful expression.

He was kinder to her, much more gentle and tender.
Though he avoided her bed, he would oftentimes hold her
close, seeming to need her arms around him, and it was
in these moments that she felt very much that he wanted
to tell her what had happened to cast a shadow over his

life, but that he could not bring himself to do so, for fear it would hurt her.

She wanted to tell him, in these moments, that whatever he had done, she was his wife and she loved him and would forgive him. Instinct—the same instinct that woke her in the night and led her to the bed of a sick child—held her back. In his own time, his own way, he would tell her. Until then, she must bide her time and be patient and go on loving him and showing him that she did.

Several months passed thus.

The river carried autumn's dead leaves upon its bosom, ran dark through winter snows. When the snows melted and the river swelled with the spring runoff, when the crocus and the squill bloomed, Edward grew restless, ill-at-ease. He seemed to be waiting for someone or something, for every time he heard a horse's hooves clattering in the courtyard, he hastened to the window, looked out expectantly.

Gunderson knew Edward was waiting for Draconas. Ermintrude guessed it.

Gunderson had not liked what he'd heard of Draconas's part in their adventures. He found many of Draconas's actions deeply suspect and he bluntly told His Majesty so. Edward admitted that he had doubts about Draconas himself, but there was no one else on whom he could rely. Gunderson would have dearly loved to tell his king to forget this woman, forget the dalliance and its possible outcome. Men fathered bastards every day and thought no more of it than the barnyard cat. Edward had not been raised to think like that, however, and Gunderson was proud of him for behaving thus honorably, even though at night, in private, Gunderson prayed to God that the woman would never be found.

Ermintrude prayed simply that whatever was going to happen would happen, as one prays on a hot and sultry day that the storm will break and bring relief.

Edward gave Gunderson orders that Draconas was to be brought to him immediately, no matter if it were day or night. Edward had just concluded hosting a banquet for his father-in-law, the king of Weinmauer, who came ostensibly to pay homage to his son for his heroics. In reality Weinmauer nosed about, whispered in the ears of several border lords and made vague promises, hoping to persuade them to shift allegiance. One and all, they held true their king, however, and Weinmauer would eventually leave disappointed.

The guests had departed. Those sober enough to walk on their own had stumbled off to their beds. Those who needed assistance had been hauled away by the servants. Edward and Ermintrude had retired to their family quarters, but they had not yet gone to bed. They sat before the fire, laughing over her father's discomfiture, for their spies had brought them all the details of his failed intrigue. Ermintrude was mulling spiced wine, when Gunderson came to the door, summoned Edward with a look.

"Excuse me, my dear," said Edward, turning to her, as she stood holding the warm mug in her hand, her smile tremulous on her lips. "Pressing business calls me away. Do not wait up for me."

He left before she could say a word. She sat down in her chair and gazed at the fire, watching the flames devour the wood, the logs crumble and dwindle and blacken.

Edward and Gunderson hastened out into the courtyard. The night was still chill, but there was a smell of spring in the air. They went to the stable, where Gunderson had stashed the visitor. He lit a lantern, flashed it about to make sure no one else was around.

"We're alone," he reported.

"Draconas?" Edward called into the darkness, into the smell of hay and horses.

Draconas stepped out of the shadows. He looked the same as he had always looked. Edward did not.

"Has Your Majesty been ill?" Draconas asked.

"Just anxious," said Edward, passing it off quickly. "What news, Draconas? Have you found her?"

"I have," said Draconas with equanimity.

"Is she . . ."

"She is," said Draconas.

"I knew it," said Edward softly. "Somehow I knew it. Is she safe? Well?"

Draconas nodded yes to all, though in that he was lying.

"You gave her the money?"

"She would not take it," said Draconas, and handed back the money pouch.

Edward absently stroked the leather with his hands. He sighed. "I hoped she might, but I didn't think she would."

His heart cried out to ask Draconas where she was, but he had promised he would not and he kept that promise.

He could not help but question wistfully, "Did she say anything about me? Send any message? Is there nothing I can do for her, Draconas, maybe without her knowing?"

Draconas did not immediately answer. His gaze shifted to Gunderson, standing silent in the darkness. Gunderson saw in the man's eyes what he was about to say and Draconas saw in Gunderson's eyes the asking not to say it.

Draconas ignored him. He had spent a most unpleasant several days in the presence of an extremely angry Anora, who had, as he had anticipated, threatened him with the loss of his ability to walk among humans unless he ceased what she termed his "regrettably weak and sentimental human behavior" in regard to Melisande.

He might well have ignored that, for much as he admired and respected Anora, she could never understand what it was like to live in two bodies, in two different worlds. Something else had happened, however, something that had hardened Draconas's heart to all humans and their little problems.

Braun was dead.

As with his father, the death had been made to look like an accident. The young dragon's gleaming-scaled body had been discovered lying in a field, his neck broken. Charred and burned patches on his body seemed to indicate that he'd been struck by lightning, as sometimes happened if dragons were caught in thunderstorms. The Parliament brought in a verdict of accidental death. Draconas knew better, and so did Anora.

Draconas had told Braun, right before his death, that he had found Melisande and he'd told Braun where she was hiding, so that the dragon could help guard her. All that information would have been plainly visible in Braun's mind, visible to his killer.

"Melisande wants only one thing from you, Your Majesty," said Draconas.

"Anything," said Edward earnestly, clasping the leather bag in his hands.

"She wants you to take her baby and raise him in your household."

"I will," said Edward at once.

"Your Majesty," Gunderson remonstrated, "please consider—"

"No, my friend. I must do this," Edward said in a tone that brooked no contraction.

"You do not need to claim the child," Gunderson persisted. "I know of a respectable peasant family who—"

Edward cut him off with a gesture. "What are the arrangements, Draconas?"

"Someone will come to fetch you or whomever you send"—Draconas glanced at Gunderson—"and take you to the baby. You will ask no questions. You will take the child and make no attempt to find Melisande. Ever."

Edward hesitated. Draconas eyed him.

"Agreed," said Edward at last, reluctantly.

Draconas pulled on a pair of leather gloves, picked up his staff.

"You will stay the night, of course, Draconas," said Edward belatedly. "I would give you a room in the castle, but my father-in-law is visiting and there would be the need for explantions—"

"Thank you, but I cannot stay," Draconas said brusquely. "It was difficult for me to get away this long, but I wanted to prepare you."

Since Braun's death, he had not let Melisande out of his sight. As for bringing the child into Edward's family, Draconas had persuaded Anora to this course of action. The one piece of information that Grald had not ripped from Draconas's mind was Edward: who he was, where he came from. Grald had not been interested in that, nor was the dragon interested in Edward now. Why should he? Grald believed that he had slain the lover.

Anora had still wanted to keep the child and the mother as prisoners, for their own safety, of course. Braun's murder had convinced her otherwise. Anora herself was in danger, for she knew too much, and there was no reason to think that she could protect the mother and the child. She might actually bring harm to them, for Grald and Maristara had seen that very plan in Draconas's mind and in Braun's.

Stashing the child in a royal human household, where he could be guarded by royal bodyguards, was the best possible solution. Draconas would have access to him as he grew, and he would be the only one. Not even Anora would know where the child was hidden.

"One other caveat, Your Majesty," said Draconas, as he reached the stable door. "You can never tell anyone the circumstances of this child's birth or its parentage. That includes the child himself."

"But if it is a boy and he favors me, people will know—"

"People may guess, but they will not know. Since you are the king, they will keep their guesses to themselves. This is for the child's own sake. Consider who might be searching for him."

"Gunderson already knows the truth," said Edward. "And I must tell Ermintrude. It's only fair. She will be the child's mother."

Draconas was frowningly dubious.

"I think she suspects anyhow," Edward added with a half-smile. "I'm not a very good dissembler."

"I am against it, but what you do in your marriage is

your own business," said Draconas with an ungracious shrug. "The child's safety is paramount. If any hint ever arose—"

"It will not," said Edward firmly.

"You will be hearing from me," Draconas promised, and he walked out the door and disappeared into the night.

Edward returned to his chambers. Ermintrude rose to meet him. At the sight of his face, so pale and troubled and care-worn, she went up to him and took his hands and folded them in her own, pressed them to her lips.

"My dear," he said softly, "could you love a child that is mine, but not yours?"

"Is that what all this has been about?" she asked him, her tone mild and gently rebuking. "Is that why you have quit eating and prowl about in the foul airs of the night? All for that?"

"I have no right to seek your forgiveness, but the child is blameless and the mother asks that I take him—"

"My own," Ermintrude interrupted, "you are not the first husband to stray, nor will you be the last. A child should be raised in the father's house. Bring the babe and I will love him or her as dearly as our Wilhelm and our Harry."

Edward could not speak, his heart was too full. He held her close and felt his great burden of shame and guilt drop off of him. He came to her bed that night and, though they did not make love, they held each other and talked all through the night until, his remorse eased, he fell peacefully asleep, his head on her bosom.

Ermintrude lay awake, staring into the gray morning and when he could not see them, the tears streamed silently down her cheeks.

The wound he'd inflicted on her bled freely, but that was good, for it meant that it would not turn poisonous.

29

IF EDWARD HAD KNOWN, HE COULD HAVE WALKED to Melisande's house, for she was living near Bramfell, in a small village known as Sheepcote, so named because its inhabitants worked with either sheep or their by-products. The village was a collection of small, snug stone houses built by the owner of the local factory where weavers assembled to turn the wool into cloth. The factory was a relatively new innovation. By custom, weavers had worked out of their homes, but that meant that the wool had to be hauled to the individual houses, which were scattered all over the countryside, and the finished goods brought back to the warehouses. Collecting the weavers together in one location saved both time and money and it allowed the weavers the pleasure of socializing as they worked.

When Melisande had discovered she was pregnant, she had insisted that they travel to Idlyswylde.

"I will not be able to care for the babe," she said to Bellona. "A son should grow up in his father's house."

Bellona had argued, but not for very long or very hard. Melisande had never truly recovered from her ordeal. Her body mended, for she was young and strong, but her spirit was shattered, like a blooming rose struck by an early, killing frost. Her pregnancy was difficult. She was constantly sick, could keep nothing down. The midwife said comfortably that this was normal in the first three months and, though it was not quite so normal in the months following, she had known such cases and the women had all delivered fine, healthy babes.

Bellona doubted, though she said nothing. She watched Melisande grow bigger and weaker every day, as though the babe was sucking the very life out of her, and fear gripped her.

When they first arrived in Sheepcote, Melisande took a job in the factory as a weaver. As her pregnancy started to become obvious, she had to remain at home, for it wasn't considered seemly for a woman in her condition to be out working. She had a talent for embroidery and fine stitchery, however, and the factory owner, quick to notice this, found her seamstress work among the nobility and the well-to-do of the upper-middle class of Bromfell.

In between her work, she wove a blanket for her baby and it was during this time, as she plied her loom, that she was happiest, often singing softly to herself, a song about springtime.

Bellona masqueraded as Melisande's husband, a role she preferred, for she had seen how women were treated in this society—as chattel and property. She adopted men's clothing and, due to her musculature and superb physical condition, she easily passed for a handsome, clean-shaven young man. She could not stand sheep, however, nor anything connected with them. Her skills as an archer won her a position as a forester, for the king had some fine hunting grounds located nearby, and her job was to see that no one poached the royal deer. Roaming the forests meant that she was often away from home, away from Melisande, but they needed the money to get them through the hard winter and Melisande assured her that she did not mind being by herself.

The two of them were closer than they had ever been before, for now they had only each other to love and think of. They were everything to each other, spent time only with each other, shunning their neighbors. But there was a difference in Melisande's love and Bellona felt it. A curtain, finespun as cobweb, transparent as sorrow, and ephemeral as happiness, had fallen between them. Not even fond affection could draw that dark curtain aside.

Melisande had one other abiding passion. She was determined to return to Seth, to tell the people the truth about the Mistress. This determination kept her going through the sickness, the weariness, the pain, and the fear. She and Bellona made plans, spoke every evening of what they would do when Melisande was recovered and able to travel.

The villagers left the young couple alone, though the wise women would often look askance at Melisande on those rare days when she ventured out of her house and whisper about how ill she looked. Gifts of venison would often appear on their doorstoop or someone would stop by with a broth to tempt "the dear thing to eat a mite."

Only one person was able to befriend the two and he was such an oddity that this strange friendship didn't seem to count as such. The cottage next door came up for lease quite suddenly, its owners moving out unexpectedly. This man moved in. Middle-aged, dark-eyed, with a full black beard and long, graying black hair, he kept to himself, said nothing to anyone, and made it plain that he wanted to be strictly left alone. He became known as the Hermit.

The Hermit did not go out to work. No one knew how he made his living or what he did all day. Bellona was distrustful of him, for she sometimes caught glimpses of him staring fixedly at their cottage. She warned Melisande to be wary of him and Melisande was wary, at first. Then came the day when she was alone and she needed water from the village pump. She was struggling to fill the heavy bucket, when a strong hand took it from her. The Hermit said nothing to her. He pumped the water, carried it back to her house for her, and left, ignoring her thanks.

After that, if she needed water or wood chopped or the fire lighted or any small task done, he would instinctively know and show up to do it. He never spoke. He refused all attempts at payment. When she tried to thank him by leaving a loaf of fresh baked bread on his windowsill, the bread remained there untouched until one of the local dogs carried it off. The villagers popularly believed that he was mute, and the rumor went about that his tongue had been torn out as a punishment for blasphemy.

No one liked the Hermit or trusted him except Melisande.

"There is something in his eyes when he looks at me," she told Bellona, "as if he understands and is sorry."

"We don't need anyone's pity," returned Bellona, bristling.

"It's not that," Melisande replied softly. "I can't explain it. It's as if he knows . . ."

Bellona looked at her sharply. "You didn't say anything to him?"

"No, of course not."

"Maybe that servant said something. The king's servant. The one who tried to give us money. I'm glad you sent him packing. We want nothing from that man."

Bellona talked on and on. Melisande didn't respond. She found comfort in the sound of the beloved voice, though she often did not hear what Bellona said. She knew this hurt Bellona sometimes. Melisande could see the hurt in her eyes and she was sorry to have caused it, but she was helpless to stop. She heard only one voice— the voice of fear. It drowned out all others.

Putting down her needle, she leaned back in the chair and closed her eyes, sighing deeply. She was in her ninth month, her belly huge and distended, so that she could not stand without help. She could not sleep for the discomfort. The only relief she found was to lie propped up against Bellona, who would gently massage her back and rub her swollen feet. What food Melisande ate all seemed to go to the baby, for she grew thinner as the child grew larger.

She could take no pleasure in the child, for whenever she felt its life stir within her, she knew only terror. She hoped the baby would be the king's, but she could not know for sure. She would not know until the birthing, and she wished desperately her time would come and bring release.

"Even the pain of childbirth will be welcome," she said softly, placing her hand on her swollen belly, "for it will be so much easier to bear than not knowing."

Babies take after their fathers, so the midwife told her: Thus does nature insure that the father will acknowledge the child. Melisande held two faces in her heart—one face handsome and smiling, with hazel eyes that glinted gold in the sunlight; the other face hard and brutal, its eyes empty of all save cruel lust.

One look at the babe's face and she would know and she would pick up the remnants of her life, stitch them together, and go on.

That midmorning in the spring when the new leaves were tiny buds on the trees, the pains came. Melisande sank down on the floor and wept for joy.

Bellona was not with her that morning. She had not wanted to leave Melisande at this late stage in her pregnancy, but Melisande had persuaded her to go to her work.

"If truth be told, you fidget me beyond endurance when you're here," Melisande said to her, smiling. "You pace about like a wild beast and look out the window and fuss with the fire, so that I'm either half-frozen or broiled like a chicken. You spoil my work by trying to help and I'm certain that you are the cause of the bread refusing to rise."

Bellona gave her such a hurt look that Melisande laughed, the first laughter Bellona had heard from her in many months.

"I'm teasing, beloved," Melisande said, nestling in her lover's strong arms.

"No, you're not," Bellona retorted. "At least, under-neath you are not. Very well, I will go, but I will have the midwife check on you."

"Really, I feel so much better today . . ."

"That's because the baby has dropped," Bellona said, with an air of wise experience, "which means your time will be soon."

"Pray God for that," Melisande whispered, squeezing her lover's hand. "Pray God."

"Are you sure you want me to go?" Bellona asked at the door.

Melisande nodded.

Bellona had not been gone long when the pains began.

The royal forest preserve was located about five miles from the village. The walk was a pleasant one, over hills white with sheep and green with grass, alive with the sounds of tinkling bells, the shepherd's call, and barking dogs. Beyond was the forest, its darker green encompass-ing the grassy green, its shadows enfolding and smoothing away the bleating of the sheep and all other sounds of the outside world.

The moment Bellona entered the wilderness that morn-ing, treading lightly on the path the foresters had worn smooth over years of guardianship, she sensed that all was not right.

Born and raised in the monastery, which was, to all intents, a small, self-contained city, Bellona had only rarely been exposed to the wilderness and that only on hunting expeditions and training exercises. What she had seen of the wilderness, she hadn't much liked. Accus-tomed to order and discipline and control, Bellona found to her intense frustration that nature deplored order, fos-tered chaos, and lived by her own rules.

The more time she spent alone among the gigantic trees, which cared nothing for her, but lived their secret lives aloof, Bellona came to realize that there was order and discipline in nature, albeit not her kind. Everything in nature lived to die and died to live. That was the order, that was the discipline. Man fit into that order, but he alone was different. He fought to escape it, to avoid it. Nature might struggle briefly, as the rabbit struggled in the teeth of the fox, but the struggle was instinctive and, in the end, accepted its fate: The rabbit does not hunt the fox to prevent its death, nor does the fox hunt the lion.

At first, this order seemed so cruel and uncaring that it terrified Bellona, as nothing else had ever frightened the stalwart warrior. But as she lived with it daily, she came to find it peaceful and soothing as the silence and the deep shadows. To know that this was order everlasting was to know God.

Stepping inside the forest that morning, Bellona sensed that God had been disturbed.

She heard it first in the silence, which was too silent. No squirrels played at games in the trees, leaping from branch to branch with a childlike sense of fun. No deer started at the sight of her and dashed off, their white tails flashing the warning of her presence. No wolf trotted across her path, keeping an eye on her, but not really minding her, absorbed in his own affairs. The animals had gone to ground.

"Poachers," thought Bellona and she drew her bow and nocked an arrow.

She had come to feel protective of this wilderness and the thought of poachers snaring her rabbits and slaying her deer angered her.

She moved deeper into the woods, watching and listening. Her vigilance was rewarded. She heard voices. She was startled by this, for the voices were not hushed or whispering, as might be expected from outlaws. They were raised in normal tones. Perhaps the king or some of his noble friends had come hunting unannounced.

She crept forward and, as she drew closer, she could hear the voices more clearly. The voices were those of women.

Truth flashed upon her in an instant. Bellona knew immediately that the warrior women of Seth had found them.

She knew because she had long expected and feared it.

Panicked instinct urged her to race back immediately to protect Melisande. Cooler logic suggested that she had time to see for herself what she was up against. Strangers of any sort were rare in the village. Accustomed to defending themselves from raiders after their sheep or bears after their food, the villagers were suspicious of anyone they did not know. They fought with crude weapons and were not trained to a soldier's standards, but they could hold their own. They would not let any armed soldiers enter their town without putting up a fight.

Bellona crept closer, moving with the stealthy care she had learned from the fox and the rabbit. She placed herself in a position to see and hear, without being seen or heard.

The first woman she saw was Nzangia.

Nzangia had twelve warriors with her. They wore huntsmen's garb to avoid attracting attention, disguising themselves as men, as Bellona had done. They had not come to do battle, for they wore no chain or plate armor, carried no shield or spear. Their helms were of leather, not steel. They were armed with bows and arrows and small short swords, as would any hunter. This was to be a stealthy operation, most likely carried out after nightfall.

"You have spied out the house?" Nzangia asked.

"We have, Commander," said one. "It is on the outskirts of the village. Several other houses are nearby and they are inhabited—"

"They will not interfere," said Nzangia. "They will be otherwise engaged. Drusilla, you take—"

Bellona waited to hear no more. If she returned to Melisande now, she would have time to take her to a place of safety, then she would return and bring help. Running swiftly, she raced back to the village.

If she had stayed one more moment, she would have heard Nzangia add, "Remember, we want the baby. Our spy sent us word that the birthing has started. Our signal is the baby's cry . . ."

30

THE PAINS WERE NOT BAD NOW, BUT MELISANDE knew they would grow worse. She'd heard the screams of a young neighbor woman who had recently given birth and she understood what she faced. She was not afraid now, however. She felt strangely exhilarated. The end was near, in sight.

Crouching on the floor, she gripped the arms of a heavy chair and managed to pull herself to her feet. She would have time before the pain came again to summon the midwife. She started toward the door, thinking she might call out to some of the children, who were always playing about the yard, when another pain hit. This was so much sharper, a red-hot wave, running up her back, that she staggered and gasped, crying out.

A shadow fell over her. The Hermit stood in the doorway.

She opened her mouth to tell him, but the Hermit came to her and took hold of her, led her back to the chair, and seated her.

"I will go for the midwife," he said and departed.

She stared after him, troubled and amazed. Those were

the first words she had ever heard him speak and there seemed something familiar about his voice. She tried to think, but the pain was too severe and she was worried that it should be this bad this soon. She sank back in the chair and panted for breath.

Bellona reached the cottage to find the Hermit leaning against the wall, his head down, his hands jammed into the pockets of his breeches. He raised his head as she approached, and regarded her with a dark and penetrating stare.

At the sight of her face, he took his hands out of his pockets, straightened.

"What is it?" he asked urgently. "What's wrong?"

Bellona ignored him, started to brush past him. He put out his arm, as though to try to halt her. She glared at him and he let his arm fall.

Inside, Melisande screamed in pain.

Bellona stood frozen, paralyzed by the sound. Her heart in her mouth, she thrust open the closed door.

The cottage consisted of a single room with few furnishings—a table and two stools, a large chair for Melisande, her loom, and a bed in the warmest corner, near the fireplace.

The midwife bent over the bed on which Melisande lay writhing in agony and moaning.

"Melisande!" Bellona cried, kicking over one of the stools in her haste to reach her.

The midwife raised her head, a scandalized expression on her face.

"What do you mean, Master, barging in like this? Men are not allowed in the birthing chamber. Get out! Get out!"

Flapping her apron as though she were shooing geese, the midwife clucked and snorted and shook her head.

Bellona stood staring at Melisande, who had ceased to scream. She lay on the sweat-soaked sheets, her face deathly pale, her eyes huge and glistening.

Bellona knew the answer to the question, but she had to ask, "Can she be moved?"

"Are you daft?" the midwife screeched. Seizing hold of Bellona, the midwife shoved her bodily out the door.

Bellona heard Nzangia's voice. *You have spied out the house.* She stood staring in the direction of the forest, gnawing her lip and wondering desperately what to do.

"Seth warriors," said the Hermit. "How many?"

Bellona at first ignored him, then the import of his words came to her and she turned to stare at him. His eyes were dark and shadowed. His face beneath the heavy beard had set in hard lines that deepened as his jaw tightened.

"I don't know what you're talking about," she began, thinking that she'd seen him somewhere.

"Yes, you do." He cast a glance to the north, to the mountains of Seth, whose snowcapped peaks were whitewashed on a blue backdrop. "And you're going to need help. How many of them are there? Ten? Twenty?"

"I counted twelve," she said, wondering, still trying to place him. "There may be more."

"Probably are. Where did you see them?"

"In the forest." Bellona stared at him, eyes narrowed. "Draconas!" she exclaimed suddenly. "The king's servant! You've been spying on us—"

"A good thing, too," Draconas interposed coolly. "The warriors will have to come through the fields to get at us and the shepherds will think they are raiders after the sheep. Go alert the villagers. Tell them you've seen raiders in the woods and they've got to mobilize the militia—"

His words were drowned out by a wild pealing of bells and the off-key blasting of a horn.

"Fire!" someone shouted. "Fire!"

Bellona and the Hermit turned in the direction of the frantic bellow to see a curl of smoke rise up into the morning sky.

"The mill's on fire!"

The call was caught up, handed from voice to voice, growing louder and more strident and more panicked. The smoke thickened to an ugly roiling gray shot through with orange flame.

"They've torched the mill," said Draconas.

"Nzangia said that the villagers wouldn't interfere with them," Bellona remembered.

"She was right," he replied grimly.

Fire, the nightmare terror of every community from tiny village to teeming city. If the fire spread from the mill it could burn down the factory, destroy every dwelling place, every shop, wipe out the entire village. In an instant the dreams, the hopes, and the very lives of the inhabitants could be reduced to ashes and charred rubble.

The villagers came running in answer to that terrified call, carrying buckets or axes or pitchforks, ready to douse the blaze and try to knock it down. All was a confusion of shouted orders, the whinnyings of frightened horses, and a crash, as of timber falling. The acrid smell of smoke wafted up the hill.

Inside the cottage, Melisande's screams grew more and more agonized. Bellona dug her nails into the palms of her hand.

"They're here after Melisande," she said hoarsely. "The Mistress sent them to kill her."

Draconas glanced at her, started to say something, then shut his mouth. Smoke from the burning mill was starting to layer over the hills, filling the valley and creeping up the slopes, where the sheep bleated in panic and the dogs barked frantically.

"She can't be moved. We'll have to hold them off here."

"We had best go inside," said Draconas. "Hide ourselves. Let them think they're taking us by surprise."

The cottages were constructed of stone with thatched roofs, each one identical to another. Each was built on a small strip of land, where the owner could grow a garden to eke out communal winter stores with vegetables of his own.

Most of the houses clustered near the factory and the mill, down by the river. As the community expanded, dwellings were added in a more random fashion, so that now they straggled along the dirt road known as Shepherd's Way. Their cottage had one small window, facing east to let in the sunlight, and a single door. The window had no glass panes, for glass was dear, but it did have wooden shutters that could be closed against the wind and weather. The shutters were usually open, for Melisande loved the fresh air. This day they were closed. The midwife wanted the cottage warm. She had built up the fire and it was now so hot that it was stifling.

A strip of garden separated their house from that of the Hermit's. Nothing grew in their garden, for Melisande was too ill to tend to it and Bellona knew little about plants. As she was wont to say, she had been taught only how to kill, not how to grow and nurture.

As Bellona started to enter the door, she paused, glanced uncertainly inside. "Melisande . . . what will I tell her?"

Draconas followed her anxious gaze. Melisande's terrible screams were coming more frequently, punctuated at intervals by almost equally terrible silences.

"I doubt she'll even be aware of what's happening," he answered. "You go on ahead. I'll join you."

He departed, hastening back to his own cottage. Bellona watched him leave and wondered if she trusted him or not. She decided that she didn't have much choice.

Back in his cottage, Draconas reached for his staff, then halted, irresolute, uncertain what to do. He knew the real reason the Mistress had sent her warriors here. They wanted Melisande dead. They wanted the baby alive.

He stared out the window, trying to catch sight of them, but the smoke obscured his view. More than ever he missed Braun, missed the dragon's eyes that would have apprised him of their approach, warned him ahead of time, so that he could have dealt with them. Now, it was almost too late.

As he saw it, he had one option.

"I could kill them. I could kill every one of them."

He'd broken the laws of his kind already, broken several, some on orders, others of his own volition. The one law, the one sacrosanct law of the Dragon Parliament, the supreme law, Draconas had not yet broken. He had never in six hundred years intentionally taken a human life. Accidently crushing that insane monk didn't count.

If he killed, Anora would have no choice but to take away his humanity. He might try to hide the deed from her, but she would see it in his mind, for he could never rid himself of the blood.

His hand smoothed the wood grain of the staff. Melisande's screams, imprisoned behind stone walls, were muffled.

He couldn't risk turning over this task to some other walker, someone who had no care for it. Draconas might lose Melisande, but he would not lose her child. He owed her that much.

Gripping the staff tightly, he left his house, headed for the cottage.

Trying to enter the door, Bellona discovered that it had been locked. She banged and beat on the door until it opened a crack and the midwife glared out.

Shoving her foot in the door, Bellona elbowed her way inside, pushing the protesting, sputtering old woman out of the way. She slammed shot the door and put her back to it.

"Raiders," she said, her taut voice slicing through the midwife's angry scoldings. "They've set the mill on fire. They're likely planning an attack on the village. They may come here and I can't defend the cottage from outside."

The midwife knew about raiders. Her face twisted in a grimace. "Murdering devils." She eyed Bellona disapprovingly. "I suppose you know what you're doing. Keep your eyes to yourself, though, and don't interfere with me."

"It's only right that I tell you that you may be in danger," Bellona said stiffly.

The midwife sniffed, turned away.

Melisande cried out, her body writhed.

"There, there, lambkin, nothing to worry about," the midwife said, wiping Melisande's forehead with a wet cloth. "Another push, my pet. Another push."

Melisande groaned and shook her head. Her face was wet with sweat, her hair soaked. The midwife had attached strips of rags to the bedposts, so that she had something to hold onto when the pains came. Her eyes were lusterless and sunken. She gazed at Bellona as at a stranger, unknowing, uncaring, wound round with the pain that was all she could see or hear or taste or feel. She arched her back and gripped the handholds and screamed.

Shuddering, Bellona closed her eyes. The screams ceased, mercifully. Melisande lay sucking in huge gulps of air. The midwife fussed around her. At least the old woman was taking this calmly, Bellona thought. But then, a midwife dealt with life and death on a day-to-day basis. Perhaps it got humdrum.

In the gasping silence, Bellona heard a tapping on the door.

"It's me," called Draconas.

Bellona hesitated a moment, then unbarred the door. He slid inside, carrying with him an oaken staff. He shut the door behind him, shot the bolt. The midwife glanced at him askance, but she was too busy to scold. Melisande's knees were drawn up, her skirts folded back over her bare legs. She stared unseeing at the ceiling, waiting in numb despair for the next agonizing moment.

Draconas looked at her and his lips tightened. He looked back to Bellona.

"You trained these soldiers. You were their commander. What's their plan?" he asked.

Bellona put herself in Nzangia's place. Nzangia was a good warrior and very imaginative. The torching of the mill as a diversion, to draw off any who might have helped them, had been inspired.

"They don't know that I saw them," Bellona said. "They'll charge the house. As you said, they'll want to take us by surprise."

She grabbed hold of him by the arm, gripped him hard, hurting. "How did they find us?"

"They went looking," he said.

She stared into his eyes, trying to see inside him and failing. Her gaze could not pierce the shadows.

"There's nothing I can say that will make you trust me, is there?" Draconas added.

"No," she returned caustically.

"So why waste time asking?"

She had no answer for that.

"Look at it this way. I'm in here with you, not out there with them. That must count for something."

Slowly, Bellona released her grip.

"Now that's settled," he said, turning away, "we better decide what we're going to do. The door opens inward. They'll rush it in a body. We'll take the bolt off."

"Why make it easy for them?"

"Because they won't expect it. I'll stand here." He took his place beside the door. "You stand there. When the door opens, they see you, not me. I'll do this." He gestured. "You do this." He gestured again.

She didn't like him, didn't trust him, didn't believe him. She was certain he had something to do with the soldiers tracking them down, though how or why was a puzzle. She didn't want their lives dependent on him, but she'd never fought in close quarters before and she'd certainly never had to defend a woman giving birth, the woman she loved better than life itself. Bellona couldn't trust her judgement, with those terrible screams tearing her apart inside. He'd devised a good plan. She could see where he was going with it.

"Is that all the weapon you've got?" she asked, disdainfully eyeing his staff.

"It's all the weapon I need," he returned, taking his position.

"But you should at least have a dagger." She reached into her belt. "Here. You can't kill with that—"

"I'm not planning on killing. Only stopping. It's a vow I took," he added.

"Some sort of religious vow?"

"Some sort," he replied.

She gestured outside. "They didn't take any such vow. They'll be trying to kill you."

"Most likely." He cocked his head, listening. "They're out there. I can hear them. Be ready. Keep them focused on you. Hold their attention."

Bellona gnawed her lip, gripped her sword, and waited.

The cottage was stifling. The midwife had built up a great roaring blaze in the fireplace. Bellona wiped sweat from her brow with the back of her hand. The air stank of sweat and blood and smoke. She began to feel stifled, closed in. The enemy was out there, creeping closer and closer. She hated waiting, hated the tension. She longed to fling open the door, confront them face-to-face, and it cost her an effort to control the impulse.

Melisande gave a shuddering scream. This time, the scream did not stop, but trailed into an agonized wail. Bellona risked a glance backward.

"Can't you do something for her?" she cried angrily.

"Push, lamb," ordered the midwife sternly, paying no attention to any of them. "I can see the crown. Push!"

Bellona shivered, the sweat chill on her body.

"One more push!" ordered the midwife. Her own hands were wet with blood, the blood of birth, not death.

Melisande gave a last push, a final cry, and the baby rushed headlong into life. With a gasping sigh of relief, Melisande sank back among the sweat-soaked pillows.

"A boy, madam," crowed the midwife in satisfaction. "Perfect as the livelong day. Not a mark on him."

She held him up, smacked him a sharp spank on his bottom.

The baby opened his mouth, gave a lusty wail.

"Here they come!" Draconas warned.

A shattering blow struck the wooden door.

31

TWO WARRIOR WOMEN SMOTE THE DOOR, KNOCKED it open, bounded inside the cottage. They halted in the doorway, startled at the sight of Bellona, standing in front of them, her sword raised. Concealed behind the door, Draconas shoved it with all his strength, slammed it on them, catching the two women in a vise between the door and the door jamb.

Bellona lunged twice with her sword, stabbed one in the stomach, the other in the breast. Neither was wearing armor. They had not been expecting to meet any resistance. Their bodies tumbled to the floor, the dirt soaking up the blood. Draconas dragged them inside, then put his back against the door, slammed it shut.

"They know now that taking us won't be easy," he said.

Bellona grunted. She grabbed hold of the bodies of the two women, rolled them over. She knew them, knew both of them, had known them since they were children together. Kicking at the corpses, she shoved them into position, trying not to look into the empty eyes.

Sheathing her sword, she emptied out her quiver of arrows, began stripping off the feathers. She jabbed the arrows into the dirt floor, points up. She glanced behind her at the baby—wet and bloody, whimpering and squirming, eyes squinched shut against the terrible light of life—then went back to her task.

"Let me see him," Melisande whispered, no voice left in her.

The midwife cut the cord that was the baby's final tie to his warm, snug, dark world, then wiped him down with a warm, wet cloth—a proceeding that caused him to give another offended cry. Over the sound of life, Bellona heard Nzangia shouting orders.

"Murdering fiends," muttered the midwife, glowering round at the two bodies on the floor. "Maybe now they'll leave us in peace."

Bellona knew better. She continued thrusting arrows into the hard-packed, dirt floor.

The midwife wrapped the wailing baby in a blanket and rested him in his mother's arms. Melisande gazed down at him in exhausted wonder.

"He's beautiful," she breathed. "I think his eyes will be hazel."

Her task completed, Bellona went to Melisande, put her arm around her and laid her face against the thin, flushed cheek.

"You are beautiful," said Bellona. She started to stroke back the sweat-soaked golden wet hair, then saw that her hands were smeared with blood. Hastily, she snatched them away.

Melisande did not notice. She held her baby, her eyes luminous with the memory of pain and the realization of joy.

"They're back," warned Draconas.

Bellona started to spring from the bed. Melisande grasped her arm convulsively, held onto her.

"My baby!" she gasped. "Don't let them take the baby."

"They're not taking anyone," said Bellona grimly. "Rest now, my love."

Melisande started to say something, then her face contorted. She gave a shuddering cry and fell back onto the bed.

"What's the matter?" Bellona demanded of the midwife. "What's wrong with her?"

An axe blade struck the wooden window shutters, chopped clean through one of them, sending splinters flying.

With remarkable presence of mind, the midwife snatched up the baby and stashed the whimpering child under the bed, out of harm's way. Melisande gave another cry. Her hands grasped and twisted the bed linens.

"Lord bless us!" the midwife said, kneading Melisande's belly. "There's another baby inside! Push, child, push!"

A second blow struck the shutters, opened up a gaping hole. Bellona started in that direction, intending to drive away the attackers. Draconas called her off.

"I've dealt with that," he said shortly. "Watch the door!"

Bellona cast a doubtful glance at the window and saw, to her astonishment, that the damage to the shutters was not nearly as bad as she had first thought. She stared at it.

"What did you do?" she demanded.

"Magic," he said, again taking up his position. "Illusion."

The shutters were whole, with only a few chop marks here and there. With the next blink of the eye, the illusion disappeared. The shutters were gone. Though the axe blade sometimes bit through nothing, the warriors outside continued to stubbornly hack away at what they perceived to be solid wood.

Before Bellona could ask Draconas if there was anything else she was seeing that she wasn't really seeing, the front door burst open. Two women barreled through, followed by a press of others, shoving and heaving. The first woman to enter saw the bodies on the floor at her feet, saw the sharp arrow points gleaming in the fire. She tried to halt her forward rush, but the others pushed her from behind. She tripped over the bodies and fell with a terrible scream, impaling herself on the arrows. She did not die immediately, but continued to scream as the blood poured from her wounds.

Draconas struck the second woman in the face with the butt end of his staff, shattering her nose. Her face blossomed with gore and bits of bone. He followed up with a jab to the knee, broke her kneecap. Her leg collapsed under her, and she tumbled to the floor, rolling around in helpless agony.

The third woman leaped over the bodies and came at Bellona, sword swinging. Melisande's cries mingled with the screams of the dying woman, who finally, mercifully, went limp, her body sagging on the arrow points.

Bellona knew her soldiers, knew their weaknesses. Feinting one way, she lured her opponent into leaving herself open, then drove her blade through the woman's body.

Bellona jerked her sword free. The warrior slid off it to her knees.

"You always did fall for that, Mari," Bellona told her. The woman pitched forward, dead.

The axe continued to chop at the window shutters that were no longer there. Draconas put his back to the door, braced himself with his legs, and heaved with all his might. He managed to shut it, but the warriors shoved back.

"I can't hold it much longer!" he grunted.

Bellona nodded, wiped her bloody hand on her breeches so she could get a better grip on her sword. Behind her, she could hear the midwife fussing and encouraging. From beneath the bed came the baby's muffled squeals.

Draconas leapt suddenly out of the way. The warriors hit the door with such force that it burst its hinges. Using the door as a shield, Nzangia struck Draconas, knocked him backward and flung the door on top of him. Warriors shoved in after her. Two attacked Draconas, but Bellona could no longer pay attention to him. She faced Nzangia.

"This is not your fight, Bellona," said her former second-in-command. "The whore betrayed you. That squalling brat is proof of her—"

Bellona struck. Nzangia swiftly parried. Steel clashed on steel, hilt met hilt. The two heaved and shoved against each other, each trying to break the other's hold.

Sunlight blazed into the room. The warriors had at last seen the truth, that the shutters had been smashed to kindling. Faces appeared in the window. Bellona saw, out of the corner of her eye, a warrior standing with a crossbow in her hand, aiming at Bellona.

Nzangia saw her, as well.

"Hold your fire!" she bellowed and flung Bellona off her.

Bellona stumbled into a stool, lost her balance, and went down.

Nzangia saw her chance, leapt at her.

"Here's the second baby—" the midwife began.

Her words ended in a gargle. She stared at the baby in her hands, then let out a piercing shriek.

The scream, sounding right on her, jarred Nzangia. Thinking someone was sneaking up on her, she whipped around swiftly to meet this new attacker.

Bellona regained her feet and lunged with her sword all in the same movement. Her blade entered Nzangia's back.

Nzangia cried out. Bellona jabbed harder, to make sure, then she yanked the sword free. Blood gushed after it. Nzangia gave a gurgling scream and dropped to the floor.

The warrior at the window cursed in anger and dismay. Bellona heard the metallic "snick" of the crossbow being fired and the vicious whir of the bolt, but she paid little attention to it.

She could think only of Melisande. The midwife's wail meant that something dreadful had happened, and she turned to go to her lover, fear twisting inside her.

Melisande lay gazing up at the ceiling, a strange expression on her face. The midwife, her mouth stretched open, held the baby and screamed.

Draconas appeared out of nowhere. Lunging between the two of them, he knocked Bellona out of his way, grabbed the baby from the midwife, seconds before she dropped it.

Wringing her hands, the midwife turned and fled toward the door. Her iron gray hair flying wildly, her face twisted in terror, she was such a frightful apparition that the warrior women fell back in alarm before her, let her go running away unmolested. She dashed off down the hill and even when she was far away, Bellona could still hear her panicked shrieks.

Draconas picked up some bloody rags, began to wrap them around the second baby.

"See to the door!" he ordered Bellona, turning away. "I'll deal with the child and with Melisande. He'll be safe under the bed. Hurry!"

Bellona hastened to the gaping aperture where the door had been. Outside, the warriors huddled together, conferring. Drusilla stood in the center, arguing with them. More than one cast dark glances at the cottage, at the bodies of their comrades.

"Nzangia is dead," Bellona called out to them. "Your mission has ended in failure. Listen to me," she continued, as Drusilla raised her crossbow and pointed it at her. "The Mistress is truly a dragon! She has duped you and duped all our people—"

Drusilla let fire. Bellona ducked. The bolt sailed past her, lodged itself in the wall opposite her.

Drusilla said something to the others, pointed emphatically at the cottage.

"Come on, then!" Bellona shouted, waving her bloody sword. "I'll take you on!"

Drusilla seemed ready, but the others shook their heads. They'd lost their leader. They'd had enough. One by one, the warriors turned and headed off. Drusilla was the last to go. Bellona could see the tears streak down her cheeks and she remembered that Nzangia and Drusilla had been lovers. At length, Drusilla turned away. Her parting look at Bellona promised that this was not the end.

Breathing a sigh, Bellona stood watching them leave, wondering if any of them would at least think over what she'd said. She doubted it.

A hand touched her shoulder.

"You better go to Melisande," said Draconas quietly.

Bellona looked at him, saw his face grave.

"What's wrong?" she gasped.

He shook his head. Shoving past him, Bellona ran to the bed.

Melisande lay among the sweat-soaked sheets, her breath coming in odd, sobbing gasps, her body stiff, her hands clenched to fists. Her face, which had been flushed with the exertion of childbirth, was a ghastly, grayish white.

Bellona knelt down beside her and it was then she saw the blood that drenched the sheet and the straw mattress. Bellona gently lifted Melisande's arm. The crossbow bolt had plowed into her chest from the side. Dark blood welled out of the wound.

Bellona gave a cry of grief and rage, and her cry roused Melisande. She turned her head in the direction of the beloved voice.

"Bellona," said Melisande softly.

"I'm here, Melis," Bellona said with a forced smile of reassurance. "Don't try to talk. Just rest."

"I can't . . . catch my breath." Melisande struggled to speak. A froth of blood bubbled on her lips. "My baby . . ."

"Babies. Twins," said Bellona.

Melisande fought to see through the shadows. She gripped Bellona's hand.

"That scream," she said desperately. "Is something wrong?"

"Nothing," said Bellona, choking on her grief.

"Nothing is wrong. The midwife was frightened by the fighting. Don't talk anymore. Rest now, Melisande. Lay your head here on my arm. Go to sleep."

Melisande smiled. The smile stiffened on her lips. With a great effort, she whispered, "Take care of my sons."

"I will, Melisande," said Bellona, tears rolling unchecked down her cheeks. "I promise."

Melisande closed her eyes. She drew in a labored breath, breathed it out in a sigh. Her head lolled on Bellona's arm. Her eyes opened, stared at Bellona, but they did not see her. Their gaze was fixed and empty.

Bellona gave an anguished cry and collapsed on top of her lover.

Beneath the bed, the two babies lay in a pool of their mother's blood and wailed as if they knew.

32

"GOD SAVE AND KEEP US!"

Draconas turned around to see Gunderson standing in the door, staring in amazement at the carnage: one body impaled on the arrows, another twitching in her final death throes, several others heaped on top of each other, as so much refuse. The floor was dark with blood that had pooled on the hard-packed earth. The stench of death and the stench of birth fouled the air in the small room.

Gunderson, the veteran soldier, turned suddenly away, and Draconas heard the sounds of retching.

Gunderson came back, wiping his mouth with his hand. "I got your message," he said unnecessarily. At Draconas's direction, he'd been staying in Bramfell, to be close at hand. "What the devil happened here?"

"We were attacked," Draconas replied, also unnecessarily. He climbed over bodies, made his way to the bed, moving swiftly. "Seth warriors found her."

"Wanted their Mistress back, huh?"

"No, they wanted her dead," said Draconas. "And they succeeded. Did you see any warriors out there?"

Gunderson nodded, mystified. "I saw some skulking

away. Looked like the fight'd been knocked out of them." He glanced at the body, clasped in Bellona's arms. "Why did they want her dead?"

"Because she knew the truth," Draconas replied. "The truth about the dragon. I know Edward told you. Or didn't you believe him?"

"I believe he believes it," Gunderson returned coolly. "Poor woman," he added, his tone softening. "What about the babe?"

He took a step forward.

Draconas raised a warning hand.

"Mind the arrows!" he warned sharply. "We've enough corpses in here without adding yours to the lot. The baby's safe. Stay where you are. I'll bring him to you."

Gunderson didn't put up any argument, but stayed in the doorway.

Bellona sat on the bed, holding Melisande in her arms. She had not looked up at the sound of voices. She could see nothing but emptiness, hear nothing but that last soft whisper. Draconas rested his hand on her shoulder, felt her muscles turn hard, rigid, as though death's chill had seized her, too.

Bending down, he said softly, for her ears alone, "We're not safely out of this yet. You have to be strong, for her sake."

Bellona shuddered at his touch and lifted her head, her eyes red-rimmed and burning. She cast an oblique glance over her shoulder at Gunderson.

"He's here for the baby," said Draconas, aloud.

Bellona stared, not comprehending.

Draconas squeezed her shoulder, bruising her flesh.

"The baby," he repeated.

Bellona looked up at him dumbly, her eyes those of a wounded animal that has no voice to speak its pain. Draconas trusted she understood him. He hoped she understood him. Otherwise . . . He didn't want to think of otherwise.

Draconas dropped down on his hands and knees, peered

under the bed. One baby lay wrapped in bloody rags, the other in the blanket his dead mother had woven to receive him. Draconas took hold of the baby in the blanket, slid him out from under the bed. Cradling the child in his arms, he rose to his feet and walked over to Gunderson. He could feel Bellona's eyes on him, but she said no word. She remained sitting on the bed, holding fast to her dead.

"She bore a son," said Draconas, placing the baby in Gunderson's arms. "He favors the king."

Gunderson looked down at the child. All babies looked alike to him and this one was no different. A round head, smashed-in nose, rosebud mouth, crinkled eyes squinched tightly shut, trying to blot out this horrifying new world into which he'd been born. The baby stirred fretfully and whimpered, wanting something and missing it and not knowing what it was.

"God forgive me for what I am about to say," Gunderson said somberly, "for it is a mortal sin. But it would have been better if the babe had died with the mother."

"You don't know that," Draconas replied. "None of us can see the future."

"Some of us can," said Gunderson. He shifted his gaze from the baby, stared fixedly at Draconas, eyes dark with enmity. "You've brought trouble enough on my king. Keep away from him. If I see you near him or this child, I'll kill you, so help me, God."

Draconas would have liked nothing better than to swear that he would nevermore set eyes on either Edward or his newborn son. He couldn't make that promise, however, for there was no way to keep it.

"I'd get rid of the blanket," he advised. "That's her blood on it."

The blood was still fresh. Gunderson felt the dampness and grimaced. "I have a woman waiting in Bramfell. A wet nurse. She'll clean and feed the babe and dress him up neat and proper."

"As befits a king's son," said Draconas.

Gunderson gave a bitter, tight-lipped smile. "If you say so."

"The boy is Edward's son," Draconas stated emphatically. "If he believes nothing else about what happened, he can believe that."

"He'll believe," said Gunderson. "More's the pity."

He drew the bloodstained blanket more closely around the child, thrust the baby beneath his fur cloak to keep warm. As he turned to leave, Gunderson glanced back over his shoulder at Melisande.

"God rest her soul," he said quietly.

He was walking out the door, trudging away, and Draconas was breathing a sigh of relief when the second baby, hidden under the bed, gave a cry—a strange cry, a low, feral wail.

Startled, Gunderson halted, looked back. "What was that?"

Draconas muttered a curse beneath his breath, shot a glance at Bellona.

"What was what?" he asked loudly.

"I heard a cry," said Gunderson, walking back.

"The cry was mine," Bellona called out. Her voice was ragged. She bent over the body, shrouding it with her long, black hair.

"It sounded like a baby's," Gunderson said, returning.

Bellona raised her grief-ravaged face. "You have what you came for! Your king has his son. Get out, and leave me to bury my dead."

"You should be going," Draconas said, blocking the door. "The child is hungry and you have a long ride ahead."

Gunderson looked from one to the other, from Bellona to Draconas. He might have persisted, but the baby in his arms began crying—the nerve-grating, insistent, demanding shriek of the newborn. Turning on his heel, Gunderson left them, clutching awkwardly the mewling baby in his arms.

Draconas watched from the doorway, watched until the

king's steward had mounted his horse and ridden off into the haze of smoke from the burning mill. The fire must be out, for he could see no flames and the smoke was starting to diminish. The villagers would be standing around staring at the ruin, as cold despair settled in after the hot excitement of putting out the blaze. The midwife would soon be among them, if she wasn't already, babbling her tale, and the people would gawk and stare in disbelief. Some would dismiss her as mad, but others would believe. She would swear by all that was holy and eventually more would start to believe her. They would come see for themselves.

Bellona had not moved in all this time. Sitting on the bed, her arm beneath Melisande's head, she gazed down at the still, pale face, so calm in death, and smoothed the fair hair with her bloodstained hand.

"You have to take the baby and leave," said Draconas.

Bellona did not look at him. If she heard him, she gave no sign.

"You promised her you would care for him," Draconas said, his voice deliberately harsh, a splash of cold water. "If you don't leave now, the villagers will find him and they will kill him. And probably us along with him."

Bellona stared up at him. "Kill him? Kill a baby? Why?"

The child had gone quiet, after that one strange wail. As Draconas knelt down to retrieve this second baby, he remembered Gunderson's words, *It would have been better if the babe had died with the mother* and he remembered his answering platitude. *You don't know that. None of us can see the future.* Well, that much was true. But he grimaced as he pulled the baby out from under the bed and saw that he was strong and healthy. Unlike his brother, this child's eyes were wide open. He stared unblinking at the light with an expression of wary watchfulness.

"Look at him," Draconas told Bellona.

She looked, but did not offer to hold him.

Still wrapped in the bloody rags Draconas had thrown over him, the baby seemed an ordinary infant, except for those oddly knowing eyes. Feather-wisp hair of indeterminate color covered his head; he held his small, clenched fists tight to his chest. His bow-curved lips were pursed shut, as though he had no expectations of this world, was not prepared to make any demands.

"He looks like Melisande," said Bellona softly. "More than the other." She reached out to touch his cheek.

Draconas thrust aside the bloody rags, revealing the child, naked.

Bellona gasped in shock, recoiled in horror.

From the groin up, the baby was normal. From the groin down, his legs were hunched like the hind legs of a beast and covered with silvery blue scales. His scaly feet had claws.

"He is her son," said Draconas, holding the baby out to her. "You promised Melisande you would care for him."

"He is not her son!" Bellona cried, averting her eyes in revulsion. "He's a monster."

"He is her son," Draconas repeated, relentless. "You promised her as she lay dying that you would take care of him."

Reluctantly, Bellona looked back at the baby. "I don't understand."

"She and Edward made love that day," Draconas explained. "They had no choice in the matter, either of them. They were meant to love, meant to create a child that day."

"I don't understand," she said again, but this time her tone was dire.

He avoided her question, kept on with what he had to tell. "The first baby born, the elder of the brothers, that child is the son of King Edward."

"And this one?"

"That was never meant to happen," Draconas continued. "Another man came to Melisande that night. His intent was also to deliberately get her with child. He attacked Edward and left him for dead and he raped Melisande."

"I know," said Bellona. "I saw him. I—"

"—attacked him from behind with your sword. He dropped Melisande and turned to face you and he would have killed you, but something stopped him. What was it?"

"How do you know all that?" Bellona demanded, staring at him.

"What stopped him from attacking you?"

"I heard a snarl. I looked up and there in the sky was a dragon—"

Lifting his hand, Draconas touched her cheek, which was wet with the tears of her grief. Her tears fell on his flesh and, as Bellona looked at him, she saw the human Draconas and, hovering over him, the spirit of a dragon with shining red-orange scales.

"Grald saw me as I truly am," said Draconas, "and he knew he could not fight me as I truly am. He would have had to change into his real form and he dared not, for fear I would recognize him. He had done what he came to do anyway. He had left his seed inside her. And so he fled."

"I saw him," Bellona said, staring far away into that terrible night. "I saw him as I saw you. He is—"

"—the same as the Mistress. The same as myself. The same as"—he sighed softly—"the blood that runs in his child. Dragons. All of us."

He placed the baby in her unresisting arms. Bellona gazed down at him, bewildered and amazed.

"I have broken the law of my kind to tell you this," Draconas went on, "for it is a secret that we have kept for thousands of years. A secret no human should know. I won't require you to keep my secret, for I have not earned the right to ask that of you. I was the one who brought this upon Melisande and when she needed me, I failed her. I ask only that you think about what I am going to say and do what you believe is right."

Draconas knelt before Bellona, looked up into her eyes.

"Melisande bore a human child, who will grow up gifted with the dragon magic. And she bore a dragon child, who may not even have a chance to grow up, if humans find out the truth about him. They will say he is cursed and they will kill him.

"Maybe he is cursed," Draconas added softly, his gaze shifting to the baby. He reached out his hand, gently touched the child's soft cheek. "Maybe he will grow up to be the curse of his people. Or maybe he will grow up to avenge his mother. I don't know. But I believe he should be given a chance. For her sake."

From outside, drifting on the air, stinging and acrid as the smoke, came voices.

"The villagers are coming," said Draconas. "The midwife has told them what she saw. The mob is forming. You can either save him or hand him over to them."

"You save him," Bellona said and she held out the baby.

Rising to his feet, Draconas took a step backward. "If I raised him, I would doom him to worse than death. His dragon father wants him and so does the Mistress. They are the ones who sent the warriors here. They were after the baby. They attacked only after they heard the baby's cry. I am the only one of my kind who has taken human form. Maristara would know to come looking for me and eventually she would find me and the baby. You are one of a vast multitude of humans. You can take the child and vanish."

Bellona brought the child back to her breast, holding him awkwardly, precariously, for her arms seemed to have gone nerveless. She couldn't feel them, couldn't feel anything anymore.

"I don't understand," she said for the third time, hard and grating. "I will never understand. What right have you and your kind to meddle in our lives?"

"None," he replied. "I know it doesn't seem like it, but we were trying to make amends."

Angrily, Bellona snatched the bloody rags from his hands. She wound them round and round the baby. "I will take him. I will raise him. To do what, to be what, I do not know. I'm doing this for Melisande," she added fiercely. "Not for you."

She placed the baby, wrapped in his mother's blood, in Melisande's chill arms. "First, though, I will bury my dead."

"There's no time. You hear the mob. They're on their way. You have to go before they see you. I will care for her."

Bellona hesitated, not wanting to leave Melisande, but she could hear the truth of his words. Outside the cottage, the clamor of the mob swelled. They had a scapegoat for their misery and they were eager for blood.

Draconas spoke to her again, said something urgent to her. She heard his voice, but it came to her as from a vast distance, drowned by the howls and shouts, drowned by Melisande's last words, *Take care of my sons.*

Clutching the baby, half-blind with her tears, Bellona turned and ran from the bed stained with blood. She ran from the death of the woman she had loved as long as she was conscious of being able to love. She stumbled over the bodies on her way out the door, kicked them aside, and paused in the doorway. She saw the mob on its way up the hill. She would not run from them, she decided. She walked calmly out the door, carrying in her arms the baby, silent and uncomplaining, as if he knew his peril. She walked down the hill behind the house, heading for the forest that would swallow her up, swallow the child.

Only later, alone and safe within the green trees, would she recall Draconas's last words to her.

On the day the dragon's son asks to know what and who he is, bring him back here to his mother's tomb.

Draconas stood in the doorway of the cottage. In his mind's eye, he watched one of Melisande's sons ride to the city of Ramsgate-upon-the-Aston, where he would be welcomed by a loving mother into a royal house, destined for a life of ease and comfort. He watched Melisande's other son fleeing death after only a few moments of life, raised by a woman who would find it hard to love him, destined for a life of loneliness and isolation, torment and anger.

Draconas watched until both faded from his view, then he returned to fulfill his promise.

Melisande lay in bloody sheets of the birthing, as her babies had laid in her blood. He placed her right hand on her breast. Lifting her left hand, he clasped the cold, white flesh in his own. He clasped her hand gently, mindful of his talons, which no one could see. No one but himself.

"I never meant for it to come to this, Melisande," he said quietly. "I am sorry."

He placed her left hand on top of her right hand, then, lifting up her body in his arms, he walked out of the cottage. He met the mob charging up the hill, and he stood in front of the open doorway and regarded them in silence. Startled by his composure and unnerved by the specter of death that he bore, a woman, whose face was so lovely and cold and whose long fair hair trailed down to brush the dirt, the villagers lowered their shovels and their rakes and eyed him uneasily.

"The babe must be inside!" the midwife yelled from the back, spurring them on. "It's a demon I tell you!"

The mob growled and several men in front lunged forward. Draconas cast a glance behind him.

The cottage erupted in flame, fire so fierce that the flames seared the faces of those in the front ranks.

The villagers gave a collective gasp, then falling and tumbling over each other, they turned tail and raced back down the hillside, shrieking that the devil was loose among them.

Draconas walked on, carrying Melisande down the road that led to the river.

ACKNOWLEDGMENTS

THE SONGS QUOTED IN THE TEXT ARE, IN ORDER OF presentation:

"Deuil Angoisseux," by Christine de Pisan

"When to Her Lute Corinna Sings," by Thomas Campion

"With Garments Flowing," by John Clare

Look for

THE
DRAGON'S
SON

BY MARGARET WEIS

Available July 2004
from Tom Doherty Associates

PROLOGUE

MELISANDE CLOSED HER EYES. SHE DREW IN A LA-bored breath, breathed it out in a sigh. The twisted grim-ace of pain relaxed, smoothed. Her head lolled on the pillow. Her eyes opened, stared at Bellona, but they did not see her. Their gaze was fixed and empty.

Bellona gave an anguished cry.

Beneath the bed, the two babies lay in a pool of their mother's blood and wailed as if they knew.

Melisande's sons.

One of them human, born of love and magic.

One of them half-human and half-dragon, born of evil.

Both of them hidden away. One in plain view for all the world to see. One in the tangled forest of grieving and embittered heart.

None of this had turned out as any of the dragons had planned.

"Killing the mother was folly," raved Grald, the father of the half-human son. "Your women should have captured her, brought her to me. She was unusually strong in the dragon magic, as proven by the fact that she bore my son and both she and the babe survived. Never before has that happened. I could have continued to make use of her, to breed more like her."

"As you said, she was unusually strong," Maristara stated coldly. "The threat she posed far outweighed her usefulness. She was the sole human on this earth who knew the truth about the Mistress of Dragons."

"The threat she posed to you," Grald grumbled.

"A threat to me is a threat to us both," Maristara returned. "Without the children of Seth, you would have no city, no subjects, no army."

"We do not yet have an army."

"We will. Our plans can go forward now that Melisande has been removed," said Maristara, with a dig and a twist of a mental claw.

"What about the Parliament?"

"The Parliament will do what it has done for a thousand years. Talk and debate. Decide not to decide. Fly back to their safe and secret lairs and go back to sleep."

"And the walker. Draconas." Grald growled the name and mumbled over it, as if it were a bone the dragon would like very much to chew. "You must concede that he is—or could be—a threat."

"That is true and we will deal with him, but all in good time. As he so cleverly arranged it, he is our only link to the children—the sons of Melisande. Your son in particular. Kill him and we kill any chance of finding them. Besides, if he were to suddenly turn up dead, think of the uproar. The Parliament might actually be inclined to do something. Best to lull them into complacency. Let the Parliament slumber and let Draconas walk the world on his two human legs."

"So long as we keep track of where those human legs of his take him," said Grald.

"That is a given," said Maristara.

*   *   *

Draconas heard two babies crying. A sound not unusual for human ears to hear, for every second that passed on earth was heralded by a baby's cry, as some woman somewhere brought forth new life. The cries of babies might be said to be the song of the stars.

What was unusual was that Draconas, the walker, the dragon who had taken human form, heard the cries of these two babies in his mind. The babes themselves were far away. The dragon blood in both linked them—all three—together.

He stood beside the cairn he had raised over the body of their mother and listened to the wails and spoke to her, who would never hear the cries of those she had brought into the world.

"There are some of my kind who believe it would have been better if your children were now lying in your arms, Melisande. Better for us. Better for them. In that instance, we dragons could yawn and roll over and go back to sleep and wake again in a thousand years. The children lived and so does the danger from those who brought all this about. We dragons must remain awake and vigilant. Your children were born of blood and death, Melisande, and I believe that is a portent."

He placed his hand upon the cold stone and wrote in flames of magic the words:

Melisande

Mistress of Dragons

Picking up his walking staff, Draconas left the tomb. The cries of the babies sounded loud in his mind until each fell asleep, and the wails died away.

Follow Mina from the
War of Souls into the
chaos of post–war Krynn.

AMBER AND ASHES
The Dark Disciple, Volume I

Margaret Weis

With Paladine and Takhisis gone, the lesser gods
vie for primacy over Krynn. Recruited to a new
faith by a god of evil, Mina leads a religion of
the dead, and a kender and a holy monk are all
that stand in the way of the dark stain
spreading across Ansalon.

First in a new series from *New York Times*
best-selling author Margaret Weis.

August 2004